He Kills Me, He Kills Me Not

He Kills Me, He Kills Me Not

Lena Diaz

AVONIMPULSE

EPub Edition August 2011 ISBN: 9780062115775

Print Edition ISBN: 9780062114556

10 9 8 7 6

To Nalini Akolekar—my mentor, my cheerleader, my rock.

To Esi Sogah—thank you for believing in my story.

To Sheila Athens and Valerie Bowman for
your friendship. You are pure gold.

To Anita, Eileen, E J, Gail, Lisa, Maria, Pam,
and Tracy—thank you for everything.

Thank you, Eileen Carr, Margaret Carroll,
Alyssa Day, FCRW, and the Unsinkables.

Thank you, Officer Glenn Morningstar, for
patiently answering my many questions.

Thank you, my wonderful son and daughter,
for loving me no matter what.

Above all, thank you, my dear husband. I
don't deserve you, but I'm keeping you.

CHAPTER ONE

The sweet music of her screams echoed in his mind as he inhaled the lavender-scented shampoo he'd selected for her. He sat cross-legged on the carpet of pine needles, stroking her hair, his fingers sliding easily through the silky brown mass he had washed and brushed.

Underlying that scent, the metallic aroma of blood teased his senses. He traced his fingers across her naked belly to the sweet center of her. The temptation to linger was strong, but the ritual wasn't complete.

He picked up the blood-red rose and tucked its velvety petals between Kate's pale, generous breasts. Molding her cool fingers around the stem, he pressed her palms together, embedding the single remaining thorn in her flesh. As he stood, her sightless pale blue eyes stared at him accusingly, just like they had in Summerville the first time he gave her a rose.

Let her stare. She couldn't hurt him anymore, not today.

A rhythmic pounding noise echoed through the trees, an early morning jogger trying to beat the impending heat and humidity of another scorching summer day. The sun's first rays were starting to peek through the pine trees, glinting off the rows of swings and slides.

Thump. Thump. Closer. Closer. A cold sweat broke out on his forehead as he listened to the jogger approach. Was Kate coming for him again, already? No matter how many times he punished her, she always came back. He'd walk around a corner and there she was, condemning him with a haughty look, taunting him with her sinfully alluring long hair.

He risked a quick glance down and let out a shaky, relieved breath. She was still lying on the ground. She hadn't come back to torture him.

Not yet.

After one last, longing glance at her body, he slid between some palmettos and followed his makeshift path through the woods. He emerged at the parking lot of Shadow Falls' only mall, next to a row of dumpsters. Exchanging his soiled clothes for the clean ones he'd hidden in a plastic bag, he quickly dressed. Then he stepped around the dumpsters, pitched the bag into his trunk, and got into the patrol car.

Loosening his tie in deference to the already sweltering eighty-degree heat, Police Chief Logan Richards did his best to blend into the shadows beneath the moss-covered live oak tree. Several feet away, Officer Karen Bingham interviewed the young female jogger who'd discovered the body. Logan had offered to help, but Karen had informed him the young woman didn't need an NFL linebacker hovering over her when she was already terrified.

He'd never been a professional football player, but he conceded the point. His size intimidated people. That had served him well when he'd worked as a beat cop here in Shadow Falls, and later as a detective in the roughest precincts of New York City. But intimidating this young witness was the last thing he wanted to do.

She sat on a wooden bench a few feet away, sheltered from the press's cameras by a stand of pine trees. Her freckled face was pale and her shoulders hunched as she wrapped her thin arms around her abdomen, shaking as if she were in the middle of a snowstorm instead of the Florida Panhandle in July.

Someone called Logan's name. He looked toward the obscenely cheery yellow tape that cordoned off a section of the park, contrasting starkly with the macabre scene within its borders. Medical Examiner Cassie Markham was waving at him, ready to share her initial findings.

Logan crossed to the tape, ducking beneath it, careful not to step on any of the bright orange tags his detectives were using to mark off their search grid.

Cassie was kneeling next to the body, sliding a brown paper bag onto the victim's hand. One of two Walton County medical examiners who rotated on-call duties for Shadow Falls and the neighboring communities, Cassie rarely had the need to visit this small rural town in her official capacity. Logan had only met her once before, about six months ago when she'd handled a domestic violence case, right after he'd moved back to take the job as chief of police.

"Hell of a way to spend a Sunday morning," he said when she looked up at him.

"You got that right." She tossed her head to flip her short blonde bangs out of her eyes. "Is she your missing college girl?"

He gave a short, tight nod. "Carolyn O'Donnell."

"How long was she missing?" Cassie picked up another brown bag and gently lifted the victim's other hand.

"A little over three days. She disappeared late Wednesday night, from this same park."

"I'm guessing a young woman her age wasn't playing on the swings. Neighborhood hangout?"

"So I hear." An uneasy feeling gnawed at the pit of his stomach as he noted the way the body seemed posed, her legs spread for maximum shock value. Ligature marks darkened her wrists and ankles. Stab wounds riddled her abdomen and extremities. Many of her bruises were deep purple or black, indicating they'd begun to heal before she was killed. Dreading the answer, he asked, "How long has she been dead?"

Cassie finished securing the paper bag before answering. "She's not in full rigor yet. Liver temp indicates about six hours, but it's hard to be specific in this heat. Might be longer."

Logan scrubbed his hand across his brow to ease the dull ache that was starting to bloom. While he and his men had been searching door-to-door, the killer was sadistically torturing this young woman. Where the hell had he stashed her? And where was he now? Was he already searching for a new victim? Logan blew out a frustrated breath. "Tell me what you have so far."

"Not much beyond the obvious." She peeled off her gloves and stowed them in her kit, then stood up beside him, her head barely reaching his shoulder. "The amount of blood doesn't fit the injuries. She was killed somewhere else and washed down before he dumped her."

Logan nodded, having reached the same conclusion. "Trace?"

"A few cotton fibers, nothing remarkable or distinctive. No hairs. No bite marks. He sliced off her fingertips. I figure she scratched him and he wanted to make sure we couldn't get his DNA from under her nails."

The perp was aware of forensic techniques. Then again, who *wasn't* these days, with all the crime scene investigation shows on TV? Logan didn't ask if the victim had been raped. The answer was painfully obvious. "Semen?"

"I'll take swabs but I doubt we'll find anything. As careful as he was not to leave any other evidence, he probably wore a condom. There's bruising on her neck, petechial hemorrhaging in her eyes."

"He strangled her."

"Yes, but I suspect that was the killer's version of 'love play'. I can't be sure until I perform the autopsy, but I'm leaning toward exsanguination as cause of death. She has deep puncture wounds in her abdomen. She would have bled out in minutes."

"What about her face?" A deep, ragged wound splayed her open from temple to jaw. Logan hoped to God she was already dead when the killer cut her.

"That's unusual, isn't it?" Cassie said. "It would have bled all over the place. Not enough to kill her, but it would have hurt like hell."

Logan's hands curled into tight fists as he struggled to tamp down his anger. Ten years ago he'd allowed his emotions to control him, and he'd made a tragic, rookie mistake that allowed a killer to go free. How many other women had suffered and died at the hands of that killer because of Logan's screwup? That question haunted him every day. The whole mess was the reason he'd fled Shadow Falls so long ago and had gone to New York City.

He'd worked in the toughest precincts to be the best detective he could be, so he'd never make that kind of mistake again. No matter how much he wished he could wrap his hands around the throat of the animal who'd tortured Carolyn O'Donnell, he couldn't let his anger cloud his judgment. Other women's lives hung in the balance if he made any mistakes with this investigation.

"Did you hear about the rose?" Cassie asked, breaking into his thoughts.

"The responding officer said Carolyn was holding a long-stemmed, red rose."

"That's right. The rose bud was nestled between her breasts and the stem was stripped clean of all but one thorn, which he embedded in her right palm, postmortem. Creepy."

Definitely creepy, but if Logan's suspicions were correct, that rose might be part of the killer's signature, his pattern. Everything about the scene told Logan this was the work of a killer who'd killed before—and would kill again.

Cassie motioned for her assistants to bring the gurney.

"When I finish the autopsy, I'll overnight the samples to the state lab."

"Hold onto the samples. I want to give the Feds first crack at the evidence."

Cassie nodded, her relieved expression telling him she was just as anxious as he was to get help with this case. Shadow Falls was a small town with limited resources. And although Logan had worked on several serial killer cases in New York, no one else in the Shadow Falls Police Department had that kind of experience. He couldn't do this alone.

Cassie gave him a friendly wave and turned to help with the removal of the body.

Once the body was carried outside the taped-off area, Logan crouched down to examine the footprints he'd noticed earlier. He followed the trail to a group of palmetto bushes. Some of the palm fronds were bent and twisted as if someone had recently passed between them. When he parted the leaves, he saw a narrow trail hacked through the woods. Someone had spent hours, maybe days, cutting this path. The killer? Had he also selected his victim ahead of time? Or did Carolyn O'Donnell just have the bad luck of being in the park when the killer made his move?

Looking back, Logan located his lead detective, David Riley. At thirty, Riley was only five years younger than Logan, but a lot less experienced. When Logan had taken the job as chief and inherited Riley as the lead, he'd assumed Riley was in that role just because the department was so small and there weren't a lot of candidates to choose from. But Riley had quickly proven his abilities.

He was smart and friendly, able to play good cop or bad

cop, depending on the need. He could charm a confession out of a suspect before they'd even seen the trap he'd set.

Unfortunately, Riley was speaking to Randy Clayton, a well-seasoned officer with a mouth that never quit. Clayton, who'd already been a veteran back when Logan began his career, wasn't a bit pleased that the rookie he'd once taunted was now his boss. Logan only tolerated his smart-ass attitude because Clayton was due to retire in a few months.

Sighing in resignation, Logan motioned for Riley to join him and wasn't surprised when Clayton tagged along, his usual smirk firmly in place.

Logan ignored Clayton and addressed Riley. "Has anyone searched this area yet?" He parted the fronds, revealing the path between them.

Riley's brows rose in surprise. "We stayed out of this section, waiting for the medical examiner."

Logan drew his gun from the shoulder holster beneath his suit jacket. He stepped between the palmettos, careful to avoid their sharp tips, keeping to the edge of the path so he didn't tread on any of the footprints. "Let's see if we have company."

Riley and Clayton glanced at each other with wide eyes and drew their weapons. The three men followed the path through the thick brush. A few minutes later they emerged at the edge of the mall parking lot, next to a row of dumpsters.

Logan motioned to the others and they fanned out, checking possible hiding places. When he was sure there was no danger, he holstered his weapon. "I'll call for another team to tape off the area. Secure the scene until they arrive."

Clayton tugged on his pants to pull them up over his protruding belly. "Riley, doesn't this seem similar to that other murder when you were a street cop? About four years ago?"

A look of realization crossed Riley's face. "You're right. I should have thought of that."

"What murder?" Logan glanced back and forth between them.

Clayton scratched at the gray stubble on his jaw. "There was another girl that went missing, and then turned up in a cabin all cut-up a few days later. There was a rose in her hands too. I can't remember her name though, something like Diana, Deana—"

"Dana," Riley said. "Dana Branson. I should have thought of her as soon as I saw the body this morning. I wasn't a detective back then, but I heard the details, saw the pictures." He shuddered, his Adam's apple bobbing in his throat. "It seems like an obvious tie-in now, but I was at the convention when O'Donnell went missing, and didn't think about it when you called me, Logan. Maybe if I'd been here a few days ago, I might have—"

Logan waved Riley into silence, impatient to hear the details about the other murder. "Clayton, tell me what you remember about the other case."

"The vic was Caucasian, mid-twenties, long, brown hair, blue eyes. She, ah . . ." He cleared his throat, his face flushing red. "She was missing for three days before we found her. Just like O'Donnell."

Logan's throat ached with the urge to shout his frustration. He wished his men had told him about the earlier case when O'Donnell first went missing. Would it have changed how he'd directed the search? Maybe, maybe not. It all depended on the details of that first case and whether there were any clues to that perp's identity. Without knowing for sure, he wasn't about to lay that kind of guilt on someone else. He was the chief. Ultimately, he was responsible. "Who were the suspects in the original case?"

"There weren't any suspects. All the leads went cold," Clayton said. "But Branson wasn't alone. There was another woman with her."

Disbelief had Logan clamping his jaw shut to avoid saying something he knew he'd regret. How could his men have forgotten a brutal, double homicide in a town of fifty thousand people? Especially since the only murders around here were usually the result of a drunken bar fight or a crime of passion between two people who supposedly loved each other. He took a deep breath and prayed for patience. "Who was the second murder victim?"

Clayton shook his head, his smug look returning. "You got it all wrong," he said. "The second girl, Amanda Stockton, she got away."

Amanda eased her tired body down onto her leather couch to take a much-needed break from her computer. Making a living by writing computer programs at home rather than having to go into an office was a blessing, but it was also a curse. She'd become the hermit her sister had once accused her of being, working inside on a beautiful weekend rather than going out. The sky—visible from her back windows—

was so blue it hurt to look at it. And she knew if she went outside she'd smell the salt in the air, might even be able to hear the waves crashing on the shore a few miles away.

She'd enjoyed the ocean once, a lifetime ago. She'd loved hearing the sand crunch beneath her feet, feeling its cooling touch between her toes, listening to the cries of sea gulls overhead. But those days were gone, a part of her past. She could never be that carefree again, that ignorant of the people around her, that exposed, vulnerable.

Wary of the all-too-familiar path her tired mind was taking, she forced those thoughts aside and curled her legs beneath her. With one click of her remote, her brand-new, sixty-one- inch, high-def TV snapped to life. A decadent luxury, it had put a huge dent in her savings. But she'd only turn thirty once, so she'd splurged.

Instead of spending her birthday last week visiting her parents' graves like she usually did, she'd watched two action flicks on her new TV, and shoveled handfuls of fattening, buttery popcorn into her mouth.

She didn't regret buying the TV.

She did regret the popcorn.

An extra hour on the treadmill had been enough to keep her from indulging again anytime soon.

After clicking through the movie guide, she selected a crime scene drama. With her past, she knew most people would think her odd to like those kinds of shows, but it made perfect sense to her. It was all about control, facing and overcoming fears.

Not letting *him* win.

But instead of the show she'd expected, the screen filled

with a live shot of the outside of the building that housed Shadow Falls' city hall and police station. A red banner underneath the picture declared "Breaking News."

When anchorwoman Tiffany Adams stepped in front of the camera, Amanda knew this was something far more important than another fluff piece on the upcoming mayoral race. Adams rarely left the anchor desk to report in the field, probably because her heavy makeup and hairspray didn't respond well to the Florida humidity.

In a tone far too upbeat for what she was saying, she informed viewers that a jogger had discovered a woman's body in the city's main park early this morning, and that the mayor and police chief were about to give a news conference.

Amanda's stomach fluttered and she twisted the hem of her pink tank top between her fingers. Four solemn policemen filed up to stand shoulder to shoulder behind a podium at the top of the steps. She shook her head at the bitter irony. If she went to a store without a written shopping list, half the time she'd come home without the very items she most needed. And yet, even though she hadn't spoken to those policemen in years, she could still remember their names. Some things she could never forget.

Even though she wanted to.

Mayor Edward Montgomery heaved his bulk up the steps and stood red-faced in front of the officers lined up behind the podium's bank of microphones. His usual jovial personality and rotund appearance had given him the nickname of Santa. He wasn't jovial today. After giving one of his briefest speeches since the start of election season, he introduced Police Chief Logan Richards and motioned toward someone off-camera.

A man with short, dark hair strode into view and stood next to the mayor, towering over him. Impeccably dressed in a navy blue suit—in spite of the stifling heat—Richards radiated confidence and authority.

The previous police chief had retired about six months ago and moved to California. Amanda knew Richards was his replacement and that he was from New York, but she hadn't paid much attention to the news reports about him when he was hired. That part of her life was over and she wanted nothing to do with any more policemen.

He looked younger than she'd expected—maybe mid-thirties—although the tiny shots of silver in his blue-black hair might mean he was older. His skin was smooth and tanned, with a slightly darker shadow along his jaw. He was probably one of those men who always looked like he needed to shave. She bet it drove him crazy; it contrasted starkly with the rest of his crisp, polished appearance.

When he spoke, his rich, deep baritone cut across the chatter of the reporters and demanded everyone's attention. His speech was short and concise, confirming what Tiffany Adams had reported earlier but adding little else.

He nodded at a reporter from the *Shadow Falls Journal*, the same reporter who'd badgered Amanda with relentless, personal questions when she was released from the hospital four years ago. After suffering through his crass, intimate questions about her abduction, she'd never agreed to another interview—not with the press, anyway. The detectives had interviewed her so many times she'd sarcastically threatened to move into the police station to save them time.

"Chief, can you confirm the body in the park is missing college student Carolyn O'Donnell?" the reporter asked.

"Until the next of kin are notified, I can't speak to the identity of the—"

"Do you actually expect us to believe the dead woman isn't O'Donnell?" the same reporter shouted.

Richards pointed to another reporter, effectively dismissing the *Journal* reporter, leaving him red-faced and sputtering.

Amanda couldn't help but grin.

"Yes, the body was discovered just off the main jogging trail in a remote section of the park," Richards said in response to a question.

"No, the jogger who found the victim isn't a suspect in the slaying."

"I can't confirm or deny sexual assault until the autopsy is completed."

"No, I can't speak to the cause of death at this time."

For several minutes, the questions continued. When another reporter repeated the question about the victim's identity, Chief Richards thanked everyone for their time and walked away, abruptly ending the press conference. Amanda smiled at his audacity.

The angle of the camera shifted, focusing again on Tiffany Adams. Quoting unnamed sources, she callously confirmed that the nude body found in the park was the Florida State University sophomore who'd gone missing while home on summer break. She quoted an unnamed source and didn't express a twinge of remorse that O'Donnell's family might be watching the broadcast.

The anchorwoman seemed to delight in going into more detail, telling the audience about the multiple stab wounds and speculating that the victim was strangled. Then she mentioned something Richards hadn't: the victim was found clutching a long-stemmed, red rose.

Amanda shivered and clasped her arms around her middle, barely feeling her fingernails biting into her skin through her thin, cotton tank.

Was the stem smooth? Had the killer removed all of the thorns? All but one?

The TV screen faded away and she was back in the cabin four years ago, lying on the hardwood floor in a puddle of her own blood, listening to the sound of Dana's terrified sobs behind her.

Amanda's attacker straddled her stomach and held a red rose above her, its sweet perfume wafting down and mingling with the metallic scent of blood. He plucked one thorn from the stem. "He kills me." He broke off another. "He kills me not."

His sickening version of the childhood chant continued as he snapped off each thorn to drop one by one onto her blood-smeared stomach. When only one thorn remained, his obsidian eyes shone through the holes of the hooded mask that covered his head and most of his face, but not the cruel slant of his lips as they curved up in a delighted smile.

He leaned down, pressing his lips next to her ear, his hot breath washing over her bare skin. She shuddered in revulsion and his hand tightened in her hair, painfully twisting her head back. "He kills me," he rasped.

Dropping the rose, he reached behind his back and

pulled out a long, jagged knife. Its wickedly sharp teeth winked in the dim light as he raised it above his head.

With a muffled cry, Amanda tore herself away from the nightmare of her past, collapsing against the couch as she struggled to breathe and slow her racing heart. The TV gradually came back into focus. Channel Ten was still covering the gruesome discovery in the park. Adams speculated on a possible connection between this morning's murder and Dana Branson's murder years earlier. A picture of Dana at Florida State University filled the screen. Then the camera zoomed in on a closeup of her tombstone.

When they showed a file photo of Amanda leaving the hospital, she flipped the TV off and dropped the remote to the floor. She reached up and ran a shaking finger down the rough edges of the long, puckered scar that zigzagged down the right side of her face, a scar that four painful surgeries had failed to completely erase, a scar that reminded her every day of the horrors she wanted so desperately to forget.

But no matter how hard she tried, she could never forget the price of her cowardice: Dana's life.

Furiously wiping at the hot tears cascading down her cheeks, Amanda wondered who had really escaped all those years ago. Her? Or Dana?

Logan thought he knew what hell was. He'd lived it for the past decade, trying to atone for a split-second decision that could never be undone.

But that wasn't hell.

Not even close.

Hell was telling the O'Donnells their daughter had been murdered. Hell was watching the light of hope die in their eyes, watching Carolyn's mother crumple to the ground, her tear-streaked face ravaged with grief.

If they'd been angry or had cursed at him for failing to save their daughter, it might have been easier. Instead, Mr. O'Donnell shook Logan's hand, thanked him for trying, and patted him on the shoulder as if Logan was the one who needed to be comforted.

This wasn't the first time he'd told someone their loved one had been killed, but it never got any easier. Every time it was like a punch in his gut, reminding him of the tragic mistake he'd once made. Had the killer he'd let go hurt anyone else? How many lives had been lost, how many families destroyed because of his lapse in judgment all those years ago?

He blew out a shaky breath and blinked his tired eyes, trying to focus on the computer screen in front of him. The most important thing right now was finding Amanda Stockton. The similarities between O'Donnell's killing and what had happened to Amanda and her friend were too overwhelming not to have been committed by the same man. She was the only living witness to his crimes. If there was any chance the killer thought she might remember something that would help the police find him, she could be in terrible danger.

None of the detectives understood Logan's obsession with finding her, but none of them could know the kind of guilt that ate at him every day. God willing, they never would.

He'd already browsed through dozens of law enforcement and government web sites searching for her, but he wasn't giving up. No one was going home tonight until he was certain Amanda Stockton was safe.

He glanced at his watch, cursing when he saw how many hours had passed since he'd begun his search. How could one woman be so hard to find? She wasn't on the tax rolls of any municipality within five hundred miles of Shadow Falls. The local utility companies didn't have her on their customer lists. Neither did the cable or satellite TV companies. If she'd gotten married or changed her name, she hadn't done it in Walton County.

Everything pointed to her not being a local anymore, which meant she wasn't in immediate danger, at least for now. But without knowing why the killer had shown up again after four years, Logan couldn't risk giving up on the search. Finding her, making sure she was safe, was his primary goal, but it wasn't his only goal.

He wanted to interview her about her abduction. Asking her to relive that horrific experience didn't sit well with him, but finding the killer before he could kill again was more important than sparing anyone's feelings. She'd been with her attacker for three days. Even though the killer had worn a disguise, Amanda had to have seen something that could help identify him. She could hold the key to the entire investigation without even realizing it.

A knock sounded on Logan's open office door, and one of the detectives helping him search for Amanda leaned in around the doorway, his eyes lit with excitement.

"Chief, I found her."

Chapter Two

Amanda woke up Monday morning to the sound of someone knocking on her front door. Blinking in confusion, she looked around to get her bearings. Fireplace, computer desk in the corner, traditional, sturdy coffee table with chunky, solid legs. She'd fallen asleep on her living room couch.

She was amazed she'd slept at all after watching yesterday's press conference, then speaking to the police when they'd called her late last night. They'd confirmed what she'd already suspected, that the man who'd attacked her was most likely back, here in Shadow Falls. They'd wanted to send a police car to her house to stand watch over her, but she'd adamantly refused. Her house was a fortress. She was safe here. But only if no one drew any attention to her. A police car out front would destroy the anonymity—and therefore safety—that she'd worked so hard to create.

The knock sounded again, startling her. She jumped up and hurried down the hallway to her bedroom to grab her robe, figuring Mrs. Fogelman was probably back to hound her again about the upcoming neighborhood block party.

Short of being rude, Amanda didn't know how to convince the well-meaning woman to give up her personal crusade to get Amanda out of the house and involved in the neighborhood.

Back in the foyer, she looked through the front door's peephole and was dismayed to see two men in business suits standing on her porch. The one on the left held up a police badge. She couldn't get a good look at the other man since he was too far to the right.

Apparently the police weren't willing to take "no" for an answer. She pulled some of her hip-length hair forward over her shoulder to help conceal her scar. Then she flipped the deadbolt and yanked the door open. "Yes?"

The blonde man holding a badge flinched and his eyes widened. Amanda tried not to let it bother her, but no matter how many times people reacted to the sight of her scar, it still hurt. She forced herself to resist the impulse to pull more hair forward or duck her head.

He lowered his badge and cleared his throat. "Good morning, ma'am. I'm Detective David Riley and this is Chief Logan Richards. Are you Amanda Stockton?"

She looked over at Richards and a shock of awareness pulsed through her. Most women would think his tanned, chiseled features and broad shoulders were appealing, and she was no exception. But that wasn't what caught her attention. Given his intimidating size and the piercing way he stared at her, she would have expected to feel uncomfortable, anxious. But she didn't. There was something indefinable about him—a presence, an intensity—as if he were aware of everything around him, on guard against any threat. Instead of making her uneasy, he made her feel . . . protected. As if no one could hurt her as long as he was here.

Confused by her reaction to him, she tore her gaze away and looked back at the other man who, although not unattractive, seemed bland compared to Richards.

"Detective Riley, I'm sure you've seen my picture in your files. You know I'm Amanda Stockton, or at least, I was. I moved to Tennessee with my sister and changed my last name to Jones before I moved back to Shadow Falls two years ago. I explained all of that last night to the officer on the phone. I also told him I wasn't interested in speaking to anyone about my case again. Unless you're here to tell me you've caught the killer?"

"Uh, no, ma'am. Not yet."

She stepped back and started to close the door.

The police chief stepped forward and slapped his palm against the door, preventing her from closing it. He anchored his left shoe in the doorway. Amanda took perverse pleasure in squeezing the door against his foot before she was forced to open the door beneath his relentless pressure. He stopped short of forcing his way inside and stood in the doorway, patiently watching, waiting, as if a woman slamming a door on the chief of police's foot was a normal occurrence. With this man, maybe it was.

Her fingers curled around the edge of the door and she couldn't help but notice she had to look *up* to meet his gaze, a rare experience for her, since she was six feet tall. His eyes were a rather remarkable shade of emerald green with little flecks of gold around the edges. And he smelled absolutely wonderful: a warm, clean, masculine scent that made her nostrils flare in appreciation.

Heat flooded her cheeks as she realized she'd been staring at him for far too long. He'd flustered her and she hated that.

"I know you don't want to speak to us," he said, his voice deep and rich. "But I believe you may be in danger. We won't take much of your time."

His respectful tone and impassive expression helped soothe her embarrassment. If he'd raised a mocking brow or grinned, she wouldn't have had the slightest twinge of remorse about kicking him off her property.

She glanced behind him to the street, and was relieved to see he'd at least had the sense to come in an unmarked car. A shiny, new-looking, black Mustang with dark tinted windows sat at the curb. Realizing she was probably drawing attention right now with these two men standing on her porch, she reluctantly stepped back to let them inside.

Hugging her robe tightly against her body, she was suddenly painfully aware of how thin the silky fabric was. "You can sit in the living room while I get dressed."

She motioned toward the end of the foyer and escaped to her left down the long hallway that led to the master bedroom of her fifties-style ranch house. She sat on the edge of the bed and hid her burning face in her hands. Had she really deliberately smashed the chief of police's foot in the door? Could he arrest her for that? Then again, she hadn't exactly invited him in, so it was his fault.

He was pushy, literally. She couldn't stand men like that,

men who used their strength and size to intimidate women. So why had her mouth gone dry and her skin all tingly when she looked into his eyes?

Before the attack she'd been attracted to tall men, mainly because they made her feel less self-conscious about her own height. But after the attack everything had changed. Big men now made her nervous, brought back feelings of helplessness she never wanted to experience again.

Shaking her head at her confusing thoughts, she dressed in a pair of faded jeans and a blue button-up blouse, then crossed to her master bath and quickly took care of her needs.

Eyeing herself in the mirror one last time, she grabbed a pale pink lipstick and added a quick touch of color. When she realized she was primping, she tossed the lipstick down in disgust and left the bathroom. Before she entered the living room, she pulled some of her hair forward over her right shoulder to cover her scar.

Detective Riley rose from the couch when she walked into the room. He gave her an apologetic nod. She smiled reassuringly and motioned for him to sit back down. She didn't know if he was silently apologizing for flinching or just for being here, but she decided to forgive him for both. He had a youthful, boyish look about him, and she doubted he meant any harm. Besides, his pushy boss had probably strong-armed him into coming here.

The boss in question stood in front of the fireplace, staring at the landscape hanging above the mantle. His profile was turned toward her, and her stomach jumped at the look of pleasure on his face as he admired the painting. The smile softened the angles, made him seem less intense, more approachable.

She must have made some kind of noise because suddenly he turned, his gaze locked on hers. She quickly moved away and sat next to Detective Riley, leaving the chief no choice but to sit in one of the two recliners that flanked the couch.

He chose the one closest to her, folding his large frame into the chair. She felt a twinge of remorse over her childishness in making him sit there. He made the recliner look like dollhouse furniture with him squeezed uncomfortably between the cushioned arms. He'd unbuttoned his suit jacket and his light blue dress shirt hugged his flat abdomen.

She glanced up and cringed as she realized he'd caught her staring at him.

Again.

Twisting on the sofa, she turned to face Officer Riley. He was shorter than Richards by several inches, far less muscular, and not nearly as appealing. She clenched her fist and vowed not to let the police chief distract her any further. "So, Officer Riley, why are you here? I specifically asked the police not to come."

"We're here, Ms. Stockton," Richards began, forcing her to turn back toward him or look impossibly rude. " . . . Or should I call you Ms. Jones?"

She shrugged. "It doesn't matter. Jones is a legal device to keep the press from finding me and to ensure my privacy. I've never gotten completely used to that name."

He nodded. "Ms. Stockton, we believe the same man who attacked you also killed another young woman yesterday morning."

She took a deep, bracing breath. "Yes, the officer told me that last night."

"We also think he may target you again."

She couldn't suppress a shiver at the expression on his face. He clearly believed she was in danger. "It's been years, Chief Richards. If he was coming after me, wouldn't he have tried sooner?"

"I'm not saying he will. It would be unusual for a serial killer. . . ." He stopped when she flinched.

She took a steadying breath and tried to smile. "Sorry. I hadn't thought of him as a serial killer until you said that. I guess it only takes two murders to qualify as a serial: my friend Dana and the woman yesterday morning, Carolyn?"

He exchanged a quick glance with the detective. "Technically, two qualifies, although some might argue with that."

"Chief Richards, what aren't you telling me?" She stared into his eyes, forcing herself not to look away, even though it seemed like he was trying to stare deep into her soul, as if he knew her terrible secret.

"I spoke to the FBI early this morning. They believe this killer has been operating up and down the East Coast for at least four years, killing several other women."

Four years. She rubbed the goose bumps that had popped up on her arms. "You think Dana was his first kill."

"I think you and Dana were both supposed to be his first kills. You were incredibly lucky to escape with your life."

Lucky, right. Just a simple twist of fate that had nothing to do with her cowardice. She squeezed her eyes shut and took a deep breath. Just a few more minutes. She could hold it together just a little while longer. All she had to do was answer their questions and send them on their way. Then she could go back to pretending her life was normal.

When she opened her eyes Richards was staring at her, his face etched with concern. He glanced at her hands and she realized how badly she was shaking. She clasped them together in her lap and cleared her suddenly constricted throat. "Since I . . . escaped, you think he came back to finish what he started. Is that what you're saying?"

He exchanged another glance with Riley. "We don't have any evidence that he's looking for you. It's practically un-heard of for a serial killer to go after a victim who got away, but he came back for a reason. I'm speculating he might have decided to go after you as a matter of pride, a job left undone he's compelled to finish. Or, it could be fear."

"Fear?" Her fingers began to go numb from squeezing her hands so tightly. She tried to relax.

Richards shifted his position in the chair, leaning for-ward with his forearms resting on his knees. "Amanda," he said, dropping formalities, "you spent three days with him. Even though you didn't see his face, you may know things about him that you don't realize. The smallest detail could be important: the way he carried himself when he walked, a phrase he repeated, whether he was right- or left-handed."

"Left," she whispered, mesmerized by his soothing voice.

"See? You know things about him. If the killer thinks so, too, he may fear you could remember something else that might lead the police to him."

"No, no, that doesn't make sense at all. If he wanted to kill me, he would have come after me long before now." She looked away from those searching eyes and concentrated on breathing in and out. Her heart was beating so fast she felt slightly dizzy. How much longer could she endure these questions, pretending to be calm, when inside she was screaming?

"You moved out of state, changed your name." He shrugged. "Maybe the killer hasn't tried to find you before because he didn't suspect you had evidence that could implicate him. Or maybe he hasn't had the opportunity to come looking for you before now. Unless he's independently wealthy, or making his way by stealing, he has a job, like anyone else. Something brought him back to Shadow Falls. Are you willing to bet your life that he didn't come back to find you?"

She couldn't breathe. She had to get out of here. She jumped up from the couch. "Where are my manners? I should have offered you something to drink. Sweet tea, anyone?"

She rushed out of the room into the foyer without waiting for a response, desperate to escape before she dissolved into a shaking mass of nerves. The kitchen beckoned to her with its bright, sunny picture window that overlooked the front yard. She hurried through the archway into the cozy room, and clutched the edge of the sink, gulping in deep breaths of air as she stared outside at a world she could never really be a part of anymore.

The little girl who lived two houses away was walking down the sidewalk, her brother following behind on a red tricycle. Their mom shadowed both of them, keeping a close watch, keeping them safe.

Amanda clutched the countertop harder. She'd always

dreamed of having her own family someday, raising a couple of kids. Dana's killer had destroyed Amanda's dreams with a quick twist of his knife.

Now she just wanted to be alone.

To forget.

Horrific images from the cabin swam in front of her. Her chest heaved. Troubling memories clouded her mind, turning the world dark around her.

"It's okay." Chief Richards' deep voice spoke softly next to her ear, pulling her back from the abyss. "You're in your house, in the kitchen. No one's going to hurt you." He clasped her shoulders gently and led her to the table where he guided her into a chair. "Take slow, deep breaths." His warm hand kneaded the muscles in her neck, soothing and calming her.

Her breathing evened out. The world stopped spinning crazily around her. The blackness receded. Her heart still raced but she could finally inhale without struggling. His touch hadn't startled her, as she would have expected. Instead, it had grounded her, pulled her back from a nightmare. She didn't know what to make of that.

She shook off his hands and he moved to stand in front of her. He picked up one of the cloth napkins from the table and handed it to her. She gratefully accepted it and blotted her cheeks. Until he'd handed her the napkin, she hadn't realized she was crying. Embarrassed at the weakness she was displaying, she laid the napkin back on the table.

"It's okay. You're safe," he reassured her.

You're safe. He didn't ask if she was all right, like most people would after she'd hyperventilated and made a complete fool of herself. No, instead, he said the one thing she needed to hear.

You're safe.

How had he known what she needed? Why did his presence comfort her and his voice reassure her? This man was turning her carefully ordered world upside down.

Anxious to put some distance between them, she scooted back in her chair. "Thank you," was all she could manage. With him this close, he could see every detail of the disfiguring scar that ran down the side of her face. She waited for the familiar look of revulsion.

It never came.

Instead, his warm gaze traveled over her face and her hair like a soft caress. He sat in the chair across from her and absently stroked his thumb across the napkin that was wet from her tears.

"Come to the station." His deep voice touched something inside her, making her ache for the life she'd lost, the life she could never have. "Talk to me about what happened. Help me figure out how to keep this man from hurting you or anyone else ever again."

Her gaze hypnotically followed the motion of his thumb across the napkin, imagining the same gentle caress across her cheek. Then his words jerked her back to awareness. Talk to him about what had happened? Didn't he realize what he was asking? She'd spent years trying to rebuild her life, to forget the past. She would not relive that horrible ordeal again. *She couldn't.*

She jumped up from her chair and crossed to the sink. Opening a cabinet, she grabbed a glass and filled it with water. After a deep sip, she lowered the glass and stared out the window at the bright sunny morning, trying to draw on its warmth and light to chase away the darkness that was never far away.

"Everything okay in here?" Riley stood in the archway that separated the kitchen from the foyer. He glanced quizzically back and forth between her and Richards.

Amanda wiped the backs of her hands across her eyes. She hadn't cried once since moving back to Shadow Falls, and here she was crying for the second day in a row. She whirled around to face Richards. "I would appreciate it if you would both leave. Now."

He looked like he wanted to argue, but he gave her a curt nod. "Come on, Riley."

Amanda followed the two men into the foyer.

Riley stepped outside but Richards paused in the doorway, so close they were almost touching. Impossibly, everything inside her ached for his touch, as if he could wrap his strong arms around her and erase her past.

As if he could save her.

"Amanda." His masculine voice whispered across her raw nerves, reminding her of everything she could never have. "If you don't fight now, you'll be looking over your shoulder for the rest of your life. You need police protection and we need your help. Come to the station. Talk to me about what happened. Help me find out who this man is. Help me stop him before he hurts someone else."

Resentment came to her rescue, drying her tears, giving her the strength she needed. This man had un-bottled her long pent-up emotions . . . emotions she wasn't prepared to deal with. And here he stood, in her sanctuary, demanding she go to the police station as if she were the criminal.

"I already spoke to the police about my abduction. They interviewed me so many times I lost count. Do you honestly think I would leave out one single detail that might help someone catch the man who butchered Dana?"

His eyes narrowed. "Don't you mean the man who hurt *you*, too? You were as much a victim as she was."

She shook her head vigorously, her throat tightening. "Get out."

A look of pity crossed Richards' face as he stepped outside. Anger flashed inside Amanda and she slammed the door shut behind him. She leaned her forehead against the cool wood, dragging deep breaths into her tortured lungs. She didn't want Logan Richard's pity and she sure as hell didn't deserve his concern. Because, in spite of his belief that she was as much a victim as Dana was, he was wrong.

He didn't know what she'd done.

CHAPTER THREE

The taller and brawnier of the five FBI agents scanned the faces of the Shadow Falls detectives sitting around the conference room table. Logan had the impression the man was cataloging each person's features and comparing them to a mental list of the FBI's most wanted. His hawklike gaze zeroed in on Logan. "Chief Richards?"

Logan nodded and stood. He'd worked with Feds before, but he was also used to working on their timetable. Since calling them this morning, he'd expected they would arrive several days, maybe even a week later, depending on their workload and whether they agreed with his opinion that he might be dealing with a serial killer. Having his secretary usher the Feds into Monday afternoon's detective meeting was a pleasant surprise. They certainly hadn't wasted much time driving in from the Jacksonville field office four hours away.

He shook the other man's hand. "Call me Logan. Thanks for getting here so quickly." He introduced Riley and the other detectives sitting around the room.

"I'm Special Agent Pierce Buchanan. We spoke on the phone." He introduced each of the men who'd accompanied him.

"Welcome to the Panhandle," Logan said, motioning to some empty chairs as he sat down. "I wish it were under better circumstances."

"Trust me, I'd rather be here than anywhere else right now. This could be the break I've been looking for."

One of the FBI agents whispered something to Pierce. He nodded and looked at Logan. "Mind if we set up some photos and diagrams around the room?"

"Not at all."

Two of the special agents set briefcases on the table, and started piling the contents onto the conference room table and sorting it into stacks. Two other men began taping photographs onto the white board that ran along the back wall.

Pierce folded his arms across his chest as he stood beside Logan's chair. "I'm convinced your killer is the same killer I've been chasing for the past couple of years."

"And the Branson case we discussed on the phone?"

"From the photographs and case notes you emailed me, the signature fits. If so, this guy has operated longer than we thought. I'm surprised we didn't hear about the Branson case before now. Is your station set up on VICAP?"

Logan hesitated. The previous chief of police hadn't bothered to link the Shadow Falls PD with the FBI's Violent Criminal Apprehension Program database. As a result, the Branson case was never reported to the FBI. If it had been, the FBI would have sent an automatic notification back to the SFPD when a similar murder occurred. The

SFPD could have teamed up with the FBI years ago. Maybe they could have solved the case and prevented Carolyn O'Donnell's death.

"We're set up with VICAP now," he said, not willing to air his grievances with the former police chief in front of his men.

Pierce gave him an assessing glance. "You weren't the chief when the Branson case happened?"

It sounded more like a statement than a question, but Logan answered anyway. "I worked in New York City for most of the past decade."

"New York? I thought your name sounded familiar. You cracked the Metzger case, didn't you? Hell of a job."

Silence filled the room, and every eye turned to Logan. Metzger was a serial killer who'd plagued New York for fifteen months, killing a dozen women before Logan was put on the case. He'd solved it in less than three weeks. But he was never comfortable with the accolades he'd received. He'd simply come at the case with fresh eyes, saw a pattern others would have seen if they weren't so close to it.

"What can you tell us about the killer?" Logan asked, steering the conversation back to what was important.

Pierce nodded, not looking the least bit offended by the gruff response. He was all business as he turned to his men and directed them at tacking up pieces of paper and pictures on the dry erase board. By now, it was covered with photographs of women who looked remarkably similar. They were all young, slim, white females with long brown hair.

A stab of guilt shot through Logan when a picture of

Carolyn O'Donnell was added to the board. He didn't know what else he could have done to find her in time, but it still bothered him that he hadn't saved her.

He now realized that even if his men had told him about the Branson/Stockton case right when O'Donnell went missing, it wouldn't have mattered. After reading through the old case file yesterday afternoon and learning that Dana Branson was killed in one of the cabins on Black Lake, he'd sent his men to search that area. The cabins were rotting and run-down, unused for years since a drought had dried up most of the lake. There was no sign that the killer had taken O'Donnell to one of those cabins. And the case files had yielded no other leads that could have helped them find her in time.

Logan looked past O'Donnell's pictures to the pictures of Amanda. The first one was her college graduation photo from before the attack. Logan didn't think she looked all that different now. She was still beautiful, even with her scar. She had the same mass of thick, cinnamon colored hair and deep blue eyes that tilted up at the corners.

The main difference between the woman in that photo and the woman he'd met this morning was her smile, or lack of one. He hated that a stranger had taken away the joy and hope that had filled her college picture.

The second photo was from the crime scene at Black Lake. Amanda was balled up inside a hollowed out oak tree where the police had found her after she'd escaped and hid from Dana's killer. It wasn't the first time Logan had seen that photo. But now that he'd met Amanda, seeing her skin so deathly pale and smeared with blood was far more disturbing. When an agent handed him a sheet of paper, Logan was grateful for the excuse to look away from that haunting picture.

"Special Agent Nelson is passing out the profile he put together on the killer," Pierce said. "We'll update it with information from the O'Donnell and Branson/Stockton cases, but we believe it's still a viable profile."

When everyone had a copy, he stepped to the white board. "We'll review the profile in a few minutes. First, look at the pictures of the women he killed, or left for dead."

"What do you mean, *left for dead?*" Riley asked from his seat on Logan's left.

Pierce drew red circles around the faces of Dana, Amanda, and another woman.

"The killer's pattern is to stab and strangle his victims, except for these three cases. He stabbed these women, but he didn't kill them. He left them to bleed to death. We don't think he cared if they lived or died. He plays a twisted game of chance with each victim, deciding whether to finish them off based on the outcome of that game."

He glanced at Logan and nodded, as if to reassure him that he'd withhold the information about the thorns. That was something Logan had insisted on when he'd called the bureau. Having information to hold back was vital for culling out false confessions, or for proving they had the real killer in custody.

Continuing, Pierce said, "It's not the killing that excites him as much as the fear he elicits from his victims."

Encouraged by the possibility of another witness who might be more willing to be interviewed than Amanda was,

Logan indicated the picture of the third woman circled in red. "Did she survive?"

"Only long enough to answer a couple of questions. She'd lost too much blood." He pointed at Dana's and Amanda's pictures. "Since these two are his first known victims, their case is crucial to our investigation. A serial killer's first murder is often the one where mistakes are made, before he hones his craft and learns from those mistakes. That's why we'll focus heavily on both the Branson/Stockton case *and* the O'Donnell case. Solving the first may very well solve the last."

"Since Stockton survived, do we have a sketch of the killer?"

Pierce glanced toward the detective at the far end of the table who'd posed the question. "The woman who told us about the game said her attacker wore a hood." He looked at Logan. "I haven't seen the Stockton interview notes yet, but I'm under the impression the witness couldn't identify her attacker, that he wore a hood when he was with her too?"

"That's right." Logan glanced around the table. "She could only describe him as a white male with brown eyes. She judged him to be about six feet tall, around one-hundred-eighty pounds."

"Hell, I guess I did it," Riley joked. "You just described me."

A few weak laughs sounded around the table.

"It's a generic description, true," Pierce said. "But you can use that to help prioritize suspects as you conduct your interviews. Don't rely on the description entirely. Eye witness accounts are notoriously inaccurate."

He pointed to each picture, naming the victims and briefly describing the details of each murder.

"How often does he kill? Is there a pattern?" Riley asked.

"That's the one thing that's consistent with this killer," Pierce said. "Every summer he abducts two women, usually in two separate attacks. Again, the Branson/Stockton case is an exception since he took two women at the same time. We can only assume he saw an opportunity and took it. Or he might have learned from that first attempt and realized it was too difficult to control two victims at once, so he didn't repeat that mistake."

"You said he kills two women every summer," a detective called from the corner. "Is there a specific time frame between kills?"

Pierce shared an uncomfortable glance with one of the other agents before answering. "It varies. The first year he killed his victims three months apart. The time frame changes every year."

Logan sat forward in his chair. "Exactly how does it vary?"

"The time between kills gets shorter."

"How much time passed between kills last summer?" Logan prodded.

Pierce cleared his throat. Logan knew from the haunted look in the agent's eyes that he wasn't going to like his answer.

"Three weeks."

"I've answered all of *your* questions," Pierce said, as he and Logan walked through the squad room to the recessed elevator lobby in the middle of the back wall. "Now it's my turn to ask *you* a question."

Logan nodded at several uniformed officers coming in for the night shift. "Ask away."

"When can I interview Ms. Stockton?"

A ripple of irritation shot through Logan. He wasn't sure why. "I spoke to her this morning. She doesn't want to discuss the case with anyone." He stopped in front of the pair of elevators and pressed the "down" button.

"She might change her mind if you tell her the FBI wants to speak to her."

For some reason, the other man's persistence was irritating. Logan frowned and punched the button again. "I don't think that will matter."

"Perhaps. But sometimes witnesses feel more comfortable speaking to the Feds, especially if they've lost faith in their local authorities. No offense intended, but from what I saw of the investigation the last chief ran, it wasn't exactly comprehensive."

Logan grudgingly admitted to himself that the agent was right, as they stepped into the elevator. The case wasn't handled well and Amanda obviously agreed, based on the way she'd acted this morning. She didn't trust the police to keep her safe and he couldn't blame her. Still, if anyone was going to interview her, he wanted to be the one asking the questions.

"I'll ask Ms. Stockton to speak to you. Fair enough?"

"Fair enough. I'd also like to read through the complete case file as soon as possible."

"You'll have full access to anything you want. We'll make

copies of everything for you to take back to the Jacksonville field office."

Pierce shook his head. "I'm not leaving. I'm staying here until this case is resolved or the killer moves on to another city and strikes again."

Logan smiled, genuinely relieved. "I was hoping you'd say that. Where are you staying?"

"We drove straight here. I'll grab whatever motel room I can find tonight and be more discriminating tomorrow when I've got more time to look."

They exited the elevator and strode through the lobby of city hall. The police station took up the entire second floor. City hall took up the first floor and an annex next-door.

"We're not exactly Miami," Logan said. "But we still have a tourist season. The few motels we have are usually booked through the summer. Are all of your men staying tonight?"

"Only Nelson, a profiler. We left in a hurry this morning, so we have a few loose ends in Jacksonville to tie up. The rest of my men will drive back tonight, set up a task force, and return with more manpower in a few days, if you're agreeable to that."

"More than agreeable. I appreciate any help we can get, especially if we have less than three weeks to stop this killer before he strikes again." He pulled his set of keys out of his pocket and worked one off the ring. "We'll work on clearing some motel rooms for your team when they return, but for now, this should help." He tossed the key to Pierce.

"What's this?" Pierce caught the key in midair.

"I have an apartment about a mile from here. You and

Nelson can use it for the duration. There's only one bedroom but the sofa folds out into a bed."

"And where will you stay?"

"I've been renovating a house outside of town. I'd planned on moving in by the end of the month anyway, so most of my things are already there." He led the way through the glass front doors and down the concrete steps to the parking lot on the side of the building. "I'll drive you to the apartment and grab a few things."

Pierce nodded. "I appreciate that. The bureau will compensate you, of course."

Logan paused with one hand on the door handle of his Mustang. "Help me catch the killer. That's all the compensation I need." He looked around, a feeling of unease passing through him as he studied the few people walking to their cars. No one looked suspicious, but he couldn't shake the bad feeling in his gut.

"Something wrong?" Pierce studied him over the roof of the car.

Logan shrugged. "Just a feeling."

"What kind of feeling?"

"Like someone's watching me."

The agent glanced around as well, his body tense, alert. "You ever get that feeling before?" he asked, as they both got into the car.

"Yes."

"And?"

Logan raised a brow. "Someone was watching me."

The metallic rasp of a blade sliding from its butcher-block holder echoed in the silence of the house. Amanda hefted the glittering knife, admiring the perfectly balanced craftsmanship, the finely sharpened edge that could cut through muscle and bone with little effort.

Knives held a morbid fascination for her. Having been on the business end of one, she was determined to master the use of them. It was another way to face and overcome her fears, another way to not let *him* win.

Raising the knife in the air, she brought it down with a resounding *whack*. The head of lettuce fell open into two perfectly sliced halves. She pulled the rest of the ingredients for a salad out of the refrigerator and set them on the countertop, next to the phone. She'd wanted to call her sister ever since the police left this morning, but every time she picked up the phone she lost her nerve.

Her time in Tennessee at her sister's home after the attack wasn't pleasant for either of them. Heather had tried to be supportive—at first anyway—but the strain of living with someone who often woke up screaming at night was hard on a family with small children.

And then there was Heather's husband, John, the real reason Amanda and Heather rarely spoke anymore. John was controlling, a pathological liar, and he thought any woman living in his house was fair game for his attentions. He'd certainly had no aversion to Amanda's scar. Of course, her face wasn't what interested him.

Amanda had tried to talk to her sister about John's inappropriate behavior, but Heather was unwilling to listen and began to treat her as if she were the one coming on to John. That's when Amanda had left, and aside from a phone call at Christmas or on the anniversary of their parents' deaths, she and Heather rarely spoke to each other.

But after Carolyn O'Donnell's murder and Chief Richards' dire warnings, Amanda longed for the love and support of the only family she had left. Before she lost her nerve, she dialed her sister's number and pressed the speaker button so she could prepare her dinner while they talked.

"Hello?" Heather's soft, southern accent came on the line.

Amanda's hand slipped and she came dangerously close to slicing off a finger. Tears started in her eyes and she realized how badly she missed her baby sister. "Heather? It's Mandy."

Complete silence greeted Amanda from the other end of the line. She had to look at the light on the phone to be sure Heather hadn't hung up.

"Amanda?" Her sister's voice was pitched low as if she didn't want anyone else to hear her. "Are you okay? Is something wrong?"

Amanda, not Mandy. She closed her eyes and swallowed past the lump in her throat. "Does something have to be wrong for me to call?"

"No, of course not. I'm surprised to hear from you, that's all."

"How are you and my two adorable nieces? How's John?" Amanda nearly gagged on her brother-in-law's name.

"We're fine, we're all fine. The girls are going to that new elementary school that was being built when you left. I volunteer in the office three days a week." A heavy sigh sounded on the other end of the line. "You didn't call to talk about my volunteer work. What's going on?"

Chop. She brought the knife down on a cucumber, then rapidly sliced it into neat little chunks.

"Amanda?"

"There was a murder in Shadow Falls yesterday." Her words rushed out so fast she wasn't sure Heather would understand her.

"A murder? How terrible. Was it someone you knew?"

Thank God, no. Not this time. She grabbed a carrot and starting slicing it into slivers. "No, I didn't know her."

"Did it trigger one of those awful nightmares?"

She paused with the knife in the air. "No, no nightmares." Of course, she was so exhausted when she finally slept she was too tired to dream.

"Well, that's good. That's really good. Sounds like you've worked through your issues."

Her *issues?*

Chop.

Her aching knuckles made her realize how tightly she was gripping the knife handle. She relaxed her fingers. "Did I mention the murdered woman had a rose in her hand?" *Chop.* "The police think it's the same man who attacked me and killed Dana." *Chop.*

"Oh, my God. They think it's the same guy? What are you going to do?"

Obviously staying with her sister again wasn't an option, since Heather hadn't made that offer. What did Amanda expect, that Heather would suddenly believe her version of what had happened at her house instead of her husband's version?

"Amanda, are you still there?"

"Yeah, sorry. I'm sure it's not the same guy. Besides, I have a great security system and I've changed my name. I'll be okay."

"Are you sure? If you need—"

"I'm fine, really. Don't worry. I have to hang up now. Some friends are picking me up in a few minutes to go shopping," she lied. "Bye, Heather." She disconnected the call but left the phone line open so her sister couldn't call her back.

Not that she would.

Swiping at the tears on her cheeks, she looked down at the countertop in front of her. *Good grief.* She'd chopped all of the vegetables into tiny pieces. Hacked was a better word. Not to mention a banana and an apple she didn't remember putting on the counter. Obviously, she still had "issues," but she would have to face them alone.

An image of Logan Richards popped into her mind, how he'd stared at her with such compassion and tenderness. If he had a sister in trouble, would he turn his back on her?

Amanda didn't think so. He seemed like the kind of man who would race in and try to help, like one of those fairy tale knights on a white horse charging to rescue a princess. Only she couldn't picture him on a white horse. He would ride an enormous, black war horse that struck fear into the hearts of the men on the battlefield, but no more so than did the fierce knight who rode him.

Shaking her head at the ridiculous image, she grabbed the kitchen garbage can from under the sink and raked the massacred food into it. Tomorrow was trash day. She might as well haul everything to the curb before it got dark. Too bad she didn't have her own fierce knight racing to her rescue on his black war horse to take out the garbage for her.

She peered out the kitchen window as she always did before going outside, but this time she was extra careful. Chief Richards' warnings ran through her mind. She didn't want to believe the killer would come after her again, especially this many years later, but she didn't want to take any chances. After making sure no one was skulking out front, she looked through the peephole in her kitchen's steel side door to make sure no one was on the carport either. Then she stepped outside.

CHAPTER FOUR

Amanda shut the kitchen side door behind her and stood still. She studied the shrubs in her neighbor's side yard, shrubs Mrs. Fogelman stubbornly insisted on not trimming because she liked the "natural" look. Amanda figured the real reason was to shield Mrs. Fogelman's view of the ugly yard next-door. No bushes decorated Amanda's landscape. No one was going to sneak up on her unless they came from Mrs. Fogelman's side yard.

Irritated anew at her neighbor's dangerous stubbornness, Amanda grabbed the handle of the oversized, green rubber garbage can she kept at the far end of the carport. She tried to pull it to the street but it barely budged. She'd missed trash day last week so the can was twice as heavy as usual.

She glanced toward the street and made sure no one was nearby. Then she turned around and grabbed the handle with both hands for better leverage. Now all she had to do was pull the monster from the end of her carport, maneuver it around her aging Honda Accord without dinging it any worse than it already was, and haul it down the driveway to the curb.

Too bad it wasn't as easy as it sounded. Maybe she should get one of those garbage cans with wheels. She'd have to add that to her shopping list the next time she ventured out. She managed to drag the can past her car but it was slow going.

"What are you trying to do? Throw out your back?" a deep masculine voice demanded behind her.

She jumped and fell backward, but an arm caught her around the waist with a vice-like grip. Jabbing sharply backward with her elbow, she stomped her tennis shoe down on her attacker's foot and whirled around to face the threat. Her mouth dropped open in dismay when she saw who her attacker was.

Chief Richards.

"Oh, no, I'm so sorry—"

"Don't. Apologize." He grimaced as he rubbed his ribs. "My fault for startling you. I am beginning to wonder, though, what you have against my shoes."

"Your shoes?"

"You keep crushing them."

Heat flushed in her cheeks at his veiled reference to their first meeting. "I really am sorry, but you shouldn't have sneaked up on me like that."

"I didn't sneak." He shrugged out of his suit jacket. "You weren't paying attention."

He tossed his jacket over his shoulder and bent down to lift the garbage can. Amanda had enough sense to grab his jacket before it brushed against the side of the can, in spite of her sudden preoccupation with the muscles bunching in his arms.

He nodded his thanks and carried the can to the street as if it weighed nothing.

Dragging her gaze from his broad shoulders, she noticed his car parked along the curb. Her mouth quirked up in a grin. Forget the black war horse. Her knight had a black Mustang. She looked back at him as he turned around. "Thank you, Chief Richards—"

"Logan."

"Thank you," she said, uncomfortable calling the chief of police by his first name. She pulled her hair forward to cover her scar. "I appreciate your help, even though it wasn't necessary."

"You shouldn't try to haul something that heavy. Why don't you have a can with wheels?"

"Never thought about it, I guess." It was hard not to smile when she'd thought the same thing a few minutes earlier.

He reached for his jacket but she held it away from him. "Uh, uh. Not until you wash your hands."

He looked at his hands, holding them out to inspect them. "They look okay to me."

"You're still not touching this nice jacket until you soap up your hands. Besides, I don't think you drove all the way over here to haul out my trash." She headed up the driveway toward the house.

"It's not that long a drive here from the police station."

She glanced at him, saw him make some kind of signal back toward the street, then quickly drop his arm when he saw her looking.

"I thought about offering them lunch earlier," she said, referring to the white Crown Victoria parked a block down from her house. "But I didn't know how they'd feel about me blowing their cover."

"You knew they were police officers?" He had a surprised look on his face.

"It's a small neighborhood. This is a dead end street. I knew that car didn't belong, so I watched it for awhile through my kitchen window and figured it out. Besides, no one could sit in a car around here for more than twenty minutes without Mrs. Fogelman interrogating them. She'd have called the cops long ago if the men in that car weren't policemen."

"You aren't angry?" He walked with her up the driveway toward her house.

"I was, at first. After all, I refused police protection, yet, here they are. But . . ." She held up her hand to stop him when he looked like he was going to interrupt. "I do feel safer knowing they're here, as long as they don't show up in a marked police car."

When they reached her kitchen door, Logan reached past her and opened it, then waited for her to precede him into the house. Murmuring her thanks, she stepped inside and bent down to get a fresh dish towel from the cabinet beneath the sink. She placed it on the counter alongside the liquid soap.

When she turned around, he was standing with his back against the door, staring at her with an unreadable expression on his face. He slowly crossed the kitchen floor, reminding her of a powerful panther. Her eyes widened at the heated look in his eyes and she moved out of the way.

As he washed his hands, he said, "Who's Mrs. Fogelman?"

"The self-appointed neighborhood-watch lady. I'd be willing to bet she already knows your men's names, badge numbers, and the names of their wives and kids."

He finished drying his hands and refolded the dishtowel, leaving it exactly where she'd placed it. "If she got all that information, I'll fire them. They should be able to give her a cover story to get her to leave them alone without revealing they're cops."

"I hope you give them decent severance pay," she smirked.

He rolled his eyes and leaned back against the sink, his long legs braced out in front of him and his palms resting on the countertop edge.

She laid his jacket over the back of a kitchen chair and smoothed an imaginary wrinkle out of the material, enjoying the clean masculine scent that clung to the fabric.

The silence grew and she looked up, surprised to see him frowning at her.

"You've been crying," he said.

She wiped her eyes self-consciously. After hanging up on her sister, she'd given in to her emotions. "Nice of you to say so," she grumbled.

"Why were you crying?" he pressed.

"Why are you so nosy?"

A slow grin spread across his face. "You're a real smart ass, aren't you?"

The comment should have annoyed her, but the way he said it with that slow, sexy grin made it sound like a compliment. "Excuse me if I don't kowtow to you like your men do. Sorry if that bothers you."

"I didn't say it bothered me." His grin widened.

Unable to hold that intense stare for long, she looked away and pulled more hair over her right shoulder to better cover her scar.

"Why do you do that?"

She froze, her fingers still tangled in her hair. "Why do I do what?"

"You're a beautiful woman. You don't need to hide behind your hair."

Beautiful? If anyone else had said that, she'd think they were making fun of her. But Richards didn't strike her as a cruel man. The way he was looking at her was the way men used to look at her, before her face was ravaged. Confused and increasingly uncomfortable beneath his scrutiny, she asked, "Why did you come here?"

"I'm supposed to ask if you'll speak to an FBI agent about your abduction."

She noted the tension in his jaw, the tightening of his fingers against the edge of the countertop. "Supposed to? You don't want me to talk to him? Or her?"

"Him. Of course I do. But I want you to speak to me first."

"Since I don't want to talk to either of you, there really isn't an issue, is there?"

He shrugged and glanced around the kitchen. She looked around too, wondering how it appeared to the eyes of a stranger. It was her favorite room in the house—bright and sunny, with a soothing, creamy yellow covering the walls.

It was an eat-in kitchen with plenty of space and a terra-cotta tile floor that perfectly complimented the color on the walls. She would have preferred it to open up into the living room like the newer houses—instead of opening into the foyer—but it was homey.

She looked back at him and frowned, wondering why he wasn't making any move to leave, not that she didn't enjoy the view. Her fingers itched with the desire to touch him, and she hadn't drawn a proper breath since he'd held her against him. The unfamiliar feelings made her uneasy and unsure of herself. She didn't want to be attracted to him, not when the sight of him standing there so tall and strong reminded her of her own vulnerability.

"Chief Richards—"

"Logan."

She sighed. "I'm not trying to be rude, but if you came here to ask me whether I'm willing to speak to the FBI, you have your answer. Was there something else you wanted?"

His gaze shot to hers, shocking her with its heat. Then he looked away and she wondered if she'd imagined that spark of attraction that had flared between them.

"I should go." He strode forward and reached for his jacket.

"Wait." His arm muscles jumped beneath her fingertips and they both looked down at her hand on his arm. She'd touched him without even realizing she'd done it.

She snatched her hand back, already regretting that she'd stopped him, but good manners wouldn't let her be so brusque. "Wait. Please. You were nice enough to help me with the trash, and you've been nothing but kind to me, concerned about my safety. The least I can do is offer you a drink. How does iced tea sound?"

He studied her with those unfathomable dark eyes, and for a moment she thought he'd refuse her offer. Then he nodded. "Tea sounds good. Beer sounds better."

She narrowed her eyes. "Are you off duty?"

The corner of his mouth tilted up in a wry grin. "As much as a chief of police is ever off duty." When she raised her brow, he added, "One beer won't impair my driving. Promise."

She crossed to the refrigerator and pulled out two bottles. "I hope this brand is okay. It's the only kind I buy."

He looked at the label and that lopsided smile appeared again, making her wonder what he was thinking.

"This will do." He took both bottles from her, twisted the cap off the first one and handed the bottle to her. Then he twisted the cap off his and they both sat down at the table.

When he tilted his bottle and took a drink, she was mesmerized by the sight of his throat working to swallow. She forced herself to look away and she searched for something to say to fill the silence. "I'm guessing you're on your way home. Where do you live?"

He set the bottle on the table and seemed to consider her question. "I was living in an apartment near the station, but as of this evening Cypress Hills is home. I've been renovating a house there. Other than finishing a downstairs half-bath, everything else is ready."

She was surprised a police chief could afford to buy a house in Cypress Hills. It was an affluent area, known for its beautiful wooded lots and gently sloping lawns. If she remembered correctly, most of the houses were set back on land that bordered a tributary with access to the Gulf of Mexico. "Cypress Hills. That's a beautiful area. Are you doing all the work yourself?"

"Most of it. I hired a roofer and an electrician. Other than that, I did the rest. It's not the first one I've done, kind of a side hobby."

"You flip houses? You're not keeping this one?"

"I've flipped a few, made a nice profit. But the real estate market isn't great right now and this house is . . ." He shrugged, making her wonder why he'd paused. "It feels like home. My sister and mom came down from New York a few months ago and spent a fortune of my money decorating it. They were worried I'd end up with a house full of electronics—and no furniture—if they didn't help."

She smiled, picturing strong, masculine Logan Richards at the mercy of two women taking over his house. "I take it your mom and sister aren't into gadgets?"

"Not at all," he said. "Unlike you."

Her fingers tightened around her beer bottle. "Unlike me?"

"I noticed this morning that you have a fondness for electronics. Your TV is state-of-the-art. Your computer is top-of-the-line. Instead of a typical printer you have an all-in-one. If I had to bet, I'd say you probably have the latest cell phone with all the options, too."

"I don't have a cell, actually." Not anymore. Who would she call? "But you noticed everything else in the ten minutes you were in my living room?"

"I noticed a lot about you this morning."

Her eyes widened at his comment and she took a nervous sip of her beer. When she set it back on the table, she realized he was watching her with one of those unreadable expressions again. "What?" she demanded, a little too forcefully.

Unfazed, he said, "I guess I'm trying to figure you out."

A spark of panic shot through her. "There's nothing to figure out."

He cocked his head. "Why did you come back to Shadow Falls when your only living relatives are in Tennessee? Did something happen between you and your sister when you stayed with her after the attack?"

She froze at the mention of Heather. It wasn't fair that he knew so much about her just because he was a cop. "That is none of your business," she snapped.

"You're right. It isn't."

Her irritation faded at his quick reply. She sighed and decided to answer his question. "I was born in Shadow Falls, spent most of my life here. My parents are buried here. It's home." She shrugged. "Besides, I couldn't impose on my sister forever." Especially when she wasn't welcome. "When I left Tennessee, I couldn't imagine going anywhere else, so I came here." Besides that, Dana was here. There was no one else to visit her grave and leave fresh flowers. Amanda owed her that much.

She pushed thoughts of Dana away and looked across the table at Richards. "What about you? Why did you move back? I remember reading about you in the newspaper when you took over from the last chief. They said you started your career here, then moved to New York. Do you have family here, or did you leave them all behind when you moved back here?"

He grinned. "Touché. No, I don't have family here." His smile faded and his eyes took on a distant expression. "Everyone I care about is in New York." He quickly finished his beer, then stood and glanced around the kitchen with the empty bottle in his hand.

"Under the sink," she said in answer to his unspoken question.

He rinsed out the bottle, then opened the cabinet and tossed the bottle in the blue recycle bin. When he straightened, he looked around as if in indecision. Then his gaze met hers and he sighed. "Not that one beer is going to make someone my size impaired, but I'd rather not hit the road right after drinking one. I could spend a few minutes checking your home security if you want. It would make me feel better about you not being under police protection."

He didn't look like he wanted to stay another minute in her house. As soon as he'd mentioned leaving his loved ones in New York he looked miserable. So why had he offered to check her security system? "I've got protection outside in an unmarked car," she reminded him.

"It would be better if someone stayed with you inside the house."

His words filled her mind with images of Logan staying in her house, watching over her, protecting her . . . sleeping on her couch. She forced the images away. He wasn't offering to stay and protect her and she wouldn't let him even if he did. She wasn't willing to give up her privacy and she hadn't decided yet if she was really staying in town, now that the killer was back.

Part of her wanted to pack her things and get on the next

plane to anywhere but here. But another part of her was just as determined not to let the killer chase her away again. She'd worked so hard to rebuild her life. She didn't want to start over. "I don't want someone staying in my house with me."

"What about work?" he asked. "My men said you didn't go to work today, but when you do, you'll need protection."

She smiled. "No one is going to attack me at work."

He raised a brow. "You seem confident about that."

"All I have to do to get to work is walk from my bedroom to the living room. I'm a computer programmer. I work remotely from home."

"Well, I guess you put me in my place." He softened his words with a smile, the first real smile he'd given her since he'd called her a smart ass.

For a moment, she was frozen by the approving look in his eyes, the way his gentle smile transformed his face and made him look like a charming rogue instead of the intimidating police chief.

The silence stretched out. Time to send him on his way. He didn't want to be here anymore than she wanted him here.

"So, how about it? Want me to check your doors and windows?" he asked.

No. "Okay." *Damn.* Why had she said that?

He nodded. "I'll start in the living room. I remember seeing a set of sliding glass doors in there. If they aren't properly secured, someone could easily pop one of them off the track and walk right in."

"I doubt that." She led the way into the living room. "I

replaced the doors when I moved in. The company that installed my alarm recommended it."

She watched him check out the security bar and the locks, and examine the alarm sensors, all the time wondering why he seemed so edgy.

"You've got hurricane glass, and you can't take one of these doors off the track from the outside, at least not easily," he said. "Good locks. I'm impressed."

"You seem surprised."

"I shouldn't be, given your past. You obviously take your safety seriously. Most people don't."

Crossing to one of the windows that framed the fireplace, he checked those locks as well, then glanced at her computer before moving to the second window. "I've never met someone who worked from home. Is it a nine-to-five type of job?"

He finished examining the locks and security sensors, so she led him down the hallway to the first spare bedroom, a room she used mostly for storage. "My schedule is flexible. I work for a consulting company and I choose which contracts I want to take on. I just finished a six-month stint. I haven't decided yet when I'll take on the next contract."

He dusted off his hands after checking the only window in the bedroom. Then he moved toward the door where she was standing.

Embarrassed about the dirt on the windowsill, she said, "Sorry about the dust. I rarely use this room."

He gave her a droll look. "I'm a guy. I don't think I've ever dusted anything."

She laughed and led him to the second bedroom. He was sweet to try to make her feel less embarrassed, but as par-

ticular as he was about his appearance, and as shiny clean as
his car was, she didn't believe for a second that his house was
anything less than pristine.

The door was already open, so he stepped inside. His
eyes widened as he looked around at all the exercise equipment. "A professional gym would be envious of what you
have here."

A picture of him shirtless and sweaty after a vigorous
session of weight lifting crossed her mind. She absently
toyed with the hem of her shirt. "I don't get out much—have
to work off the occasional Haagen-Dazs indulgence somehow."

His gaze slid down her body in a slow, leisurely caress,
as if he was evaluating the effects of her workout routine.
When his eyes met hers again, the heat in his gaze nearly
scorched her. She wanted to encourage him, wanted to
throw back some kind of flirty comment to let him know
the attraction was mutual.

She couldn't.

She was too scared, but not of him. She was scared of
herself. In the years since her attack she'd built a solitary,
safe life. Until Logan, she wasn't tempted to enjoy the com-
panionship of a man again. Now that he'd awakened all
those dormant feelings, she didn't trust herself.

Could she act like a normal person with him? What if
he tried to hold her, kiss her? Would she welcome his touch
or would the image of her attacker loom in her mind and
send her screaming from the room? Seeing him look at her
like she was crazy would hurt even more than when people
looked at her scar and flinched.

She couldn't bear it.

Deciding it was time for him to leave, she pivoted on her heel and hurried back to the kitchen to usher him out.

He followed her, stopping behind her, close, but not touching. "Amanda, look at me." His deep voice was patient, soothing. "Please."

She blew out a frustrated breath and turned around, looking up into his eyes as she leaned back against the same countertop where he'd leaned earlier.

"I'm sorry I scared you," he said.

She shook her head. "You didn't scare me. You don't scare me." And it was true. She felt so safe with him she wanted to wrap herself in his arms and lock out the rest of the world. She barely knew him. He was powerfully built and no doubt could easily hurt her if he chose. She was alone with him, with no one else to help her if he did want to harm her. So why wasn't she afraid of him? It didn't make any sense.

"No?" His searching gaze held hers. "Then why did you run?"

She sighed and automatically started to pull her hair forward, then stopped self-consciously when she remembered what he'd said about her hiding behind her hair.

"Amanda—"

"I'm sorry. Really. I can't . . . it's just that I . . ." She blew out a frustrated breath.

He reached out his hand toward her but dropped it when she jerked backwards. She awkwardly folded her arms over her chest, her automatic reaction reminding her she was right. She couldn't handle a relationship, no matter how tempting.

His eyes were sad as he looked at her. "Don't apologize. My actions were inappropriate. I don't know what got into me." His eyes took on the far-away look he had earlier when he talked about his loved ones in New York. "I really don't."

He shrugged into his jacket, then pulled a small white card from his pocket and laid it on the kitchen table. "My business card. If you change your mind about speaking to the FBI, call me." His gaze captured hers. "Even if you don't change your mind, if you need someone to talk to, about anything, call me. No strings."

He crossed to the side door, gave her another one of those heart-achingly sad smiles, then stepped out onto the carport.

By the time the taillights on Logan's car faded in the distance, Amanda was shaking so hard she had to sit down at the table. For a few minutes tonight, Chief Richards—Logan—had made her feel attractive again. She'd forgotten how good it felt to have a man look at her with hunger in his eyes.

Not that it mattered. She couldn't encourage any kind of relationship between them. Her own seesawing emotions were too much to deal with.

Let alone his.

At times tonight, he'd looked like he was scared to death of her.

Logan shook his head in disgust, tilted his beer, and took a long, deep drink. He slammed the empty bottle down on the top rail of his back deck, mildly surprised the glass didn't shatter. The gold label sparkled up at him in the porch light, mocking him, reminding him Amanda drank the same brand of beer.

They both had the same brand of TV, the same kind of computer. About half of the DVDs in the rack beside her TV were the same movies he had next to his—action movies, not chick flicks.

He wiped a bead of sweat from his forehead and looked down at the picture frame he held in his left hand. Victoria's soft brown eyes stared up at him with that adoring look she'd once reserved only for him. God, how he'd loved her. He still couldn't believe she was no longer his. They'd been happy together, or so he'd thought, until she asked for a divorce so she could marry someone else.

In the year since the divorce he'd been convinced he could never love another woman like that. He'd never meet someone and again feel that hot rush of attraction, that sense of connection when he looked in her eyes, as if he'd known her forever. He never thought another woman could make him burn for her, yearn for her, the way he'd once burned for Victoria.

Until he met Amanda.

The moment he'd looked into those haunted blue eyes he was lost. He'd wanted to pull her into his arms, protect her, ease the hurt that caused the shadows in her eyes. Even now he wanted nothing more than to rush back to her house and make sure she was safe, even though his men were outside watching over her.

He cursed and crossed the deck to the set of French doors and went inside. He set the alarm, discarded his beer bottle in the kitchen, then glanced at his watch. He should have been in bed long before now, but he was too keyed up to sleep. He needed something to take his mind off Amanda, because no matter how much he might want her, he couldn't have her. Might as well do what he did most nights when he couldn't sleep, which was often. He headed toward the front of the house to his study.

The top of his desk was covered with stacks of files. Aside from the cold cases his former team in New York occasionally sent to get his advice, he now had files from both the O'Donnell case and the Branson/Stockton case piled across his desk. He grabbed the nearest folder and flipped to the first page, but the words swam in front of him, making no sense. He couldn't focus, couldn't concentrate, not with thoughts of Amanda still swirling through his mind.

She was a witness in a murder investigation. Logan knew he had no business even thinking about getting personally involved with her. If he couldn't concentrate now, it would only get worse if he allowed this insane attraction to go any further. What if he missed something important and another woman died? At least with his rookie mistake, he could tell himself maybe the killer hadn't killed again. Maybe the killer knew his victim and it was a crime of passion, a one-time thing.

Carolyn O'Donnell's killer was different. He'd killed before and he would kill again. He was probably already stalking his next victim. Logan had to do everything he could to stop the killer, or the next woman's death would be on him. There wasn't any room in his life for a relationship right now, especially with Amanda.

Even if he didn't have the case to worry about, Amanda had been horribly brutalized, both physically and emotionally. She wasn't ready for a relationship either, as evidenced from their discussion earlier tonight. The best thing for her right now was for him to respect her wishes, treat her professionally, and find the killer who'd nearly destroyed her four years ago.

He shuffled through the pages in the current file, pages he'd already read dozens of times today without seeing anything new. What he'd really like to have is the Anna Northwood file to look through. Looking through the case he'd screwed up ten years ago would give his mind a break, free his subconscious to work on the details of Amanda's case to look for a pattern.

Unfortunately, his search for the file earlier today in the department's online database had yielded only one line that read "archived to off-site storage." The file was too old, had never been keyed into the online system. He'd have to pay a visit to the storage warehouse sometime soon and find that file, but for tonight, he'd just have to review the Branson case again.

He sighed and flipped another page.

Kate was back.

He could barely believe it, even though he knew it was true.

She'd never come back that soon before. *Damn it*. Why wouldn't she leave him alone? He'd found peace, blessed peace, and he'd hoped it would last this time.

She'd called herself Carolyn earlier, and she'd been so perfect, so sweet, that he'd believed maybe, just maybe, she'd finally go away for good this time like she'd promised. He'd foolishly hoped she might finally let him live his life without fear, without worrying she'd find him again.

He should have known he couldn't trust her. Kate always lied.

And this time, like once before, she called herself Amanda.

CHAPTER FIVE

Guilt was a powerful motivator. Amanda fought its relentless pull for two days, but it was a losing battle. Wednesday afternoon she sat in her car, parked outside the building shared by city hall and the police department, trying to work up the courage to open the door and go inside.

She didn't want to dredge up her past and endure another round of police interviews. The ugliness of what had happened to her stared back at her every day when she looked in the mirror. The killer had left his mark on her in so many ways, ensuring she could never forget, never truly escape. And she'd already told the police everything—or, at least, everything relevant to their investigation.

But what if Logan Richards was right and she knew something she didn't even realize she knew, something that would help them stop the killer before he hurt anyone else? Dana had died because of Amanda's cowardice. Could she really live with another person's death on her conscience?

She already knew that answer. Since Logan's visit, the nightmares had returned: vivid images of the inside of the

cabin, the wink of light against the killer's jagged blade,
Dana's cries of terror when Amanda ran from the cabin,
leaving her behind.

Amanda shivered and rubbed her arms, her chill having
nothing to do with the cool air blasting from the car's air-
conditioner. She fervently hoped if she answered Logan's
questions, the nightmares would go away again. She could
return to her sanctuary, live her quiet life, and go back to
trying to pretend the past had never happened.

She grabbed her purse, got out of her car, and hurried
up the steps into the building before she could change her
mind. The crush of people in the first floor lobby had her
pulling her hair forward to hide her scar. She kept her
eyes downcast, hoping no one would try to talk to her, and
pressed the button for the elevator.

A few moments later a low beep signaled the elevator's
arrival. She rushed inside, relieved when no one joined her.
As the doors closed, she punched the button for the second
floor.

Nausea churned in her stomach as she stepped out into
the elevator lobby, a small alcove set back from the squad
room. She wiped her palms on her long, denim skirt and
stared out at the hauntingly familiar scene. The walls were
still a depressing battleship gray. Row upon row of paper-
strewn desks still filled the cavernous space. The combina-
tion of phones ringing, the clicking of computer keyboards,
and people talking still produced the same low hum she
sometimes heard in her dreams.

Some of the faces had changed, but most were familiar,
as if the last four years had never happened. But time *had*

passed. In spite of the crying jags she'd gone on the past few days, she wasn't the broken woman she was back then. She refused to cower now.

She straightened her shoulders and looked down at the threshold that separated the elevator lobby from the squad room. That thin black grout line looked so small, so insignificant, but she knew once she crossed it there was no going back.

She took a deep breath and crossed the line.

"Miss, can I help you?"

Amanda finger-combed her hair over her scar and turned toward the freckle-faced police officer who'd approached her. Her heart squeezed in her chest at the youthful innocence on his face. He looked like he should be renting a tux for his senior prom instead of wearing a gun and a badge. How many crime scenes would it take before that innocence was shattered and gone forever?

For her it had only taken one.

She smiled, keeping her face partially averted so he wouldn't see her scar. "I'm Amanda Stockton. I'm here to see Chief Richards, if he's available?"

"Sure, follow me. He's in the main conference room." Before she could stop him, he charged off through the maze of desks toward the right side of the room, his eagerness to please showing in every bouncing step he took.

She caught up with him at the door. "Please, wait. He's not expecting me. I don't have an appointment. Does he have an assistant who could see whether he has an opening, or—"

"Mabel's off today. I'm sure it's not a problem. I'll let him know you're here." He tapped on the door, then pushed it open and stepped inside to speak to someone she couldn't see.

As the door swung further into the room, a wall of horrific photographs swam into view, including one of her, covered in blood, squeezed into the impossibly narrow, rotten tree trunk she remembered so vividly.

She could almost smell the damp, rotting wood, feel the insects crawling over her skin, in her hair, biting and stinging, the paralyzing fear as a twig snapped nearby, fear that the killer had found her.

Blackness swirled at the edges of her vision. Her breath came out in sharp, choppy pants. Her pulse pounded in her ears, drowning out the sounds around her. Panic flooded through her. What had made her think she could relive that nightmare again? She wasn't ready. She had to get out of here.

Whirling around, she rushed through the squad room, no longer caring that anyone could see her scar as her hair flew out behind her. She skidded to a stop in front of the elevators and punched the "down" button.

Too slow, too slow. Can't breathe.

She punched the button again and frantically looked around. A door to her left had a red sign marked "stairs." She lunged toward the door, her high heels slipping on the polished terrazzo floor.

"Amanda, wait." Strong hands grasped her shoulders, pulling her back.

"No, leave me alone." She kicked back with her heel, striking her attacker's shin. A pained grunt sounded behind her. A powerful arm circled her waist and pulled her back against a solid chest.

"Amanda, it's Logan," a deep voice whispered next to her ear. "No one's going to hurt you."

Logan. It was Logan. Her panic drained and she collapsed against him, inhaling his comforting, familiar scent as her labored lungs struggled for air.

He turned her in his arms and gently pressed her head against his chest while he whispered soothing words to her. She squeezed her eyes tightly shut and clung to him, reveling in the feel of his strong arms around her. *She was safe. With Logan she was safe.* The dark shadows began to recede. The dull roar in her ears faded. Sounds returned. Phones ringing. Papers shuffling.

"Back to your desks, everybody," Detective Riley's voice called out. "There's nothing to see."

Amanda's eyes shot open. She gasped and shrank back from the crowd of detectives and uniformed policemen watching her from a few feet away. Logan's arms tightened around her.

The young policeman who'd led her to the conference room stared at her, his eyes wide, his freckles standing out in sharp contrast against his pale face. Riley shoved him to get him moving and ushered the other men back into the squad room.

Amanda squeezed her eyes shut again, her face flushing with heat. "Can you get me out of here, please?" she whispered miserably.

"Do you want me to carry you?"

Carry her? He sounded serious, as if he was about to lift her up in his arms in front of the entire police department. Her face flushed even more as she shoved out of his arms and took a step back. "Don't you dare. I'm embarrassed enough already."

He tilted her chin up and leaned down, his brows drawn together in a hard line. "You've been through hell and back, endured more than most people could ever imagine. You don't owe anyone any explanations and you sure as hell shouldn't feel embarrassed."

His declaration of support had her throat closing up. It had been so long since anyone had shown any concern about her. She offered him a wobbly smile. Her smile faded as she noticed a man in a dark suit standing a few feet away, studying both of them. She instinctively tucked herself closer to Logan.

Logan squeezed her shoulders. "This is Special Agent Pierce Buchanan," he said. "He's the FBI agent I told you about."

Pierce, who looked strikingly similar to Logan, held out his hand and offered her a reassuring smile.

"Amanda Stockton," she said, as she reluctantly shook his hand. The feel of his strong fingers clasping hers sent a tremor of dread through her. She snatched her hand away, then flushed with embarrassment and leaned back against Logan. Both of these men towered over her. Both of them were powerfully built. But for some reason she couldn't explain, she felt completely safe with Logan. His size didn't make her uncomfortable like the FBI agent's did.

"It's good to meet you, Ms. Stockton," Pierce said, glancing from her to Logan, obviously wondering if there was something going on between them. "I apologize that you saw those photographs," he continued. "They were never intended to be seen by civilians."

At the mention of the pictures, she swallowed against the bile rising in her throat.

Logan's deep voice sounded next to her ear as he leaned down behind her. "I'll take you home."

Her heart clutched in her chest at the way he kept his arm around her, unfazed by what the agent might think of him. Even though she hadn't told Logan that she was here to let him interview her, he must have figured it out. And yet, he was willing to give up his chance to ask her questions. He was more concerned with making sure she was okay.

The temptation to take the comfort he offered and ignore her responsibilities was nearly overwhelming. But the reprieve would only be temporary. The guilt that had haunted her since Monday morning when he'd first asked her to come to the station would dig its tentacles into her again, forcing her to come back. And since she had no intention of ever coming back after today, she needed to face her fears and get this ordeal over with.

"No, I'm okay." Her voice sounded shaky and weak. She cleared her throat and tried again. "I'm fine," she said, her voice clear and strong this time. She stepped away from Logan again and faced him. "I came here to speak to you." She looked over at Pierce. "And you too. I'm here because Chief Richards said he wanted to ask me some questions. He thought I might know something that can help with your investigation."

"Let's go into another conference room," Pierce suggested, his voice eager.

Logan frowned at him. "Are you sure, Amanda?"

She nodded and pasted what she hoped was a serene smile on her lips.

He hesitated, giving her a doubtful look.

"I'm really okay," she assured him, hoping he couldn't tell how much she was shaking inside.

He still didn't look like he believed her, but he gave her a tight nod and led her through the squad room, turning left this time instead of right. Flanked by the two large men, she was shielded from any curious stares.

Pierce stopped in front of a frosted glass door and held it open while she and Logan stepped inside. Since there was a table and chairs in the room, it could technically be called a conference room, but it was so small a closet was a more apt description. With Logan and Pierce inside, it was filled to capacity.

"Do you want something to drink?" Logan asked.

"No, thank you. Let's just get this over with."

He reached across the table and squeezed her hand. "If we ask any questions that make you too uncomfortable, let us know."

She nodded and tried to relax back against the chair. She tugged her hand away from his, not because it bothered her, but because she couldn't think with him touching her. Instead, she clasped her hands in her lap beneath the table.

"Let's start with the week before the abduction," Logan said. "We need to know exactly where you went, who you saw. We need to know why he chose you and Dana."

"Okay." The week before the abduction was safe territory. She could handle that.

A hundred questions later, she wasn't so sure. She felt like a tennis ball tossed back and forth across the net, never knowing where the next swing would come from or where she might land. She answered most of their questions, but every time one of them veered toward the details of the attack itself, she steered them away to safer territory. She could tell they were both frustrated, but she couldn't bring herself to discuss those intimate details again. Her throat closed up every time she tried.

Pierce finally pushed his chair back and stood. "I appreciate your patience with our questions, Ms. Stockton. You've been a tremendous help."

"I have?" She didn't think she'd given them anything new.

"You've filled in gaps in the reports I've read. If you want to come back and talk again, please do so. I'd like another opportunity to question you further, when you're ready."

Meaning, when she was ready to talk about what her attacker had done to her, not just the events surrounding her abduction. He left the room, leaving the door open behind him.

"You did a great job," Logan said.

She ignored the little rush of pleasure his praise sent through her, especially since he was just being polite. Nothing she'd told them seemed like anything new or significant, even though she'd tried her best to think of any details she might have missed before. "I'm sorry I couldn't answer the questions you really wanted me to answer. I wanted to. I really tried, but I . . ." Her voice trailed off and she looked up at him, frustrated at her inability to face her fears.

"It took tremendous courage to come here, and even more to put up with our badgering."

Courage? She didn't agree, but it felt good to have someone talk to her like she mattered. Until she'd met him, she hadn't realized how much she'd missed interacting with other people, or how much that bothered her. Other than going to the post office or to the occasional store when she absolutely couldn't get what she needed delivered to her house, she was always alone.

"Why are you frowning? The inquisition is over," he teased as they both stood.

"I didn't mean to. I was just thinking." She was thinking about how she'd still feel just as guilty when she got home as she did now, since she hadn't really helped with the investigation. She hadn't had the courage to help Dana when it mattered most, but maybe there was something else she could do, some way to help catch Dana's killer. "I'd still like to help, somehow."

Logan's eyebrows rose in surprise. "You want to help with the investigation?"

"Absolutely. I'm great with computers. Is there something along those lines you need? Maybe I could help catalog the case files into a database, index them, build an algorithm to cross-check interviews for commonalities, look for patterns, something like that."

"You could do that?" Pierce called out from the doorway. He glanced at Logan. "Sorry for interrupting. I came back to tell you Riley has a new lead: a friend of Carolyn's who might have remembered someone suspicious hanging around a couple of weeks before she was abducted."

"Someone local?" Logan asked.

"No, someone at FSU. Riley took Clayton with him. They're driving up to Tallahassee now. Should be back by morning."

"Sounds good." Logan turned back to Amanda, a thoughtful look on his face. "Most of the data is already in a database, but that algorithm you mentioned might be useful. How long would it take to build something like that?"

"Not long, depending on the kind of computer system you have, and depending on the amount of data. A day or two, at most. If I can remote in from home, use my own equipment, I could get it done faster."

"Sounds like a great idea," Pierce said. "Nelson could show her the files and how they're organized right now. He's the closest thing to a computer expert on my team. And you could give her an overview of the investigation."

"Not so fast," Logan said. "Can you give us a minute?" He stared pointedly at the door.

Pierce looked reluctant to leave, but he nodded. "I'll be in the main conference room." He stepped outside, closing the door behind him with a sharp click.

"Why are you doing this?" Logan asked.

"What do you mean? I told you, I want to help."

"I know what you said, but I also know what happened when you saw those photographs. The data, as you called it, is just as graphic as those pictures. I'm not so sure that letting you read the reports is a good idea."

She straightened her shoulders, not at all pleased with the impression she'd obviously given him. He probably thought she was weak. She really couldn't blame him since he'd seen her at her worst from the moment he'd met her. Was she weak? Perhaps, in some ways, but she truly believed she could help if he'd only let her. "I wasn't prepared before. I am now. I can handle it."

He looked skeptical, like he didn't believe her, but she could tell he wanted to.

Irritation had her clenching her fists. "Look," she said. "I want to find Dana's killer as much as you do. After the attack, I kind of . . . checked out. It took a long time for me to get to a place where I could really function again. And when you came to my house the other day, I was still getting over the shock of finding out the man who'd attacked me was back in town. But I'm over that now. I'm really okay. And I'm the best damn programmer around. Please, let me do this one thing. Let me help you find Dana's killer before he kills someone else."

His lips twitched and his mouth curved up in a half-smile. "The best damn programmer around, huh?"

She couldn't help but respond to his smile with one of her own. "The very best."

"All right. You've convinced me." He opened the door. "Let's go see Agent Nelson."

"Are you hungry?" Logan asked.

Since he and Amanda were the only ones in his office, she had to assume he was talking to her. Was he asking her out? Dread pooled in her stomach even as her pulse leaped with excitement. The sound of crinkling paper made her realize she was crushing the computer printout in her lap.

She smoothed out the paper and looked across the desk at Logan, not sure what to say.

He held both his hands up as if to stop any crazy thoughts going through her head. "I'm not asking you out on a date. I thought you might want a bite to eat since it's getting late. My treat, to thank you for putting up with the interrogation earlier, and for agreeing to help organize all this mess." He pointed to the printouts of files they'd both been poring over in preparation for her to start working online with all the information.

"I promised to take some evidence to the sheriff in Okaloosa County this afternoon to pay back a favor." He stood and shrugged into the jacket he'd hung on the back of his chair. "You could go with me and we could stop somewhere out of the way for dinner, somewhere private where you don't have to worry about being recognized."

Relief flooded through her that he wasn't asking her out. At the same time, a flash of disappointment shot through her. Why? Hadn't she already told herself she couldn't deal with a relationship right now? She glanced at her watch, surprised to see she'd been at the police station for the better part of the day. The sunlight coming in through the lone window in Logan's small office was already fading. "I should get back home, start working on that algorithm."

He looked like he wanted to argue, but then he shrugged and took the pile of papers from her, setting them on the desk. "Maybe some other time." He opened the door and waited for her, then accompanied her to the elevator. When he stepped inside next to her she glanced up questioningly.

"You didn't think I'd let you walk to your car alone, did

you? I have to make sure my best computer programmer
stays safe," he teased.

She smiled and looked down, clasping her hands together. As they'd walked next to each other from his office
to the elevator, she'd actually forgotten about the killer.
She'd allowed herself the fantasy of pretending she was a
normal woman walking next to a handsome man who was
interested in her. The reality was far less appealing, far less
flattering. There really was a killer out there, probably looking for her. And the man next to her probably only seemed
interested in her because she might know something that
would help with his investigation.

So why not have dinner with him? It wasn't a date, so there
wouldn't be any awkward dating conversation or pressure on
her to say something interesting. And even though she loved
to cook, she remembered the days when she'd enjoyed the
occasional meal out, trying new dishes, watching the people
around her. She wasn't a hermit by nature, only necessity.

Logan would keep her safe. So why not come out of her
shell for an hour or two? She could fantasize that she was
normal, that she hadn't been forced to change her entire life,
and that she didn't have to live in fear. For a few hours, the
fantasy would actually be true.

When the elevator opened they stepped into the lobby
of city hall. The women they passed aimed admiring glances
at Logan but he seemed immune, as if he didn't even notice
them. Amanda ducked her head, letting her hair cover her
scar. But she couldn't resist a secret, gloating smile that the
other women were probably jealous of her because of the incredibly appealing man next to her.

They exited through the front doors and turned left toward the parking lot on the side of the building. They went down the steps and she said in a rush, "I guess I could spare the time for a drive and dinner." When she risked a quick glance up at him he was smiling.

"Good," he said. "I'll get one of the detectives to bring down the boxes I need to take to Okaloosa. Mind if we take my car?"

"I don't want you to have to come back here for my car later. I'll just follow you."

"I won't have to come back. We can take my car and one of my men can drive your car to your house." He waved at someone in the parking lot and she realized the white Crown Victoria that was normally sitting on her street was now sitting in the parking lot. Two men had just reached the car, probably because they'd been inside the building all this time watching her, without her knowing. Logan waved them over.

"I didn't even know they'd followed me here." Amanda was vaguely alarmed that she hadn't noticed them trailing behind her to the station this morning, but she was also impressed that they were able to tail her car without her noticing.

Logan grinned. "Maybe I won't have to fire them after all."

Amanda shouldn't have to live in fear, afraid to step outside because the killer might find her. That was no way to live. Logan had hoped to put her at ease by choosing an out-of-the-way diner, several miles outside of town. So far she was anything but relaxed.

She chewed on her bottom lip while she read the laminated menu. Even though her back was to the rest of the diner and only Logan could see her face, she kept playing with her hair, finger-combing it over her scar.

He sighed. "Do you want to go somewhere else?"

She glanced up, her eyes wide and questioning. "Why?"

"You seem uncomfortable."

"No more uncomfortable than I would be anywhere else. I haven't been to a restaurant since I moved back from Tennessee."

Stunned, he looked back down at his menu as he tried to digest what she'd just said. She'd moved back from Tennessee two years ago. In all that time, she'd never been out to eat? That must mean she hadn't dated either, since going out to eat was the main thing people did on first dates. Did that mean she didn't have any friends? Was she totally alone, with no one to talk to? Hoping he was wrong, he probed for more information. "What do you and your friends do for fun?"

She chewed her bottom lip again and flipped the menu over as if she were suddenly interested in the senior specials listed on the back. "I keep busy . . . with work and all. I . . . watch movies a lot."

At home. On TV. Even without her saying it, he knew that's what she meant. He noted the tension in her shoulders, the way her knuckles whitened as she held the menu.

She didn't have any friends. She probably never went

anywhere unless she absolutely had to. The only reason for her to seclude herself that way was if she was scared to go out.

Logan suddenly felt like kicking himself. He was the world's biggest jerk. He'd pressured her to do something that seemed ordinary to him, but to her was probably like climbing Mount Everest. All because of his selfish desires, both for the information she could provide and the enjoyment of her company. She was a beautiful and intriguing woman. He liked her, too damn much. He'd allowed his feelings to blind him to hers.

He studied her posture. Embarrassed, uncomfortable, but not scared. Maybe he could still salvage the evening for her. If he could help her have a good time, maybe she wouldn't regret her decision to come to the station or to drive with him out of town.

And maybe he wouldn't feel like such an ass.

Amanda stood just inside her kitchen while Logan lounged in the doorway that led to the carport, one shoulder resting against the doorjamb.

"I had a wonderful time," she said. She cringed inside as she realized how intimate that had sounded. She looked down at the floor.

"Amanda?"

"Yes?" she said, still unable to look him in the eyes.

"I had a wonderful time, too."

Surprise had her meeting his gaze again. He was smiling

and she couldn't help but smile back. He raised his hand as if to touch her face, and she stiffened before she could stop herself. His smile turned sad and he lowered his hand.

Amanda died a little bit inside, wishing she could take back her automatic reaction. He'd touched her at the station, put his arms around her after she'd seen those horrible pictures. She hadn't flinched then. Why had she flinched now?

"Thanks for coming to the station today," he said, smiling that sad smile. "And thank you for having dinner with me. If you have any trouble accessing the station's computer system from home, let me know. Or if you just want to talk, my offer of a shoulder is always open."

Before she could respond, he turned away. She shut the kitchen door, set the alarm, and trudged into her living room. Collapsing onto the couch, she wondered what would have happened if she'd let him touch her. Did he really have feelings for her apart from his desire to know more about her abduction? Would he have run his thumb across her lower lip the way he'd run his thumb over the cloth napkin that day in her kitchen? Would he have slid his hand behind her neck and pulled her forward for a kiss?

For the past few years she'd convinced herself she didn't need anyone else, didn't need to feel the touch of another human being. All she needed was to be safe. But meeting Logan had reawakened a part of her she'd forgotten ever existed.

She rose from the couch and paced back and forth in front of the fireplace. Her entire body shook and her hands fisted at her sides. She couldn't think straight, couldn't focus with so many thoughts and emotions pulsing through her.

A nameless, faceless killer had stolen so much from her, far more than she'd realized until now. She'd thought she'd won with her little victories. She continued to wear her hair long just to prove the killer's obsession with her long hair hadn't forced her to cut it. She'd learned self-defense, how to shoot a gun, how to use knives. Her home was safe, secure—a place where no one could hurt her.

Lies. They were all pathetic lies. She'd lied to herself, told herself she was in control, but all along the killer was in control. He was the one with the power. He'd destroyed her life, made her cower in fear, and forced her to give up everything and everyone that mattered. Somehow, she had to make a change. She couldn't let him win anymore.

She stopped pacing and hurried back into the kitchen where she'd left her purse. The yellow sticky note with her user ID and password beckoned her like a beacon of hope. She grabbed the Post-it and hurried back to her computer.

No more lies, no more excuses. It was time to take her life back. It was time to catch a killer.

CHAPTER SIX

"They have temps for this, you know." Pierce flicked a ball of dust and hair from his suit jacket in disgust. "I still don't see why we have to search through this nasty warehouse ourselves, especially before breakfast." He shed his jacket and laid it over a partially shredded leather chair that used to decorate the city hall lobby.

Logan decided not to tell him the chair wasn't shredded from age. It had been shredded by rats. He exchanged a grin with Riley and tossed another box marked "Miscellaneous" onto the growing stack in the middle of the concrete floor. Both men were enjoying seeing the city-slicker Fed acclimate himself to a rural town and all its charms.

"Just be glad we didn't stumble across any gator nests this close to the swamp." Logan tossed another box, enjoying the alarmed look that flashed across Pierce's face. "Besides, every cent of my budget is going to this case right now. I'm not going to waste precious resources hiring a temp for something that will only take a couple of hours. And I sure as hell am not pulling your team or mine from the investigation for this."

Riley grunted as he tried to move one of the heavier boxes marked "City Hall." Pierce helped him, and together they heaved the box back several feet.

"Chief." Riley motioned toward the stack of smaller boxes that were now revealed. "I think we're in the right spot. These boxes are labeled "Police Archives.""

Logan straightened and wiped sweat from his forehead. "Do they have any categories? Dates?"

"Nope."

"We'll have to look through all of them then. How many boxes total?"

"Four here." Riley braced a hand against the concrete wall and leaned around the boxes to see the others stacked behind them. "At least ten more over here with the same label."

Pierce threw up his hands. "Haven't you people ever heard of computers? Or Sharpies to write meaningful labels on the boxes? Your filing system sucks."

Logan laughed as he helped Riley lift the desired boxes and start a new stack next to one of the old, discarded conference tables they'd set up when they arrived. "I agree. But we're still going to look through all of these boxes."

In spite of his complaining, Pierce dove in, helping stack all the boxes by the table. Then he pulled up a rusty metal chair and, after dusting it off, sat down to start sorting through the contents of each box. He squinted in the dim light from the grimy windows as he tried to read the label on a thick file. "Remind me again exactly what we're looking for?"

Logan sobered, his grin fading. "Any missing person, abduction or murder case file within the past decade. Shadow Falls is the only place our perp has struck twice that we know of. I'm hoping to find some earlier case that will lead us to a suspect. Maybe he grew up here and that's why he returned. I'm particularly interested in the Northwood case."

Riley dropped a thick file on the table. "Northwood? When was that?"

"Ten years ago, almost to the day."

"Ten years . . . ten years," Riley mumbled as he tore into another box.

"What's so special about the Northwood case?" Pierce asked. He added another folder to the small stack.

"Anna Northwood was murdered in a motel room a couple of miles from here. I was involved in that case."

Riley paused and looked up at him. "Was she abducted first?"

"No."

"Did the killer leave a rose at the scene?"

"No."

The room grew silent and Logan sighed beneath the weight of Riley and Pierce's stares. "I know that case is most likely not related to our current case, but while we're here I'd like to get that folder to look through it and see if anything was missed the first time around. I was a rookie back then, made a stupid mistake, and because of me the suspect got away."

Riley let out a low whistle. "Man, that sucks."

"Yeah, it does." Logan pulled one of the folders toward him and flipped it open.

"What kind of rookie mistake?" Pierce asked. He sat

with both elbows on the table, no longer interested in the files or boxes.

Logan's gut churned. He didn't want to talk about this, but he wanted that folder, and it would be a lot faster finding it with Riley and Pierce's help than by himself. Looking for other similar cases wasn't exactly a ruse, but it was close.

"I pulled over a white van on a routine traffic stop. I'd probably remember that van to this day even if there hadn't been a murder. It had writing all over the back doors, quotes from scriptures twisted into different meanings. The one I remember most was, "Do unto others before they do unto you."

Riley stumbled and dropped the box he was carrying. "I'm okay," he called out as he reached down to retrieve the box.

"You were saying?" Pierce urged.

"I pulled the van over because it didn't have a license plate. It had a piece of cardboard in the tag holder that read "lost tag." I was walking up to the driver's door when a call came in about a murder, two blocks away. I waved the driver off before I even got to his door, and went to the scene."

Pierce studied him for a moment. "Let me guess. The killer was the one driving the van."

Logan nodded stiffly. "I had a bad feeling about that van. My internal radar was going nuts from the minute I saw those twisted scriptures and the black curtains in the back windows. I knew in my gut something was wrong. He'd been driving too carefully, like he had something to hide. But even if I hadn't been suspicious, I should have radioed back to the murder scene to see if there was a description of a getaway vehicle. Standard procedure. If I'd followed the rules I would have known I'd just pulled the suspect over."

"How certain are you the killer was driving the van?" Pierce asked. "Maybe someone saw the van near the hotel when the body was discovered and assumed—"

"There was a witness. A maid at the motel saw a man run from the room. She was too far away to give a good description of him, but she saw him get into a white van that matched the same description as the one I'd pulled over, right down to the scriptures."

The quiet in the room was palpable. Logan glanced over at Riley. He was standing next to a stack of boxes with a thoughtful expression on his face. Before Logan could ask what that expression meant, his cell phone rang.

He answered and listened quietly to Officer Karen Bingham, his hand clenching into a fist as she reported what had been found.

"We'll be there in fifteen minutes," Logan said. He flipped his phone shut and shoved his chair back from the table. Pierce and Riley looked at him expectantly.

"They've found the primary scene where Carolyn O'Donnell was killed."

Before evil had invaded her world and changed her life forever, Amanda used to visit the cemetery once a week and leave a dozen roses on her parents' graves. It took two years of therapy and a philandering brother-in-law to give her the courage to move back to Shadow Falls and resume her weekly visits.

But she'd never brought roses again.

Instead, she brought pink carnations. She'd read somewhere that pink carnations meant you missed someone and that you would never forget them. That seemed appropriate. And since the number seven was supposed to be lucky, she always placed seven carnations on her mother's grave, seven on her father's.

And seven on Dana's.

Knowing the killer was back, Amanda had debated not coming to the cemetery for her weekly visit. But her parents had devoted themselves to her and her sister, Heather. If it weren't for the plane crash that had unexpectedly taken their lives, Amanda had no doubt they would have continued to support her and help her. The least she could do was put fresh flowers on their graves.

And she owed far more than that to Dana.

Besides, she should be safe. The two plain-clothed policemen who normally sat outside her house had followed her here. One of them was getting out of his car to keep watch over her as she walked through the cemetery. She gave him a small wave to let him know she appreciated his protection. Then she walked up the slight hill to Mr. Reynolds' flower cart where she always bought her flowers.

The vendor smiled and reached down for the pink carnations already wrapped in tissue paper, waiting for her. "Your usual order, Ms. Jones." He handed the flowers to her and took her money.

The name "Jones" gave her pause and she realized she'd grown used to "Stockton" again in the past few days, since the policemen always used that name.

"Thank you, Mr. Reynolds," she murmured. Another group of mourners was approaching the flower cart so she hurried past them, keeping her head bent. Usually she chatted with Mr. Reynolds. He was always nice to her and lived in her neighborhood, but he understood her shyness about her scar. She was sure he wouldn't hold it against her that she hadn't stayed to talk today.

The sound of crunching gravel startled her, but it was just one of the undercover policemen keeping pace about twenty feet away.

She turned down a dirt path between the graves and stopped under an oak tree with delicate fingers of Spanish moss dripping down. Her mother had loved oak trees, which was why Amanda had chosen this spot when she buried her parents. The shade was nice, too, lowering the stifling temperatures by several degrees. Still, it was so hot outside today that her lungs felt like they were sticking together every time she breathed. Her policeman shadow wasn't faring any better in the heat. He stopped under another tree, loosening his tie as he took advantage of the shade.

The hot breeze did little to help, but it did bring out the scent of freshly mown grass. Combined with the sweet, delicate scent of the carnations, it reminded Amanda of better times, summers spent with her mom, dad, and little sister.

Amanda leaned forward and used the pink tissue paper to brush off the black granite headstone that marked the two graves. Then she filled the two vases with carnations. Normally she spoke out loud, telling her parents what she'd done the previous week. Or, on the rare occasions when she had news about Heather, telling them about her sister.

She shivered in spite of the heat. There was nothing about this past week she wanted to share. And with a police officer only a few feet away, she wasn't comfortable speaking out loud. Instead, she sat on the thick grass between the graves and allowed herself a few moments of silence to quietly remember them.

Growing up in Florida had been fun. Her dad's nine-to-five desk job at an insurance company didn't buy a lot of extras, but it paid the bills, kept a roof over their heads. Mom stayed home to raise her two daughters, taking them to the beach every chance they got. Weekends were for cookouts on the back deck, or sometimes they'd go to a neighbor's house and enjoy their pool.

Amanda smiled again as she remembered how excited her father was when he got a promotion and a bonus. Heather was a senior in college. Amanda had already graduated and started her career as a computer programmer. For the first time since her parents' honeymoon twenty-four years earlier, her parents could afford to go on a real vacation. They'd been so excited about their upcoming trip to Italy.

Amanda's smile dimmed. The plane crash had not only taken her parents' lives, it had driven a wedge between her and her sister. It didn't help that Amanda was the one who'd suggested the trip in the first place. And then there was John, Heather's husband.

Shaking her head, Amanda pushed away the unpleasant thoughts. The policeman leaning against a tree a short distance away was trying not to be obvious about watching her. But the disapproving look on his face, and the way he kept glancing around, told her he didn't like her being here out in the open.

She didn't either, but sometimes responsibility outweighed other considerations. She sighed and pressed a kiss against the cold headstone. "I love you, Mom and Dad," she whispered.

After climbing to her feet, she brushed off her jeans and carried the last of the carnations to Dana's tombstone only a few graves away. Amanda replaced the dried up carnations from her last visit with fresh ones. Keeping her voice low, she told Dana what she told her every week. "I'm so sorry, Dana. Please forgive me."

Channel Ten anchorwoman, Tiffany Adams, stared down at the fresh flowers on Dana Branson's grave. She waved her cameraman over. "Get a shot of this. Did you see anyone by this grave?"

"Nah, no one's been over here since we got here."

She stepped back so he could get a shot of the flowers. Looking around the cemetery, she didn't see anyone who might have placed them on the grave. The only person she saw was the flower vendor, Mr. Reynolds. She'd spoken to him on Sunday after the O'Donnell murder and had asked him if he knew who put flowers on Dana Branson's grave. He'd claimed he didn't know, but the flowers today were far too fresh for him not to have seen who put them there.

"Look in that trash can," she said, pointing to a garbage can near a tree. "See if someone left the packaging from the flowers in there."

He lowered the camera from his shoulder and gave her an arch look. "You want me to dig through the trash?"

She narrowed her eyes. "I want you to dig up a story. Now."

His shoulders slumped and he mumbled beneath his breath. Tiffany didn't care what he said as long as he did what she told him. A minute later he ran back with some tissue paper in his hand.

"Jackpot," he grinned, holding the pink paper up in the air. "It's got that flower vendor's logo on it." He pointed to Reynolds' flower stand.

A slow smile spread across Tiffany's face. "Call the station. See what they can find out about our flower vendor. I need leverage."

"This is one royally screwed up perv," Pierce said.

Logan raised a brow. "Is that the FBI's official assessment?"

"Hell, yes." He stepped past one of the technicians who was dusting the boxcar for prints. "He went to enormous trouble to make this torture chamber."

Bile rose in the back of Logan's throat as he took in the black, dried blood that had sprayed across the walls and formed sticky pools on the floor. There were small holes drilled into the sides of the abandoned railroad car to allow ventilation, but even partially shadowed beneath the huge branches of an oak tree as it was, the temperatures inside had to be close to a hundred degrees.

"I'm surprised Carolyn O'Donnell didn't bake to death in this hell hole," he said.

One of the techs pointed to some of the holes drilled higher up near the top of the car. "There's a hose hooked up to that hole. The other end is hooked to a generator outside, and a small air-conditioning unit. We think he used that to keep the temperature more bearable, at least while he was here."

The tech stepped around Logan and began dusting the next section of the wall for prints.

"Let's get out of here," Logan said. "We're just in the way."

He and Pierce stepped out of the steel tomb, their shoes kicking up dust as they crossed the dirt, away from the hive of activity. The Feds were examining every inch of the forty-foot steel shell while Logan's detectives walked the grid outside searching for evidence.

Officer Karen Bingham was taking the witness's statement. She was sitting on a fallen log beside a white male about twenty years of age. Dressed in camouflage shorts, he wore a white t-shirt that boasted a picture of a marijuana plant.

Logan glanced around as he and Pierce strode toward Karen. "Where's Riley?"

"He's directing your men in the grid search," Pierce said.

Logan spotted Riley then, about fifty feet away, walking with one of the other detectives around the abandoned boxcar, pointing to various spots in the dried-out grass and dirt as he spoke to the man beside him. Logan didn't know why Riley felt he needed to walk the grid. There were more than enough techs doing that already.

"Chief," Karen called out, capturing his attention. "This is Gerald Mason. He's the hiker who found the boxcar."

Logan shook the hiker's hand and introduced Pierce. "Mr. Mason, we appreciate you calling the police when you found the boxcar. I'm sure you already answered a lot of questions from Officer Bingham, but would you mind telling Special Agent Buchanan and me what happened?"

The young man looked over at Karen as if asking permission. She nodded and smiled reassuringly. His neck bobbed as he swallowed. "I used to hike through these woods when I was a kid. I'm home on break and—"

"You're a college student?" Pierce asked.

"Yeah. FSU."

Logan exchanged a glance with Pierce. Mason was from the same campus as Carolyn O'Donnell, Florida State University. "Go on, Mr. Mason. Tell us how you found the boxcar."

"It's been here forever, even when I was little. The railroad left a couple of them in this field and another field a little ways from here when they pulled out years ago. Anyway, I wanted to get away from the house—away from all the relatives, you know?"

Logan nodded encouragingly and wondered when the kid would get to the point.

"I hiked up here and then I remember that old car. I thought it'd be fun to look inside, maybe see if any of my old army men or matchbox cars were in there." He shuddered and shut his eyes.

"Was the door open or shut when you got here?" Pierce asked.

"Shut. But it wasn't locked. I just opened it and . . ." He shuddered again, making a gagging noise in his throat.

Logan stepped back, out of gagging range. "Thank you, Mr. Mason. Be sure to give Officer Bingham your addresses both at school and home, and any phone numbers where she can reach you if we have more questions."

"O . . . okay."

Pierce and Logan moved away to stand beneath a towering oak tree where they could keep an eye on the agents and detectives working the scene. The doors to the boxcar were propped open and several men were inside processing the evidence. One of the techs wasn't dressed like the others. When he turned, Logan realized who he was.

"What the hell is he doing?"

Pierce gave Logan a surprised glance. "Who?"

"Riley. He's in the boxcar. I specifically told him he didn't need to go inside, that the techs are busy in there. I don't want him contaminating anything."

"What are you worried about? He knows what he's doing."

Logan crossed his arms over his chest.

"Spill it, Logan. Something's bothering you."

"It's crazy."

"I'm used to crazy."

"Okay, but let's get out of this hot sun. Besides, I don't want anyone else to hear this." He led the way to his Mustang parked under a shade tree fifty yards back. He sat behind the wheel and started the engine, turning the air-conditioner to full blast as Pierce got in beside him.

Logan watched Riley through the windshield. "Riley was a rookie cop when Dana and Amanda were abducted. He wasn't a detective then, but he was on the force, a newbie.

In a town like this we only get half a dozen murders a year, usually domestic disputes. What are the odds that a rookie cop would forget about a case as memorable as the Branson case? What are the odds that every detail wouldn't be burned into his brain?"

"He did remember the case. He and Clayton are the ones who told you about it."

"Only after Carolyn O'Donnell was found murdered."

Pierce watched Riley through the windshield, too. "Didn't you say he was at a conference when she was abducted, in Alabama? And he'd only returned the morning she was found dead?"

"Yes, but he knew about the abduction. I called him when she went missing. He's my lead detective. I wanted to pick his brain, see what suggestions he might have for trying to find her. It didn't occur to him to tell me about the earlier case until *after* O'Donnell was killed. Three days later."

"Which means?"

"Which means, maybe he didn't want her found alive."

Pierce stared at him as if he thought he'd gone crazy. "Are you suggesting your lead detective is the killer?"

"I'm not suggesting anything. I'm just thinking out loud. Things aren't adding up."

"What things?"

Logan drummed his fingers on the steering wheel.

"Come on, Logan. You've got my attention. Spill."

Logan already regretted mentioning his suspicions. He didn't want to put a stain on Riley's reputation, not if he was innocent. But if there was even a chance Riley could be involved, he had to look into it.

Pierce was watching him expectantly. Logan blew out a frustrated breath. "First of all," he said, holding up one finger, "He meets the general description Amanda gave of the killer. Second," he ticked off another finger, "He didn't notice the trail of footprints leading from the O'Donnell crime scene into the woods until I pointed it out."

"Half the male population of this town meets the general description Amanda gave. And Riley was waiting for the medical examiner. You told me that."

Logan ignored the interruption and continued. "Third, he didn't mention the Branson case when Carolyn was abducted. Fourth, by walking through the grid and inside the boxcar, he's given himself a perfect alibi if we find any trace leading back to him."

"Go on."

Logan dropped his hand. "That's it. I don't have anything else. Just my gut."

Pierce sat silently for several moments, considering. "From what you told me about your gut this morning, about when you stopped that white van because you thought something was off, I'm inclined to trust your instincts. I'll call the field office in Birmingham, have them check out the conference alibi, make sure Riley was really there. Do you want to send any of your men to Alabama?"

"No. I don't want Riley or anyone else to hear about this, especially without any evidence. I don't want to hurt his career or his reputation if I'm wrong. Can someone out of your Jacksonville office run a quiet investigation into Riley's background? See where he was at the time of the other murders during the past four years?"

"You bet. In the meantime, we could put a tail on him."

"It wouldn't work," Logan said. "I may have been born here but I moved away for over a decade. To my men, I'm still an outsider until I prove myself. Riley's one of them, a local. None of them could keep this a secret from him."

"Then I'll have one of *my* men tail him."

"Can you spare the manpower?"

"I'll get the manpower. If there's even a slight chance Riley could be our man, I want to know."

"You don't think I'm nuts?"

Pierce's mouth quirked up in a wry grin. "I think you're desperate. I don't think Riley has anything to do with the murders. But I'll humor you. In a few days I'll have proof, one way or the other."

CHAPTER SEVEN

One of Amanda's constant shadows opened his car door down the street from her house, apparently thinking she was about to go for a walk. She waved him back and pointed to her mailbox at the end of the driveway to let him know she was just checking the mail. He waved to let her know he understood and closed his car door.

A white Camry turned the corner onto the street. Amanda glanced at the unfamiliar car. A flicker of unease passed through her. She hurriedly grabbed the mail, quickly noting there were only bills, not the new movie from her mail-order movie club that she'd been expecting. Maybe tomorrow. She had plenty of movies in the house she could re-watch. No big deal.

The sound of the car's engine was much louder now. Amanda closed the mailbox and hurried up the driveway, back toward the safety of her house. Tires squealed behind her, and she jerked around to see the Camry barreling into her driveway. She gasped and dove out of the way, hitting the ground hard and rolling onto her back as the car screeched to a halt, its front bumper narrowly missing her.

A man holding a camera jumped out of the car, along with a familiar-looking blonde woman. Amanda's stomach lurched with dread.

"Ms. Stockton, Tiffany Adams, Channel Ten News," the woman announced as the man who'd gotten out of the car shoved his camera toward Amanda's face.

Car doors slammed down the street. Shouts of "Police, stop!" were accompanied by the sounds of shoes slapping against the pavement.

Amanda desperately raised her hands to hide her face, and struggled to get up with the camera so close to her. "Back off," she bit out through clenched teeth. The man stepped back, giving her just enough room to stand, but not offering to help her up.

"Ms. Stockton," the blonde continued, as if nearly running someone over was nothing to worry about. "Can you comment on the recent murder of Carolyn O'Donnell? How does it make you feel to know that the man who attacked you and killed your friend may be back in town killing again?"

Amanda's face flushed hot as she shoved past the anchor-woman. How did they think she felt? That had to be the dumbest question ever asked and it was usually the first one out of a reporter's mouth when interrogating a crime victim.

When the reporter stepped in front of her, Amanda took childish relish in stepping on the toes of the woman's designer high-heeled shoes and seeing the woman flinch. "Get off my property," Amanda told them as she ran to the carport.

"Hey, what are you doing? Get your hands off the camera."

Amanda heard the commotion behind her and knew the undercover policemen had reached the news crew. She jerked open her side door and rushed inside the kitchen, slamming the door shut behind her.

"I hate morgues." Riley stepped into the elevator. "Even hospital morgues. They smell."

Logan rolled his eyes and punched the button for the parking garage level.

"I've smelled worse," Pierce said. "At least the medical examiner's tests were able to confirm the burn marks on Carolyn O'Donnell's body were from a taser, just like the taser he used in the Branson/Stockton case."

"Yeah, but it's not like he'd use the same taser four years apart. No one's that dumb. I sure wouldn't do that," Riley said.

Logan exchanged an uneasy glance with Pierce. He hated being suspicious of Riley, but once the doubt had planted itself in his mind, he couldn't shake it. Everything Riley did or said now made Logan more suspicious. He hoped the Feds would finish their investigation into Riley's alibis soon. If Riley wasn't involved, then Logan could clear his mind of that worry and concentrate on other leads.

What few leads they had.

When the elevator opened and they stepped out into the parking garage, Logan's cell phone started ringing. He reached into his jacket pocket just as Pierce and Riley's phones began to ring. The three men shared a startled glance, then took off in a sprint toward Logan's car.

"**Y**ou're a material witness," Pierce said to Amanda from his perch on the couch next to Logan. "We can force you into protective custody."

Amanda's nails dug into the arms of the recliner. "If you're going to lock someone up, lock up that reporter for trespassing."

"No one's going to jail," Logan said.

"But, Pierce said he would—"

"He's bluffing. He can't declare you a material witness without a suspect in custody. No one's going to make you do anything you don't want to do."

"Thank you," she said to Logan. She narrowed her eyes at the FBI agent, letting him know she didn't appreciate his threats.

"Pierce," Logan said, his voice hard. "See if Riley has found out who leaked Amanda's address to the press."

"Riley doesn't need my help," Pierce said, his voice equally hard.

Logan slowly turned to face the FBI agent. Something silent passed between them. Pierce mumbled beneath his breath and threw his hands up in the air. He left the room without another word, the front door closing behind him with a sharp click.

"Sit with me," Logan said. He stood and held his hand out. "We'll figure out what to do. Together."

She didn't hesitate or flinch away like she'd done that

night he'd stood in her kitchen doorway. She put her hand in his, immediately feeling secure as his warm fingers wrapped around hers. He led her to a seat on the couch beside him, surprising her by not pulling his hand away.

"How bad is it?" she asked. "Does the entire Panhandle know where I live now?"

"It's worse than that. You've gone national. All the major networks picked up the story. Your front lawn is full of reporters and the street's lining up with news vans."

She groaned and shook her head. "What are my options?"

"Obviously, staying here in your house isn't viable anymore. We need to put you in a safe house."

"Hawaii would be nice."

Logan's mouth tilted up in a lopsided grin, doing funny things to her heart. "I'm afraid that's not in my department's budget. How about somewhere close by, like Tallahassee or Pensacola?"

"Why do I have to leave Shadow Falls? Can't I just stay in a motel or something?"

"I thought you'd be thrilled to get out of town. It's the safest option."

She tugged her hand from his and stood, too keyed-up to sit still. She crossed to the fireplace and paced in front of the couch, hugging her arms around her waist. Logan sat, quietly watching her, waiting. He probably thought she was crazy to hesitate about leaving. Maybe he was right.

When she'd mentioned Hawaii she'd only been half-joking. The idea of leaving town *was* vastly appealing. But leaving would delay the computer work she was doing to help Logan with the investigation. Still, she wasn't a martyr. She didn't want to make it easy for the killer to find her. "Do you think I should leave town? You still think I can help with the investigation don't you? Besides the database, you think I might still remember something that will help, right?"

He considered her question for a moment, his mouth drawn into a tight line. "I'd be lying if I said I wanted you to leave. There aren't many leads in this case. Right now you're my best chance at catching this guy. I have to believe that after being with him for three days there's something else you know about him, some kind of clue that will help me nail this bastard." He shrugged. "But it's your life. You're the one taking risks if you stay. This has to be your decision."

His voice sounded matter-of-fact, like he was willing to accept any decision she made, without argument.

"What would you do?" she asked. "If you were me?"

His eyes were hard and unreadable, remote . . . as if her questions took him far away, to another place or time. For a moment she thought he wouldn't answer, but then his expression changed, as if he'd just made an important decision. He stood and stepped over the coffee table to stand directly in front of her by the fireplace. He reached out to take her hands in his. "May I?" he asked.

She nodded her permission and he entwined his fingers with hers. Her pulse leaped at the feel of his warmth surrounding her.

"I started my career as a beat cop, here, in Shadow Falls. I made a rookie mistake, one that had terrible consequences. When I realized what I'd done, I quit the force, moved to

New York, tried to start a new life. But running didn't do any good. I think about the mistake I made every day. That's why I came back, to face what I'd done." His hands tightened around hers. "Whatever you decide, just make sure you do it for the right reasons. Don't do something you'll regret for the rest of your life."

Tears burned at the backs of Amanda's eyes. "I already have," she whispered, her voice breaking on the last word as the memory of Dana's screams echoed in her mind.

Logan's eyes narrowed. "What do you mean?"

The front door opened and closed, followed by the sound of shoes on the foyer's tile floor. Pierce and Riley entered the living room, their faces drawn and tense.

"Chief," Riley said. "Got a minute?"

Logan didn't move or respond to Riley's question.

"Amanda?" he asked, his voice pitched low so only she could hear. "What did you do that you regret?"

Panic flowed through her. No, she wasn't ready. She couldn't tell him what she'd done. She couldn't bear to see the disgust that would twist his face if he knew. She shook her head and tugged her hands from his. "Never mind. Go, see what Riley wants."

"Chief?" Riley repeated, his voice sounding urgent.

Logan's expression mirrored his disappointment, as if he'd expected Amanda to tell him something that would help with the case. If it were that simple, she'd tell him everything. But what she'd done wouldn't help. It would only make him hate her.

"This isn't over," he assured her. Amanda shivered at his words and fervently wished she hadn't said what she'd said.

He crossed to the far end of the room to join Pierce and Riley at the opening to the foyer. They spoke too quietly for Amanda to hear them, but she didn't have to hear the words to know Logan didn't like what they were telling him.

He shook his head and heatedly mouthed the word "no" several times. Riley appeared to be the calmer of the three. He spoke to Logan for several minutes and then Logan's mouth tightened but he gave one short, crisp nod. Pierce immediately turned and rushed out of the house, slamming the door behind him.

Amanda warily watched Riley and Logan cross the room toward her.

"Riley found the leak," Logan said. "Mr. Reynolds, a flower vendor at the cemetery."

Amanda recoiled in shock. "Are you sure? I can't believe he would tell the reporters where I live. He's always been so nice to me."

"Reporters can be quite persuasive," Riley said, "especially if they threaten to report someone to the IRS. Selling flowers is a side job for Mr. Reynolds. Apparently he hasn't reported any earnings from his flower sales on his tax returns."

"You need to make a decision, Amanda," Logan said. "Do you want to stay in town or go somewhere else?"

"I'm staying."

Riley looked pleased with her answer. Logan's face was harder to read. She wasn't sure if he was glad or not.

She rubbed her hands up and down her arms, feeling chilled by the change that had come over Logan since she'd mentioned her regrets. "So, what do we do next? Do I go to a motel?"

"Unfortunately, it's not that simple," Logan said. "In a town this small it would be too easy for the killer, and the press, to find you in one of the local motels. No matter how careful we are, someone is bound to notice the extra police presence, even if my men don't wear uniforms."

"Besides that," Riley added. "Pierce isn't comfortable with the setup around here. He said all our motels are old and lack modern security features."

"You're staying at Logan's house," Pierce's voice called out from the entryway, announcing his return. He strode across the room and stood beside Logan. "Only a handful of people know he owns that property. It's not even in his name. It's listed under a real estate investment company he set up. I've already made the arrangements. All you have to do is pack a suitcase."

"Wait, wait. I'm confused," Amanda said. "What are you telling me? That I'm staying at the chief of police's house? That's . . . unusual, isn't it?"

"Ms. Stockton," Riley said, drawing her attention. "It might be unusual but it's an excellent alternative. Most of the department still thinks the chief lives in town in an apartment, but he loaned that out to the FBI and moved outside of town when this case started."

"A police officer would stay with you during the day," Pierce said. "Logan would be there at night. You'd have 'round-the-clock protection in a secure location. Close enough that you can continue to assist with the investigation. But perfectly safe."

"I guess it makes sense," she allowed, watching Logan

carefully. He'd remained silent during the entire exchange, watching her with a solemn expression on his face. "But I don't think Logan wants me there."

His mouth tightened. "I want you safe. That's what I want."

"What's the problem then? Wouldn't I be safe at your house?"

One of his brows arched up, as if she'd asked a ridiculous question. "Of course you'd be safe."

"Good, it's settled." Pierce said. "We have two unmarked cars waiting on the street behind your house to escort you to Logan's house. A female officer is on her way here to act as a decoy for the press out front."

In spite of her decision to be brave, panic filled her at the thought of leaving her sanctuary. "I didn't say I would go to Logan's house."

Logan's expression softened and his eyes filled with concern. He reached out and took her hands again, oblivious of the two men watching. "I think having a witness living at the chief of police's house is a conflict of interest. I need to concentrate on solving the case and I'm worried my attention will be divided."

She started to interrupt but he squeezed her hands to let her know he wasn't finished.

"For now, though, if you're determined to stay in Shadow Falls, then staying at my house is the best alternative."

She noticed the tension in the tiny lines at the edges of his eyes for the first time. Riley looked agitated too. It dawned on her that what they'd been arguing about earlier had nothing to do with the decision about where she should stay. "There's something else, isn't there? What aren't you telling me?"

He hesitated, as if carefully weighing his words before he spoke. "There's no easy way to say this."

"What? Tell me."

"There's been another murder."

Frank Branson didn't mingle with the reporters in front of Amanda Stockton's house. He remembered some of them from four years ago, and he was afraid they might remember him. Drawing attention to himself was not part of the plan.

The overgrown shrubs on the property next-door gave him the perfect vantage point. Hiding beneath the bushes, he could see both Amanda's side door that opened onto the carport, and the sliding glass doors in the back. When the press got tired of their vigil out front, and the cops thinned out, he'd pay the Stockton bitch a visit.

Two hours later he was stiff and sore, he'd drained the last of his six-pack, and he really needed to take a piss. He stumbled through the bushes, away from the cops and reporters, and relieved himself behind the neighbor's house.

Later. He'd come back later, maybe tomorrow, or the next day, when there weren't so many people around.

For the second time in less than a week, crime scene tape cordoned off a section of the park and a young woman's body lay broken and discarded among the pine needles. Detectives walked the grid, shoving evidence markers into the ground, and Dr. Cassie Markham processed the body.

Logan approached the tape, Pierce at his side. They'd both stayed behind at Amanda's to ensure the decoy worked. Riley had gone ahead to the crime scene and now hurried over to give them his assessment. His constant FBI shadow was there, too—only Riley thought the man was there to assist him. Instead, he was there to keep an eye on Riley.

"What are we looking at here?" Logan asked as he ducked under the tape.

"The vic has short blonde hair, hazel eyes. She was killed here, not killed somewhere else and dumped. The only similarities between her and O'Donnell are that both bodies were found in the park and both vics were holding a red rose."

"What about the thorns? Was the stem stripped?" Logan held a low-hanging pine branch up for the other two men to walk beneath.

"No," Riley said. "It had all its thorns."

"COD?" Pierce asked.

"Gunshot wound. One bullet through the chest, close range. The perp tried to mask the bullet wound by stabbing her post-mortem."

"Copycat," Logan said.

"Yep," Riley agreed. "Not a very good one either."

Logan frowned. Had Riley's voice sounded boastful? Or was he just imagining that slight inflection? "Did the vic have a boyfriend?"

"Husband. Detective Reid is interviewing him at the station. No alibi, fidgety, not too broken up about his wife's tragic death. Reid's sure he'll crack soon."

Logan sighed in relief that another woman hadn't been brutally tortured like Carolyn O'Donnell, although if she had, it would have been quick proof of Riley's innocence. He'd been under surveillance since leaving the boxcar scene earlier today.

But regardless of whether this woman was killed by a stranger or by a supposed loved one, she deserved the same professionalism and attention to detail the O'Donnell case was getting.

He glanced at the lights his officers had rigged. "We'll need more lights, better lights, to comb a scene like this at night." Six months as chief of police hadn't given him enough time to squeeze city hall for a better budget and better equipment.

"Already on it," Riley said. "Department of Transportation is bringing some lights. They might have to halt construction somewhere for one night, but they didn't give me any grief over it."

"Good thinking. Let's get those reporters further back. I don't want any shots of the vic on the evening news."

"You got it." Riley headed toward the reporters lining the street in front of the park's main entrance.

Logan mentally prepared himself for the gruesome scene.

"Ready?" Pierce asked.

"As I'll ever be."

CHAPTER EIGHT

Amanda bolted upright in bed, panic shooting through her at the unfamiliar furnishings in the room, the unfamiliar smells wafting in from the hallway. Was that coffee? She didn't drink coffee. Wait, last night, the reporters. She'd had to leave her house.

Officer Karen Bingham and two FBI agents had escorted her here last night, to Logan's house, in unmarked cars. Karen was an old family friend and had been in Logan's house before. She knew where everything was and had insisted on settling Amanda into the master suite.

In Logan's bed.

If Logan came home last night, Amanda hadn't heard him, and she didn't know which of the other bedrooms he'd slept in.

She lingered on the massive four-poster bed, smoothing her fingers across the luxurious, mocha-brown comforter, enjoying the faint scent of soap and aftershave that clung to the silky, rich fabric. The room was decorated in muted golds and browns, entirely masculine, like its owner.

A glance at the bedside clock told her it was half past seven, an obscenely early hour for her, but she imagined the local police chief would leave for work soon, if he hadn't already. The ominous words he'd spoken to her last night ran through her head, *there's been another murder.*

She threw the covers back and hopped out of bed, heading toward the master bath. Hopefully she could still catch Logan before he left, so he could tell her what had happened. After a quick shower, she threw on a pair of shorts and a teal blue t-shirt from the suitcase she'd packed last night, and headed downstairs.

She automatically started to pull her hair forward, but Logan's admonitions to stop worrying about her scar echoed through her mind. If he didn't mind her scar, she'd try not to mind either. She flipped her hair back over her shoulder and hurried down the last few steps. Turning toward her right, she followed the smell of coffee to the back of the house where she and Karen had entered last night into an informal eating area next to the kitchen.

To her disappointment, Logan wasn't there. Karen was. She was sitting at the round, mahogany table in front of the French doors that led onto the back deck. Amanda remembered there was a matching porch on the front of the old Victorian, but she'd noticed little else last night because the agents had rushed her inside.

"Good morning," Karen greeted her as she lowered a coffee mug and a copy of the *Shadow Falls Journal*. "I hope I didn't startle you. I did tell you last night I'd be here today, didn't I?"

Amanda pulled some of her hair forward. "You didn't

startle me. I'd hoped Logan was still here though. Seems kind of early in the morning for you to start babysitting duty."

Karen laughed, the deep-seated lines crinkling around her eyes. "Babysitting huh? I guess you're not too thrilled about this arrangement."

"Nothing personal. I'm used to being alone."

"Some fresh coffee will make you feel better. Always works for me." Karen pushed back from the table and went around the black granite bar into the kitchen. "How do you take it?"

"I appreciate the offer, but I'm not a coffee drinker."

Karen's brows raised in surprise, as if someone not drinking coffee was a mortal sin. "Water? Soda?"

"Soda would be great. Thanks."

"Coming right up." Karen opened the refrigerator. She came back carrying a can of Dr. Pepper, which she set on the table in front of Amanda. "Is that okay?"

Amanda blinked, surprised Logan had her favorite drink on hand. "That's perfect, actually. Thanks." She sat down at the table.

Karen didn't sit. Instead, she took a long sip of coffee and picked up her newspaper. "I'm here to protect you, not babysit you. I'll try to stay out of your way most of the time. Lord knows I have plenty of paperwork to catch up on. I've set my laptop up in the mother-in-law suite in the front of the house. Yell if you need me."

"Wait." Amanda softened her request with a smile. "I was wondering, about last night, do you know anything about . . . the murder?"

Karen shook her head. "Not really. By the time Logan got in, it was close to two in the morning. We were both too tired to talk shop. I ended up crashing in the mother-in-law suite instead of going home to Mike, my husband. Logan was gone before I got up."

Amanda pulled the soda can towards her and ran her finger across the condensation. "Do you think Logan would mind if we called him?"

"I don't see why not." Karen's brow crinkled with concern. "Are you worried about your safety? I assure you Logan's got the best security system around. The entire perimeter of the yard has sensors and cameras. If anyone steps on the grass, we'll know it. Besides," she tapped the gun holstered on her belt, "this isn't just for decoration."

"No, no, that's not it at all," Amanda hastened to reassure her. She was relieved to hear about the security system, but she was more concerned right now with the murder. She wanted, needed, to know what had happened. Had the same man who'd attacked her killed another woman? Just the possibility had anger pulsing through her. Had she waited too late to offer her help? Could she have prevented the murder? "I just need to talk to him."

Karen shrugged. "Sure, I'll call the station first and see where he is. I don't want to call him if he's interrogating someone and doesn't want to be interrupted."

"Thanks. I appreciate it."

Karen nodded and punched some buttons into her cell phone.

Amanda drummed her nails on the table.

The call ended quickly. "He's not in the station. He's out

in the field, off Mill Cove Road on Black Lake. Not sure why. I'll go ahead and call his cell."

Panic churned in Amanda's stomach but she fought it down.

"No," she said, wincing at how loud her voice sounded. "I'm sorry," she said, lowering her voice.

"Something wrong?"

Yes. Black Lake was where the killer had taken her and Dana, right off Mill Cove Road. Was Logan looking for clues? Was he in the same cabin she'd been in four years ago? The soda can pinged because she was squeezing it so hard. She forced herself to relax her fingers.

"Amanda, what's going—"

"I'm fine." Amanda shoved the can back and stood. If there was any chance she knew something, going back to Black Lake was probably her best shot to remember whatever it was she might have forgotten.

Karen obviously didn't know about her background, at least not enough to realize the significance of where Logan was. Good, that would work in Amanda's favor. Because otherwise, there was no way Karen would agree to do what Amanda was about to ask her to do.

Calling Logan now wasn't an option either. Even though he wanted her to talk about her past, he wouldn't want her to go to Black Lake, to revisit the cabin where the torture had taken place, where the old Amanda had died and the new one was still struggling to figure out who she was.

She took a deep breath and forced a smile onto her face. "Karen, I need a favor."

"We're done here." Logan glanced around the interior of the cabin. He'd hoped that coming to Black Lake, walking off the crime scene, would give him a new perspective, new insight into what the murderer had thought when he'd brought Dana and Amanda here. But the crime scene was too old. The cabin was dry-rotting. The metal bed Dana had died upon had been hauled away long ago along with anything else that might have helped set the scene.

"It was worth a look," Pierce said. "Even this many years later, we could have found something that was missed the first time around. But you know that already. As many courses as you've taken at Quantico, you probably know more than me. What did you do, spend every vacation for the past ten years training at the FBI academy?"

Logan narrowed his eyes at him. "Did you run a background check on me?"

"Let's just say I was curious to know why the guy who solved the Metzger case would settle for a chief of police job in a little backwater town like Shadow Falls."

"Watch the insults. This is my hometown."

Pierce held up his hands in a placating gesture. "No insult intended. Hell, I grew up in Savannah, only moved to Jacksonville a few years ago. Trust me when I say both those places, in spite of their size, have a lot of similarities to this little town. But both of them have enormous opportunities for a career in law enforcement. Shadow Falls doesn't. So tell me. Why did you come back? And don't tell me it's because of that rookie mistake you mentioned the other day."

"I didn't lie when I said that's why I came back."

Pierce leaned back against the lone window and crossed his arms. "That's one reason. Not the only reason. What happened in New York? Why'd you leave?"

"Is this going somewhere? Because I have a hell of a lot of work to do if this doesn't have something to do with the case."

"Was it a woman?"

Logan strode across the cabin and stopped a few feet in front of Pierce. His fists clenched at his side. "You got something to say, Buchanan, say it. Quit pussyfooting around."

"All right." Pierce shoved away from the window sill. "I know you left New York right after your divorce."

"So much for respecting my privacy," Logan sneered.

"I've seen friends go through that rebound stage, fixating on the first pretty woman that passes their way."

"I care about this why?"

"I've seen the way you look at Amanda Stockton. I want to be sure that you can keep it professional with her staying at your house. Too much is riding on this investigation to let anything personal get in the way of your thinking."

Logan hadn't been this tempted to slug anyone in years. The only reason he hadn't hit Pierce yet was because he knew Pierce was only being an ass because he wanted to catch the killer just as badly as he did.

"What I feel for Amanda is none of your concern. I'm not going to do anything to jeopardize this case. All I care about right now is finding the bastard who killed Carolyn O'Donnell." Logan shoved Pierce.

Pierce shoved him back.

"Um, excuse me, boss?"

Logan and Pierce both whirled around at the sound of Karen Bingham's voice in the open doorway. Logan let out a string of curses when he saw who was behind her.

Amanda.

It took every ounce of courage Amanda had to stand her ground as Logan strode across the cabin toward her, his face as dark as a thundercloud. Her own face felt as hot as the summer sun beating down on her back. She hadn't heard much, but what she did hear when Karen opened the cabin door was enough for her to realize that Pierce thought Logan was interested in her.

And Logan hadn't exactly said he wasn't.

"Amanda, you shouldn't be here." Logan grabbed her arm and started out the doorway.

She yanked her arm away from him, gasping when it felt like she'd left half her skin behind. She rubbed her arm and stepped inside the cabin. "Karen didn't drive me all the way out here for you to send us right back home. I came here for a reason."

Logan's eyes filled with regret. He stopped in front of her and gently reached out, his fingers brushing across her arm, soothing away the burn. "I didn't mean to hurt you."

"It doesn't matter. I'm fine." She pushed his hand away and took a step back to put some much needed distance between them. "The murder last night, was it . . . the same man who came after me?"

He shook his head. "No. That woman's husband killed her. He staged the scene to make it look like our serial killer, but it wasn't." He glanced aside at Karen who stood next to Pierce closely watching them. "This could have waited. You shouldn't have left the house."

"Don't blame Karen. I tricked her."

"Tricked me?" Karen said, sounding surprised. "How?"

Pierce leaned back against the windowsill. "She didn't tell you this is where she and Dana Branson were taken when they were abducted."

Karen's shocked gasp sounded loud in the tiny cabin. "Boss, I'm sorry. I wouldn't have come out here if I'd known. Come on, Amanda. Let's go."

Amanda evaded Karen's hand. "No, stop it, all of you. Quit trying to push me around and decide what's best for me. I'm sick of being coddled and pitied. I'm sick of being treated like a victim. I don't want to leave. You can't make me." She stomped her foot in frustration.

Pierce coughed into his hand. Karen's eyebrows were climbing into her hairline. Logan's mouth twitched. Amanda suddenly realized how silly she'd sounded, yelling "you can't make me" and stomping her foot like a child. Her face flushed with heat and she glared at Logan, daring him to laugh.

He cleared his throat, twice. "Okay. Now that we've got that settled. Besides asking about the copycat killing last night, why else are you here?"

The walls of the cabin suddenly felt like they were closing in on her. She wrapped her arms around her middle and took a good look around the cabin for the first time since she'd been here with Dana. She swallowed against the sudden lump in her throat. "Last night, when you said there was another murder, I was so scared. I thought another woman had been killed, that it was my fault, because I couldn't tell you about what happened."

"What that maniac does or doesn't do isn't your fault," Logan said, his voice hard.

"I understand that, I do, but I still feel guilty." She shrugged. "I know it doesn't make any sense."

His eyes darkened. "It makes more sense than you know. Are you sure you want to do this? Maybe you should wait—"

"No. I'm ready." She leaned in close. "Can Pierce and Karen wait outside? If I start talking about . . . what happened . . . I don't want them to hear—"

"You don't have to explain. Give me a minute." He crossed the room and spoke low to Karen and Pierce. They both left, but a moment later Pierce stepped back inside with two folding chairs, the kind people threw in their trunks for quick trips to the beach. He handed them to Logan, nodded at Amanda, then stepped back out and closed the door.

Logan set the chairs up in the center of the room then motioned for Amanda to take a seat. He sat down across from her, so close their knees were touching. He didn't pull away, so she didn't either.

"How do we do this?" she asked, her stomach already clenching with dread. "I'm not sure how to start."

He studied her, clearly worried. "Let's start with how you met Dana."

"Didn't I tell you that at the station the other day?"

"Humor me."

She shrugged. If he wanted to start by going over what they'd already discussed, she could do that. "When my parents died, I had to sell the house to settle their debts and finish paying for Heather's education. She was in Knoxville, going to the University of Tennessee, and her only income was from my parents. I auctioned off the house and everything in it. It was just enough to pay tuition and most of her expenses. She still had to get a part-time job but she made it through, earned her degree."

"You gave everything to her, saved nothing for yourself?"

"Don't make me out to be a Good Samaritan, Logan. I'm not." *Far from it.* "I had already graduated and had a job. It was the logical decision. But it was still early in my career and I didn't have much money. Mom and Dad had still been helping me here and there. With them gone I needed a little extra cash, so I looked in the paper for a roommate."

"Dana put an ad in the paper."

"Yes. She was going to the local technical college and needed someone to help with expenses, so I rented a room from her."

"Apartment, right?"

She nodded. "Her last roommate skipped on the rent. Dana was getting desperate."

"Didn't she have family?"

"Her mom and dad. But Dana made a lot of poor choices, burned her bridges. Her parents were trying tough love, trying to wake her up and get her to stand on her own feet. They were devastated when she was killed, blamed themselves for not helping her more."

He asked about her routine with Dana. After answering several questions, she said, "I don't know why he targeted us, why he chose us."

"Figuring that out is my job. You're doing fine." He leaned forward with his forearms resting on his knees. "I want to talk about the abduction now."

She took a deep breath. "Let's get it over with."

"Tell me about the morning you were abducted."

"It was Wednesday. I know that because that's the only day Dana didn't have classes. I worked from home, even back then, so my schedule was flexible. Dana wanted to go shopping, so I said I'd go along."

"How did you get to the mall?"

"Dana's car. She drove."

"I know it's been a long time, but can you remember if anyone followed you?"

"There wasn't much traffic. I don't remember any other cars."

"Had anyone called you that morning? Or in the weeks before that? Threatening calls? Hang up calls?"

"Not that I know of." She shrugged. "If they called Dana, she never said anything."

"Go on."

"We parked." Her hands shook and she swallowed hard. "We parked near the end of the mall parking lot, near the trees and dumpsters. She had vinyl seats that got really hot, so she liked to park in the shade and crack the windows. Anyway, we went into the mall."

"Can you remember anyone watching you, following you? Maybe you saw the same person in more than one store."

She frowned and mentally traced their trip through the mall, surprised at how easily the details came back, easier than at the station the other day. "No, nothing like that. Everything seemed fine, a perfectly normal day. We bought a few things, stupid stuff—body lotion, a bracelet. Dana bought a pair of yellow polka-dot socks. I bought a pink tank top. We walked out of the mall and I was going to call my sister. That's when I realized my cell phone wasn't in my purse. I remembered using it at the last store we were in, so Dana told me she'd get the car and pick me up. I walked back inside to look for my phone."

Logan's fingers tightened around hers, helping ground her, chasing away the shadows.

"When I came out, her car was still parked at the end of the lot. The trunk lid was up so I thought she was standing behind the car, rearranging all the junk." She smiled, remembering how much of a slob Dana was.

"You didn't see anyone else near the car?"

"No, not even when I got to the car and went around to the back of it. I expected to see Dana standing there. I called out her name, but no one answered. When I rounded the bumper I saw her lying in the trunk. Before I could react, he zapped me."

"Taser."

She nodded. "That's what they told me later anyway. At the time, I didn't know what had happened. I dropped to the ground. For a few seconds I couldn't think beyond the pain. Everything was fuzzy. Then he tossed me into the trunk beside Dana, slammed the trunk lid shut."

Logan flinched but quickly schooled his features. "Did you see him when he picked you up? Maybe you saw his face for an instant?"

She chewed her bottom lip as she tried to recall, but it was no use. She'd tried hundreds of times and never could form a clear image in her mind. "I got the impression of a tall, white male. Nothing else."

"When he opened the trunk you were at the cabin? This cabin?"

Her eyes darted around and she shivered. "Yes."

"He didn't stop anywhere on the way?"

"No."

Logan stroked her hand with the pad of his thumb. "Do you want to stop?"

She shook her head back and forth. "No, no, I need to do this."

He stared at her intently. "Look around you. Try to remember the cabin the way it was that day. Tell me the things I can't see in the police photographs. What did you smell?"

"Smell?" She wrinkled her nose. "Blood. I smelled blood."

"Before that, when you first went inside the cabin, what did you smell then?"

"Musty, dirty, like now."

"Good. What else?"

She sighed and nodded toward the window. "The pine trees outside. Nothing else."

"What about sounds?"

She cocked her head, listening. "Birds, the same ones I hear today. The woods are full of them."

"Try to block that out. Think about what you heard *inside* the cabin. Did the man speak to you? Did he have an accent?"

"He whispered."

"The whole time? He never raised his voice? Think back, think about all the times he spoke to you."

She pursed her lips together and tried to picture herself back in this cabin. Over there, in the corner, the metal bed bolted to the floor. The hook, also bolted to the floor, here in the center of the room. She glanced down, expecting to see dark stains on the wood, blood. But someone must have replaced the boards. There was no blood, no metal hook where the killer had taken turns chaining her and Dana. She'd lain on that floor with him crouched above her as he whispered his commands. "He hummed," she said, surprised to suddenly remember that.

Logan squeezed her hand. "Good. Was it something random or a song?"

"A song, definitely, but nothing I knew. It was distinctive, slow, creepy. Like a chant or something."

Her hair had fallen in front of her face. Logan leaned forward and brushed it back, his fingers skimming through the curls and running down the length of the strands as if he couldn't resist touching it.

"He loved my hair, too," she whispered.

He snatched back his hand as if he'd been burned.

"I'm sorry," she said. "I didn't mean to—"

"It's fine. Go on," he urged.

She sighed. "He brushed my hair for hours. Washed it every day. Combed out every single tangle. And all through that he hummed. I can't believe I forgot that."

"Sometimes we block out details like that, to cope. If you

think of something else about the song that might help me identify it, let me know."

"You think a song can help you catch a killer?"

He shrugged. "It's a piece of the puzzle. You never know what tiny clue will break a case wide open. Is there anything else you can think of?"

She looked around, pictured the cabin again the way it was that day. The man with the hood, sitting above her, holding the rose, twisting off a thorn. The sick game he'd played.

He kills me.

She squeezed her eyes shut.

"Amanda?"

She opened her eyes and met his concerned ones. It was time to tell him the truth, what had really happened in this cabin. She opened her mouth to tell him, but nothing would come out. All she could think was that once he knew, he'd despise her.

Suddenly the tight, hot space was too confining. She had to get out of here. "I can't think of anything else," she lied. "I'll go get Karen." She tugged her hands from his and ran from the cabin.

Logan started to run after Amanda, but Pierce caught him just as he reached the doorway.

"She's fine. Karen's with her. We've got bigger problems."

Logan could see Amanda on the other side of the clearing, getting into Karen's car. He waited until the car was heading down the dirt and gravel road that led away from

Black Lake before he gave Pierce his full attention. What had he said? Something about bigger problems? "What are you talking about? Has there been another killing?"

"No, a fire."

Logan's nostrils stung from the smell of charred wood that filled the air. The warehouse that he, Riley, and Pierce had been in yesterday morning was now just smoldering rubble. The roof had burned away, leaving blackened concrete blocks rising into the sky like the legs of a dying spider. The firemen were stowing their hoses, packing to leave. They'd put the fire out quickly, but there was nothing left to save.

"I don't suppose you guys have backup copies of all those files," Pierce said.

"Those *were* the backups." Logan shook his head in disgust.

"I do have some good news. The report came back from our little side investigation. Riley's alibi checked out. He's not the man we're after."

"Are you absolutely certain? I have a hard time believing vagrants started this fire, especially since we didn't see any signs of vagrants near the warehouse when we were here."

"Riley was at the conference. I can tell you every workshop he attended, every meal he ate, when he arrived, when he checked out."

"Okay, okay. He didn't kill Carolyn. What about the other women?"

"Has anyone ever told you you're stubborn?"

"Every day." Logan turned away from the burned-out structure and trudged toward his car.

"I can prove where he was for half the murders."

Logan paused with his hand on the door handle. "Prove?"

"Absolutely."

"Damn." Logan slid behind the wheel and slammed the driver's door shut.

Pierce got into the passenger seat and gave him a sideways glance as he fastened his seatbelt. "Why do you look so disappointed? I would have thought you'd be happy to know your lead detective isn't the killer."

Logan gunned the engine. "Yeah, but now I don't have a suspect anymore. The killer is probably out there right now stalking his next victim. If we don't figure out who he is, soon, another woman is going to pay a horrible price."

Chapter Nine

Two weeks after Carolyn O'Donnell was killed, Logan stood with Riley and Pierce in the same spot where her body had been found. The yellow crime scene tape was only a memory, but Logan couldn't help thinking the park had a desolate, mournful feel, as if the trees themselves were weeping at the horrible injustice that had taken place here.

On this beautiful Sunday morning, this park should have been full of children laughing and playing, but families no longer brought their children here. Joggers didn't travel the manicured paths of which the city had once been so proud. What had been a place of joy was now a place of fear.

"You don't expect to find any more evidence here, do you?" Riley asked. "The entire area has been picked clean, by our guys and Pierce's guys."

"No, that's not why we're here."

"Then why did you ask us to meet you here?" Pierce asked. He wiped his forehead with the back of his hand and leaned back against one of the majestic oaks that dated back to the days of the Civil War.

"I wanted to get us away from distractions."

"A conference room wouldn't have been sufficient?" Riley snickered.

Logan gave him a sharp look and Riley quickly sobered.

"It's been nearly two weeks since Carolyn O'Donnell's death and we don't have any leads. Based on the profile, the next murder is due any time now. I've been walking the scene for over an hour, trying to put myself in the killer's mind, trying to think like he does. But I'm not getting anywhere. We need to take a fresh look at the case. We're missing something."

Pierce shoved away from the oak tree and joined the others next to a strand of palmettos. "After finding out Gerald Mason was from FSU, I had my team re-look at everything we'd gathered from the school. We couldn't find any connection to Carolyn, and he had alibis both for the day she was abducted and the day she was killed."

"What about Carolyn's friend you re-interviewed," Logan asked Riley. "The one you and Clayton drove up to Tallahassee for? Did you re-interview any of her other friends or professors while you were there? Did anyone see her talking to someone they didn't know? Maybe somebody was calling her, emailing her."

Riley shook his head. "False alarm on the friend. I reviewed everything from the school too. We subpoenaed cell phone records, internet accounts, and interviewed everyone she came into contact with the past semester. She was popular, well-liked, so that was a lot of interviews. But through all of them, nothing came up to point to her having contact with anyone suspicious. Nothing."

Pierce wiped a bead of sweat from his forehead. "We traced every call in or out of her dorm for the past six months. No red flags."

"Visitors to the dorm?" Logan asked.

"Not even a fake name on a visitor log that couldn't be verified," Pierce replied. "It all checks out. If she caught the perp's attention on campus, he didn't do anything to make himself noticed by anyone."

"So, you're convinced the killer didn't target her at school," Logan said.

Pierce shook his head. "FSU has thousands of students, but the investigation into the circle of people Carolyn associated with was thorough. In my opinion, there isn't any evidence to suggest he targeted her from school and then followed her here."

"But there isn't any evidence to suggest he targeted her here, either," Logan said.

Pierce frowned but didn't respond.

Riley was staring at the ground, apparently deep in thought.

"No one has any fresh ideas? A new direction?" Logan asked.

"What about the algorithm Amanda was putting together? Did anything come of that?" Pierce asked.

"What algorithm?" Riley glanced back and forth between them.

Logan flushed, realizing he'd never confided in Riley about the work Amanda was doing. He wasn't sure why he'd never told him. Maybe he'd been subconsciously suspicious of Riley even before that day at the boxcar.

"Amanda organized all the evidence into a new database and cross-referenced everything. She came up with a program to scan for similarities and patterns. That's how Pierce's men eliminated some of the potential suspects from the stacks of interviews. Amanda's still fiddling around with her program, trying to come up with something better."

Riley nodded, suddenly looking distracted.

"We should review all of the interviews again," Pierce said. "Maybe there's a nugget of information we missed. Or someone we should have interviewed that we didn't. I can go back to the office and look through all of them again."

Logan shook his head. "There has to be something else to pinpoint how he chose Carolyn, or how he chose Dana and Amanda. That could be the key. I think we should look into Frank Branson."

Riley's head shot up, a look of surprise on his face. "Dana Branson's father?"

"You do realize," Pierce said, "that we ruled him out as a suspect? He discovered Dana's body in the cabin and called 9-1-1, yes, but he had an ironclad alibi during Dana's time of death."

"Yeah, so did a lot of murderers I've put away over the years," Logan said. "Never completely trust an alibi, or a profile for that matter. We need to review his alibi again, see how ironclad it really is."

"Why do you want us to look at Branson?" Pierce asked.

"As part of revisiting Dana Branson's murder, Frank Branson was re-interviewed. I met him, briefly, and I didn't get a good feeling about him." Logan shrugged. "Probably nothing."

Pierce gave him a sharp look. "If it was nothing, you

wouldn't have brought it up. It certainly wouldn't be the first time a father killed his daughter; happens a lot more than people realize."

Riley shook his head. "No, it wouldn't be the first, but can I say, ick? His own daughter? She was raped."

"Dana was his stepdaughter, if that makes any difference," Pierce clarified.

"It doesn't." Riley shuddered in distaste.

Logan flinched as his thoughts turned to Amanda. The police reports stated she wasn't raped, at least not in the traditional sense of the word, probably because the killer preferred to rape his victims at the moment of death and Amanda had gotten away. But what had happened to her was just as brutal. "What about forensics from the Branson murder?" he asked Pierce. "Did your men find anything the state lab missed?"

Pierce shook his head. "No trace from the perp, only the victims. And all of the blood collected at the scene was either Dana's," he looked at Logan, "or Amanda's."

Logan winced then quickly schooled his features. Every mention of what Amanda had suffered was like a knife slicing into him. Judging from the expression on Pierce's face, and their earlier confrontation in the cabin, he obviously wasn't hiding his feelings very well.

A flash of movement had Logan looking toward the front end of the park. Several men were milling around, talking in a small group and watching the three of them. "Looks like we've caught the attention of some of the neighbors. We'd better go introduce ourselves before they flood the station with suspicious-person calls."

"What do all of the victims he killed in the past four years have in common?" Logan asked as the three of them walked along one of the pine-needle-strewn paths. "Most were in different states so they couldn't frequent the same businesses. Did they vacation at the same places?"

"Not that I could find," Pierce said. "About the only things linking the victims are their physical characteristics. They were in their mid-twenties to mid-thirties, had long brown hair and blue eyes. He doesn't kill prostitutes or the homeless, people who wouldn't be missed. He only goes after white, middle-class victims."

"Go on," Logan said. He knew the profile, had read it dozens of times, but hearing it again might make him think of something, an angle he hadn't thought of before.

Pierce sighed and continued. "He's probably blue-collar, or if he's white-collar it's in a low-paying job. Either that job gives him opportunities to travel, or he quits and easily finds another similar job in any town he lives."

"Like a waiter?" Logan asked.

"Or a truck driver?" Riley said, his voice holding an edge of excitement.

They all stopped, ignoring the hostile looks of the growing throng of neighbors thirty feet away.

"Exactly like a truck driver," Pierce said. "You have something?"

Riley glanced back and forth between Pierce and Logan. "Frank Branson is a truck driver."

Since attempts to locate Frank Branson had failed so far, Logan had decided to embark on a different search. He moved down a row of rusty filing cabinets in the first-floor storage room in the city hall annex. He'd overheard some admin assistants talking about the warehouse fire that had happened, saying they were glad their invoices were stored downstairs. Logan was anxious to take a look and see if any of the police department's case files were also down here. It was a long shot, but he had to try one last time for a copy of the Northwood file.

Solving that case had become an obsession, he knew it. But he also knew he was better at solving cases when he let his subconscious work on them. Sometimes he needed another case to review to help him get his mind off the current case. That's when the patterns started making sense. That's how he'd solved the Metzger case. He couldn't think of another old case file he'd rather study right now than the case he'd screwed up.

With the disastrous warehouse fire fresh in his mind, he'd decided to search the storage room by himself. At this point, he didn't trust anyone.

Stopping at a cabinet marked "property of SFPD," he yanked the drawer open and started thumbing through the files. Five drawers later with nothing to show for his efforts, he moved to the next cabinet. The rusty metal drawer screeched its displeasure as he forced it open. Dust flew up from the top and he waved impatiently to clear the cloud out of his way.

"What are you doing down here, Chief Richards? Is

there something I can help you with?" His secretary's sensible pumps echoed on the concrete floor after she descended the last of the stairs into the storage room. Mabel's gnarled hands were wrapped around an open-topped box full of computer printouts.

Logan hurried forward and took the box from her. "You shouldn't carry something this heavy, let alone down those stairs. Have one of the men do that for you."

"Bah," she grumbled. "I've been going up and down those stairs longer than you've been alive. Haven't managed to fall yet and don't plan to." She raised a perfectly plucked, bluish-gray brow. "Put that box over there against the wall and tell me why you're snooping around down here without asking for my help."

He carried the box to the spot where she'd pointed, careful to hide his grin at her scolding. When he turned around, she was thumbing through the files in the drawer he'd coaxed open.

"I can't imagine what you'd find interesting in old expense reports," she said. "I've got a whole cabinet full of requisition requests and travel reimbursement invoices that are much more interesting."

"I wasn't looking for expense reports," he admitted.

She crossed her arms. "You don't say."

"I was hoping to find a copy of an old case file that burned up in the warehouse fire."

"Then you've come to the right place. The backups are over here." Her puffy blue hair bounced in rhythm to the click of her heels as she headed to the far side of the cavernous room.

"Backups? I thought the warehouse had the backups." He rushed across the room and joined her beside a wall lined with more rusty metal file cabinets.

She huffed and stared at him over the top of her glasses. "I never agreed with putting my files in that moldy firetrap. Of course I have backups. Now, which file are you interested in? I'll find it a lot faster than you will."

Hope flared in his chest. He'd come down here without any real expectations of finding anything. "There was a case about ten years ago, a woman was murdered in a motel—"

"Anna Northwood." She moved down the line of file cabinets, scanning the labels on the front of each one.

"You know about that case?"

"Of course. I pay attention around here. I'm not just a pretty face, you know." She winked and stopped in front of one of the cabinets. "Here we are."

Logan stepped forward to force the drawer open but she waved him off.

"They open much more easily when you unlock the cabinet first."

His face heated as she fished her keys from one of the pockets of her long, pleated skirt. It hadn't occurred to him that the screeching cabinet he'd opened earlier was locked. He'd assumed it was rusted shut because it was so old.

She unlocked the cabinet and pulled the drawer, which slid open on well-oiled rails without a hint of protest. She raised a brow but didn't bother to chastise him further. Her unspoken command was clear. Next time, ask her first before infringing on her domain.

A quick flick of her sensibly short nails across the tops

of the folders and she located the one she was looking for. "Here you go." She heaved the thick file up out of the cabinet.

Logan took it from her and scanned the first page to confirm it was the right one. He closed the folder and leaned down to press a quick kiss against Mabel's cheek.

She blushed, her pale, wrinkled skin turning the bright pink of youth. "What was that for?" she said, clearing her throat and smoothing her skirt.

Logan grinned and gave her another quick kiss. "That, my wonderful, efficient Ms. Mabel, was a thank you. May I assist you upstairs or did you have more work to do down here?"

He offered his arm and she raised a brow before linking her arm through the crook of his elbow. Her eyes sparkled. "I don't need your assistance, young man, but I'll take it anyway." She leaned forward conspiratorially. "And I'll take another "thank you" at the top of the stairs, right in front of Mayor Montgomery's prissy administrative assistant. Betty Lou has a terrible crush on you. I'd like to take her down a peg or two."

Logan laughed and led his delightfully sassy secretary toward the stairs.

Sunday was supposed to be a day of rest, but Logan was betting the serial killer he was after wasn't resting. So he wasn't going to rest either. After spending all day working with his team, he'd come home and secluded himself in his study. He'd begun reading through the Northwood case, several hundred pages of interviews and reports. So far he hadn't found anything new. He'd also pored through reports and interviews from the O'Donnell case, looking for the elusive clue that would make everything come together.

And he was also trying to forget that Amanda was in the next room.

Living with her under the same roof had proved to be a much bigger strain than he'd expected. He was trying to ignore his body's inconvenient response to her every time she entered a room. He wanted her, desperately, but it was so much more than that.

She made all his protective instincts go into overdrive. He wanted to help her, keep her safe, hold her close and make sure she knew she never had to be afraid again.

He shook his head, amazed at how quickly his thoughts could stray to Amanda. He needed to concentrate on the case. Their best lead, Frank Branson, wasn't panning out. No one seemed to know where he was. The trucking company he worked for said he was hauling a load up to North Carolina. But he never made it to his destination. Pierce's men were staked out, watching his apartment. Logan hoped Branson was their man, but he didn't want to risk losing time on any other leads if Branson turned out to be innocent.

"Are you going to work all night?"

All thoughts of the case evaporated when Logan glanced up to see Amanda standing in the doorway to his study. She was so beautiful it hurt to look at her. He noticed she'd pulled her hair forward again, hiding half her face. He hated that she felt so self-conscious.

He glanced at his watch, surprised to see it was so late. The sun had gone down hours ago and he hadn't even noticed. "Sorry, I didn't realize the time. Did you eat?" He started to get up from his chair but she waved him back down as she walked into the room.

"You don't have to fuss over me. I've been feeding myself for quite a while now, without anyone else's help. I had a sandwich earlier."

He grimaced. "I haven't been much of a host since you got here. Is there anything you need? I could go to the store—"

"Karen has been keeping me stocked with everything I need. I certainly don't expect you to wait on me. You have far more important things to do." Her smile faded as her gaze fell to the papers strewn across his desk. "Unless you snuck past me sometime today, I don't think you've eaten since breakfast. I haven't wanted to disturb you, but you've got to take a break sometime. I could fix you something to eat. Are you hungry?"

Yes. But not for food. He cleared his throat and made a show of straightening his papers while he reminded himself she was a witness, staying under his roof because she needed protection. No matter how much he wished he could have met her under different circumstances, he hadn't. She was off-limits. Period. "I'll eat later. Thanks."

She moved farther into the room, her gaze lightly touching on the walls of bookshelves, the grouping of chairs in front of the fireplace, the flat screen TV over the mantle. "You didn't answer my question," she said, stopping in front of his desk with a half-smile on her face.

Logan stared into those deep blue eyes and tried to remember what question she was talking about, but it seemed that every one of his brain cells had taken a vacation when she walked into the room. "What question was that?"

"I was wondering how late you were going to work. You have to take a break sometime or you won't be able to function tomorrow. There's an old Miami Dolphins game coming on TV in a few minutes. I thought you might like to watch a few plays, take your mind off . . . things."

"You like football?"

Her eyes widened. "You don't?"

"Hell yes, I like football. It's sort of a genetic requirement, being a guy and all."

She put her hands on her hips. "So, being a woman and all, I'm not supposed to like sports? Is that what you're saying?"

He laughed and held his hands up in mock surrender. "Please accept my apologies. My chauvinism is showing."

The smile that curved her lips had him groaning inside. The woman had no idea how appealing she was.

"You're forgiven. But only if you watch the game with me." She plopped down in one of the stuffed armchairs next to the desk.

He looked down at the stack of interviews he hadn't read through yet.

"Half an hour. You can spare that much time, can't you?" she said. "We'll just watch the game for a few minutes, give your mind a break. It will help you see things differently once you get your mind on something else. I've spent hours in front of my computer before trying to solve a problem. I've found that when I step away for a few minutes, I come back at the problem with a fresh perspective, and I can usually solve it much more quickly that way."

That's exactly what he did when working on a case. "All right, I'll defer to your wisdom. You sound like you know what you're talking about." He shoved his chair back and stood. "We can watch the game in here if you want." He grabbed his remote control out of the top desk drawer and handed it to her. "I've got to run upstairs for a minute. I'll be right back."

He strode across the room to the door.

"Logan?"

Amanda's soft, hesitant voice had him turning back around. "Yes?" he asked, hating that the sadness that had disappeared from her eyes a moment ago was back.

"Thank you."

"For what?"

"For letting me stay here. For keeping me safe."

He wanted to cross the room and pull her into his arms, hold her close and tell her no one would ever hurt her again. But he wasn't sure if she'd welcome his comfort or if she'd withdraw back behind the wall she often used to block the world out.

His fingers curled around the door jamb and he forced himself, against every protective instinct he had, not to run back into the room and scoop her up in his arms. "Any time."

Like a rubbernecker on the highway, unable to pass a horrendous crash without looking, Amanda inched toward Logan's desk to see what he'd been reading when she entered the room. She leaned forward to look at the papers when a stack of envelopes caught her eye. Her name and address were on the top one. A utility bill. Logan must have picked up her mail for her. She hadn't even thought about her mail since she'd temporarily moved into Logan's house.

She picked up the stack and flipped through it. Bills, loan offers, the usual assortment of junk mail. The last envelope didn't look like the others. It had her name on it, but it was addressed to the police station. Why would someone send her mail there? Curious, she ripped open the envelope and pulled out the small folded piece of paper inside.

Logan threw some water on his face and stood gripping the sides of his bathroom sink as if it was a life preserver. He'd been trying to convince himself that his fascination with Amanda was just physical, but her innocent remark about the football game had made him start to panic. They had so many things in common. They liked the same foods, the same beer, the same movies, and now he knew they both had the same favorite football team.

By now he'd almost grown used to the way his body reacted every time she walked into the room, the way he hardened and ached for the relief that he instinctively knew only she could provide. But tonight, his constant desire for her had paled next to his desire to see her smile finally reach her eyes, to hear her laugh, to hold her close and keep her safe. He'd caught a glimpse of the carefree woman she once was and he wanted more.

He pitched the towel on the countertop and shut off the

water. There were only two things he should be focusing on right now: keeping Amanda safe and finding the killer. He was letting his concern for her cloud his judgment, affect his decisions.

The man in the mirror stared back at him and Logan knew he couldn't ignore his duty anymore. Amanda hadn't told him everything that day at the cabin. She was holding something back about her abduction, something that he sensed could be the missing piece of information that would make everything else fall into place. It was time to confront her and get her to tell him the truth.

After changing his clothes, he started down the stairs, but he paused halfway down. The house was quiet. Too quiet. The light blinking on the alarm panel by the front door should have reassured him, but it didn't. Something was wrong. He could feel it.

His gun was out of its holster before he reached the bottom step. As quietly as possible, he made his way to his office, praying harder than he'd ever prayed before that he hadn't let Amanda down, that he hadn't missed something, and that she wasn't now paying the price for his mistake.

Careful not to step on any of the boards that were prone to creaking, he crept to the open doorway. Amanda was sitting in one of the overstuffed brown leather recliners beside the dark, rarely used fireplace, her feet curled up beneath her. Relief filled him as he realized she was okay, that no one else was in the room. He holstered his gun before she saw it and stepped through the doorway.

He was shocked when she turned to look at him and he saw how pale she was. He rushed over to her chair and dropped to his knees. When he took her hands in his he was alarmed at how cold they felt.

"What is it? What's wrong?" he asked.

She took a ragged breath. "He found me," she whispered, her voice breaking on the last word.

Logan looked down at the envelope in her lap and saw the rose petals and thorns.

CHAPTER TEN

Amanda sat in the recliner, watching Pierce sitting at Logan's massive desk, studying the note. Logan hovered over him, his frown creased with worry whenever he glanced over at her, which was often.

She was wrapped up in a blanket, Logan's endearing attempt to comfort her even though it was the middle of summer.

Thank God for air-conditioning.

Even with the blanket, she couldn't suppress an occasional shiver, which was why he'd wrapped her up in the first place.

But she wasn't cold.

She was scared.

Pierce grasped the note between his latex-gloved fingers and held it up to the light.

"You think it's him?" Logan asked.

Pierce shrugged. "Hard to say. There's no history of the killer threatening any of his victims before he abducted them. It's certainly not what I would have expected."

"But you think it's him."

He pursed his lips and considered the question. "If I had to say one way or the other, I'd say yes, but only because whoever sent this note knows about the game. Very few people do, unless the killer's a police officer. I've considered that possibility but it doesn't seem likely. The profile says the killer has a problem with authority. He'd never make it in law enforcement."

"Are your profiles ever wrong?"

"Of course. But Nelson's the best profiler we've got. I can't imagine him being wrong about something that significant." He set the letter down. "Why didn't you open this at the station?"

Logan's jaw tightened and Amanda spoke up. "He was going to ask my permission before opening my mail. I saw that envelope sitting on his desk and opened it before he had a chance to warn me."

"I should have locked it in my drawer as soon as I got home," Logan said, shaking his head. "I knew something was off, since it was mailed directly to the station. Amanda's given me permission now to open all her mail at the station. I'm going to forward it there from now on."

Amanda rubbed her hands up and down her arms. She certainly wasn't in any hurry to open any more mail, not after the surprise she'd had tonight. The note had echoed her attacker's words all those years ago, "He kills me, he kills me not," with "he kills me" underlined as if the decision had already been made.

"I'll have Nelson run the evidence to the FBI lab tonight," Pierce said. "Maybe we'll get lucky and they'll find a fingerprint. We could have a suspect by morning."

"I don't believe in luck," Logan said.

"Unfortunately, neither do I." Pierce clapped him on the back and took the evidence envelopes containing the thorns, rose petals, and note. He paused beside Amanda's chair. "We'll catch this guy, Ms. Stockton. Count on it."

She nodded. "Call me Amanda, please. And thank you for your help."

Pierce nodded and walked to the door with Logan.

Amanda looked away as unshed tears stung the backs of her eyes. The cowardice she'd shown at the cabin had to end right now. The one thing she hadn't told Logan yet was exactly what the killer had done to her, and the horrible thing she'd done to Dana. Neither of those seemed relevant to him catching the killer, but she couldn't take that chance any longer. The killer had just announced his intentions. She had to fight back. Telling Logan the truth was the only way she knew how to fight.

"You know I'll keep you safe, don't you?"

She glanced up. Logan had come back in the room so quietly she hadn't heard him. "I know you will. You're a good man and you're fighting hard to help me." She swallowed against the lump in her throat. "You're fighting more than anyone else ever has. It's time I did the same."

He crouched down next to her. "What do you mean?"

"I'm ready to tell you what *really* happened four years ago."

After what felt like an eternity later, but was really only a few minutes, she was sipping a glass of wine that Logan had insisted on getting for her. She didn't really care for wine, but she wasn't going to tell him that since he was trying so hard to help her. In typical male fashion, he had to *do* something to fix things when sometimes there was no fix.

He moved the coffee table out of the way and slid a matching recliner in front of hers. If she needed him, all she had to do was reach out.

He leaned forward, worry creasing his brow. "What did you mean, what *really* happened?"

She hugged her arms around her waist and tried to prepare herself for the moment when he would shrink away from her in disgust. "I never told you what the killer did. What I did." She closed her eyes, partly to avoid seeing the condemnation on his face that would soon be there, partly to put herself back in the cabin as she tried to remember anything that might help.

"He took off our clothes that first day. With a knife. The floor was slippery with blood by the time he'd finished."

Logan didn't say anything. She took a deep breath and continued. "There was only one bed. An iron bed, bolted to the floor. He made Dana sit on the floor, shackled her arms to the foot rail. He threw me on the bed—"

"You don't have to tell me this," Logan said, his voice sounding strained.

"—but he didn't rape me. I don't think I . . . excited him . . . in that way. Instead, he cut me. When he was . . . finished . . . he did the same things to Dana. And then he left. We spent the night tied to a blood-soaked bed in a pitch dark cabin with boarded up windows, crying and holding onto each other, wondering if we'd make it out of there alive."

"Concentrate on him, not on what he did to you. I know he wore a hood, but you saw part of his face, his hands. Can you describe those? Did he have any tattoos, rings?"

"His eyes were . . . black. Almost. Dark with hate." She swallowed, cleared her throat. "He didn't have any tattoos, birthmarks, jewelry. God, I wish I could have seen something that would help, but I didn't. Nothing."

"That's enough. You don't need to say anything—"

"The second day was worse," she interrupted, determined to finish. She didn't want to talk about it later. She wanted this over with. After tonight, she'd never talk about it with anyone else ever again. "He got . . . creative, like he was testing out a new set of knives. He sat on my back, carved me up, flipped me over and cut me some more, over and over. I have scars, big ugly scars—"

"Stop it, Amanda."

"Then he did the same to Dana. When that mad look left his eyes, he'd take us outside, one at a time, and hose us off like he was washing a dog. It burned, all those open cuts. He'd take us back inside and he'd sit for hours on the floor, looking off into space while we huddled together on the bed. He hummed that eerie tune." She shook her head. "I can't believe I'd forgotten that part."

"That's because you didn't want to remember and you didn't think it was important. You've been through enough for one night. We can talk about this some more tomorrow," he urged, his tone pitched low as if he were trying to soothe her.

But it wasn't working. Not this time.

"He'd sit for hours, then he'd turn and that mad light

would come back into his eyes, and he'd start the whole thing all over again."

Logan gently shook her shoulders. "You don't have to do this. The interview is over."

She opened her eyes and stared into his haunted ones. "I didn't know until later, of course, in the hospital, but he took away any hopes I had for a family." Her voice broke and he reached for her, but she shrank back from his touch.

"Stop talking about this," he entreated.

She laughed bitterly, knew she was close to losing it, but she didn't care anymore. Once she'd started she couldn't stop. "But you haven't heard the best part. I have to tell you about the game. The one with the rose. The thorns."

"I know about the game, Amanda. It was in the reports."

"No, you don't know everything about the game, Logan."

He grew very still. "What do you mean?"

"You were right all along. I did hold something back. Not on purpose, not at first when everything was so jumbled in my mind. Later, I felt so guilty, I *couldn't* tell anyone."

A sob escaped her lips and she pressed a fist to her mouth. Logan reached for her again and she slapped his hand away.

She ignored the hurt look in his eyes and twisted her hands in her lap. "When he showed up that last day, he brought two long-stemmed red roses. He played the game with each of us. When it was my turn, he made me lie down on the floor. He sat on my stomach, held up the rose, twisted off a thorn. Do you know what he said?"

"Yes. It's in the report."

"He said, '*He Kills Me*'. Weird how he talked about himself in third person, don't you think?"

Logan stared at her, his mouth pressed firmly shut, his fists clenched where they rested on top of his thighs.

She laughed again. "Then he twisted another thorn off and dropped that one too. He said, *'He Kills Me Not'.*"

Logan blanched white but didn't try to touch her again.

"He sang his little chant until he'd twisted off all of the thorns but one. He left that one. Don't know why."

"Amanda, the interview is over. He played his sick little game and ended with *"He Kills Me"* for Dana and *"He Kills Me Not"* for you. You were very lucky that he gave you a chance and you were able to escape."

Another hysterical giggle bubbled up from her lips and she shook her head violently. "Oh Logan, you don't get it, do you? It was the other way around. Dana was supposed to live. I was supposed to die."

CHAPTER ELEVEN

Logan swore beneath his breath and reached for Amanda. She tried to push his hands away, but he ignored her attempts, scooped her up in his arms and carried her out of the study.

She shouldn't let him carry her like she was helpless, but it felt so good to be held that she wrapped her arms around his neck and snuggled against his chest. If the man didn't care that her tears were soaking through his shirt, she wouldn't care either.

He carried her into the master bedroom. After gently laying her down on the cool cotton sheets, he disappeared into the bathroom. She heard the sound of running water and a moment later he sat on the edge of the bed, wiping her tears away with a warm damp washcloth.

His eyes had darkened to a deep forest-green, and she wondered what he was thinking. He'd heard her confession. Even without knowing the details of how she'd gotten away, he knew she had and that she shouldn't have. "You think I'm a horrible person, don't you?" she whispered as she hiccupped into the pillow and breathed in the clean familiar scent of the soap he used.

The washcloth continued its slow, comforting strokes across her cheeks, her brow. "I think you're a wonderful person," he whispered.

She shook her head "no" but she didn't have the energy to argue. She was so tired. Her eyelids felt sandpapery, heavy.

Something else kept niggling at the edges of her mind, a shadowy memory that struggled to surface. Finally, she remembered. As her eyes slid closed, she murmured, "He called me Kate."

He called her Kate?

Logan didn't know the significance of that, didn't really care at the moment. He was still reeling from everything she'd told him. The torture and devastation she'd suffered were far greater than he'd imagined from reading the police reports. And after she escaped with her life, the cruelest punishment of all was that she could never bring another life into this world, never have children.

He never should have asked her to talk about her abduction. Putting her through that again was too much to ask of anyone. He'd give anything to take it back, but he couldn't. What was done was done, and all he could do now was help her in any way possible.

He continued the gentle strokes of the washcloth until he was certain she was asleep. He set the cloth aside and stared down at her pale, tear-streaked face, her brow delicately knit with tension even in sleep. Her fists were knotted in the sheets, clutching them to her chest like a security blanket.

Stroking one of her clenched fists with the pad of his thumb, he murmured soothing words like he'd done for his little sister when she'd had bad dreams. Madison's nightmares were the typical stuff of a small child, full of dragons and other imaginary monsters. He suspected Amanda's nightmares were about real monsters, the kind that didn't go away when you woke up.

When the lines of worry smoothed out on her brow and she relaxed into a calmer, deeper sleep, he moved to the chair next to the bed. He ran a shaky hand through his hair as he thought about what she had, and hadn't, told him both tonight and that day back at the cabin.

Most of what she'd said he already knew from the police reports. That the killer hummed was new. It didn't seem like a significant piece of information, but it had been rattling around in the back of his mind ever since she'd told him. He knew he'd heard something like that before. Maybe not humming, specifically, but something about a killer and music.

It would come to him eventually.

That the killer had called her Kate seemed far more significant. Tomorrow, finding out who Kate was would become a top priority for his detectives. If anyone they had even remotely identified as a person of interest had a Kate in their lives, their name would move to the top of the list.

Amanda's breath caught and she mumbled something in her sleep. He started to go to her but she calmed and snuggled back into the pillow.

He didn't know how she did it, how she functioned each day with the memories that roiled around inside her mind, knowing the man who did those horrible things to her was still out there, stalking and murdering other young women. Just the suspicion that the killer Logan had let go had probably killed other women made it hard for him to function some days. Considering what Amanda carried around in her mind every day, he was amazed she functioned at all.

His fingers dug into the soft cloth of the arms of the chair as he remembered the hospital pictures of her after the attack. It was difficult enough viewing them before he'd met her. Thinking about them now sent a jolt of fury coursing through him. How could anyone, no matter how sick, look at that angelic, heart-shaped face and want to hurt her?

The killer had better hope he was captured by someone other than Logan, because the way he felt right now he knew he'd kill him, probably with his bare hands. It would be a pleasure to smash his fist into the bastard's face, feel the bones crunch beneath his knuckles. Unprofessional, petty, sure . . . but it would make Logan feel a hell of a lot better.

Later, when Amanda knew the killer could never hurt her again, would she be able to go on with her life? Could she be happy again? The picture he'd pieced together of her past was of a woman who had withdrawn from the world, done everything she could to avoid human contact and lock herself away in her safe little cocoon.

He understood her need to be alone, to do everything she could to avoid being hurt again. Leaving Shadow Falls ten years ago was his way of withdrawing, of running away from his problems. None of the other officers seemed to blame him for his mistake, but it wasn't his peers he'd run from. He'd run from himself. It took him a full decade to realize that.

Looking back at her, he watched the gentle rise and fall of her chest, her dark curls framing her delicate cheeks and falling across the bed like a satin drape. There was no denying there was something special about her, a kindred spirit he'd recognized the moment she'd crushed his foot in her door. Everything he'd learned about her since then had only deepened his respect for her.

When her parents died, she was legally entitled to half their estate. She was struggling financially at the time. The money would have made her life much easier. Instead, she'd given it all to her sister to fund her education.

He'd called Amanda's sister, Heather, as part of the investigation. Heather painted a picture of a big sister who'd always looked out for her, although they'd had some kind of falling out that Heather wouldn't elaborate on.

Logan couldn't imagine how Amanda must have felt, still mentally healing from a horrendous attack, the only family she had left had abandoned her, turned away in her moment of need. And yet, she sent generous checks to her sister on the anniversary of their parents' death and Christmas, using some bogus excuse about proceeds from a trust.

Alone, she'd done everything she could to keep the ugly world at bay, to isolate herself. And yet, once she knew the killer was back in Shadow Falls, she'd insisted on staying, to help in any way that she could to find the killer.

Most women he knew would have left, not given a second thought to helping the police. Amanda was scared, but she'd done everything she could to help. She had the same desire for justice that he had, the same sense of family loyalty.

She was resting comfortably now, so he tucked the covers around her and pressed a soft kiss to the top of her head before shuffling off to the guest room where he was staying.

An hour later, he was awakened by a scream so chilling he was certain the killer had broken in and was torturing Amanda. He grabbed his gun and ran into her room, expecting to see a man standing over her with a knife. Instead, he found her in the bed, alone, whimpering in her sleep. He stroked her arm, whispered soothing words until she calmed. She let out a soft sigh before snuggling back under the covers.

He'd just reached the doorway when she let out another agonized scream.

Rushing back to the bed he stood in indecision. She whimpered and thrashed back and forth, her face a mask of fear as her legs kicked at the covers.

"Ah, hell," he swore. He checked the safety on his gun and put it in the nightstand drawer before climbing into the bed and laying down on top of the covers next to her. Crawling under the covers would be far too tempting. Circling his arm around her slim waist, he pulled her tightly against him and spooned his thighs behind hers. She immediately calmed and snuggled into his embrace, her fingers entwining with his.

She would probably be furious in the morning when she discovered him in bed with her, but if he heard one more of those blood-curdling screams, *he'd* be the one having nightmares.

When she wiggled her bottom against his groin, he gritted his teeth. It was going to be a long night.

The smell of bacon had Amanda hopping out of bed and rushing through her shower the next morning. She couldn't imagine Karen cooking breakfast, but her nose told her otherwise.

After last night's grueling interview, she didn't relish the idea of being alone to relive the vivid memories that were already swirling through her mind this morning. So even though she wasn't particularly hungry and wasn't much of a breakfast person, she hurried through her morning routine.

Glancing at the clock before she left the bedroom, she was glad to see it was after eight. Logan would have left for the office a few hours ago, giving her time to gather her defenses before she saw him again. She didn't know how she would face him, what she would say, and she needed time to think about it.

He'd seemed so concerned about her last night, tucking her into bed, staying with her until she fell asleep. She had vague impressions of nightmares but she hadn't woken herself up screaming like she usually did when those disturbing dreams haunted her. She'd slept the best she could remember in a long time.

As she descended the last step, she called out, "Karen, you should have waited. I could have helped you cook." She walked into the kitchen and came to an abrupt halt when she saw who was standing in front of the stove.

Logan turned around and even though Amanda's stomach flipped as she realized she'd have to face him earlier than she'd hoped, she couldn't help but smile at his ensemble.

He was immaculately dressed, as usual, in perfectly pleated navy blue pants, shiny black shoes, a light blue dress-shirt tucked into his waistband and the ever present gun holstered beneath his left arm.

But he'd rolled up his sleeves and instead of the suit jacket he normally wore he had a white towel hanging from his waist from hip to hip, apparently his homemade version of an apron to keep the grease from splattering his clothes.

Returning her smile, he used a pair of tongs to lift out several slices of burned bacon and laid them on a plate. Not a napkin or paper towel in sight to absorb all that grease. Honestly, she didn't know how men survived their own cooking.

"I hope you like bacon and eggs," he said as he turned off the stove and set the pan on a cool area of the glass top stove. "I have biscuits, too."

"Sounds wonderful," she lied, as she suppressed a shudder at the thought of all that fat. A bagel was her usual fare, but he looked so awkward she'd bet he almost never cooked. He certainly hadn't cooked since she'd started living here, but she'd assumed that was because he usually got home so late. The fact that he'd cooked for her this morning made her determined to eat whatever he'd made and to pretend she loved it, regardless of how fatty or burned it was.

"Breakfast is the only meal I know how to cook," he continued, confirming her earlier thought. "Well, besides cookout."

"Cook-out?" She smiled.

"Hamburgers, steak, ribs."

"Ah. Man-food."

He gave her a grin and placed a platter of eggs, bacon, and biscuits on the table. "I have coffee, but you prefer soda, right?"

Since he was already grabbing a soda from the refrigerator, she didn't bother to answer. She nodded her thanks when he set it and his cup of coffee on the table.

"So, why aren't you in the office?" she asked, hoping he hadn't heard the nervous catch in her voice.

He stepped behind her, startling her until she realized he'd pulled out her chair so she could sit. His mama had taught him well. This wasn't the first time she was the recipient of his ingrained southern manners.

Nodding her thanks, she sat and scooped some scrambled eggs onto her plate. Apparently Logan only knew how to cook breakfast one way, well done. The eggs were as dry as they could be without being brown.

Rather than sit in the chair across from her, he chose the one next to her. "I asked Karen to come over a couple of hours late today. I'll go into work after she gets here."

He hadn't really answered her about why he wasn't in the office, but she decided not to push him. She probably didn't want to know his real reason for being home. She didn't want to rehash last night's events, and she fervently hoped he hadn't stayed home to grill her with a few more questions about her abduction.

They sat and ate in companionable silence. Neither of them seemed anxious to fill the void with conversation, which was fine with her.

After forcing down the minimum amount of food she thought was necessary to make him feel like she appreciated his efforts, she set her fork on her plate and took a sip of her soda.

Logan put his fork down right after she did, as if he'd been waiting for her to finish. She glanced at his plate and only then realized he hadn't eaten much more than her. Apparently he didn't have an appetite this morning either.

"I wanted to make sure you were okay before I left for work," he said. "I know last night was . . . difficult."

Why couldn't he let it drop? She took another sip of her drink.

"Are you okay?" he asked.

Sighing, she set the can down. "I don't know how I feel. You've kind of knocked me off balance."

"What do you mean?"

She waved a hand at the food on the table. "Breakfast. You, here, being nice to me."

He sat back with a lopsided smile. "I'm not supposed to be nice to you?"

"You know what I mean."

"Yes, I think I do." His face lost all signs of amusement. "You think because you survived some lunatic's twisted sadistic game and your friend didn't, that you're somehow to blame. That's bullshit."

"Excuse me?"

He pitched his napkin on the table and stood. "Let's go for a walk. There's something I want to show you."

He stepped behind her chair to pull it out, not giving her a chance to argue.

They went out through the French doors, across the back deck, and stepped into another world. The grass was spongy and soft beneath Amanda's sandals. The air as they neared the edge of the lawn was surprisingly comfortable in the shade of the towering pines and moss covered live oaks.

"It's the creek," Logan said, noticing her surprise. "It runs along the back of the property, cools the air. Beyond that is deep-water access to the Gulf, which sends even more breezes this way." He reached out his hand. "Come on."

She placed her hand in his and was rewarded with an affectionate squeeze of his fingers.

He pulled her behind him down a twisting path through the pines, a path she hadn't noticed from the house.

"Are you sure you have time for this?" she asked, wondering how far they were going.

"I'm the boss. I'll write myself a note," he teased. "We're almost there."

The path ended abruptly at the edge of the creek Logan had mentioned. Amanda was walking so fast to try to keep up with his long strides that she couldn't stop. She would have fallen into the creek if he hadn't grabbed her.

Once he'd steadied her, instead of letting her go, he wrapped his arms around her waist and pulled her back against his chest.

She stiffened at first, then she relaxed against him, and his arms tightened around her. Delicious heat spiked through her as she breathed in his familiar scent, the same scent that clung to the comforter on her bed. It felt so right standing there with his arms around her.

"This is my private sanctuary," he said, his voice pitched

low as if they were in church. "It's where I go when I need to think, or get away."

The creek was no more than twenty feet wide but it had a strong current as evidenced by the little eddies and swiftly moving pine needles that blanketed its surface. It was dark, with the towering pines and oaks sheltering the glade, but that's why it felt so cool and comfortable even in the midst of the hot Florida summer. Jasmine scented the air and a cooling breeze blew across the water.

"It's beautiful," she breathed, her voice as low and respectful as his was.

He took her hand and pulled her to the quaint wooden bench that sat in the middle of the clearing with a perfect view of the creek. He sat down and patted the bench beside him.

"Sit," he ordered. When she hesitated, he added, "Please?" and gave her hand a gentle tug.

Shaking her head at his irresistible charm, she sat, her thigh pressed tightly against his in the narrow space. "How many women have you taken here to your cozy little retreat?"

"Just one. You." He turned his intense gaze upon her.

Her breath caught at his whispered words. Unable to bear his scrutiny, she looked at the water, concentrating on the beauty of its motion as it rushed over the little rocks and branches that drooped down.

"Why did you bring me here?" she asked, barely able to get the words out past the tight constriction in her throat.

He sighed, the sound loud in the silence of the forest. "I should never have asked you to tell me about your abduction. I put you through torture. Gave you nightmares."

"Nightmares?"

He glanced at her as if searching for something in her expression. "I heard you cry out."

"Oh. Well, I do that sometimes, have nightmares. It drove my sister crazy." After several minutes of silence, she said, "I'm not upset at you for last night. If you brought me here to apologize—"

"That's not why I brought you here."

"Then why did you?"

He raked his hand through his hair. "You bared your secrets to me last night, secrets that were difficult for you to talk about. I don't take that lightly and I want to return the favor."

"What do you mean?"

"Ask me anything you want, anything at all. I'll answer as honestly as I can."

She stared at him, surprised again at his generosity, how he put her needs above his at every turn. At first she thought she'd turn down his offer, let him off the hook, but there was one thing she wanted to know more about.

"What was the rookie mistake you said you made, the one that made you leave Shadow Falls and go to New York?"

His glance shot to hers. "Ouch. How did you know where to strike?"

"I'm sorry. I shouldn't have asked. It's just that you told me at my house, about making mistakes, and regrets . . . so I was curious. Forget it, I shouldn't have—"

"Hey." He gently lifted her chin to look up at him. "A deal's a deal." He dropped his hand and sighed, looking out over the creek. He told her about a murder, a traffic stop, a split-second decision gone wrong.

"I screwed up," he continued. "I made a bad decision that has haunted me ever since. And I knew the only way for me to move past it was to get better training, better experience than I was getting here. So I moved to New York City, took a job in the most violent precinct, traded my vacations for FBI courses at Quantico, did everything I could to make myself a better cop."

"That sounds admirable."

He shook his head. "No, it's what I had to do. It was the least I could do. My mistake, no matter how small it might sound, had tragic consequences. A killer went free." He clenched his fists against his thighs. "It's something I have to live with, knowing if I'd taken two more minutes, followed my instincts, followed standard procedure, I could have stopped him. Who knows if he's killed again, or hurt anyone else?"

"Thank you for telling me." Amanda reached out her hand to hold his.

He looked at their entwined fingers resting on his thigh before turning the full wattage of his gaze on her. The pain was there, etched in lines around his mouth, but there was also a raw hunger in him that made her gasp in recognition as the same hunger burned through her. She looked at his mouth, leaned slightly forward.

His body tensed and he reached for her, but in spite of the heat in his eyes and the tension in his body, he was ever so gentle as he wrapped his arms around her, pulling her against him. He lowered his lips toward hers, slowly, as if to give her time to change her mind. She waited for the panic to come, but all she felt was the same raw hunger, the same answering need. She reached her arms up and wrapped them around his neck, pulling his lips down to hers.

He groaned deep in his throat. When she moaned beneath the gentle pressure of his lips and parted hers in invitation, his restraint vanished and he swept his tongue inside to mate with hers.

Without breaking their kiss, he twisted, pulling her onto his lap. She straddled him between her thighs, her stomach clenching as she felt the hardness of his erection beneath her. She couldn't stop herself from arching against him.

He jerked beneath her and thrust his hips in response. His hand slid along her thigh, up beneath the edge of her khaki shorts, squeezing her bottom. His other hand snaked up between them, beneath the hem of her tank top to the lacy edge of her bra. He cupped the fullness of her breast and she cried out when his thumb brushed across her.

His mouth broke free from hers and he slid his lips along the bottom of her jaw, tracing a heated path down the side of her neck. When he reached the upper curves of her breasts where they swelled above her top, he kissed his way to the valley between them and delved his tongue inside.

Amanda shivered beneath his fiery caresses and ground her hips against him. She ran her fingers across the planes of his chest, unable to get enough of him, desperate to feel his skin against hers. Frantically working the buttons of his shirt, she gasped when his hot mouth closed around her, not realizing until then that he'd worked her top and bra down, completely exposing both of her breasts.

"You're exquisite," he breathed against her.

By now she had his shirt unbuttoned and she moaned in

delight when she smoothed her hands across the wiry hair of his chest and followed the dark line to where it disappeared beneath his waistband. The muscles of his stomach rippled and jumped as she raked them with her nails.

She was burning up and wanted nothing more than to rip his clothes from his body and drive him as crazy as he was driving her. He jerked beneath her when she ran her hands on the outside of his pants, down the impressive length of him, and then back up, her nails raking against his hard ridge as she struggled to undo his belt.

He reclaimed her mouth and slid his hands around her back, diving them deep into her hair, playing with the silky strands as his tongue tangled with hers.

Suddenly she was in the cabin again, and she heard the humming as the hooded man ran his fingers through her hair.

She whimpered and shoved him but she couldn't break his hold.

In desperation, she raked her nails across his chest and screamed.

"Amanda!"

Her eyes flew open and she was staring into Logan's eyes. He held her arms in a vice-like grip, lightly shaking her. "Honey? Are you with me now? Say something."

"Y . . . yes, I'm here," she whispered, her throat oddly raw and aching. Her gaze traveled down his chest and she saw the red angry scratches across it, oozing blood.

"Oh, my God, Logan. Did I do that? I think I'm going to be sick."

Logan turned her to the side as she threw up her breakfast.

"It's okay, honey. Everything is okay. Do you know where you are?" His voice was low and soothing.

Amanda shuddered and crawled off his lap, pushing away from him so she could stand up. "I know where I am," she whispered, unable to meet his gaze.

While she straightened her clothing, he stood and repaired his as well. When he reached out to take her hand she shoved it away. Taking a steadying breath, she met his searching gaze. "I did that to you, hurt you." She pointed to the red dots of blood that were soaking through his shirt.

"I've survived far worse. It's nothing."

"Stop being so damned understanding. Don't you see? He screwed up my head. There's something wrong with me. I'd given up on having a normal relationship again, and then, then I met you, and then . . ."

"Then what?"

"There's no use, can't you see? I actually hurt you. And I didn't know I was doing it."

"Let me help. I'm a great listener—"

"No," she sobbed, shaking her head back and forth. She whirled around, her long hair rippling out behind her as she ran into the forest.

Logan jogged behind Amanda. He knew she needed some time alone but he wasn't about to let her out of his sight until she was safely back in the house and Karen arrived. She wasn't due to be here for another hour but he'd call and see if she could come over now. No point in waiting.

He couldn't shake the image of Amanda's pale face, eyes

wild and unfocused as she clawed at him and screamed with such heart-wrenching terror.

When he woke up this morning in bed beside her, he was struck by how right it had felt. Now he wasn't so certain. Not because his feelings had changed. They hadn't. But he'd misjudged her, underestimated how scarred she was inside.

He'd brought her to his sanctuary by the creek, determined to share it with her, bring some peace to her after the difficult night she'd had. The kiss had been a terrible mistake. When she'd looked up at him so trustingly, he'd gotten lost in her eyes. Then when she'd looked at his mouth and leaned forward he'd lost all control, and scared her to death.

All along he'd struggled with his attraction to her, worried it would interfere with his job, worried that he might not be any better for Amanda than he had been for his ex-wife. That worry was justified. He wasn't any good for Amanda. He needed to back off, keep it all on a professional level.

But now that he'd had a taste of heaven, how was he going to give her up?

Chapter Twelve

Amanda knew she was a coward, running away from Logan like that, but as she stood at the window in his bedroom and watched him drive away, she knew she'd had no other choice.

And running from the woods wasn't the only running she was going to do.

She was going home.

For a few minutes, anyway, to get some more clothes and her passport. Then she was leaving—not just Shadow Falls. She was leaving the country. There was nothing else for her to add to the investigation, no reason to stay.

The memory of Logan's sweet, sexy smile shot a stab of pain through her so intense it almost brought her to her knees. How had he wiggled his way into her heart so quickly? She shook the image away and finished stuffing her last few belongings into the suitcase on the bed.

Leaving made perfect sense. It was the right thing to do. She couldn't bear to face Logan again, knowing she wasn't coming back.

Getting away from the house would be easy. She'd eavesdropped earlier when Karen arrived and she'd heard Logan tell Karen she was upstairs and wanted to be alone. Karen wouldn't expect her downstairs anytime soon.

And since Logan had stored her car next to his garage, all she had to do was wait until Karen did one of her patrols around the property and drive away.

With luck, she'd get what she needed from her house and be on her way to the airport before Logan realized she'd left. By the time he figured everything out, she'd be on an airplane and there'd be nothing he could do to stop her.

Would he care? She doubted it, not after the way she'd acted this morning. He'd probably be glad to be rid of her and all her emotional baggage, but he was a man of honor. His misguided sense of duty might force him to try to stop her from leaving, which was why she was going to sneak out now.

After shutting her suitcase, she looked around the room, memorizing it, taking a picture to hold in her heart when she looked back on what might have been.

She sat on the bed and stared out the window, waiting for Karen to leave the house.

A few minutes later, Karen stepped into her line of vision and began her patrol of the perimeter of the property.

Amanda hefted her suitcase and hurried through the house. She turned off the alarm, slipped out the back door and re-armed the alarm before heading for the garage. She didn't relax until she was in her car and out of the driveway on her way to her house.

When she was ten minutes from home, she pulled over at a convenience store and convinced the clerk to let her use their phone. Yes, she wanted to go home and get a few things before leaving town, but she wasn't stupid. If the killer was watching her house, she needed protection. But if she'd asked Karen for help, Karen would have tried to stop her and would have called Logan.

She didn't know if the unmarked police car was still down the street keeping an eye on her house, and she didn't want to rely on men she didn't know—even if they were police.

No, what she needed was someone she could trust: someone who would trust her and believe the lie she was about to tell.

"SFPD, how may I direct your call?" an elderly voice asked upon answering the phone.

"Detective Riley, please."

"One moment."

She clutched the phone as she waited, guilt already riddling her for what she was about to do. Riley was a nice guy and she hated to deceive him, but she couldn't think of any other way.

"Detective Riley."

"Riley? It's Amanda Stockton."

"Amanda? Is something wrong? Logan's in his office. Do you want me to get him for you?"

"No, no, I'm sure he's busy and I don't want to bother him. Actually, I was hoping you could do me a favor."

When Amanda drove up to her house, Riley was just getting out of his car. Perfect timing. She pulled into the driveway behind him.

He slammed his door shut and stood with an incredulous expression on his face.

As soon as she shut her car door, he stalked up to her and grabbed her arm. His face was red and he looked like he was struggling to control his temper.

"Riley, before you yell at me, give me a minute to explain."

"Oh, for God's sake, I'm not going to yell at you. You can explain why you lied to me once I get you inside. It's not safe out here, and I value my life too highly to face Logan if something happens to you." He pulled her toward the house, forcing her to jog to keep up with him.

He kept looking around as if he expected an attack any second. His nervousness started transferring to her and she suddenly felt very foolish.

"Riley, I know it was wrong to lie to you, but I needed to get some more clothes and my passport so I thought if I asked you to get them—"

"You did ask me to get them. I was supposed to bring your things back to Logan's where you promised you'd be waiting. Why did you come here?"

They stood on the front porch as she tried to put her key into the lock on the front door. Riley stood with his back to her, his jacket thrown open to expose his gun. Amanda's hand was shaking so hard now she couldn't seem to get the key to work. "I'm sorry about lying," she said. "It's just that I'd decided to leave and—"

"You're leaving without telling Logan?" he asked, glancing back at her. Perhaps noting her expression, he shook his head. "I see. That's the point, isn't it? You're not a prisoner,

Amanda. If you'd leveled with him, he would have taken you himself. And he would have made sure you were safe. None of this was necessary."

"You don't understand," she said, catching her ring of keys as they dropped from the lock.

"Here, let me." He reached his arms around her, shielding her with his body as he unlocked the door. "When we go in, stay in the foyer. If something happens, press the panic button on your alarm."

"If you're trying to scare me, you've succeeded."

"I'm not trying to scare you. I'm trying to protect you." He pulled out his gun and shoved the door back, then entered the foyer with her close behind.

She entered her security code to turn off the alarm, closed and locked the door behind them.

He nodded his approval. "Wait here."

He glanced into the kitchen, then hurried to the living room and disappeared around the corner. A few seconds later he came back into the foyer. In response to her questioning look, he said, "Clear so far. I'll check the bedrooms."

She nodded and waited.

And waited.

Something had to have happened to him or he would have been back by now, wouldn't he? Part of her wanted to run out the front door, but Riley was here because of her, and she couldn't deal with any more guilt if he were hurt.

She chewed her bottom lip. Should she call out his name? If the killer was there, he'd hear her. She began shaking so hard she was afraid the killer would hear her teeth chattering. As quietly as possible, she reached down and picked up a heavy paperweight from the decorative table against the foyer wall.

Suddenly Riley rushed around the corner from the hallway. As soon as she saw his pale, drawn face, she whirled around and slammed her palm against the alarm's panic button.

Logan braked so hard that his car skidded sideways and hopped the curb before settling to a stop on Amanda's front lawn. Ignoring the cursing coming from Pierce in the passenger seat, Logan threw open the driver's door and vaulted over the hood.

He probably looked like a madman, sprinting across the lawn and taking the porch steps two at a time, but he didn't care. All he could think about was getting to Amanda.

He'd already spoken to Riley on the phone. Even though Riley had assured him Amanda was okay, that she'd fallen and bumped her head when he'd frightened her by running around the corner into the foyer, he had to see for himself.

Once inside, he pushed and shoved his way through the uniformed policemen milling around to get into the living room where the activity appeared to be centered. As he paused to survey the room and find her, Pierce came to a halt beside him. His jaw was set and he punched Logan's arm.

"Is this how you protect a crime scene in your town? Let every cop and his brother crawl all over it and compromise the evidence?"

Logan flushed. He knew Pierce was right, but it still

wasn't going to keep him from getting to Amanda. He glanced around, located Riley. "Riley," he called out. "Clear the room, secure the scene."

Riley nodded and Logan surged through the group of officers surrounding the couch, pushing them aside so he could see what they were looking at. Pierce cursed behind him and Logan knew the man thought he was a backwoods fool. Maybe he was, because nothing else mattered but seeing Amanda, seeing how badly she was hurt.

Suddenly Pierce was beside him, helping him shove everyone out of the way and shouting at them to quit mucking up the crime scene and to get out of the house.

If Logan wasn't so frantic to get to Amanda, he would have laughed at the startled looks on his men's faces and at how quickly they snapped to attention, obeying the FBI agent as if they'd taken orders from him all their lives.

The room quickly emptied and at last Logan saw Amanda. She was lying on the couch, holding an ice pack to the side of her head while an EMT cleaned blood off her face.

She was all right. That's what he kept telling himself as he took a shaky breath. He tried to calm his raging emotions before he did something stupid, like pick her up and haul her out of here, lock her up and keep her prisoner until the killer was found.

"You're all right?" Logan asked after the EMT left. He held Amanda's hand as he sat beside her on the couch.

She looked into his eyes, comforted by the concern she

saw. "I'm fine. It's stupid, really. I panicked and slipped. Just a bump, nothing serious."

"What happened?" Logan asked, as Pierce slid the coffee table back a couple of feet and perched on its edge to face her. Riley took one of the recliners next to the couch.

Glancing uncomfortably at Pierce, Amanda turned back to Logan and spoke to him in a hushed voice. "After this morning, I decided there was no reason for me to stay at your house anymore. I wanted to get as far away as I could, but first I needed to get more clothes and my passport. So I asked Riley—"

"*Tricked* Riley," Logan corrected.

She frowned. "Yes. I tricked him. I told him I needed some more clothes, and asked if he could pick them up for me and bring them to your house. I made it sound like no big deal, nothing to bother you about, and he was nice enough to come over here."

"And instead of you staying at my house," Logan interrupted, "like you promised him, you came here. My God, Amanda. What if you had gotten here earlier, when the killer was still inside? You could have been killed. And Riley."

She felt the blood drain from her face. "I'm sorry, Riley. I wasn't trying to hurt anyone."

"And you didn't," Pierce assured her. He leaned toward Logan. "Can I speak to you for a minute?"

Logan clenched his jaw. "This isn't over," he whispered. He stood and left the room with Pierce.

Amanda shivered at the cold anger that had radiated in those three little words. She looked up and met Riley's concerned brown eyes. "I really am sorry, Riley. I shouldn't have lied to you."

He smiled and sat beside her on the couch. "Look at the bright side."

"Bright side? What's that?"

"If you hadn't conned me into coming out here to begin with, we wouldn't have found the presents the killer left in your bedroom. And honestly, the way the case is going, we need all the evidence and clues we can get, so I'm glad you got me over here."

"I'm not sure I agree with all of that, but thanks for trying to make me feel better. Do you mind if I ask you a question?"

"Sure."

"It's just that, well, when we entered the house and you disappeared down the hall, you were gone so long. And then, when you ran around the corner . . ."

"Yes?"

"The look on your face. You looked . . . scary."

He laughed awkwardly. "Don't you mean I looked scared? When I saw what the killer left in your bedroom, I have to admit it scared the shit out of me." His face turned red. "Sorry. Anyway, I've never seen anything like that and I sort of zoned out. I'm sorry I scared you when I ran around the corner. I was expecting to find the killer."

"I'm the one who's sorry. If it weren't for me you wouldn't be in the middle of this mess."

He smiled again, a boyish, youthful smile that made her wonder how she could have ever been afraid of him, even for a second.

"I'll forgive you, on one condition."

"Anything."

"Next time, call Logan instead."

Logan still smarted from the argument outside with Pierce. Pierce had read him the riot act on preserving crime scenes, and tried to get him to leave the scene to those less emotionally involved. Although he knew Pierce was right, he wasn't leaving without Amanda. But he did give his men orders and organized the scene. If it was anyone else talking to him the way Pierce had, he'd have knocked them on their ass. But he respected Pierce and he knew he was right.

When Logan walked back into Amanda's living room with Pierce at his side, he nodded at Riley standing by the fireplace and joined Amanda on the couch. Pierce sat on the recliner to her right, having as much trouble as Logan had over a week ago when he'd had to squeeze his body into the slim chair.

"Amanda," Pierce said. "Did detective Riley tell you what he found in your bedroom?"

"He said there were some pictures of me."

"There were a lot of pictures of you, hundreds, taped all over the walls."

"How many people know about the game the killer played with you and Dana?" Logan asked.

"The police, of course. Dana's father, my therapist—"

Logan exchanged a startled glance with Pierce. "Dana's father knows?"

"He visited me in the hospital. He wanted to know everything that had happened to Dana. I didn't want to tell him, but he was emphatic, said it was his right as her father to know. You seem surprised. Should I not have told him?"

"No, no, you did the right thing," Logan said. "That's a detail we've held back from the press, and I didn't know Branson knew. Go on. You said your therapist knows. Anyone else?"

She frowned in concentration. "No one else I can think of. Why?"

"Because there was a long-stemmed rose on your bed. It only had one thorn. And there was a note that said, '*He Kills Me, He Kills Me Not.*'"

Pierce took his Blackberry from the breast pocket of his suit jacket, opened it, and punched some buttons. "What's the name of your therapist?"

"My therapist didn't leave that note," she insisted.

"His name?" Pierce repeated.

"*Her* name is Joanne Bateman. She practices out of Pensacola now."

Pierce glanced at her, shrugged, and typed in the name. "We'll still check her out. Maybe there's a tie-in."

"Riley," Logan said. "Have they found anything else? Fingerprints? Witnesses?"

"Plenty of prints on the pictures. And a neighbor nextdoor was getting her mail early this morning and said she saw a man dressed in blue coveralls on Amanda's property. She thought he was the cable guy."

"I don't suppose you snuck out for an appointment with the cable company?" Logan asked her.

Her cheeks flushed red. "No."

"I'm on it," Pierce said. "Which neighbor, Riley?"

Riley told him and Pierce left the room.

"Riley?" Logan asked, his eyes riveted on Amanda. "Now would be a good time for you to check on the men outside, make sure they've got the scene taped off correctly."

"Um, yeah, sure." Riley left the room.

When they were alone, Logan tried to keep in mind how Amanda had responded the last time he'd pushed her. He didn't want to hurt her, or make her panic again, but the urge to yell at her was so strong it was making his throat ache. She'd put her life in danger by coming back here, knowing there was a killer out there, knowing the killer probably knew where she lived.

But looking into her eyes, seeing the fear mirrored back at him, his anger quickly faded. He held out his hand, palm up, and sighed in relief when she put her hand in his. "Why did you leave my house?"

She stared at their hands joined together, resting on the top of her thighs. "I made a complete fool of myself . . . with you. I was embarrassed and didn't want to face you again. Besides, there wasn't any point in staying. I told you everything I know about the case. The computer program I wrote did all it could do. There was no point in me staying any longer."

He gently lifted her chin until she met his gaze. "I don't want you to leave."

She swallowed hard and her eyes widened. "You don't?"

"Not even a little." Not wanting to make her panic again, or bring back any bad memories, he pulled back his hand, even though it practically killed him. What he really wanted to do was pull her close and protect her and chase the fear from her eyes. Instead, he tried to reassure her. "Staying at my house is safer. Only a handful of people know you're there, and you always have a police officer with you—either me or Karen."

Her eyes widened, and for a moment he thought she looked disappointed. But then she smiled. "Well, there's a lot to be said for 'round-the-clock cops watching over you."

"Right," he agreed. "I know you want to leave, get away from all of this, but I'm asking you to stay with me for a couple more days. If I don't crack this case by then, I'll take you to the airport myself."

"Why?" she asked. "Why should I stay?"

Because I can't imagine coming home and you not being there. Because I'm falling in love with you. He cleared his throat. "Because I may have more questions, and it's easier to ask them in person. Plus, until this killer is caught, I'd feel much better knowing you were at my home, guarded by Karen or me, rather than trust someone else to protect you."

She shivered and wrapped her arms around her waist. "All right. I'll stay, for a few more days. Then we can reevaluate."

"Thank you," he whispered. Unable to resist the urge to touch her again, he pressed a tender kiss against her forehead and quickly pulled back before he made her panic.

CHAPTER THIRTEEN

"Nice. You'd think someone would pick up around here
once in a while," Riley said. His lips curled in disgust as he
kicked a discarded fast-food bag out of the way, and stepped
over the ant trail that led to some indefinable sticky mass on
the stained concrete.

The stakeout had finally yielded results. Pierce's men
had called in to report that Branson showed up at his apartment less than an hour ago. Pierce, Riley, and Logan were
hoping to surprise him.

Following behind Riley, Pierce stopped to rake his shoe
on the edge of the concrete. Logan didn't ask what Pierce
had stepped in but he could guess any number of unpleasant
things.

Riley knocked on the rusted front door that might once
have been white but now was a mixture of blistering, yellow-
ing paint and grimy black handprints. He made a show of
wiping his hand on his pants as if to wipe off any germs he'd
picked up from the door. Logan gave him a warning look.

The door creaked open and a disheveled Frank Branson

greeted them with bloodshot eyes and several days' growth of stubble on his face. The khaki shorts and white cotton t-shirt he wore were horribly wrinkled but appeared to be clean.

Logan braced himself against the urge to slam his fist into the other man's face. Instead, he extended his hand. "Mr. Branson, I'm Chief Richards."

Branson eyed his hand as if it were a serpent. "What do you want?"

Logan was more than a little relieved that he hadn't had to shake Branson's hand. "We'd like to ask you a few questions, and thought it would be easier to meet you here than to haul you back to the station. May we come in?"

Branson pursed his lips as Logan's veiled threat sank in, just as Logan had intended. He planned to haul Branson back to the station, anyway, to get his fingerprints, but he wanted inside his apartment to see if the man was foolish enough to leave evidence lying around. If Branson let him in without a warrant, it would save them all time.

Branson shrugged and left the door open as he retreated inside and plopped down on a vinyl recliner positioned in front of a tiny TV set.

He didn't bother to turn off the TV, which was currently tuned to a rerun of CSI Miami. Logan thought that was an odd choice for the father of a murder victim, but he knew Amanda liked the same show, and God knew she had every reason not to. People were complicated.

The apartment consisted of a small kitchen separated from the main room by a cracked laminate countertop. There were two doors set into the wall and Logan guessed those led to a bathroom and a bedroom. The apartment was tiny enough to be an efficiency, but there was no sign of a bed or even a futon where Branson could sleep out in this main room.

It was cleaner on the inside than Logan had expected, given the way it looked outside, but not by much. Dirty dishes overflowed the sink and discarded clothes littered the floor in small piles as if Branson had undressed and left them wherever they happened to land.

The only place to sit besides the recliner was a stained brown couch with piles of dirty clothes scattered across it. Branson didn't offer to clear a place for them, and Logan wouldn't have sat if he did.

Instead, he leaned down and turned off the TV, then stood beside Riley in front of the screen. Pierce strolled around the apartment, quietly studying everything.

Branson frowned and tossed the remote on the Walmart-variety end table next to him. "What do you want to ask me? Hurry up. I'm missing my favorite show."

"It's a rerun," Riley offered. "The limo driver did it."

Branson's face grew red and Logan gave Riley a warning look. "Mr. Branson, where were you yesterday morning, around eight-thirty?"

Branson's eyes opened wide and Logan thought his face paled a bit beneath the stubble on his cheeks. "I was at work."

"That's interesting, since the trucking company you work for hasn't seen you in quite some time. Did you get a new job?"

"That's right, yeah. I'm hauling for another company now."

Riley pulled out his phone. "Can you give me the name of that company so I can verify your claim, Mr. Branson?"

Branson's face reddened again. "My daughter was murdered and my wife left me. You've got no business harassing me, and I don't have to answer any of your questions." He looked past Logan and seemed to finally notice Pierce, who was studying a pile of envelopes and pieces of paper lying on the kitchen bar. "Hey, what are you doing? Don't be going through none of my things."

"Someone called the station a few days ago, Mr. Branson," Logan said, trying to divert his attention. "They asked a lot of questions about Amanda Stockton. The man on the phone didn't give his name, but the police officer recognized the voice. He'd interviewed you after Dana's murder. He was quite certain you were the one who called. But when he asked your name, you hung up."

Branson's eyes widened and a light sheen of sweat broke out on his forehead. "Okay, so I called. No big deal. I was checking on the investigation. It's been years, and you still haven't caught the man that killed Dana."

Logan leaned toward him, taking advantage of his size to intimidate the much smaller man. "I wasn't on the case back when your daughter was killed, but I am now. I promise you, I will find the killer. And I'll find the man who broke into Amanda Stockton's house yesterday and tried to scare her."

Branson sank back in his chair, his eyes darting around as if he was looking for somewhere to run.

A wisp of a noise had them both looking toward the kitchen where Pierce was standing. The pile of papers he'd been studying had fallen to the floor. "Oh, sorry, must have bumped them with my elbow," Pierce said as he bent down to gather the envelopes and papers.

"No, no, I'll get them. Leave them alone," Branson sputtered as he jumped up from the recliner.

Pierce was studying a receipt but Branson swiped it away. "Give me that," he said. He leaned down to grab the other envelopes and paper.

"That was a florist receipt, Mr. Branson. Looks like you bought a dozen roses yesterday. And these blue coveralls on the floor right here? They match the description of the clothing worn by an alleged cable man seen at Amanda Stockton's home, right down to the ripped front pocket that a very observant neighbor noticed."

Logan growled and took a step forward. Pierce stepped between him and Branson while Riley pulled out his handcuffs.

"You're under arrest, Mr. Branson," Riley said cheerfully, as he jerked Branson's arms behind him and cuffed him. The mail and receipt dropped from Branson's fingers.

"What for? Buying some stupid flowers?" he demanded.

"Good question," Riley said, looking at Logan. "Stalking or murder, boss?"

Pierce placed a restraining hand on Logan's arm. "You don't have enough for murder yet. He'll lawyer-up and be out by morning. Stalking might hold him longer until we can pull together more evidence."

Logan nodded, not trusting himself to speak. He wanted to rip Branson apart. Whether he was the murderer or not, at the very least he'd terrorized Amanda.

Riley patted Branson down, then grabbed his arm and

led him to the door. "Stalking it is. By the way, did you know Florida has some of the toughest anti-stalking laws in the country?" He led Branson out the door, chatting amiably about the penalties of stalking.

Pierce released Logan's arm. "Can you handle this? Maybe you should take yourself off the case. You've made this a personal vendetta instead of a search for justice."

"I haven't done anything wrong, haven't crossed any lines."

"You haven't crossed any lines? You're the chief of police and you're working this case as if you were still a detective. Tell me, if Riley and I hadn't been here, what would have happened to Branson?"

Logan scowled. "I need to see this through. I can handle it."

Pierce sighed. "I can't tell you what to do, but I'm asking you to be careful. If you let your personal feelings affect your judgment, you won't be doing anyone any favors, least of all Amanda."

"He did it," Riley insisted. "I don't know how he got around Amanda's security alarm—not yet, anyway. He doesn't seem smart enough to know how to disable one, but he did it. I know it."

"Sure he did," Logan said. "He's responsible for the pictures, notes, rose, thorns—all of that—and we can prove it. But murder? I'm not convinced." He let out a frustrated breath, weary from arguing. The other two men believed Branson was the killer. Before the interrogation, so had

Logan, but not anymore. He had serious doubts about Branson's ability to plan and carry out the crimes, and remain undetected all these years.

Besides that, Pierce's lecture at Branson's apartment had struck a chord. Logan had realized he was falling into the trap he'd vowed all along not to fall into. He'd let his attraction to Amanda cloud his judgment. No more. He was determined to prove he could focus on the case in spite of the feelings he could no longer deny to himself. Amanda mattered to him. Somehow he had to focus on the case regardless of that.

The first thing he'd done after Branson's arrest was try to seal his emotions away and come at the evidence from a logical viewpoint. Once he'd done that, it became painfully clear that Branson couldn't be the murderer.

He glanced across the conference room table at Riley. "Why are you so determined to label Branson a killer?"

Riley's eyes widened and he looked like he was trying to figure out how to respond.

"And why are *you* being so stubborn?" Pierce interjected. "I'd think you'd be jumping at the chance to put away the man who hurt Amanda." He tossed his pen on the table. "You're still not being objective or you'd see the facts right in front of you."

"What facts?" Logan asked. "The facts are the same as before you and Riley interviewed Branson. He didn't tell you anything you didn't already know. You're both allowing your dislike of the man to influence you."

"Hold on," Riley said. "The man's a disgusting jerk, but

that alone wouldn't sway me to brand him a murderer. The evidence tells me he did it."

Pierce pointed at Logan. "You're the one who told us to look at Branson again, and we've gathered a mountain of evidence that shows his guilt. The interview was just icing, and proves he couldn't come up with a reasonable explanation for his actions today or better alibis for the other murders."

"You say we have a mountain of evidence, but it's entirely circumstantial," Logan said. "There isn't one solid piece of forensic evidence to tie him to any of the murders. You can't get a judge to indict based on the flimsy facts we've put together."

Pierce leaned forward in his chair, his eyes dark and intense. "What we have is a man who fits the profile in every way—"

"Profiles aren't evidence."

"—and," Pierce continued as if Logan hadn't interrupted, "we can place him in the same towns at the same times as three of the murders."

"What about the other murders?" Logan asked.

"He's worked for a variety of trucking companies. We're still looking for documentation but I'm sure we'll find it."

"Motive?"

"He's a serial killer. His motive is he's a sick bastard," Riley said.

"You're partly correct," Pierce said. "We don't know what the trigger was when he killed Dana and attacked Amanda, but after that, his wife left him, he was laid off from his job at the bank. He lost everything he had. Those pressures are the classic types of triggers. Trucking pays the bills but it doesn't get his wife back, or give him his self-respect again. It just gave him opportunity for the other murders."

Incredulous, Logan glanced back and forth between the two other men. "And you accused me of not being objective," he said to Pierce. "The man is five-foot-four and probably weighs less than a hundred pounds. How do you think he would be able to control a woman like Amanda? And besides that, she thought her attacker was at least as tall as her, which means our suspect has to be six feet or taller."

Pierce looked undaunted. "He was much heavier four years ago. We both know men as a rule are stronger than women, even women who are taller than them. And she can't have a good sense of his height since she was, by her own admission, either lying on the bed or the floor most of the time during her attack."

Logan winced but Pierce relentlessly continued. "He initially used the taser to subdue the women. After that, they were weakened by blood loss. It's entirely plausible he could manage them."

"Did you find a taser at his apartment?" Logan asked.

"Not yet, but they're still searching. It could be hours before they're done. But even if he doesn't have one now, that doesn't mean he never did."

"It's reasonable doubt," Logan said, thumping the table to emphasize each word.

"I disagree." Pierce crossed his arms over his chest.

They were at an impasse. Logan's lead detective and an FBI agent were 100 percent convinced they had the killer, that it was Frank Branson. So why wasn't *he* convinced?

Was he really too close to the case to see what they were seeing?

"I still don't like it," he said. "But do what you have to do to build a case. We'll hold him on the stalking for now, up the charge to murder if we can get enough evidence to convince a district attorney."

"What about the rest of the investigation?" Riley asked.

"We keep working on the other leads as if Branson weren't in the picture. I'm not willing to let anything drop just because we have a suspect in custody."

"That will take more manpower than we have," Riley complained.

"I can take most of the Branson research under the FBI budget, bring in more resources," Pierce said. "Logan, if you'll give me Riley to coordinate efforts with a couple of your detectives, you can have the rest of them for the other leads."

"Is that what you want, Riley?" Logan asked.

Riley shrugged. "I believe Branson is the murderer. I'd like to work with Pierce on that. But if you need me on something else, I'll do it."

Logan drummed his fingers on the tabletop. Riley was his best detective and he didn't have a large team to draw upon. Could his feelings for Amanda be making him paranoid? Unable to believe it was that easy, that Branson was the one?

Was he willing to risk being wrong again? What if Branson really was the killer and he went free because Logan persuaded his men Branson was innocent? He looked up at the line of pictures marching across the top of the whiteboard.

But instead of seeing those women, instead he saw the shadowy faces of the women who might have been murdered by the killer he'd already let go. How many were there? Six, eight, more?

He shuddered and scrubbed his hand across his face. No, he couldn't risk it. He had to assume, for now, that Pierce and Riley were right. But he also had to pursue other leads, just in case they were wrong.

"I'll keep two detectives working on the other evidence. You two can take the rest and work the Branson angle, but make sure the stalking charge sticks regardless of where else your investigation leads. I don't want him terrorizing Amanda again."

Pierce nodded, his relief obvious. "Thanks, Logan. I appreciate you keeping an open mind."

"I don't know how open it is, but I trust you and Riley enough not to strangle-hold the investigation. I hope to God you're right and we've got the killer."

Logan headed for the conference room door but before he reached it, the door flew open and crashed back against the wall. Mayor Montgomery stood in the opening, his rotund body stuffed into a suit so tight the buttons looked ready to pop. His close-set eyes zeroed in on Pierce and Riley before looking to his right where Logan was doing his best to blend in with the wood paneling.

"Chief, what's this I hear about an arrest in the Red Rose Ripper case?"

Logan flinched at the grotesque name the press had dubbed Carolyn O'Donnell's murderer. "We've arrested Frank Branson for stalking."

"Stalking? Who cares about stalking? The press is hounding me night and day about the O'Donnell case. Why haven't you charged this Branson fellow for that?"

"Just a little thing called evidence," Logan mumbled.

Pierce coughed behind his hand and the mayor's hawk-like gaze turned to him. "What's the FBI's position on this? Do you think Branson is the killer?"

Pierce shot Logan an apologetic glance. "Everything points to Branson. If I had to give an opinion, then yes, I believe he's the killer. But," he held up a hand to stop the flood of words the mayor looked ready to spew, "I agree with Logan that there's not enough evidence to arrest him for murder. Yet."

The mayor frowned, not pleased with that answer. "What about you, detective?" he said, addressing Riley, who was slouching down in his chair and looked like he might slide underneath the table any minute. "Is Branson our man?"

Riley straightened and shrugged. "I don't have the experience that Logan and Pierce have, so I don't know that my opinion makes any difference."

"Drop the bullshit, detective," the mayor said. "Do we have the right man or not?"

Logan watched the expressions crossing Riley's face and knew before he spoke that they were in trouble. Riley honestly believed Branson was guilty, but he didn't know politics, didn't realize the mayor was looking for the slightest excuse to divert attention from his office. If that meant branding an innocent man a murderer in the eyes of the press, Logan knew the mayor wouldn't hesitate. Not because he was a bad person. He was just weak, too weak to withstand the daily calls from concerned parents and the kind of pressure he was under.

Especially with an election coming up.

"Well? Guilty or not?" the mayor demanded, his face turning a florid color as he waited impatiently for Riley to respond.

"I think we've got the right man, sir," Riley said. He lowered his eyes to the table as if the wood grain pattern was suddenly fascinating.

The mayor clapped his hands together, a smug smile on his face. "I'll set up a press conference immediately. Shouldn't be hard to do since the bastards are camped out on my doorstep every freaking day." He glanced at his watch. "Twenty minutes? Is that enough time for you three to join me on the front steps?"

Logan shoved away from the wall. "Riley and Pierce can make up their own minds on this, but I won't be there. I'm not going to mark a man a murderer without proof."

The mayor sputtered, his eyes widening as Logan headed toward the door. "How am I supposed to announce we have a suspect without you there? You're the chief of police, for God's sake. You have to be there."

"No, I don't. If you're going to call a press conference, you're doing it without me."

Logan left the room and headed for his office. He understood the mayor's position. All of the evidence they had, what little there was, did point to Branson. But no matter how many times he tried to picture him as the killer, he couldn't see it.

After grabbing his jacket and some files from his desk, Logan turned to leave. His cell phone buzzed, so he stopped and took a look at the caller ID. When he saw it was from his sister, Madison, he sighed and dropped the files onto his desk and plopped down in his chair.

His baby sister had lost her husband in a tragic accident in New York a year ago. Ever since, she'd been traveling around the world, running from her pain. One day she would realize she had to face her problems to put them behind her, but in the meantime she would call him or their mother every few months and announce she was still alive.

He flipped open his cell phone. "Hey, trouble. Where are you this time? Rome? London?"

Thirty minutes later he hung up the phone with a rueful grin. Leave it to Madison to trick him into revealing more than he'd meant to about Amanda. He'd purposely not told her anything about the serial killer or the case because he didn't want to worry her, but he'd admitted he had Amanda in protective custody.

From that statement his sister had leaped to the conclusion he and Amanda were a couple. She wanted to come to Shadow Falls to meet her but he was adamant that she not, assuring her that he and Amanda were not a couple and that he was working an important case and couldn't afford any distractions right now.

His sister was astute. His protestations about his feelings for Amanda not being serious didn't fool her. Thankfully she was three states away, vacationing in Louisiana. He was safe from her prying and her avowed role as matchmaker in his life.

After the call with his sister, he hurried out of his office and down the elevator, but paused as he opened the front door of the building. The mayor was standing behind a podium set up on the landing at the top of the steps. Flanking his sides were Riley and Pierce.

Logan exited to his left, taking care to stay close to the building and avoid drawing anyone's attention as he hurried toward the parking lot.

Riley looked miserable. He was sweating profusely and kept shoving his hair out of his eyes. Pierce looked bored, resigned.

As the mayor rapped a gavel on the podium to signal the start of the press conference, Logan hurried down the last steps.

His car was parked in the slot marked "Chief of Police." A man in an oil-stained, tan jumpsuit leaned against the brick side of the building. Logan didn't know him, but he recognized the uniform as the type worn by the mechanics who maintained the police cruisers. A half-smoked cigarette dangled from the man's lips. A baseball cap was pulled down low over the right side of his face and he wore his hair shaggy, shoulder-length. Logan nodded in answer to the man's wave, then put his briefcase in the Mustang and started the engine.

He backed out of his space and put the car in drive, but instead of pulling out onto the street, he stopped. The smoking area for employees was in the back of the building, not the side. And something about the man put him on edge. Logan looked back toward the building, but the mechanic was gone.

The shrill sound of a microphone brought his attention to the front steps. The press conference was starting. One of the reporters glanced his way and excitedly gestured to the cameraman beside him. Logan pressed the gas and sped away.

Chapter Fourteen

When Logan arrived at home, he climbed the stairs to the
back deck and found Karen and Amanda sitting at one of
the umbrella-topped round tables, hunched over a board
game.

Amanda's back was facing him and she didn't hear his
approach. Karen glanced up, but Logan shook his head
and pressed a finger to his lips, motioning for her not to let
Amanda know he was there.

She smiled and looked back down at the game board.
Logan was carrying a basket and he set it beside the French
doors before stepping behind Amanda's chair.

Curious to see what had her so engrossed, he peered over
her shoulder. Scrabble. Karen must have brought the game
with her, because the only games he had at his house involved cards, poker chips, and when a woman was playing,
as little clothing as possible.

The thought of playing strip poker with Amanda was
a tantalizing one, but not something he wanted to think
about with Karen sitting three feet away.

He leaned down next to Amanda's ear. "Honey, I'm home."

Startled, she jumped half out of her chair, bumping the table and sending her tiles flying.

Karen laughed, shaking her head as she set the Scrabble box on top of the table and started to rake the tiles off the board into the drawstring bag.

Amanda scooted her chair back from the table and stood next to Logan with her hands on her hips. "I could have won if you hadn't done that."

"Really?" he asked as he looked at the score pad. "Did you have an eighty-three-point word you were about to put on the board?"

She smirked and shoved him out of her way. Logan's breath caught as he watched her crawl under the table to retrieve the tiles that had dropped to the deck, her shorts tightening around her shapely rear.

The sound of a throat clearing had him jerking his gaze back to Karen. She gave him a wink. "I'll leave the game here, Amanda. I'll see you two later."

"Oh, okay," Amanda called out from under the table. "Maybe I'll have better luck tomorrow. Thanks for playing."

"Good night, Logan," Karen said as she struggled unsuccessfully to suppress a grin.

Logan gave her his sternest glare but she only rolled her eyes, chuckling as she walked across the deck to her car.

"Got you, you slippery little devil." Amanda crawled out from under the table, triumphantly holding up a wooden tile.

Clearing his suddenly-dry throat as her gaping tank top

revealed far more than she probably realized, Logan forced himself to meet her gaze. "If you're through crawling around on your hands and knees, I thought you might like to get out of here for the evening." He grasped her hand and pulled her to her feet.

She dusted off her knees then pitched the tile into the Scrabble box. "What do you mean, *get out of here?* Go into town?"

"Not exactly." He retrieved the basket and placed it on the table, flipping the top open to reveal the food packed inside.

"A picnic?" A delighted smile lit up her face as she rummaged around in the basket. "It looks and smells wonderful."

He swatted her hand and she jerked it back, allowing him to close the lid. "You can look at all of that later. Daylight's wasting."

After grabbing her shoes, Amanda followed Logan across the deck and down the steps that led to the backyard. "Uh, Logan, your car is the other way."

"Who said we were taking the car?"

She rushed to keep up with his long stride as they stepped down onto the grass. With her hand in his, she followed behind, her brows shooting up when she realized where they were going, the path that led to the creek. Remembering the disaster that had been last time, her delight over the prospect of a picnic began to fade.

When they reached the creek, instead of turning to the

right as she expected, he turned in the opposite direction. "Where are we going?" she asked, slightly out of breath from trying to keep up with his pace.

He looked back and immediately slowed. "We're almost there."

The path led to a narrow wooden footbridge that arched about three feet high across the creek. Rope handrails were strung between posts placed every few feet on each side.

Being dragged across the deck and through the woods was one thing, but Amanda wasn't about to be forced across that rickety-looking bridge. She tugged her hand from Logan's grasp.

He turned around with a questioning look on his face. "Something wrong?"

She crossed her arms and rolled her eyes. "Are you kidding? That old bridge looks like it would fall into the water in a stiff breeze, and you haven't even explained why we need to cross it. Either tell me where we're going or I'm turning around."

"I bet you never liked surprise parties when you were a little girl," he teased.

"You're right, I didn't. When you're a kid, your whole life is wrapped up in what other people think of you, so it's important to always look your best. If the party is a surprise, you might be caught without makeup or wearing some ratty old outfit you wouldn't ever want your friends to see you in. I like to know what's going to happen and plan for it."

He leaned back against a post and swept her with an assessing glance. "If I'd given you more time, what would you have done differently?"

"More time?"

"Instead of trying to surprise you, which is proving to be very difficult."

"Surprise me with what?"

"If I tell you, it won't be a surprise."

"Oh, good grief," she said, pretending exasperation. Knowing he wanted to surprise her put everything in a different light. She was suddenly looking forward to whatever he wanted to show her, even if it meant crossing that sorry excuse for a bridge. The water didn't look all that deep, should she have to go for an unexpected swim. And she was confident Logan would keep her from drowning if it came to that. He seemed capable of just about anything. "Let's just get on with whatever you want to show me," she huffed. "If you don't hurry up I'll starve to death."

He gave her a smug smile, as if he knew she was bluffing, and took her hand again. Matching his stride to hers this time, he tugged her along beside him across the bridge.

Thankfully the bridge didn't even wobble as they crossed. "Did you build this bridge?" she asked as they stepped off on the other side and continued on another path through the woods.

"My dad. He owned this property when I was growing up, but he sold it after he retired. When I moved back here, one of the first things I did was buy the property back. The bridge was still in good condition. All I had to do was re-string a new rope handrail."

"You mean, the house you live in now—"

"Is the one I grew up in. Yes."

She studied his profile as they walked along the path.

Knowing he'd gone to so much trouble to buy the house he'd grown up in surprised her. Who would have thought tough-guy Logan Richards was a sentimental softy on the inside. "What did your dad do for a living?"

He pushed a small branch out of her way. "He was a regular guy, blue-collar. Married mom right out of high school, didn't go to college. Worked for thirty years at the paper mill."

"Sounds like he was a good man, took care of his family."

"You make him sound boring."

"I didn't mean—"

"I'm teasing." He shrugged. "Most people would probably think his life was boring, but he was happy. We never had a lot of money, growing up. The only reason he was able to afford this place was because it was handed down through the family. As it was, he had to sell it to pay the taxes later on. We never did the Disney thing, or Six Flags, places like that, but we did things as a family. The beach, picnics, movies."

"You've never been to Disney?" she asked, genuinely shocked. Her parents hadn't had much money, either, but she'd been to Disney so many times she'd lost count. She'd considered it a rite of passage for all Floridians. Everyone went to Disney.

"Is that a sin?" he teased.

"If it's not, it should be. When I have kids, I'll take them to. . . ." She choked back the rest of her reply. Something about being around Logan made her relax, forget. For one moment, she'd actually forgotten she couldn't have children.

He set the basket down on the path and gently gripped her shoulders. When she looked up she saw his teasing grin was gone.

"It's a horrible thing what that man did to you," he said, his voice low and gruff. "I don't pretend to understand how you feel. But I do know there are an obscene number of kids out there who don't have homes, kids who are shuffled around the foster system from family to family. There's no reason in the world you can't become a mother to one or more of them. You deserve that kind of happiness, the love of a family, and a man who will love you and adopt an entire houseful of kids with you."

He hesitated, as if he wanted to say more, but then he abruptly grabbed the picnic basket and pulled her after him.

Before Amanda could recover from his surprising speech, they turned a corner in the path. Her mouth dropped open in astonishment when she saw what was waiting for them. The path ended at the beginning of a long dock. Tied to a massive wooden post at the end was a red and white boat. Low and sleek, it had twin motors and was built for speed. Not surprising for a man who chose to drive his personal Mustang GT to work instead of the typical sedan the police department would have provided.

"She's beautiful," Amanda said.

"Yes, she is."

Amanda looked up and met Logan's deep green eyes. He wasn't looking at the boat. She swallowed hard. "I'm . . . ah . . . surprised you aren't down here more often."

"I don't keep the boat here," he said, walking with her down the dock. "She's usually dry-docked at a marina. When I want to take her out I call ahead and have them gas her up and stock her with supplies. At the end of the day, they clean up the boat. All the fun of ownership without the work."

Butterflies began racing around Amanda's stomach. Logan had obviously gone to a lot of trouble to have the boat brought out here, just for her.

As it turned out, he'd gone to even more trouble than she'd realized. The picnic basket held an assortment of delicious pasta dishes, salad, and fine wine—prepared and packed by an exclusive Italian restaurant back in town.

After they ate and enjoyed some of the wine, Logan drove the boat almost all the way to the Gulf, pointing out different birds and plants to her as they rode by. A narrow waterway opened up on their right. He slowed the boat, turned, and cut the engines. They drifted on the slow current deeper into the marsh, with vegetation growing up so close they almost touched the boat.

The mud and grass and occasional swamp oak spread out as far as she could see, as if she and Logan were the only people for miles around. With anyone else, she'd have felt uneasy, but with Logan she was just . . . curious. She was about to ask him why he'd brought her here, but the words clogged in her throat when he pulled a pistol out of a storage bin.

"Logan, what are you doing?"

He checked the loading before handing it to her. "Take it."

She eyed the gun with distaste. "Why?"

"Because I'm going to teach you how to shoot."

Amusement swept through her and she couldn't help but smile. "What makes you think I can't shoot already?"

His brows shot up. "Can you?"

She took the gun, popped out the clip, checked the loading herself. She popped the clip back in and chambered a round. "Where's the target?"

Logan eyed her thoughtfully and pointed out past the port side of the boat. "That tree stump."

Amanda shook her head. "Too easy." She raised a hand to shield her eyes from the glare of the setting sun. "There, that clump of driftwood."

"That's too far away. You'd need a rifle to accurately aim—"

The sound of her shot filled the air. A chunk of the driftwood snapped off and flew into the marshy grass.

Logan shook his head and his mouth curved in a wry grin. "Hell, you shoot better than I do. I guess you don't need shooting lessons." He took the gun from her and pulled out a cleaning kit. "Where'd you learn to shoot like that?"

Amanda wrinkled her nose in distaste. "Tennessee. My brother-in-law took me to a shooting range every day for months, insisting I needed to learn to defend myself after . . . what happened."

"Sounds like a decent guy."

"He wasn't."

Logan's head snapped up. He slowly lowered the oil rag in his hand. "What do you mean?"

"When I moved to Tennessee I never planned on coming back here. Heather, my sister, is the only family I have. I wanted to stay with her, maybe buy my own house and move down the street once I was back on my feet. Her husband made that impossible."

Logan's eyes narrowed. "Did he hurt you?"

She shook her head. "He didn't try to force himself on me, if that's what you mean. He made it very clear that he wanted to sleep with me, but he never touched me." She shivered and rubbed her arms. "Can we go back now? It's getting kind of creepy out here with the sun going down."

"I'd like to meet your brother-in-law someday." Logan stowed the gun and cleaning kit beneath the seat and crossed to the captain's chair.

"Why would you want to meet him?"

"He needs a lesson in manners."

Amanda grinned as Logan eased the boat forward through the small channel. Wouldn't John be surprised if Logan showed up at his house! She'd like to see that.

The waterway suddenly widened and curved to the right. Logan gunned the engines, sending the boat racing back toward his property. By the time they were within sight of the dock, the moon was out, and the sun had long ago sunk beneath the horizon.

Expecting him to bring the boat on in, she was surprised when he cut the engines again and let the boat drift lightly on the current.

At her questioning glance, he sat back in his seat next to hers and raked a hand through his hair. "I wanted you to enjoy yourself, get your mind off everything going on. But I need to tell you something before you hear it on the news or from Karen in the morning."

A sick feeling settled in her stomach. "Tell me what? Has there been another murder?"

"No, thankfully, not that. We arrested Frank Branson today."

"Dana's father?"

He nodded.

"Why?"

"He's the one who left the rose and pictures at your house, and mailed you the threatening note."

"Are you sure?"

"Positive. He wasn't good at covering his tracks. Even if we didn't have fingerprints tying him to the pictures, we found the receipt for roses at his apartment. The paper the note was written on matched a pad of paper in his truck. And on top of all that there was a witness. Your neighbor, Mrs. Fogelman, identified him as the man she saw outside your house."

She brushed her long hair back from her face. "Why would he do that? Is it because he blames me for Dana's death?"

"If Pierce and Riley are to be believed, it's because he's the killer."

She laughed. From the look on his face she guessed that wasn't the reaction he'd expected. "You can't be serious. I know the man who attacked me was wearing a hood, but his body type was nothing like Frank Branson's. There's no way he could be the killer."

"Pierce seems to think you wouldn't be able to judge the killer's height accurately."

"Because I was on my back most of the time?"

He grimaced. "Yeah, that pretty much sums it up."

"Well, that's just stupid. I can tell if someone is tall or short even without standing next to him. Even if I were off a few inches, there's no way he's the killer."

"Maybe, maybe not. Riley and Pierce are convinced he's their man."

"And you're not?"

He shook his head. "No. I don't think Branson is the killer."

"Good. I know you'll figure out who he is and you'll catch him. If anyone can, you can."

His gaze shot to hers. "Thank you."

She smiled. "You're welcome. I'm relieved it was Mr. Branson who left the notes, though. At least I know the real killer isn't the one who was stalking me." Her smile faded. "Poor Mr. Branson. He came to see me at the hospital after Dana's death. He wanted to know anything I could tell him about Dana's last days." She rubbed her hands up and down her arms, suddenly feeling chilled in spite of the hot summer night air. "He was really angry with me. I think he believes if I hadn't escaped, Dana would still be alive."

"It's not your fault. You know she would have been killed regardless of what you did, don't you?"

She shrugged. "Probably. I don't guess I'll ever know for sure."

He shook his head, his jaw tight with strain. "You're a good person, Amanda Stockton Jones. You need to let go of all that guilt. Nothing that happened to you or Dana was your fault."

Her throat suddenly felt tight as she looked up at him, saw the trust and faith in his eyes. "Thank you," she whispered.

"You're welcome." He started to lean forward, and for a moment she thought he might kiss her. But then he pulled back. She swallowed her disappointment. Part of her wanted him so badly, but she understood his reluctance, considering she'd acted so crazy when he'd kissed her before.

"It's getting late," he said. "I'd better take us on in." He reached for the key to the ignition, but she stopped him with a hand on his arm, reluctant to let the evening end.

"You spent the whole evening talking about me, finding out every boring little detail. I haven't learned hardly anything about you."

"What do you want to know?"

"Something, anything. What's your favorite color?"

"Blue. Midnight blue. With little blue-green flecks around the edges."

He'd just described her eyes. A delicious feeling settled in the pit of her stomach but she tried to ignore it. Determined not to let him get her off track she continued with her questions. "How old are you?"

"Old enough to know you don't want to know my age or my favorite color—"

"Yes, I do."

"—and that you're trying to work up the courage to ask me something else. Go ahead. Ask."

"You won't tell me your age?"

"Thirty-five. Now what do you really want to ask me?"

Dropping her gaze to the picnic basket on the floor between their seats, she fingered the rough, wicker handle. She thought about that day at her house when he'd talked about the loved ones he'd left behind, the raw, far-away look in his eyes. A mom and a sister wouldn't make a man look like that. "Who did you leave behind in New York?"

He sighed and looked out at the dark water, toward the light burning on the end of the dock as the boat rocked gently on the current. Jasmine scented the warm breeze. "I'm divorced, Mandy." He turned back and looked at her. "It was for the best. I know that now."

Mandy? Her heart did a little flip, hearing her old family nickname on his lips. Her pleasure was tempered by the unwelcome image of him putting a ring on another woman's finger, pledging to love her and protect her.

"Do you want me to tell you about her?" he asked.

"No. Yes."

He laughed, his deep voice rumbling in his chest.

"Did you love her?" she asked, immediately regretting her question.

"Yes, I loved her. It's a long story. Are you sure you want to hear this?"

He loved her. A sick feeling twisted Amanda's stomach, but she'd started this. She wasn't going to back down now. "I'm sure."

He let out a long sigh. "When my father died, he left a hefty insurance policy and a hell of a 401(k). My mom had a decent retirement pension already, so she insisted that my sister and I split the insurance money and the investments between us. Madison and I put a third of the money into savings for my mother, in case she ever changed her mind. We invested the rest."

He grinned wryly. "To put it mildly, the investments did well, very well. Madison had champagne tastes. She bought her way into the upper social circles in New York, and dragged mom and me with her. We made appearances at

Madison's parties when she badgered us enough, and that's where I met *her*."

"What was her name?"

"Her name is Victoria. And if you ever meet her, don't call her Vicki. Not if you care for that pretty little hide of yours."

His backhanded compliment had her face heating with a blush. "She sounds like a snob."

He laughed. "Not really. She liked the high life. I fell for her, hard, married her a few months later." He looked out over the dark water. "I wanted children. When it didn't happen, we both got tested. There was nothing wrong with either of us, except that she hadn't gone off the pill. Turns out she wanted kids, too, just not with me."

He wanted children. She thought back to what he'd said about adoption earlier and wondered if he was the kind of man who could be happy not having his own children. "What happened to her?"

He frowned and tapped the tops of his thighs. "She married another cop. Last I heard she had two kids and had moved to the suburbs."

"That's why you left? To get away from her?"

"It was one of the reasons."

She cleared her throat and brushed an imaginary speck of lint from her shorts. "It's getting late. We probably should get back."

The silence stretched between them but she refused to look up, afraid he'd see the yearning in her eyes. Imagining him as a husband, a father, had her thinking all kinds of thoughts she had no right to be thinking. He was everything she ever thought she'd want in a man, but she knew she wasn't everything he wanted in a woman. She was damaged goods. Her scars were far more than skin-deep, and she was a fool to hope for what could never be.

Finally, he started the engines and turned the boat toward the dock. When they were back on solid land again, he led the way with a flashlight and guided her through the path in the woods back toward the house.

Tension coiled inside her as they crossed the footbridge. They would be back at the house in just a few minutes, and this feeling of closeness, of intimacy, would be gone. He'd go into his study and work on the case. She'd spend another night alone, watching TV or reading a book in the living room, wishing her computer algorithm had been more successful.

And she'd go to sleep, wondering what would have happened if she hadn't panicked when he'd kissed her by the creek. Suddenly she didn't want to wonder anymore. She wanted to know, needed to know. And the only way to know was to try again.

She stopped at the end of the bridge where the moonlight shined through a break in the trees overhead. She could see Logan's surprise, his concern, and she hated that the killer had made her such a victim. She wanted Logan to look at her with desire, not pity. "Kiss me," she whispered, stepping close, wanting to touch but afraid to in case he turned her away.

His nostrils flared and she heard the sharp intake of his breath as he stared down at her. His hands shook as he reached out his fingers and slowly ran them down the sides of her face, a slow, soft caress that feathered lightly across her scar, a scar she almost never thought about anymore when she was with him. Almost.

"Are you sure?" he asked, his voice as soft as hers, but deeper, huskier than she'd ever heard him before.

"Yes." She closed her eyes, shivering when his thumb caressed her bottom lip.

He cupped the sides of her face. "Mandy," he whispered, his voice hoarse, rough. "Look at me."

Her eyes flew open and she stared questioningly at him. As she watched, he slowly, ever so slowly slid his fingers into her hair, his intense gaze holding hers, never wavering.

The first prickling of panic squeezed her chest. She reached up and grabbed his forearms.

He stopped, but didn't remove his hands. "Trust me," he whispered. "Look into my eyes. Trust me."

She wanted to, so much, but suddenly her boldness of a moment ago was gone. She was afraid again, afraid she would shatter into a thousand pieces, afraid she would run screaming like a crazy woman if he didn't stop.

"Mandy, fight. Don't let him win."

She stared into his eyes, her chest tightening as confusion roiled within her.

"Breathe, Mandy. Breathe with me, look into my eyes. Don't close your eyes."

She took a deep breath, felt some of the tightness ease in her lungs. His hands still cradled her face, his gaze locked onto hers, a lifeline to the panic rippling through her. He was so patient, and he was looking at her with desire, not pity.

Forcing her fingers to relax their grip on his arms, instead she wrapped them around his waist. He was so warm and hard. She shuddered as her fingers splayed out across his back. Her eyes slid closed. . . .

"Open your eyes. Don't close your eyes."

She forced her eyes open, stared into his, watched him as he leaned down and pressed an achingly sweet kiss to her lips. Then he pulled back, just far enough for her to focus on his eyes again.

"Have I told you how incredibly beautiful you are?" he murmured. His eyes locked on hers as he told her, in vivid detail, exactly how beautiful he thought she was. Then he leaned down and pressed a whisper-soft kiss against her lips. She shivered and flexed her fingertips against his chest, reveling in the warmth of his skin that radiated through the soft cotton fabric of his shirt.

"There, now, that wasn't so bad, was it?" he asked.

She blinked, realizing his hands were buried deep in her hair. She waited for the panic but it didn't come. Suddenly they were wrapping themselves up in each other. His mouth clamped down on hers and she struggled to pull him as close as possible. He growled low in his throat and lifted her up against him so she stood on her toes, her core centered against his firm ridge. The kiss went on and on, hotter and hotter until she was shaking with need.

When she shifted her legs to cuddle him more intimately against her, he tore his mouth free and shuddered. "We have to stop."

Disappointment flared inside her but she knew he was right. He was probably afraid she would have a flashback again. She pulled out of his arms and started back down the path.

He caught up to her quickly, put his hand through hers to guide her as he lit the way with a flashlight. "Don't you want to know why I said we had to stop?"

"I'm not an idiot, Logan. I know you're worried I'll freak out again. To tell you the truth, I'm worried, too. You were right to stop us. I shouldn't have allowed myself to dream, to hope that we could . . . share ourselves in that way. I probably couldn't handle it, no matter how much I want to."

They stepped out of the trees and onto the soft, springy grass of his back yard. She increased her strides, anxious to get back into the house, to forget this incredibly wonderful evening had ever happened. She couldn't allow herself to dream of a future with Logan. It hurt too much, knowing it could never be.

"Amanda, wait." He caught up to her on the back deck. He gently turned her around, pressed his hand beneath her chin, forcing her to look up into his eyes. "I didn't *want* to stop, Mandy. I *had* to stop. Karen went home to have dinner and spend a few hours with her husband, Mike, but she's coming back." He glanced at his watch. "She'll be here in a few minutes. They're transferring Branson to the county lockup tonight to avoid the press. I have to be at the lockup to sign the paperwork when he gets there."

"Oh." She was still stuck on the part where he'd said he didn't want to stop. Her gaze lowered to his mouth and she licked her suddenly-dry lips. "Well, then, ah . . . thank you for a . . . wonderful evening." She turned and ran into the house.

Logan didn't make it to the county lockup. Neither did Branson.

Pierce walked up beside Logan and stood shoulder-to-shoulder with him as they both watched the detectives collecting evidence from the road surrounding the crumpled Ford Explorer and the T-boned patrol car.

"The officer at the scene didn't tell me much on the phone. Can you fill me in?" Pierce asked.

"I'll tell you what he told me, which probably isn't much more than he told you. Two officers were transferring Branson to county lockup. It's only ten miles from the station. When they didn't show and didn't respond to dispatch, another officer was sent to look for them and this is what he found." He nodded toward the mangled cars.

"How many victims?"

"Two, that we know of. Both Branson and the driver of the Explorer are unaccounted for. The two officers who drove the patrol car are both in the hospital."

A muscle ticked in the side of Logan's cheek. One of the officers, Redding, a young rookie, was in a coma. Logan had met the officer's young wife at the academy's graduation ceremony a couple of months ago. He remembered her name was Julia.

The rookie's partner was Clayton. Although he was unconscious at the scene, his vital signs were strong and steady. The EMTs were optimistic about his prognosis.

"This is a busy road. Someone had to see the crash." Pierce glanced at the line of cars being diverted onto the shoulder of the rural highway to get around the scene.

"Not as busy as you think. This traffic is unusual, mostly curious kids with nothing better to do than to see where all the fire trucks were going when they sped through town."

"Knowing you," Pierce said. "I'll bet you've got a theory already."

Logan crossed his arms and shrugged as a tow truck arrived to take one of the cars away. "You can look at this several ways. The most obvious is that it really was an accident. The driver of the Explorer panicked when he realized he'd hit a police car, so he took off. Branson saw an opportunity to escape and he took it."

"Sounds reasonable." Pierce cringed at the ear-piercing shriek of metal on metal as the tow truck driver, with the aid of some firemen, began pulling the two vehicles apart. "But you don't think that's what happened."

"Do you still think Branson is the killer?"

"No. I don't," Pierce said.

"Earlier today you were adamant that we had the right man."

Pierce raised a brow. "Is this where you say I told you so? Even I can't swallow a coincidence this big. We arrest a man for the killings, and he just happens to be involved in a traffic accident and is able to escape? Nope. Not buying it. I'll lay a hundred to one odds the Explorer is stolen and it was driven by the real killer."

"There's hope for you after all."

Pierce gave him a good-natured shove. "We're back to ground zero. Branson's either dead or will be soon, and we don't have any leads on the real killer's identity."

"We know more about him than we did before," Logan countered.

"Such as?"

"He probably saw the press conference and didn't want someone else taking credit for his kills. He may not want to be caught, but he doesn't want someone else taking the glory, either. That's why he took Branson."

Pierce raised a brow. "Are you suggesting we bait a trap?"

"That's exactly what I'm suggesting. Use his ego against him. We can make a fake arrest, announce we've caught the real killer. Can you bring in a Fed to play the role of our suspect?"

"I can. We'll have to work out the logistics, how to leak his whereabouts without being too obvious. Set up a stakeout. It's worth a shot."

Logan nodded. "I'll leave the details to you. I've got to go to the hospital to check on my officers." He stopped and looked around. "Have you seen Riley anywhere? He should have been here by now."

"I heard he called the station, said he couldn't make it. Car trouble."

Logan frowned. Riley's car was practically brand new. What kind of car trouble would he have?

CHAPTER FIFTEEN

After spending the entire night at the hospital, sitting in
the waiting room with the families of the two police officers
who'd been hurt, Logan took a quick nap at home. Then he
showered and headed back to the office. Other than a quick
greeting, he didn't get a chance to speak to Amanda.

He knew it bothered her, especially after the way he'd
left her so abruptly after that scorching kiss last night, but it
couldn't be helped. He went back to the hospital and stayed
until he was certain both his men were going to be okay.
Then he went to the station for a full day of meetings, reviewing interviews and evidence, brainstorming with his
men, trying to find a new angle. The elusive clue he needed
to make the puzzle pieces fit seemed to be just beyond his
reach.

There were only a handful of lights on in the house by
the time he got home. Karen met him at the door, and after
a quick report about her day watching over Amanda, she
rushed to her car to get home to her husband. Logan felt
guilty for keeping her so late and decided he'd ask her to-

morrow if she wanted to switch bodyguard duties with someone else for a while.

He flipped the deadbolt on the French doors and set the alarm, then leaned back against the wall. He blew out a frustrated breath and closed his eyes.

"You look tired."

Logan slowly opened his eyes at the sound of Amanda's soft voice. Then he promptly forgot how to breathe.

She stood in the opening to the breakfast nook wearing one of his dress shirts. It hung to mid-thigh. The sleeves were rolled up to keep from flopping over her wrists. The thin material clung to her breasts. Logan's mouth went dry when he saw the dark shadows of her nipples thrusting against the fabric.

His eyes dipped lower and it was all he could do not to rush forward and carry her off like a conquering barbarian when he saw the slightest hint of a shadow at the juncture of her thighs.

"I hope you don't mind me wearing one of your shirts. I need to do laundry and ran out of night gowns."

Logan reluctantly dragged his gaze up to meet her eyes. He had to clear his throat twice before he could speak. "You can wear anything of mine you want." *Wear me.*

She frowned and looked away, crossing her arms over her breasts. "I didn't get to see you much today. I wanted to make sure you were okay."

He silently cursed himself for staring at her. He'd obviously made her nervous, and that was the last thing he wanted to do. Having her panic or be afraid of him wasn't something he could stomach. He wanted her, desperately, but he wanted her to want him just as much, and he didn't want to scare her.

He smiled and slowly walked toward her, hoping to keep her from looking down. If she did, she wouldn't have any doubts about what he was really thinking. "Why don't you go sit in the living room and I'll grab us a couple of beers?"

"Sure. Sounds good." She returned his smile and turned away.

Logan ran a shaking hand through his hair and slowly counted to ten.

So much for her pathetic attempt at seduction.

Amanda felt like an idiot.

She had plenty of clean nightgowns, but she'd purposely chosen one of Logan's silky shirts because she thought it might look sexy on her. It worked in the movies. Why hadn't it worked for her? When he'd stared at her so long without making a move toward her, she'd started to feel self-conscious. Maybe he thought she looked ridiculous in his oversized shirt. She didn't have a clue what he was thinking and she'd crossed her arms self-consciously, turning the conversation to hide her embarrassment.

He walked into the room, carrying two beers. After handing her one, he sat down beside her on the couch. They faced each other, each with a leg drawn up and an arm resting on the back of the couch.

They both took a few sips of their beers, then set them down on the coffee table. She put her hands in her lap and waited for him to say something. He stared at her so long she started to feel nervous again.

"Karen told me there was an accident last night, but she didn't give me many details," she finally said.

He blinked as if to bring her into focus, as if he'd been deep in thought. "The accident. Yeah, it had to do with Branson, actually. A car T-boned the police cruiser that was taking him to lockup."

She fisted a hand against her chest. "That's terrible. Was anyone hurt?"

"Two of my officers, but it looks like they're going to be fine. We don't know about the driver of the other car though. It was a hit and run."

"What about Mr. Branson?"

He loosened his tie and unbuttoned his collar. "Frank Branson is missing."

"Oh, my gosh. I can't believe he escaped. That's so weird that something like that happened. What are the odds, huh?"

He gave her a funny look as if he was surprised at what she'd said. "Yeah, what are the odds?"

She drummed her nails against her thigh and looked toward the dark, empty TV screen. She thought about turning it on but she really didn't want to watch anything. She wanted to *do* something, but apparently she was the only one.

His warm hand gently closed around hers, stopping her nervous tapping. "Is something wrong?"

She looked up, hoping to see some hint of the passion

he'd displayed last night, after their kiss in the moonlight. But instead he was looking at her with concern. She clenched her fists in her lap. Had she really thought he would still want her after having time to calm down and think? She wasn't beautiful, and she was damaged, inside and out. She was foolish to think he would ever really want to make love to her. "Nothing's wrong. I guess I'll head up to bed now."

"Me, too." He stood at the same time she did. He moved back to let her pass ahead of him, and she walked toward the stairs with as much dignity as she could, knowing the thin shirt revealed more than it hid, and knowing that he didn't want her now.

She held her head up, refusing to worry about the peep show she was probably giving him as he followed her up. After living for years by herself with no prospects for a love life she didn't exactly have any sexy underwear. Her purchases were ruled by comfort and her pocket book. Tonight, rather than wear sensible white cotton panties, she'd worn nothing.

Let him look. She didn't care.

Midway up the stairs she thought she heard him groan. She stopped and turned around. His gaze jerked up to meet hers and he gave her a tight smile.

She turned back around before he saw her answering grin. He certainly wasn't looking at the stairs when she'd turned around, and his jaw was clenched so tight when he smiled it looked more like a grimace.

Maybe wearing his shirt wasn't a bad idea after all.

She hurried up the last few steps, knowing the shirt would bounce higher that way.

Logan cursed behind her and it sounded like he'd stumbled on the stairs.

At the top she turned. "Are you okay? Did you lose your footing or something?"

"Or something," he mumbled. He climbed the last few steps and swept his hand out for her to precede him down the hallway.

She was still ensconced in his master bedroom, which meant he would be going into the guest room he was staying in.

Unless she did something about it.

Now that she knew he was affected by her display, she was going to press her advantage. At the entrance to the guest room, she stopped and turned. She raised a hand high on the doorframe and leaned a hip against the wall.

His eyes widened and his gaze dipped down where the shirt rode high on her thigh. Sweat broke out on his forehead as he jerked his gaze back up to meet hers. "Goodnight, Amanda." His voice was raspy and hoarse.

"Aren't you going to give me a goodnight kiss?"

His brows climbed into his hairline. "A kiss?"

"Just one. Well, unless you want more than one. I suppose that would be okay."

"Unless I want . . ." His brows drew down in a frown. "Are you teasing me?"

"Maybe."

His gaze bored into hers as if he could divine her thoughts if he looked closely enough. But he still didn't make a move toward her.

She stared back and realized this was the moment she'd

been both yearning for and dreading since she'd first met him, since she'd first felt his strong, gentle hands grasp her shoulders and pull her back from a world of darkness, since she'd first heard his deep, sexy voice telling her what she'd longed to hear. *You're safe.*

She wanted him, more than she'd ever wanted anyone or even thought she ever could want anyone. But it wasn't enough. He had to want her just as much, and that meant he had to be able to look past her scars. He'd already seen her at her worst, seen how confused and scared and irrational she could sometimes get when her fears overwhelmed her.

He hadn't run. He was still here.

There was another hurdle to overcome if there was even a chance that there might be something deeper between them. Until this moment, she wasn't sure she could face it, but now that the time was at hand, she knew she was ready.

She just didn't know if *he* was ready.

"Logan," she whispered as her hands moved to the top button of her shirt.

He swallowed, hard, and his gaze followed her fingers as she opened the top button and glided her fingers down to the next.

"Yes?" he rasped.

"The scars, they're—"

His eyes looked up at hers. "You're beautiful, Mandy. All of you."

"But you haven't seen—"

"I've seen everything that matters. *You* matter."

She blinked back the tears in her eyes. Then she grinned

and dropped her hands. "Well, in that case, if you've seen everything that matters—"

"That doesn't mean I don't want to see more." He reached down and whisked her shirt up over her head, throwing it to the floor before she realized what he was doing.

She froze before him even though her instincts told her to grab the shirt and hide the ugly, puckered scars that crisscrossed beneath her breasts all the way to her navel.

He looked her over with the intensity of a hawk, not missing a thing. "You're amazing, Mandy. Perfect." When his eyes finally met hers, the raw hunger and anticipation in his gaze reassured her in a way that words never could.

How he could see her battered and scarred body and still look at her with such appreciation was a miracle she wasn't going to question. Instead, she simply gave thanks and sank into his kiss when his lips touched hers.

Suddenly his hands were everywhere, sliding across her skin, cupping her breasts, spanning out across her lower back to cup her buttocks, pressing her tightly against his erection.

He broke the kiss, panting for breath. "If you want me to stop, tell me now, while I still can."

She watched his chest heave, listened to his ragged breathing, and felt an answering tightening in her lower belly. He looked pained, like he was struggling for control. She smiled and reached out her hand and splayed her fingers across the hard muscles of his chest.

"Don't stop." She leaned forward and lightly sucked the curve of his neck where it met his shoulder. She ran the tip of her tongue across his skin, reveling in the salty flavor.

His sharp intake of breath was her only warning. Suddenly she was in his arms and he was striding down the hall toward the master bedroom.

When he reached the bed, he stripped off the covers with one hand and gently laid her down on the cool, soft sheets.

He stood back, shucked off his shoes, and yanked off his socks. Next came his jacket and tie. Cuff links flew, pinging across the wooden floor somewhere behind him when he ripped his shirt off over his head.

In a matter of seconds he was completely naked. Amanda gasped at her first glimpse of him in all his glory. He was extremely . . . impressive.

He crawled into the bed and lay on his back. He wrapped his hands around her waist and lifted her so that she straddled his stomach.

She reached down and ran her thumb across his lower lip, shivering when he lightly bit down on her finger. "You're so . . . well-proportioned. I'm not sure you'll fit," she teased.

He laughed. "You do know how to flatter a man." He reached up and slid his hands into her hair, pulling her forward until she lay with her breasts pressed against the soft wiry hair of his chest. His lips moved across hers in a slow, sensual slide, and his tongue swept inside, branding her with its heat.

Without breaking their kiss, he rolled with her, pinning her back against the mattress. His forearms supported his weight and his knees anchored her on both sides of her thighs. When he pulled back, she opened her eyes and looked into his. She wondered at the serious look that drew his brows down into a frown.

"Is something wrong?" She wasn't innocent but she might as well be. Her experiences were limited and happened so many years ago she could barely remember them.

"I want this to be perfect for you, Mandy. Promise me if I do anything that makes you afraid or uncomfortable, you'll tell me. I'll stop." The corner of his mouth lifted into a sardonic grin. "Even if it kills me, I'll stop."

She flushed self-consciously. He must be worried she would freak out again. It worried her, too, but she wanted him so much. She didn't want to spend the rest of her life wondering what it might have been like to be with him if she backed out now. "I will. I promise."

His brow smoothed out, and he leaned down and kissed the tip of her nose. Then he slid further down her body so he was face-to-face with the scars that crisscrossed her abdomen.

She reached for the sheet and started to pull it over her, but he stopped her with a gentle, firm hand around her wrist. "Don't. Let me look."

She didn't understand why he wanted to look at her scars, but she trusted him. She released her grip on the sheet, and he flipped it out of the way. He leaned down and placed a soft kiss against one of the scars on the underside of her breast. The action was so tender, so sweet, that tears filled her eyes. He moved to the next scar and gave it the same, careful attention. Then he moved to the next, and the next, kissing and caressing each hurt, as if he could take away all the pain she'd ever suffered, telling her with his actions—far more than words ever could—that the scars didn't matter. Not to him.

By the time he'd finished, the tears were flowing hotly down her cheeks. He looked up at her and his face filled with dismay. He slid up her body, settling over her as he gently wiped her tears. "Don't cry, Mandy. Please don't cry," he whispered, his eyes searching hers.

"You make me feel beautiful." She reached her arms up behind his neck.

He pressed a whisper-soft kiss against her lips. "You *are* beautiful. Nothing and no one can change that." He kissed her again, then gently turned her over so he could press a kiss to one of the scars on her back. He worshipped every nick, every cut, and she started to believe, really believe, that he might actually mean what he'd said. He thought she was beautiful. He wasn't just lying to try to make her feel better.

A peace unlike anything she'd ever felt settled over her—and joy, such tremendous joy—that she nearly burst with the feeling of it. She twisted in his arms, ignoring the surprised look on his face when she plastered her body against him and kissed him with abandon, worshiping his mouth the way he'd worshiped her body. Telling him with her actions what she couldn't yet put into words, feelings she wasn't even ready to admit to herself. She wanted him, so much it hurt, and he wanted her. For now . . . that was enough.

Gone was the gentle lover. Suddenly Logan was wild, his skin burning hers with his heat as he kissed a fiery path down the side of her neck. His hands were everywhere, sliding across her skin, massaging, squeezing as he slid back down her body. There wasn't a place he didn't touch, a curve he didn't worship. She writhed beneath him, her head twisting on the pillow when he reached the very heart of her and gave her the same, maddeningly slow attention he'd given her scars.

She screamed as her climax rippled through her and she writhed against him, drawing her knees up and throwing her head back against the pillow as waves of ecstasy surged through her. Before the last wave of pleasure began to fade, he was kissing her again, slowly building that incredible pressure.

"Now, I can't wait any longer," she breathed, opening for him, reaching down to position him at her entrance. When her hands covered him, he sucked in his breath and jerked beneath her.

"You're killing me," he gritted out. He pulled her hand away, kissed the tips of her fingers. Positioning himself above her, he gyrated his hips, pushing into her ever so slightly.

She groaned and pushed her hips up against him. "Do it, Logan," she gasped. "I need you inside me. Now."

He shuddered against her. With one, quick, thrust he was inside her, filling her so fully that the sensual haze surrounding her began to dim. Attuned to her so completely now, he stilled, giving her body time to adjust to his size. Capturing her lips with his, he fanned the sensual flames again, expertly playing her body like a fine instrument, stroking her skin, building the tension until she had to move against him. The pleasure her movement caused was so exquisite, she moved again.

Suddenly they were moving together, straining against each other, building the delicious pressure. His hips pumped against her as his thickness filled her, wringing every ounce of pleasure from her that he could, driving into her with abandon.

He hardened even more, and she knew he was close to his climax. He reached his hand down between them and quickly brought her to that same frenzied edge, hovering on the precipice with him.

He drove forward again in one, long, powerful thrust, grinding his hips against her and sending both of them over the edge into ecstasy.

When her heartbeat finally slowed and she could draw a normal breath, she opened her eyes. He was leaning on his forearms, looking down at her with an expression she could only describe as arrogant. "You look awfully smug, Logan Richards."

"You screamed my name four times. And you called me God twice."

She punched him in the arm. "I did not."

He grinned and pressed a quick kiss on her lips. He lay down beside her and pulled her up against him with his groin resting against the curve of her buttocks. "Go to sleep, woman. I need at least half an hour to recover before we make love again."

"Half an hour? Are you kidding?"

"Well, maybe not that long. We'll see."

CHAPTER SIXTEEN

Amanda awoke sore, exhausted, and hopeful for the first time in years. She'd faced her fears and had overcome them. The killer hadn't won after all. And although no words of love had been exchanged between her and Logan, she had no doubts about her own feelings.

She was hopelessly, irrevocably, pitifully in love with the man.

She couldn't quit smiling.

Or humming.

Which had Karen giving her funny looks over the break-fast table.

But the glow didn't last long. There was a dark pall over her happiness, evil waiting in the shadows to snatch away her dreams. Until the killer was caught, until she knew the man who'd brutalized her and had killed Dana could never hurt her or anyone else ever again, she'd never truly find peace.

When Karen headed outside for one of her patrols around the perimeter of the yard, Amanda headed into Logan's study. He'd set her computer up on a side table and she'd used it when she'd cataloged the evidence and created her program to help the detectives, but his laptop was sitting in the middle of his desk. For once, he hadn't locked it away before going to work.

She ignored the little voice in her conscience telling her she shouldn't look. She knew Logan had information on his computer that he felt was too disturbing to share with her. But she was stronger than he thought she was. What if that information was the one thing that would trigger a memory, make her think of that elusive key Logan kept talking about, the one puzzle piece he was looking for?

Finding the killer was just as important to her as it was to him. He didn't think she knew when he got up in the middle of the night and went down to his study to pore over his files. But she did, mainly because she couldn't sleep either. She was just as worried about identifying the killer as he was, for much the same reason. They both had their personal demons to slay, and solving this case might be the key to freeing them both.

With that justification egging her on, she sat at his desk. She ignored the laptop for now, pushing it out of her way. Instead, she concentrated on the stacks of files. After looking through each stack, Amanda realized that Logan was a stickler for detail and organization. Every report, every interview, was meticulously documented. No sloppy police work here. No case he handed the DA would be resulting in a mistrial because someone didn't follow procedure.

There were twelve different cases in all. Apparently, Logan was reviewing other similar abductions and murders, including two missing persons cases, looking for a pattern. Since she wasn't familiar with those other cases, she decided instead to focus only on the ones she was certain were connected—Carolyn O'Donnell's and hers. There were several new interviews and reports she hadn't seen yet. She'd read those first, see if she could find that elusive connection her computer program had failed to find.

She opened the top drawer in Logan's desk and was unsurprised to find everything neatly organized inside: envelopes, stamps, pens, a tray that kept paperclips from scattering all over the inside of the drawer. She took out a pen and opened the second drawer. A stack of legal pads and spiral notebooks sat side-by-side. Taking one of the legal pads, she set it on the desk and closed the drawer. With her pen and paper at the ready, she dug into the files.

When she came across an older report that described the scene where Carolyn O'Donnell's body was found, it struck her how pristine everything was. No trace evidence of any kind that could be linked back to a specific person was found. No fingerprints, not even DNA. The killer had to be smart, methodical, and hyper-aware of evidentiary techniques so he wouldn't leave any evidence behind.

Comparing that to the description of Frank Branson's apartment when he was arrested, she couldn't reconcile the two. There was no way Branson could be the killer. His apartment was a goldmine of trace evidence. He would have had to transfer something to the victim, something that could be used to identify him. He was too disorganized and didn't appear to have the intelligence to pull off the immaculate scene where O'Donnell was found.

Amanda drew a column on the legal pad and labeled it "Potential Suspects." Frank Branson's name went underneath the heading. She drew a line through his name, crossing it out. Beside it she listed her reasons for eliminating him as a suspect.

Flipping another page in the file, she began to methodically go through the interviews of people who'd known Carolyn.

When her back started aching she straightened and stretched, surprised to see that the sun was high in the sky. It was late afternoon. She'd been working over the files for hours. Her stomach rumbled, demanding attention.

Karen checked on her a few minutes later. They shared a quick lunch of ham sandwiches and chips on the back deck. Then Karen headed back into the mother-in-law suite she'd commandeered while Amanda went back into the study.

As she reread the list she'd compiled on her legal pad, one conclusion kept popping up in her mind. The killer was a cop, or someone who worked with cops. He had to be, or how else could he keep the crime scenes so pristine? He'd have access to stun guns, too. And how better to move around and target victims than in a police car? No one called in suspicious person reports on a cop car driving around in their neighborhood. That would explain how the killer had selected his victims without anyone noticing.

On the top of the page she wrote "cop?". What if it wasn't a police officer, though? Who else would have access to a police car? She wrote "mechanic?" on the page as well.

Assuming Logan was right, that the first case was the most important and told the most about the killer, she wrote "grew up in Shadow Falls or neighboring community." She wished she could review the human resources files on each of the policemen in Shadow Falls. She could compare their vacation days to the dates and times of the other murders outside of Shadow Falls.

She tapped her fingers on the desk and glanced at Logan's laptop. Without knowing his ID and password, there was no way she could get into the HR files. Maybe she'd ask him later about it, see if he'd already thought of that angle. She added a note about reviewing the HR files to her list and pulled the laptop in front of her. She might not be able to look up their vacation schedules, but she could go to the SFPD website and at least see if any of the officers had the same physical characteristics as the man who'd attacked her.

The light began to fade in the window. The sun was going down. If Amanda was going to keep at it, she'd have to get up and flip on a light switch. She was just getting out of her chair when the doorbell rang.

A flash of unease went through her. In all the time she'd been here, no one had ever stopped by. This house was on several acres of land, surrounded by trees. It wasn't exactly on a traveling salesman's route.

Karen stepped to the archway that separated the study from the foyer, and gave her a reassuring smile. "Don't worry. I already know who it is. I think you'll be pleased."

Pleased? Amanda closed the laptop and listened intently as Karen opened the front door. The sound of feminine laughter floated through the house. A minute later, Karen led a petite brunette into the study.

Logan's sister. Madison. There could be no mistake.

Even if Amanda hadn't seen her picture plastered all over Logan's family albums that she'd looked through earlier this week, she would have known this woman was related to him. She had the same blue-black hair and piercing green eyes. And when she grinned, it was the same lopsided expression Amanda had seen on Logan's face on those rare occasions when he actually let himself relax. She was the spitting image of him, except that she was a foot shorter and a few years younger.

"You must be Amanda. Oh, my God. I love your hair. I could never grow mine that long. Goodness, it must reach all the way to your hips." The young woman practically bounced across the hardwood floor to the desk. Amanda couldn't help but smile at her energy.

"And you're either the Energizer bunny or Logan's sister, Madison," she teased as she stood to shake hands.

Madison stopped in front of her and instead of shaking her hand she wrapped her in a surprisingly strong hug for such a tiny woman. "I'm so happy to meet you."

Karen laughed from the doorway. "I guess I don't need to make introductions. I'll be in the front room, if anyone needs me."

Madison released Amanda and stepped back. "Thanks, Karen. We'll chat later about that hunky husband of yours."

The policewoman's laughter floated back to them and Madison gave Amanda a quirky grin. "Sorry. I know I can come on a little strong."

"Just a tad."

"Maybe we should start over. Hi. I'm Madison Richards-McKinley." She held out her hand.

"And I'm Amanda Jones, I mean, Stockton." Amanda shook her hand.

"So which is it? Jones or Stockton?"

"I guess it's Stockton. I changed my last name to Jones a few years ago, but it hasn't really stuck. Everyone around here always uses Stockton."

"I like Stockton better. It's more sophisticated."

Madison grabbed Amanda's hand—just like Logan was wont to do—and tugged her across the room. "Let's go in the living room and chat. I like that room much better than this stuffy old study of his."

Amanda didn't bother to disagree or argue. Madison was like a drill sergeant, marching them both across the hall to the other room. Madison plopped into a recliner so Amanda sat on the couch.

"I guess you're wondering why I'm here," Madison said.

"You're probably wondering the same thing about me."

They both smiled. Madison curled her legs up in the chair beneath her. "Actually, I spoke to Logan on the phone the other day and he told me he had you in protective custody. I went to his apartment first, but no one answered the door. He wasn't at the station, either, so I took a chance he might be out here."

"Do you want a soda or something?"

"Oh no, I'm fine. Grabbed some takeout on the way through town and scarfed it down in the car."

"You drove all the way from New York?"

Something dark passed behind Madison's eyes but was quickly gone. "I don't go to New York much anymore. I've been slumming in Louisiana for the past few months.

Haven't decided where I'll go next. Wherever the road takes me, I guess. But I didn't drive from Louisiana. That would take way too long, and my curiosity was killing me. I jumped on the first plane available to Pensacola, then rented a car and, well, here I am."

Amanda studied the bubbly woman in front of her. On the surface, she seemed carefree, but Amanda sensed there was far more to her, a depth and seriousness she tried to hide that stared out from eyes that looked much older than they should. She was the opposite of Logan, who was serious most of the time and hid his carefree side.

Madison noticed the stack of albums on the side table where Amanda had left them. "You've been looking through the family albums?" She hopped up from the chair and grabbed the top album on the stack.

"I hope you don't mind," Amanda said.

Madison plopped down on the couch next to her. "Don't be silly. I'm sure my brother doesn't mind one bit and I sure don't. Want to look at the pictures together? I can tell you all the family secrets, all those little details we sisters like to use to embarrass our big brothers." She winked and flipped the album open, and started to tell Amanda all about Logan Anthony Richards.

Logan glanced in his rearview mirror to back out of his parking space, but a commotion outside the police garage on the other side of the parking lot caught his attention. Riley was standing on the side of the building in an obviously heated discussion with one of the mechanics. Riley, like

Logan, chose to drive his personal car rather than a patrol car or one of the Crown Vics the department offered. So why would Riley go to the police garage? And why would he be upset with one of the mechanics?

Something about the mechanic seemed familiar. He was too far away for Logan to see any details, or read his name printed on the front of the tan jumpsuit he wore, but his shaggy, shoulder-length hair sparked a memory. He was the same mechanic Logan had seen hanging around the side of the police station the day of the press conference.

Logan threw his car into park and cut the engine. He got out and jogged across the parking lot. Riley looked his way, waved, and said something to the mechanic. The mechanic nodded and slipped around the corner into the garage. Riley stepped forward to meet Logan as he reached the garage entrance.

"Hey, chief. What's up?"

"Who were you talking to?" Logan asked, peering past Riley into the garage, trying to catch a glimpse of the man he'd just seen.

Riley raised a brow. "One of the mechanics. Why?"

"Looked like you were arguing. Everything okay?"

"Oh, that. I asked him if he does work on the side. Some of the mechanics do. He wanted to charge me a fortune for an oil change. Screw it. I'll do it myself. Hey, if you don't need me for anything, I'm meeting one of the Feds to re-interview someone about Carolyn O'Donnell's abduction."

"Sounds good," Logan said, without any real enthusiasm. None of the O'Donnell interviews had yielded any viable suspects and he didn't hold out much hope another re-interview would yield anything better.

Riley's silver Chevy Malibu was sitting a few feet away. The paint gleamed with a fresh coat of wax, and Logan knew from experience the inside was just as neat and clean. "Hear you had some car trouble the other night, when Branson escaped."

Riley followed Logan's gaze. His grin faded and the skin around his eyes tightened. "Flat tire, no big deal. But I didn't have a spare so I called Triple-A. Took forever. I didn't think you needed me, not with Pierce there. Was I wrong?"

Logan studied Riley's face. He looked genuinely concerned, as if he was worried he'd let Logan down. The sincerity in the other man's eyes had Logan feeling silly for his misgivings. Riley wasn't the killer. He had an alibi for Carolyn's murder. Logan knew that. So why did he feel so unsettled and suspicious? "No, no, of course not. You'd better get going. Those Feds don't like to be kept waiting."

Riley laughed and clapped Logan on the back. "You got that right. I'll catch you later."

Logan stood by the garage while Riley got into his car. He rolled his window down and waved as he exited the parking lot and turned onto the street in front of the police station. When Riley was out of sight, Logan turned around and headed into the garage.

Frustrated with his lack of success in locating the mechanic who'd been arguing with Riley, Logan sped up his gravel driveway less than an hour later, and had to slam his brakes and swerve to the right to avoid the unexpected car parked in his usual spot.

A cherry red Mercedes convertible.

There was only one person Logan knew who would drive a flashy car like that.

Madison.

Damn it. He'd told her not to come. He should have known she wouldn't listen.

Normally, he'd welcome his baby sister with open arms. Not today. Her timing couldn't be worse.

The entire day had been hell. At the hospital he'd been relieved to find that Redding had come out of his coma and his prognosis was good. But Clayton had made up for that joy by spending the better part of an hour complaining about his aches and pains. He'd followed that up by threatening a lawsuit against both the city and Logan for putting him into a dangerous situation. Right. Like being a cop didn't automatically mean you were in danger every single day.

Logan's attempt to locate the mechanic Riley had argued with had been just as futile as his conversation with Clayton. There was only one mechanic in the garage when Logan went inside and he wasn't the man Riley had been talking to. Apparently that other mechanic had headed out the back door for his dinner break while Riley was driving away.

There were no clues about where Frank Branson was, no new leads about the killer's identity. And now Logan's sister had put herself in danger by coming into town.

The one bright spot in Logan's day—the anticipation of coming home to Amanda and letting her beautiful spirit wash away all the dirt and filth of a horrible day—was now gone. Instead, he'd have to put up with his fireball of a sister and somehow convince her to get the hell out of town.

Convincing Madison to do anything she didn't want to do was next to impossible.

He took a deep breath and got out of his car. He slammed the door and trudged up the steps to the back deck. Karen was waiting at the door when he came inside, her purse already on her shoulder. She didn't normally meet him so quickly. Alarmed, he looked past her into the house. "Is something wrong?"

"Not at all. I saw you drive up and it took you a while to come in. I'm in a hurry to meet Mike, dinner plans. What about you? I heard it was quite the mad house today back at the station and the hospital."

"Not the best day in SFPD's history. Frank Branson is still unaccounted for, and we don't have any suspects in his disappearance." He spoke in a low voice so his sister and Amanda wouldn't hear him. Their laughter trilled in from the living room.

"I heard you think he was abducted, that he didn't escape on his own. You think the killer has him?" Karen asked in the same hushed tone.

"I can't afford not to think it. We're doing everything we can to locate Branson, and we're also operating on the assumption he could be armed and has an accomplice." He stood back so she could step outside. "I appreciate you keeping an eye on Amanda all this time. I can get someone else to trade off if you want to get back in the office for a few days."

"I'm fine with the way things are right now. My commute here is shorter than the office. Besides, I enjoy hanging with her. She's a great lady. And I'll enjoy talking to your sister tomorrow. I didn't get to catch up with her today because she and Amanda were having such fun together."

"Fun?" Knowing his sister, that didn't bode well for him.

"They've been going through photo albums and laughing like they've known each other for years. Today is the first day I've seen Amanda so lighthearted. Even before Madison got here." She grinned at Logan. He felt his face flush like a horny teenager caught necking with his girlfriend in the backseat of his car.

Except he'd been doing a hell of a lot more than necking.

He met her grin with his best scowl, but she only laughed and headed to her car. Logan waited until she was speeding down the driveway before locking the door and resetting the alarm.

Another burst of laughter from the living room had him swallowing his disappointment. Any remaining hopes that he could kick his sister out and have some time alone with Amanda dissolved. If Madison was bringing some much needed laughter to Amanda, he wasn't about to interfere.

She deserved, needed, to get away from the fears and worries that plagued her.

He couldn't put it off any longer. Time to see what kind of damage his baby sister had done. She'd wreaked havoc with his love life in the past, telling one of his girlfriends in high school that he had herpes. Madison thought the lie was hilarious. His girlfriend didn't. That was the end of their relationship.

Not letting Madison see how he felt about Amanda would be a challenge. Not letting her know how furious he was about her coming to Shadow Falls when he'd asked her not to would be even more challenging.

Then again, maybe it was a good idea to let her see how furious he was. It might knock some sense into her, make her see that he had serious concerns about her safety. But he didn't want to scare Amanda, make her dwell on the killer again. It was a hell of a situation.

"I haven't told you yet about Logan's date to the senior prom and his alleged medical condition." Madison laughed.

"And you're not going to." Logan strode into the room.

Amanda looked up at Logan standing on the other side of the coffee table, hands on his hips, scowling at his sister.

"Logan," Madison said. "You're home."

"And you're not. Why is that?"

"I'm on vacation. You knew that."

He leaned forward, placing his palms on the coffee table, his scowl even darker. Amanda was glad his anger was targeted at Madison instead of her. She wouldn't want to face him in his current mood. His sister was grinning, not daunted in the least.

"You were on vacation the last time I talked to you," he said. "I told you to either stay where you were or go back to New York. I specifically told you not to come here."

"Since when have I ever done what you told me to do?"

He gritted his teeth together and straightened. "I'm serious, Madison. You shouldn't have come. It's not safe."

"But it's safe for Amanda to be here?"

"That's different."

"Why? Because you don't want her to leave? You would put your own desires over her safety?"

A tic started in his cheek. "Do you really think I'd put anything above Mandy's safety?"

Madison grinned at Amanda. "He calls you Mandy? How sweet."

"Oh, for God's sake," he growled.

"Oh, for God's sake, yourself," Madison said. "I haven't seen you in months. At least give me a hug before you go all cop on me. I've missed you."

She jumped off the couch and charged around the coffee table toward him. Amanda thought she was going to tackle him but at the last second, he opened his arms and caught his sister against his chest.

"I missed you too, trouble." He gave her a hug and kissed the top of her head. His anger seemed to evaporate as soon as she hugged him, but lines of worry still crinkled his brow.

He looked over her and gave Amanda a slow, sexy wink.

Instantly her pulse sped up and an ache started in her belly.

Oh, boy, did she have it bad.

Madison pulled back and looked up at him, her face serious for once. "If it makes you feel better, Amanda already lectured me about coming here. She explained what was going on and that I should have listened to you. And if I'd known all the details, I would have followed your advice. But as usual, you tried to protect me by dancing around the issue. All you did was make me curious, which is why I came. So, it's really your fault that I'm here."

"I told you not to come. That's the only detail you needed."

"You hear that, Amanda? My brother thinks *telling* a woman to do something is the same as *asking*. It's going to take a special woman to put up with his archaic views and bring him into the current century."

Without giving Amanda a chance to respond, Madison pointed her finger at Logan's chest and poked it against him with every syllable to emphasize her words. "Amanda is a very special woman. I hope you appreciate her."

She turned and strode toward the archway. "I'm going to go upstairs and get ready for bed. I chose the blue bedroom on the opposite side of the house from yours, Logan. I'll turn my iPod up really, really loud. Good night, you two. Have fun."

Amanda's eyes widened at Madison's parting words.

"She's a real force of nature, isn't she?" Logan sat in the recliner opposite the couch.

"I like her," Amanda said. "I can't always follow what she's talking about, but I like her. She's sweet."

"You think she's sweet?"

"I do."

He laughed, obviously not agreeing with that statement.

"Logan, I hope you don't mind but I looked through your files today. The ones on your desk in the study."

His grin faded. Tension lined his brow with worry. "I wish you hadn't done that."

"I know, I'm sorry, but I wanted to help. Since my computer program didn't yield much, I decided to take another stab at it myself. I made a list of suspects based on the interviews and descriptions in the files. If you don't mind looking at it, I can go grab it." She started to get up but he waved her back down on the couch.

"In a minute. First, I want to discuss what Madison said. She has a good point, about me putting my needs above your safety, because God knows I need you. And I can't stand the thought of you not being here with me. I thought I could keep you safe, but with Branson missing, maybe I should take you to a safe house after all."

She frowned at him. "You've kept me safe here this long. I don't see any reason to go anywhere else. About that list I made. If you'll just take a minute—"

"You've only been safe this long because no one knows where you are. It's only a matter of time before someone figures that out. Madison's right. You need to be somewhere safer while I work on the investigation."

Pain knifed through her. Last night they'd shared their bodies and their souls. How could he want her to leave? "If you think you're getting rid of me that easily, you'd better think again. I'm not going anywhere."

"Get rid of you? Is that what you think I'm trying to do?"

"Is it?"

"Hell, no. I want you here, in my house, in my bed. But with Branson missing, and the killer possibly escalating, I can't risk him finding you. I should turn you over to the Feds tomorrow."

"Turn me over? Just like that? Don't I have any say in it?"

His face hardened and his eyes took on a flinty color. "No, you don't."

She wasn't about to back down, not when her heart was at stake. "The answer is no."

His knuckles whitened where his hands clenched the arms of his chair. "I didn't ask. I've made my decision. I'll call

Pierce, ask him to come over in the morning and take you to a federal safe house out of town. I'll have Madison pack your things, and I'll see that they get to you."

Panic sent butterflies swirling through her stomach. "None of this makes sense. I was safe here before, but now that Branson is missing, I'm suddenly not safe? Did something happen to compromise my location?"

"No."

"Then why are you trying to send me away?" she whispered, unable to hide the pain in her voice this time.

Logan flinched but he didn't waver. "If I screw up again, if I miss anything . . ." He raked a hand through his hair. "I couldn't bear it if something happened to you and it was my fault. I need to get you out of here, so I can focus on the case."

She felt the blood drain from her face. "I'm a liability now?"

"Damn straight. I can't think with you here."

"Fine." She stood, swallowing hard against the tears that threatened to fall. She had to get out while she still had some dignity intact. "Last night obviously meant nothing to you."

"The hell it didn't," he growled. His eyes narrowed dangerously. He stood and she decided a tactical retreat was in order. She hurried to stand behind the couch. With both the coffee table and the couch between them, she felt relatively safe.

"It's okay," she said, trying to calm his anger and at the same time struggling not to let him see that her heart was breaking. He wanted to send her away. How could he be so cruel after making such sweet love to her last night? "I understand. I put too much importance on what happened between us. It was just sex."

"The hell it was," he gritted out. He shoved the coffee table out of the way. It slid across the wooden floor and banged against the wall.

She yelped when she realized he wasn't slowing down. He vaulted over the couch and she ran for the stairs.

She'd only made it to the third step before she was yanked off her feet and thrown over his shoulder. Her breath left her with a solid whoosh.

He didn't pause. As if she weighed nothing he jogged up the stairs. She was so surprised she didn't say a word, not that she could have. His shoulder knocked the breath out of her with every step he took.

At the top of the stairs he headed down the hallway, turning right, toward the master suite. Amanda tried to grab the banister, but he was going too fast and her hands slid off the polished wood.

"Put me down," she demanded, wiggling to get out of his grasp.

He stalked into the bedroom and kicked the door shut with his foot. He didn't slow as he approached the massive four-poster bed.

"Put me down," she insisted again.

"As you wish." He dumped her unceremoniously on the bed. The mattress hadn't stopped bouncing before he followed her with his body, pressing her into the mattress, chest to chest, thigh to thigh, groin to groin.

His dark, angry eyes bored into hers as he stared down at her. She stared back, amazed at this side of him she'd never seen before, wondering what he was going to do. His eyes dropped to her lips. The tension in him suddenly changed and she felt the pressure against her abdomen increase as his growing erection pressed against her.

"Mandy, what the hell am I going to do with you?" The words sounded like they were torn out of him, filled with frustration, anger, and something else.

"*Love me?*" she whispered, reaching up and gently running her fingers along the side of his face.

He shuddered beneath her touch. She saw the surrender in his eyes a moment before he leaned down and covered her mouth with his.

Lora Dean

Chapter Seventeen

"Wake up, sleeping beauty."

Amanda groaned at the sound of Logan's cheerful voice. She was lying on her stomach with one arm hanging off the edge of the bed. "Too early." She threw the sheet over the top of her head.

He chuckled and relentlessly tugged the sheet back down in spite of her efforts to hang on to it. "My curious sister is already downstairs, asking me all kinds of questions about why you're so tired this morning. What do you think I should tell her?"

She cursed and opened her right eye to glare at him.

"What was that? I didn't quite understand you, sweetie."

The sheet continued its relentless slide down her bare back. Had she actually thought this man was kind and sweet when he'd kissed her scars and made her feel beautiful and cherished? She cleared her throat and spoke louder. "I don't care what you tell her. Leave me alone. Must . . . sleep. Go away."

Logan whisked the sheet off the bed and slapped her bare bottom.

She shrieked in outrage.

"Like it or not, we've got company. And unless you want me to tell Pierce why you're so tired, you'd better get hopping."

"You wouldn't dare." She reluctantly sat up, grabbing a pillow to cover her breasts and block Logan's view.

His eyes dipped down to her lap and he gave her a lecherous leer. She gasped and grabbed another pillow to cover up.

Laughing, he bent down and pressed a quick kiss against her lips. "If you're not downstairs in ten minutes, I'm going to join that luscious body of yours in bed. I don't care what Pierce and Madison think."

She shoved him off the bed but he caught himself before he fell. When she grabbed a knickknack from the bedside table and threatened to throw it at him, he grinned but hurried from the room, closing the door behind him.

It wasn't until she was in the shower that what he'd said sank in. *Pierce* was here? In spite of the wonderful night she and Logan had shared, had Logan called Pierce this morning to take her to a safe house as he'd threatened to do last night?

The rest of her shower was taken amidst a series of stomps and curses as she vented her anger. She purposely took longer than ten minutes just to see if he would dare to come upstairs, now that she was awake enough to realize what he'd done.

When he failed to show, she grudgingly admitted he

knew her better than she thought. She reluctantly headed downstairs.

Amanda located Pierce, Madison, and Logan on the back deck, sitting at one of the round tables with an assortment of bagels and cream cheese.

Logan stood and pulled out a chair for her next to him. She ignored him and grabbed another chair, scooting it in between Madison and Pierce, forcing them to move over to let her sit down.

"Good morning, Pierce, Madison." She forced a cheerfulness into her voice she didn't feel.

Madison exchanged a quizzical look with Pierce. "Good morning, Amanda."

Logan stood beside his chair with a scowl on his face. "Wouldn't you rather sit over here? You're crowding the others."

"Pierce? Am I bothering you sitting here?" Amanda asked sweetly, turning her sunny smile on him.

He shot a glance at Logan then looked back at her. "Uh, no, not at all. There's plenty of room."

"Good. Let's eat. I'm starving."

Logan sat. He leaned back with his long legs spread out in front of him and crossed his arms over his chest. "You're normally not much of a breakfast person. You must have worked up quite an appetite last night to be so hungry."

Madison choked on the water she was drinking.

Amanda stabbed at a container of cream cheese and

smacked a glob of it onto the top of a blueberry bagel. "Actually, I must have slept through the whole night because I can't remember anything . . . well . . . memorable."

His face darkened and he leaned forward, his jaw tensed. "Do you need me to remind you what we were doing? Sweetheart?"

Her face flushed but she returned his glare with a smoldering one of her own.

Madison smacked her hands on the table and stood. "You two obviously need some privacy to work out whatever is bothering you. Pierce, would you join me inside, please?"

She crossed to the French door and yanked it open. "Pierce?"

He glanced at Logan. "Am I still going to take her to the—"

"Yes," Logan said.

"No," Amanda said at the same time.

Pierce held his hands up in surrender and followed Madison into the house.

"What was that about?" Logan demanded.

"I'm sure I don't know what you mean." She grabbed the can of Dr. Pepper he'd obviously brought out for her and took a deep swallow.

"Let's take a walk," he said.

"I'm eating."

"No, you're not. We need to talk."

She dropped her bagel on her plate. "There's nothing to talk about. I'm not going with Pierce. Period. You're not getting rid of me that easily."

"I don't *want* you to leave. I *need* you to leave, so I know you're safe. If something happened to you . . ." He shook his head and looked away, his fists clenched on the table.

She felt her anger draining away. She was being childish, she knew it, but it was so difficult to think about leaving him after everything that had happened in the past two days. Her love for him was so new, her need for him so raw she couldn't stand the thought of not being with him.

It wasn't fair for her to be angry at him for wanting to protect her when that was one of the reasons she was drawn to him in the first place. He had a sense of honor and duty, and put everything he had into his work. And no matter how much it galled her, right now she was part of that work, and she needed to let him do what he felt should be done. If leaving was what it took for him to be able to do his job, then she would have to leave.

That didn't mean she was happy about it.

She shoved away from the table and he was suddenly behind her, pulling out her chair.

"Can you at least tell me where I'm going?" she asked. "And tell me how long I'll be gone, before you send me away?"

"I wasn't going to toss you in the car without discussing anything." He sighed and raked a hand through his hair.

She noticed his hair was starting to look a little ragged, longer than he normally wore it. He needed a haircut. There were shadows beneath his eyes too. Not just since last night. She'd noticed them several days ago.

He was tired, wasn't sleeping well, and wasn't putting himself first. Instead, he was putting her first: working long hours and still coming home and making time for her, like when they'd gone boating, even though he was running on adrenaline and exhaustion.

And here she was giving him a hard time. She wanted to kick herself.

"Is that offer for a walk still open?" she asked, hoping he would want to go to the bench by the creek, or maybe even all the way to the dock. They could sit and watch the pelicans and seagulls fly by, take off their shoes and let their feet hang in the cooling current.

It would be a wonderful way to say goodbye, because that's what she had to do. Say goodbye, go to the safe house so she didn't distract him any further, so he could work on the case without worrying about her.

He leaned down and tenderly kissed the top of her head. "Let's go."

They held hands and walked across the deck, down onto the soft carpet of grass. She smiled as he led her toward the now-familiar opening in the pines.

When they neared the woods, a small section of bark erupted from the tree near Logan's head, accompanied by a loud cracking noise.

Logan wrapped his arms around her, pulled her tightly against his chest as he lunged toward the protective cover of the trees. He twisted in midair so he landed on his back with her on top of him.

Before she could gather her wits and figure out what was happening he yanked her to her feet and pulled her with him down the path in a mad dash, weaving like a drunken sailor from one side to the other.

Another puff of bark exploded on a tree next to him. The loud crack was enough for Amanda to finally realize what was happening.

Someone was shooting at them.

The trees to the right of the path were so close together and thick with underbrush, there was no escape. Logan pulled her with him toward some trees to the left of the path where the underbrush was thinner, but a shot near his foot had him weaving back to the right.

They had no choice but to run down the path toward the creek. The shooter was herding them along, a trap. From the cursing coming from Logan, Amanda knew he'd come to the same conclusion.

The next shot was so close that splinters of tree bark flew at his face. Amanda tried to stop to check on him, but he wouldn't let her. His right arm was wrapped around her shoulder and he had her glued to his side so none of her was exposed to the shooter.

"Let go of me so you can use your gun," she cried out.

"I have to get you to cover first. Come on, run," he urged. "The brush is thinner near the creek. We'll be able to get into the trees there."

"But you're hurt. My God, you're bleeding." Blood was pouring from a cut on his cheek but running like they were—continually zigzagging—she couldn't reach up to check how bad it was.

The next shot wasn't as close as the last one. It drove into the dirt a few yards to their left but it was close enough for her to realize that none of the shots seemed directed at her.

The shooter wasn't aiming at her.

He was aiming at Logan.

They reached the creek and just as he was pushing her toward an opening in the trees on the right side of the path, she saw the silhouette of a man deep in the pines on their left, raising his arm and aiming his gun straight at Logan.

This close, there was no way he would miss.

She ducked beneath Logan's arm and twisted around to his left side, wrapping her arms around his waist just as a shot rang out.

Logan lunged with her toward a clump of palmettos, anchoring her to his chest as they rolled on the ground until they were securely off the path.

She squealed when a shadow broke away from a tree behind him, but Logan pressed his hand against her mouth to silence her. Without turning around he said, "It took you long enough."

"Excuse me, Daniel Boone. I don't know these woods and had to double back to find an opening."

Amanda relaxed in relief when she recognized Pierce's voice.

Logan dropped his hand from her mouth. "What were you thinking? Why did you throw yourself in front of me?" His voice was low and angry, his eyes dark, almost black.

"He was shooting at *you*. Not me."

"Don't you think I know that?" he said, exasperation evident in his voice.

"Then why didn't you let me go so you could use your gun to defend yourself? I would have been okay. He wasn't trying to shoot me."

"I couldn't risk it. You would have been too exposed." He turned to Pierce. "Do you think you got him?"

"I only got one shot off. If I didn't hit him, I came damn close. He knows there are two of us now. He's probably on the run."

"Call for backup."

"Already done."

"Then take this little spitfire back to the house before she gets herself killed."

She gasped in outrage and sat up. As she wiped the pine needles from her shirt, she said, "I can take myself back to the house. I don't need Pierce's help."

"I'll be sure and tell Logan you said that when he gets back."

She looked up, stunned to see that Logan wasn't there. Instead, Pierce was standing over her with his gun in his right hand, pointed away from her. He held out his left hand to pull her to her feet.

"Where did he go?" she demanded as she accepted his help and stood.

"To catch the bad guy."

"Shouldn't you be helping him?"

"Yes. And just as soon as I have you safely in the house, I will."

She felt the blood rush from her face as she realized Logan's prediction had come true. She was a liability. Cold fear settled in her stomach. She turned and ran with Pierce faster than she'd ever run in her life, praying she could get to safety quickly enough for Pierce to help Logan before it was too late.

Logan squatted next to Frank Branson's still-warm body. The bullet had gone clean through his temple. Since Logan hadn't fired his gun, either Pierce had made one hell of a lucky shot earlier, or the real killer had just claimed another victim, execution-style.

Easing back into the trees, he scanned the thick forest around him, searching for signs of the shooter. Adrenaline pumped through his veins making it difficult to remain still and quiet, when he wanted to rush into the trees and find the bastard who'd hurt Amanda four years ago. He desperately wanted to eliminate this threat to her so she could live her life out from under the cloud of fear that had loomed over her for so long.

The soft crack of a twig sounded from the copse of trees directly in front of him. A slow smile spread across his face as he made his way deeper into the woods.

Amanda and Madison sat in two Adirondack chairs in the corner of the deck, watching the dwindling army of policemen and FBI agents. The men left in small groups, each one stopping to check in with Logan or Pierce before getting in their cars to drive back to town.

The wait earlier this morning had been excruciating. She and Madison were forced to sit in an interior hallway away from any windows, guarded by a pair of Shadow Falls police officers. When she complained they'd be more comfortable in the study or the living room, the older of the two shook his head and insisted they were safer here, and proceeded to tell her he valued his life far too much to take any chances with hers.

From the goofy grin on the other police officer's face and Madison's burst of laughter, Amanda wondered if the whole police force had figured out that she and Logan were sleeping together.

She didn't appreciate her personal life being made public knowledge, but that wasn't what bothered her the most. What bothered her the most was waiting to find out whether Logan was all right.

She'd paced the hallway for what seemed like hours, and every time she asked one of the officers whether Logan was okay, he simply told her what she already knew: that several other officers had gone into the woods to assist him, including Special Agent Pierce Buchanan.

Finally another officer came to let them know the perimeter was secured, and they were free to move about the house.

She and Madison had taken that order to its extreme and sneaked out onto the back deck. They sat in a corner on the far left side to watch what was going on.

Minutes later a group of officers emerged from the forest. They were carrying a stretcher with a white sheet draped over it. Amanda clutched Madison's hand as she watched that stretcher, and prayed like she'd never prayed before that it was the shooter—not Logan—lying there.

Relief flooded through her when another group of men stepped out of the trees, and even from this distance she could see Logan and Pierce standing several inches taller than those around them.

Her relief was short-lived, however, when he got close enough for her to see the blood on his face and shirt. She would have run to him right then, but he glanced over at her and the look in his eyes kept her in her seat.

He was furious.

At her.

But why?

An EMT pulled him toward one of the ambulances in the driveway while the stretcher was loaded in the other one.

Pierce stepped onto the deck and approached their table.

"Is Logan okay?" Amanda asked.

"He might need a few stitches. The blood is from the tree bark that exploded near his face when one of the shots got too close. He's fine."

"Can I go see him?" Amanda asked.

"I wouldn't recommend it right now. An EMT is sewing him up, and then he'll be busy for a while."

"EMT? Why doesn't he go to the hospital?"

"He refused, says he doesn't have time." Pierce shrugged. "He's a stubborn man."

Madison squeezed Amanda's hand beneath the table. "Who was on the stretcher? Did Logan get the shooter?"

He hesitated. "The dead man is Frank Branson, but Logan didn't shoot him. He was dead when he found him." Pierce spoke to them for a few more minutes before he left to direct his agents and speak to Riley, who was overseeing the detectives.

Hours later, with most of the police gone—except for a contingent who were patrolling the edges of the property—

Amanda and Madison remained at the table, waiting for a chance to speak with Logan about what was going on.

"After being willing to sacrifice his own life for mine this morning you'd think he'd want to stop and check on me at least once today," Amanda complained. Logan stood on the opposite end of the deck, near the stairs that led to the driveway and garage. Pierce and Riley were talking to him, and it seemed like he was making a concerted effort not to even glance her way.

"I think this is where I'm supposed to reassure you that he's probably just really busy. But even I can't lie that well," Madison said. "Pierce didn't have a problem updating us several times today, and he's got at least as many responsibilities as Logan. He is a federal agent, after all."

Amanda glanced at her friend and raised a brow. "Well, well. Interesting. Pierce did go out of his way to reassure us today, but now that I think about it, he spoke mainly to you. Not me."

Madison grinned. "He's a hottie. I flirted outrageously with him this morning over bagels before you showed up and ruined the fun."

"Ouch. Sorry. I was furious with Logan. Now, I just want him to talk to me." She looked at him and willed him to turn her way.

"He's mad about something all right," Madison said. "He was furious this morning too. I could tell by the tic in his left cheek. Have you ever noticed that?" Not waiting for Amanda's answer, she continued. "But now he's moved on to that dark and moody stage all men devolve into at one time or another. Yep, no doubt about it. He's pissed at you about something."

"Great."

Madison shrugged. "You still have the advantage. You're sleeping with him. Just don't put out until he makes nice again."

In spite of Amanda's sour mood, she laughed out loud.

Logan glanced over at her, but quickly looked away without a smile or even a nod. It was as if she didn't exist.

It hurt.

Too damn much.

Logan watched Amanda go into the house with Madison. It was difficult not going to her and grabbing her when he came out of the woods and saw her sitting next to his sister. But he was so angry he couldn't trust himself to speak without yelling, so he tried the opposite approach. He'd ignored her, not an easy task when she sat outside in that sexy white tank top and khaki shorts that revealed far too much skin. The way that glorious dark hair of hers spilled over her shoulders to curl around her hips was damned distracting. He'd caught several of his patrolmen gawking at her today.

They wouldn't make that mistake again.

"Logan? Are you listening?" Pierce punched him in the arm.

"What?" Logan asked.

Pierce rolled his eyes. Riley laughed.

"You know you're going to have to speak to her, tell her why you're so upset," Pierce said.

"Upset? She threw herself in between me and a bullet. I

wear a vest, for God's sake, and she's out there in a tank top and she throws herself in front of me. Is she insane?"

"She seems to like you. That probably qualifies as a kind of insanity," Pierce conceded.

Logan shoved him, then crossed his arms and leaned back against the railing. "Riley, when you get the bullet out of Branson, put a rush on the ballistics. I want proof it didn't come from Pierce's gun." He glanced at Pierce. "You do have another gun you can use for now, don't you?"

"Of course."

"I'd like to know how the shooter found this place. I always drive the long way home and make sure I'm not followed."

"What about Karen?" Pierce asked.

"Karen doesn't live far from here. She drives between here and her house. There's no reason for someone to follow her, since she never goes into town these days. And other than you," he gave Pierce a pointed glance, "no one else has come here from town."

"Except your sister," Pierce said. "She did say she looked for you at the police station. How many people know she's your sister?"

"Ah, hell. Everyone. She's not exactly the meek and mild type. She's like a cyclone blowing into town. Everyone in a ten-mile radius of the station probably knew she was there. And if someone was following her, she certainly wouldn't have noticed."

"Do you want me to take Amanda to the safe house tonight or wait until morning?" Pierce asked, glancing up at the darkening sky.

Logan sighed heavily. "Riley, how many men are patrolling the property?"

"Four. They're keeping in contact via radio every fifteen minutes. I'll rotate them out in the morning around eight o'clock with a fresh team."

"Don't bother with a new team. I'll let her stay here tonight, give her time to pack her things. She can leave at first light for the safe house. Does that work for you, Pierce?"

Pierce nodded. "I'll drive her there myself. What about Madison?"

Logan flushed. Getting Madison to safety hadn't even occurred to him with all his worries about Amanda. Some brother he was. "I hadn't even thought about her," he admitted.

"I can take her into town with me," Riley offered.

"So can I." Pierce aimed an irritated look at Riley.

Logan's brows rose. "You're interested in my sister?"

Pierce folded his arms over his chest. "That a problem for you?"

"I don't know. I'll have to think about it." He grinned and shoved Pierce. Pierce shoved him back.

Riley looked at them, his eyes darting back and forth. "So I'm not taking her back with me?"

"No," Logan and Pierce said at the same time.

"Okay, okay." Riley held his hands up. "If that covers everything, I'll head back to town. I'm going to be up half the night as it is, filling out reports."

"I'll help you tomorrow. I have to fill out one of my own on the shooting," Logan said.

"I'll go take Madison off your hands," Pierce said as he eagerly strode back toward the house.

Logan stayed on the porch until well after Riley drove away. The side of his face was throbbing where he'd had a handful of stitches, and his mood was still too dark to want to go inside.

He was so angry with Amanda he wanted to shake her until her teeth rattled. But at the same time he wanted nothing more than to hold her and assure himself she was okay. She'd come so close to being killed today. If Pierce hadn't come along when he had and took that shot, she'd be dead. He'd seen the shadow of a man off to his left a split second before Amanda threw herself in the way, a split second too late if Pierce hadn't been there.

The sound of a door opening had him jerking his head up in time to see Madison and Pierce stepping out onto the deck. Pierce held a suitcase and nodded at Logan before continuing to his car.

Madison stopped in front of him and instead of the lecture he expected for ignoring her all day, she surprised him by wrapping her arms around his waist and squeezing him in a bear hug.

He returned the hug and kissed the top of her head. "What was that for?" he asked

"Oh, let me see. You were shot at. You could have been killed today. What do you think?"

"Touché."

"Of course it would have been nice if you'd bothered to take a few minutes out of your day to say hi."

"Now this is what I expected."

She sighed. "I love you, big brother, and I'm glad you didn't get shot, but if you don't go in there and fix my new friend's broken heart, I'm going to shoot you myself." With that she marched off the deck without a backward glance.

Broken heart? What was she talking about? How had he broken Amanda's heart?

For the first time since that God-awful moment when he'd almost lost her to a killer's bullet, his haze of anger began to fade. In its place he started to see the events of the day from Amanda's perspective.

She'd thrown herself in front of him, willing to give her life for his even though it wasn't necessary. She knew he wore a vest. So why had she done it? Why had she risked her life?

The only answer he could think of was that she hadn't thought. She'd simply reacted on instinct. She'd risked her life for his.

And he'd done nothing but glare at her since.

"Ah, hell."

CHAPTER EIGHTEEN

When Madison and Pierce walked out the French door and closed it behind them, an overwhelming sense of loneliness crashed down on Amanda.

With Logan ignoring her, there was no reason for her to hang around downstairs, so she headed upstairs and retired to one of the guest rooms. She didn't think he would seek her out, so she could have stayed in her own room, but the thought of sleeping in that big bed without him was far too depressing.

Instead, she chose one of the smaller rooms with a single bed. It was decorated in warm browns and subtle hues of creamy yellow. Not a rose or any other flower in sight. She loved it. She especially liked that it had a chaise lounge on the far side of the room shoved up beneath a large picture window. It was a cozy reading spot and she intended to make full use of it tonight. Her nerves were so on edge she doubted she'd be able to sleep.

After pulling the shades and drapes closed, she grabbed

a blanket off the end of the bed, snuggled into the oversized chaise, and settled down to read.

A few minutes later she heard Logan coming up the stairs. His footsteps echoed down the wooden hallway toward the other end of the house where both of their bedrooms were located.

When he didn't immediately come down the hall looking for her, she ruthlessly squashed the twinge of disappointment that shot through her, and flipped the page of her novel. It wasn't like she wanted him to come looking for her. It was just that it would make her feel better to hear him beg her to unlock the door, beg for her forgiveness.

Was it too much to hope for a little groveling? After the day she'd had she felt like she deserved it. Not that she'd open the door even if he did grovel. But it would be nice just the same to hear him whining for her affection through the locked bedroom door. Irritated that she couldn't seem to concentrate on anything but Logan, she flipped another page.

"You must read really fast. You turned the last page no more than ten seconds ago."

She jerked around toward the sound of Logan's voice, stunned to see him standing in a doorway she hadn't even noticed before, a doorway that apparently adjoined this bedroom with the one next to it.

"Can you forgive me for being such an ass?" he said, even as he leaned down and scooped her into his arms.

"Put me down," she demanded, as her book tumbled to the floor.

"If you insist." He turned and plopped lengthwise onto

the chaise with her still in his arms. She bounced against his chest and he pulled her even more tightly against him as he straightened his legs out and sat back.

"I didn't give you permission to come in here," she said as she struggled against his hold and tried to slide off his lap.

"I didn't ask." He gently but forcefully tilted her chin up until she had to look at him. "If you'll stop squirming I'd like to try to explain why I acted the way I did today."

The longing in his eyes was so intense she felt an answering longing deep within her. Then she caught sight of the stitches running down the left side of his face near his hairline. Her hand flew up—as if of its own accord—and her fingers shook as she lightly feathered them down the cut that ran from his temple to just past his eye.

He reached out his hand and lightly ran a fingertip down the scar on the side of her face and smiled. "It's just a scar. It doesn't matter."

She knew he was referring to *her* scar instead of *his*, and it was difficult not to let him turn her attention when she was so touched by the way he used every opportunity to remind her he thought she was beautiful.

"It does matter," she insisted. "You could have been blinded if the cut was a little more to the left, not to mention maimed or killed."

"But I wasn't."

She shook her head in exasperation and pushed back to put more distance between them. She would have jumped up but his arm around her shoulder held her firmly in place on his lap.

"Logan, what would you have done if I wasn't with you when that man started shooting at you today?"

His jaw tightened and a look of unease flashed in his eyes. "It's a moot question. If you weren't with me, I wouldn't have been in the woods."

"You would have taken out your gun and gone after him. But you didn't because you were afraid you would leave me exposed if you stopped to do that. Isn't that right?"

"I didn't come in here to argue with you."

"Oh? Then why did you come in here?"

"To apologize. And to explain why I ignored you all day."

"You didn't just ignore me, Logan. You glared daggers at me the few times you actually looked my way."

His hand curled into a fist where it rested on top of her thigh. "I was angry. No, I was furious. I still am."

"Why?"

"Why?" His eyes blazed out at her and he looked incredulous. "Someone was shooting at us and you threw yourself in the line of fire."

She waited for him to continue, but he just glared at her like he'd been doing most of the day. She sighed and tried again. "I understand you being angry about that, but you treated me like a pariah all day. How do you think I felt when everyone around me saw how embarrassed of me you were—"

"I wasn't embarrassed."

She threw her hands in the air, then crossed them over her chest. "We're getting nowhere."

They sat in silence for several minutes. She did her best to ignore him, not to mention the growing erection beneath her bottom. How could he be thinking about sex at a time like this?

"I'm sorry, Mandy." He leaned forward and nibbled on her earlobe.

She jerked away and struggled to maintain her anger, in spite of the jolt of desire that one little touch had evoked.

He sighed. "I'm not very good at controlling my anger when it comes to you. That doesn't excuse it. I know that and I'm sorry my behavior embarrassed you, but if you ever do something like that again, I can't promise I won't act like an ass again. I'll try," he said, holding up a hand to halt the angry words she was ready to spill. "I can't promise I won't do that again but I can promise that I'll try. Fair enough?"

It was a lousy apology but she knew it came from his heart. She would have preferred a promise that he'd never do something like that again, but he was too honest for that. He knew his limits. She grudgingly nodded her agreement.

He pulled her back to lie against his chest, tucking her head beneath his chin, stroking her hair and massaging her scalp. "I've made a promise to you. Can you make one to me?"

"Depends on what it is."

He chuckled, a deep rumbling sound that tickled her ear where it rested against him.

"Promise me you won't ever put yourself in danger like that again."

She shook her head. "I didn't do it on purpose. I reacted. Just like you can't promise me you'll never get that angry with me or shut me out like that, I can't promise not to try to protect the man I love, even if it means danger to me."

His fingers stilled where they rested in her hair. She suddenly realized what she'd said, and hoped he hadn't noticed. She hadn't intended to be the first to say it.

He cupped the sides of her face, tilting her head up to look at him. "You love me?" he asked, his voice husky and low. His hands shook and his eyes had turned so dark they were almost black. As much as she regretted saying it first, she couldn't let him think she hadn't meant it.

She turned her head slightly and kissed his palm. "Yes. I love you."

He crushed her against himself, covering her mouth with his and thrusting his tongue inside, stroking in and out in a frenzied rhythm that left her clutching his shoulders and drawing up her knees to cuddle him against her.

When her tongue stroked lightly against his and she sucked his tongue, he shivered against her and groaned low in his throat.

Suddenly he twisted and pulled her beneath him, frantically tearing at the fastenings to his pants as he continued to ravage her mouth.

She strained against him, jerking off his tie, struggling with the buttons on his shirt until she gave up and ripped it open. Buttons flew against the wall and onto the floor.

He broke their kiss so he could work her shorts down her hips. She eagerly lifted for him so he could slide them off, even as she struggled to push his own pants down his thick muscular thighs.

She'd never felt so consumed with raw hunger before, not even on that first night they'd made love. She was wild for him. He tugged her tank top and bra over her head and leaned down to delve his tongue into the valley between her breasts, squeezing and molding them with his hands.

"Logan, your pants, take them—"

"No time, can't wait." He thrust inside her with his pants tangled around his knees.

She bucked beneath him, her head thrown back against the chaise, matching his rhythm with her own. Pushing and straining, they frantically raced toward their shared goal.

She felt him tighten inside her and knew he was close. She was close, too, and when the first flutterings of her impending climax rushed through her, she threw her head back against the lounge, her fingers digging into his back, reveling in the sensation as it built within her.

He sucked in his breath and grew even harder, thrusting with quick, deep strokes into her. "Come with me, Mandy," he urged. "Let yourself go." He leaned down and grazed his teeth against her nipple, pulling the swollen tip into his mouth, sucking in unison with his deep, long strokes.

"Logan!" She screamed as her climax rippled through her and she convulsed against him. He joined her a few moments later, as waves of ecstasy consumed them both.

He collapsed on top of her, his chest slick with sweat, heaving with each ragged breath. The wiry hairs brushed against her swollen breasts sending tiny ripples of pleasure through her.

"That was—"

"Amazing," he said, finishing her sentence.

She was going to say *incredible*, but *amazing* worked, too.

Just when her heartbeat was returning to normal and she could finally breathe without rasping, she felt the stirrings of his growing erection deep inside her. "You can't possibly—"

"I'm not finished. Not even close," he said, and proceeded to prove it.

It wasn't until much, much later when she was drifting off into an exhausted sleep in the tiny twin bed—where they'd managed to move the third time they'd made love—that she felt a twinge of unease.

She'd told him she loved him.

But he hadn't told her that *he* loved *her*.

Just before sunrise, Logan carried a nearly comatose Amanda to the much more comfortable bed in the master bedroom. He tucked her in and stood watching her for several minutes, awed by the ethereal picture she presented.

She looked like an angel with her full pink lips curved in a delicate smile, and her hands clasped together beneath her soft cheek as if in prayer. Her glorious hair surrounded her like a halo, but he knew what lay beneath that cherubic exterior.

She wasn't an angel. She was a tigress. A demanding woman who'd surprised him yet again with the depth of her passion. Little dark circles beneath her eyes attested that he hadn't been able to keep his hands off her all night.

When she told him she loved him, he was so overwhelmed he went crazy, showing her how much he loved her by wringing out every ounce of pleasure from her that he could. The last time they'd made love, he'd brought her to climax three times before she cried out for mercy and he plunged inside her, joining her in ecstasy in three quick strokes.

He marveled at the way they made love as if their bodies were created solely for each other, fitting together so perfectly with every thrust, every kiss, every slide of her skin against his.

She was nothing like Victoria, nothing like his preconceived notions of what he wanted in a woman. And yet, she was absolutely perfect for him.

At the doorway, he turned back to make sure she was still sleeping peacefully. When she was this tired, the nightmares usually didn't come, and for that he was grateful. He hoped one day he could banish those nightmares forever.

Confident she would sleep a few more hours, he showered and dressed in one of the guest bathrooms. He called Pierce from his study to make sure he was on his way. Pierce answered his cell phone on the first ring and assured Logan he would be there in about twenty minutes.

Yearning for coffee but not wanting to brew any for fear the aroma would awaken Amanda, he drummed his fingers on his desk.

He started to straighten some papers and the Northwood case file caught his attention. There were only a few pages left in the thick folder for him to review. Might as well do it now. He pulled the folder toward him and flipped it open to the section he'd marked with a paper clip to keep his place.

One of the papers was an interview with the motel manager. Anna Northwood had worked as a maid at the motel where she was murdered. The brief interview was light in details and didn't tell Logan anything he didn't already know.

He read two more reports before turning to the end of the folder. The last page was clipped to a clear plastic envelope with a CD inside. Curious, Logan unclipped the piece of paper. It was a far more in-depth bio than he'd seen in the folder until now. This one was recorded several days after the murder by a detective whose name he didn't recognize.

Listed on the top of the form was the full name of the victim, Anna Katherine Northwood.

Logan froze, the blood chilling in his veins as he read the name again. Anna. *Katherine.* Northwood. Next to her full name was a box marked "nickname." Inside that box were four letters, K-A-T-E. Her family had called her Kate.

The same name Amanda's attacker had called her.

It had to be a coincidence.

Because anything else would destroy him.

His hands shook as he unclipped the CD holder and read the Post-it note taped to the back. The note said the CD was playing in the motel room when the victim's body was discovered. Alarm bells started going off in Logan's head.

Amanda had said the man who attacked her hummed a strange tune, something she'd never heard before or since but would recognize if she ever heard again.

"Logan?"

He jerked his head up at the sound of Amanda's sweet voice, surprised to see her standing in the doorway, even more surprised to see Pierce standing next to her.

He longed to go to her, to wrap his arms around her and

ask her to give him those three precious words again, to tell him she loved him. But he didn't. He couldn't.

Pierce strode to the desk. "Amanda let me in. I guess you didn't hear the doorbell."

Logan pushed his chair back and stood with the CD in his hand. "Amanda, do you remember the case I told you about?" he rasped. He cleared his throat. "The case where I let the killer go?"

She nodded and joined Pierce in front of the desk. "You didn't know, Logan. You can't possibly still blame yourself for that."

"She didn't have long hair, but her eyes were blue. Her family called her Kate."

Amanda's eyes widened. She glanced at Pierce then back at Logan. "That's a fairly common name, isn't it? Yes, I think it is."

He heard the doubt in her voice, that little note of uncertainty.

"I was looking through the old file from that murder and I found a CD. The report says it was playing on the stereo when the police found Kate's body."

He slowly walked across the room to the CD player built into the wall beneath the TV.

"Logan, don't. Please." Her voice broke on the last word.

His heart squeezed in his chest at the pleading note in her voice, but he had to know if his terrible suspicions were true. He took a ragged breath and pushed the CD into the slot.

He slowly turned around, his eyes fastened on hers as he waited for his fate to be decided.

"What's going on?" Pierce glanced back and forth between Amanda and Logan.

Logan ignored him, frozen in place like a man strapped into the electric chair, watching the second hand creep toward midnight, knowing the call that could save him wouldn't come in time but desperately hoping it might.

Deep, mournful tones erupted from the speakers. Amanda's face turned white. A look of panic entered her eyes. "No." Her voice was filled with anguish. "Logan, no."

She covered her ears and ran from the room, her sobs echoing back as she fled up the stairs.

"I can't believe you haven't checked on her." Pierce shook his head in disgust.

Logan gripped the pen tighter and scrawled another line on the paper in front of him.

"What's wrong with you?" Pierce asked. "Why aren't you upstairs with her right now? I thought you cared about Amanda."

Logan clamped his jaw tight and jerked open his bottom desk drawer. He grabbed the stack of photographs out, the ones he looked at every night, and dropped them on top of his desk. "What I want and who I care about doesn't matter anymore. Don't you see?" He fanned out the pictures, copies of the same pictures that were posted on the whiteboard in the conference room at work. "Everything I've feared for the past decade has come true."

"What are you talking about?" Pierce narrowed his eyes at him.

"The only thing that got me through every day after I let that white van go was the hope that maybe, just maybe, the killer had never hurt anyone else after that day. I tried to fool myself into thinking no one else got hurt because of me."

He jabbed his finger at the photographs. "Now I know the truth. All of these women were brutally tortured, raped. . . ." His voice broke and he scrubbed a hand across his face. He dropped back down into his desk chair. "I have to stop him. I can't let anyone else die, don't you see?"

"Not that I agree with anything you just said, but what does this have to do with Amanda? You should be upstairs, right now, helping her through—"

Logan slammed his fist on his desk. "You saw the look on her face. She knows the truth now. She knows if it weren't for me, she'd never have been attacked. Everything she's suffered is because of me." He tore the piece of paper off the yellow legal pad he'd been writing on earlier.

Pierce shook his head. "For the record, I think you're way off-base. You're letting your own impressions cloud your judgment."

"I'm thinking more clearly than I've ever thought in my life. I know exactly what needs to be done now, finally."

"At least tell me what you were writing. I can't read your chicken scratches." Pierce turned his head sideways to try to read the notes on the yellow piece of paper. "That looks like an address."

Logan handed him the paper. "It is. Anna Northwood grew up thirty minutes from here in a rural area called Summerville. Her parents moved to Pensacola when she was fif-

teen. The police never interviewed anyone in Summerville.
They didn't think they needed to look back that far, since
she was twenty-three at the time of her death."

"They had no reason to believe the killer was someone
from her past," Pierce said.

"Anna Northwood didn't have long hair when she was
murdered. But I'll bet she did when she was younger, the
first time she and the killer crossed paths. We're going to
Summerville."

"**B**ut why are you taking me to the safe house, Karen?"
Amanda clutched the armrest and tried not to give in to the
anguish roiling inside her. "I thought Pierce was going to
take me. Where is Logan?"

She took a deep breath and tried to calm down. After
hearing that horrible music, she'd panicked and run upstairs
to escape the images running through her mind. By the time
she'd calmed down, Pierce and Logan were gone. A few
minutes later, Karen had ushered her into an unmarked car.
Now Karen was driving Amanda down Interstate 10 with
two more policemen following in the car behind them.

"Logan will explain everything later," Karen assured her.
"He said he had an important lead and Pierce insisted on
going with him." She glanced over at Amanda. "Don't worry.
We're almost there. Once we get to the motel, the officers
will continue on so they don't bring attention to us. An FBI
agent is waiting in the motel room."

Worried? Was she worried? Yes, but not about the safe
house. She was worried about Logan. He'd looked so dev-

astated right before she ran from the room. She shouldn't have run— wouldn't have—except she'd been so scared she hadn't stopped to think about what running out of the room would do to him.

She knew how it must have looked: as if she blamed him for not capturing the killer when he'd had the chance, the same one who'd attacked her years later. His guilt over what he thought of as his rookie mistake had haunted him for a decade. She couldn't imagine how he must be hurting, now that she realized the same killer he'd let go was the one who'd attacked her, the same one after her now.

She had to tell him she didn't blame him. Because she didn't, not even for a second. He'd had no way of knowing who was in that van, or the consequences of letting the driver go. The only person to blame for everything that had happened was the driver of that van, and the choices he'd made.

"I have to speak to Logan. Can I borrow your phone?"

"I don't think that's a good idea. Why don't you give me a message, and I'll see that he gets it once I'm back in Shadow Falls."

"I just need to talk to him for a few seconds. *Please.*"

Karen's brow furrowed and she shook her head as she checked her mirrors. "I'm really sorry, but I can't let you do that. Logan left me strict instructions to make sure you were safe. One of those instructions was to avoid using my cell phone while I was transporting you."

"And you always do what Logan tells you to do?" Amanda said, frustration and sarcasm heavy in her voice.

"Always."

Amanda fisted her hands beside her as Karen turned the car down the next exit. A few turns later and they were in the parking lot of what appeared to be an exclusive condominium complex. Each condo had a separate entrance, with decorative wrought-iron gates.

The two officers in the patrol car behind them waved as they turned around and headed back toward the interstate, back toward Shadow Falls.

Karen slowed the car and rolled her window down. "This place is huge. Help me find building ten."

Amanda looked out her window trying to find the numbers that would tell them which building was which. She felt a rush of relief as she saw the one-zero painted on the side of the building to their right. "Over here, Karen. I think we just passed it."

Karen leaned over to look out Amanda's window. "Damn. They never put addresses where they're easy to find, do they?" She pulled into a parking spot to turn around.

Amanda glanced over at her. Her eyes widened in horror when she saw a man running toward the car with a short metal pipe in his hand. "Karen, look out!"

Chapter Nineteen

Logan shook his head as he stared at the ragtag collection of rotting hovels that called themselves Summerville. There wasn't even a courthouse, and from what he'd seen driving in, the only stores were a Piggly Wiggly grocery store and a gas station.

Even Walmart hadn't discovered this part of the world yet.

As Logan pulled the car to a stop in front of the address he was looking for, Pierce whistled long and low next to him. "I see why the Northwood family left. What on earth would make anyone want to stay in a place like this?"

"Low crime?"

Pierce grimaced. "Good point."

They got out of Logan's Mustang and strode up the tired path of cracked concrete and patches of weeds to the front porch. Before they braved the sagging boards, an elderly woman opened the screen door and stepped outside.

Her white hair was neatly pulled back into a tight bun. A clean, white apron covered the faded blue dress she wore.

From the delicious aroma wafting through the screen, Logan guessed she was baking an apple pie. He couldn't help but smile. She reminded him of his own grandmother.

"What brings two handsome young men like yourselves out my way today. You lost?"

"No, ma'am," Logan said. "If you're Mrs. Whitman, then we're at the right place. I'm Police Chief Logan Richards from Shadow Falls, and this is FBI Special Agent Pierce Buchanan."

She shook Pierce's hand first. "What's so special about you, Agent Buchanan?" His eyes opened wide and he looked like he was trying to think of something to say. "I'm teasing, Mr. Buchanan. I know what a special agent is. I watch TV." She winked before turning to Logan.

When she shook his hand she didn't let go. Instead, she held on as she descended the two steps to the yard. "I can't imagine why you'd want to talk to me, but it's time for my daily walk so you'll have to come along."

"Yes, ma'am." Logan started to pull back his hand but she steadfastly held on. Pierce hid his grin with a cough. Logan elbowed him in the ribs. If Mrs. Whitman wanted to hold onto him, he'd let her—anything to find out the information he needed.

He tucked her hand into the crook of his arm and she beamed her approval.

"Now, what do you young men want to know?"

"Well, ma'am—"

"Call me Sadie."

"Sadie, we're here to find some information on a family that lived in this town a long time ago. We were told you were the best person to ask."

"Who told you that?"

"The manager of the Piggly Wiggly."

She rolled her eyes. "Mr. Simmons. It's a wonder he can even dress himself in the morning without help. But he was right this time. I've been here longer than anybody, and I imagine I can tell you whatever you need to know."

"I appreciate it. We don't have a lot of time—"

"Then why aren't you asking me your questions?"

Pierce coughed again and Logan shot him a glare. "The family's name was Northwood. We're specifically interested in Anna Northwood."

"You mean Kate."

A frisson of excitement shot through him. "Yes, Kate."

"How's she doing? I haven't heard a whisper of gossip about that family for the longest time."

"I'm sorry, Sadie. Kate died several years ago."

She stopped and looked up at him. "And how did that happen?"

"She was murdered."

"Well, can't say that I'm surprised. It's a shame, though. She was a good girl. A little willful—"

"Why aren't you surprised, Sadie?"

"My, my, you are in a hurry. I suppose I've shown you off long enough." She turned back toward her house, pulling him with her, Pierce following behind.

As a suddenly spry Sadie Whitman hustled him back to her front porch, he looked around and only then realized they were the center of attention. Residents of various ages sat on nearly every porch, trying to pretend they weren't staring at him. He guessed Sadie didn't get many visitors.

"You've got your own fan club," Pierce teased. He backed away before Logan could elbow him again.

"Well? Are you going to ask me some questions or not, young man? I'd offer you some apple pie, but I can see you're in an all-fired hurry."

He looked up and realized she'd climbed her front steps, with no assistance, and was standing by the front door watching him.

He shook his head and couldn't help but grin. Sadie had fooled him into thinking she was a feeble old woman.

She winked and returned his smile.

"You said you weren't surprised Kate was murdered. Why is that?"

"Because of that boy that lived next door to her. I always worried he'd go after her again someday."

"Again?"

She nodded. "He was sweet on her and she tolerated him because he was her boyfriend's brother. I guess she felt sorry for him, too. He was never quite right in the head, got teased horribly by the other kids. Didn't have many friends."

"What was his name?"

"Tom. Tom Bennett."

The name didn't sound familiar to Logan. He turned to ask Pierce to call in the name, but Pierce was already walking to the car with his cell phone to his ear.

"What happened, Sadie, that made you think Tom might go after Kate someday?"

"The last summer she was here, she and her boyfriend, David, took a walk in the woods and Tom tagged along without them knowing. They disappeared for three whole days. Everybody was looking for them."

Three days. The same amount of time the killer always kept his victims before killing them. When Sadie paused, Logan encouraged her to continue her story.

"Tom's father found them. They'd gone exploring, got lost. Apparently they didn't get along too well, everybody being scared and upset and trying to find their way home. Kate got mad at her boyfriend, blamed him for getting them lost. She told him she didn't want to see him anymore. I guess he tried to change her mind. He gave her a wild rose he found growing in the woods, but one of the thorns cut Kate and she threw the flower at him. That's what set Tom off."

"Set him off? What did he do?"

"I guess he had a crush on Kate, and when she broke up with David, Tom got this crazy notion in his head that she'd want him. He tried to kiss her and touch her where he had no business touching. I guess he scared her. She hit him with a rock. When the boys' daddy found them, he had to take Tom into town and get him stitched up. Kate had laid open his face from here," she touched her right temple, "to here." She ran her finger down the side of her face to her chin.

The same cut the killer left on his victim's faces.

The same jagged scar that marred Amanda's face.

"Hey, pipe down, everybody. I can't hear Pierce." Special Agent Nelson waved at the other officers and detectives in the squad room until he was satisfied with the noise level before cradling the phone back to his ear.

Riley paused, his fingers curled over the keys of his computer, where he was typing up his handwritten notes from another interview he'd conducted that morning. He looked over at Nelson, two desks away.

"Yeah, I got it," Nelson said into the phone. "Bennett. Tom Bennett. I'm keying the name in now."

One of the uniformed officers called across the room. "I know a Tom Bennett. He's one of the mechanics in the garage. Is that the guy Pierce is looking for?"

A sick feeling settled in the pit of Riley's stomach. His fingers curled into fists and he cursed beneath his breath. He shoved back from his desk and hurried across the room to the bank of elevators.

"Hey Riley? Where ya going? Pierce has a hot lead to follow up on," Nelson called out.

"I've got a hunch," Riley called out.

The elevator door opened and he stepped inside.

Excitement pulsed through Logan, and he was impatient to hear what, if anything, Pierce's men could come up with on a search for Tom Bennett in the FBI databases.

"You've been a tremendous help, Sadie. One more question. Did Kate wear her hair long when she lived here?"

"I can do better than answer that question. I've got a picture of little Kate. Come on in and I'll show you."

Logan motioned to Pierce to let him know he was going inside. Pierce waved back, still on the cell phone, pacing back and forth beside the Mustang.

Though small, the inside of the house was as neat and

tidy as Sadie herself. She led the way through the living room to an upright piano tucked into the corner. Both the top of the piano and the wall above it were full of pictures in varying sizes. She lifted an eight by ten silver framed picture from the piano and handed it to him.

"That's a picture of a church picnic back when the Northwoods still lived here. This is Tom." She pointed to a tall, freckle-faced teenager standing off by himself. "And this is Kate." She ran her finger across the photo, following the direction where Tom was looking, toward the right side of the picture. She tapped the young girl who was standing in a white cotton dress with a group of other girls her age.

She had blue eyes.

And hip-length brown hair.

Anna Kate Northwood could have been Amanda's twin.

He leaned down and kissed Sadie's cheek. "Thank you, Sadie. You may have saved several lives today."

"Well." She looked nonplussed and a rosy blush spread across her weathered cheeks. "Then you're very welcome. I do hope you'll come back and see me when you have more time to visit."

"Count on it." He started to turn away when another picture captured his attention. It was a picture of Kate standing in front of a white house, holding hands with a boy who looked vaguely familiar. Logan picked the picture up and held it out for Sadie. "Who is this boy standing next to Kate?"

"That was her boyfriend. It's such a shame, what happened that day in the woods. David was crazy about her. I always thought they'd end up married. But even if she could have gotten over what happened, he couldn't. I think he hated her for what she'd done to his brother, scarred him for life. He didn't see Tom try to kiss Kate, and he never believed her that she'd hit Tom in self-defense."

"What do you mean he didn't believe her? He was there."

"After Kate got mad at him, he took off, left her and Tom behind."

Pierce leaned in around the screen door. "Logan, we have to leave. Now."

"Just a minute." Logan studied the boy in the picture. The face was so familiar. "Sadie, what did you say the boy-friend's name was?"

"David, his name was David Riley Bennett."

David Riley. Logan's gut clenched and he looked up at Pierce. Alarm coursed through him when he saw how pale he was. "What is it?" Logan asked. "What's happened?"

Pierce glanced pointedly at Sadie. "Outside. I'll tell you in the car."

Logan quickly thanked Sadie again and rushed outside.

Standing in the opening of the driver's door, his face tight and drawn, Pierce said, "Toss me the keys. I'm driving."

Logan didn't waste time arguing. Whatever Pierce had found out had completely rattled him. Logan had never seen Pierce rattled before. He dug the keys out of his pocket and tossed them over the roof of his car. As soon as the doors closed, Pierce gunned the engine and punched the gas, throwing Logan back against the seat.

"Damn it, Pierce, what's going on?"

Pierce's knuckles whitened against the steering wheel. "When I gave Bennett's name to one of my men, he repeated it out loud as he wrote it down. One of your officers overheard him and mentioned that he knew someone named Tom Bennett. He's a mechanic at your police garage."

A mechanic? Riley had argued with a mechanic outside the police garage. Cold fear settled in Logan's gut as the pieces of the puzzle snapped into place. "Have they found Bennett yet?"

"No, but they will. I've put out a BOLO. Every cop in the state will be on the lookout for him. We'll get him."

"I want Riley picked up immediately and put in a holding cell until we get back to the station."

"Riley?" Pierce's voice held a note of shock. "Why?"

"He's Bennett's brother."

Pierce's face went white. "Oh, shit."

Dread coiled in Logan's stomach. "Riley's missing, isn't he? That's what you wanted to tell me, that Bennett and Riley are in on this together."

Pierce shook his head. "No, that's not what I wanted to tell you, but you're right. No one knows where Riley is right now. He said he had a hunch and he took off. But he's not the killer. He doesn't fit the description the witnesses gave."

"What witnesses? What happened? Damn it, Pierce. Spit it out."

"Man, I'm so sorry," Pierce said. "Karen was transferring Amanda to the safe house. Tom Bennett attacked them before they could get inside."

Logan paused in the doorway of the hospital waiting room. He spotted Madison sitting near a bank of windows, cradling a paper cup between her hands. Her eyes looked bleak as she watched him approach.

"Hey, trouble," he said, trying not to let his despair show in his voice. He kissed her on the cheek and gave her a tight hug before sitting beside her. "Heard anything?"

She shook her head. "Karen's been in surgery for over two hours. No updates yet. Mike is getting another cup of coffee. I would have gotten it for him but I think he needed a few minutes alone."

"I'm surprised you're the only one here."

"Oh, plenty of officers have been here, trust me. But every time someone tries to stay, Mike tells them they need to be out there catching the man who did this to Karen. I'm sure he'll tell you the same thing."

"I had to come check on her."

"I know."

"I heard you were out of town when Karen and Amanda were attacked," Madison said. "Mind sharing some details with your baby sister? All of your police officers are tight-lipped. They don't like to share information with us civilians and I'm not about to ask Mike."

He glanced at her, noted the worry lines etched on her face. He took her hand and tucked it beneath his elbow. "I was tracking down a lead, a very good lead, as it turns out. We know who the killer is." He realized he was crushing her hand and he forced himself to ease up on the pressure. He gave her a sanitized version of the attack, that a man ran up to the car and hit Karen over the head. "From what I hear, Amanda tried to warn Karen. She put up a good fight.

But she was no match for a taser and a lead pipe." His voice broke on the last word.

Madison clutched his hand, her face a mask of misery. "I'm so sorry. I know how much you cared about Amanda."

He pulled his hand from hers, shaking his head. "Don't say it in the past tense. She's not . . . we're going to find her in time."

Madison didn't answer.

Karen's husband rounded the corner into the waiting room with a steaming cup of coffee in each hand. Madison jumped up and took the cups from him, setting them on one of the side tables.

Logan rose and shook Mike's hand. "Is there anything I can do, someone I can call?"

Mike waved him back down and took the seat Madison had left open for him next to her. "There isn't anyone to call, chief, but thank you just the same. I already told the other officers not to waste their time here with me either." He patted Madison affectionately. "I've got this sweet girl if I need anything."

Madison smiled through the tears trickling down her face.

"Chief," Mike said. "I know you care about Karen and I appreciate the gesture, but you have a young lady of your own you should be searching for instead of sitting here with me."

"A young lady of my own?"

Mike smiled, a gentle, sad smile. "Karen knew Amanda had feelings for you, and Karen was sure you felt the same."

Logan drew a ragged breath and scrubbed his face with his hands. Feelings? What a pathetic word. What he felt for Amanda was so much more than just "feelings." When he tried to picture a world where she didn't exist, all he could see was a black void.

"You have responsibilities," Mike continued. "I'm sure there are more important things you could be doing right now than trying to console an old man, like finding the man that hurt Karen, and making sure that whatever happens to her, it isn't in vain. Karen cares about Amanda. She wouldn't want you sitting here when you could be out there doing something to find that young lady."

A feeling of relief shot through Logan because he wanted to go help look for Amanda so desperately. But it was quickly washed away by the guilt that followed close on its heels.

Mike gave him an understanding look and patted his shoulder. "You're a good man. I don't blame you for what happened. Karen is a cop. She knew the dangers. There's only one thing I want from you right now and that's a promise that you'll catch the man who hurt her. Don't let him do this to someone else. Go catch him."

Logan was humbled by the sincerity in Mike's eyes. He meant what he'd said. He didn't want Logan to sit there with him. He wanted him to go after the man who'd hurt his wife. Swallowing against the lump in his throat, Logan stood and shook Mike's hand. "I promise I'll do everything I can. Madison, call me if either of you need anything, or when you hear word about Karen, okay?"

"Go. Do what you need to do." She added an encouraging smile along with her words.

Logan nodded, turned on his heel, and rushed from the waiting room.

As soon as he cleared the doorway he broke into a run, ignoring the startled looks of the people he passed as he sprinted down the hallway and out the front doors of the hospital.

"He fits the profile perfectly. Absolutely perfectly." Pierce folded his arms over his chest and leaned back in the conference room chair, watching Nelson update Bennett's details on the white board.

Logan bleakly watched Nelson write, but he couldn't focus on the words. All he could think about was Amanda. Where was she? Was she hurt? He clenched his hands into fists and tried to concentrate on the lists on the board. There had to be a pattern. There was always a pattern, something to tell him where Amanda had been taken. But damned if he could see it.

Detectives were clustered in small groups around the room, strategizing, planning new searches. A pair of them on the other side of the table leaned over a map of Walton County, writing the names of the men leading search parties in each area.

"His father drank and beat his wife," Pierce continued. "That's why she left him. There's also evidence Tom and Riley's father abused them, too, although charges were never filed. Tom was a social outcast at school. After Anna Northwood rejected him and cut his face, his father moved them to a small town in Alabama. Five years later the father disappeared. No trace of him was ever found. I'll bet Bennett killed him."

Logan critically eyed the board, reading what Nelson had written. "You've established Bennett in the same towns, at the same time five of the attacks occurred. What about the other four? Why are you being so stubborn about agreeing that Riley might be guilty?"

"Because witnesses identified the security badge picture of Bennett as the man who attacked Karen and abducted Amanda. They didn't finger Riley. Bennett had access to police cars and could have pretended to be a cop to abduct his victims. Everyone who knew Tom Bennett said the same thing. He was "off," antisocial, talked to himself half the time. He was a brilliant mechanic, which is the only reason they didn't fire him, but everyone who worked with him said he was nuts."

"Which means he probably couldn't focus enough to plan the murders and leave the scenes so clean we didn't find any forensic evidence. Even if he was involved, someone else had to have helped him," Logan said.

Pierce shook his head. "All right, all right. Go ahead, Nelson. Put up what we've found about Riley."

Nelson added five more bullets to the board.

* Victim #3—Riley on vacation; Credit card records show him in same town as victim

* Victim #6—Riley on vacation; Hotel records show him in same town as victim

* Victim #8—Riley on vacation; no receipts yet, but was out of town, had opportunity

* Frank Branson—Unable to establish Riley's where-

abouts at the time of Branson's abduction and later murder

* Born David Riley Bennett, legally changed his name to David Riley at age eighteen

* Dysfunctional family (evidence of abuse, abandoned by his mother), intelligent, organized

"It looks damning, Logan, but even if you think Bennett and Riley are some kind of serial-killer tag team, which is extremely rare, Riley doesn't fit the profile. He's a police officer, no reprimands on his record, no trouble with authority."

"Profiles can be wrong." Logan held up his hand to stop Pierce's response. "He's not answering his phone and he disappeared after hearing that we suspected Bennett. He knew Bennett would lead us to him. That's the only reason he would have run off."

"Or maybe Riley realized his brother might be the murderer and he went off to find him on his own, to stop him. There's no reason to think Bennett didn't commit all of the murders. We just haven't proved it yet," Pierce insisted.

"And Riley just happened to be on vacation and in the same towns when three of the killings occurred. And he had time to drive back and forth between some of the other victims' locations and Shadow Falls and still make it in time for work each day." Logan grabbed his jacket off the back of a chair and shrugged into it. "If Bennett killed Branson, how do you think he found my house? He wouldn't have been in the station when my sister came looking for me. He wouldn't have known to follow her. Either Riley told him where I was, or Riley was the shooter. Like it or not, Riley's in this up to his neck." He headed toward the door.

"Bennett could have just as easily put a GPS locator on

your car while you were at work. He could have followed you, figuring you'd eventually lead him to Amanda," Pierce called out. "Will you stop for a minute? Where are you going?"

"I can't sit around here doing nothing while Amanda's out there enduring God only knows what kind of torture." His voice broke and he cleared his throat. "I have to find her."

"Use your brain, Logan. Not your emotions. We'll find her more quickly if we work together, evaluate the facts, figure out where she's being held. Our men have been searching for hours and haven't had any luck. What makes you think you'll do any better out there?"

Logan ignored him and strode through the outer office, which was filled with detectives on phones, shuffling papers, typing on their computers. He tried to ignore the sympathetic looks everyone gave him, as if it was a foregone conclusion that Amanda was already dead.

He refused to believe that. He'd failed her once all those years ago by letting Northwood's killer go free. He couldn't fail her again.

Once inside the elevator, he pulled Amanda's list of suspects out of his jacket pocket. He'd found it earlier today when he went home to get the Northwood file, hoping to find some clue that would tell him where Bennett, or Riley, would have taken Amanda.

She'd drawn circles around the words "cop," "mechanic," and "Riley," with question marks beside each one. Each conclusion was explained with meticulous notes referring back to the exact report or interview in each file that made her reach that conclusion. In a matter of hours she'd done a better job of analyzing the data than any of the detectives on his team—including him—had done in weeks.

He drew a ragged breath and crumpled the paper into a ball, shoving it back into his pocket. Twice she'd asked him to look at it yesterday, but he hadn't. If only he'd listened to her, given her five minutes, she'd still be safe. It was entirely his fault that Karen had been hurt, that Amanda had been abducted again. And worse than that, the man who had her was the same man he'd let go. Amanda would never have been hurt if it weren't for his incompetence. She'd still have her dreams, still be able to have a family.

The elevator doors opened and he shoved his way past the people in the lobby, racing through the building to his car. He was backing out of the parking space when someone tapped on his passenger side window. Pierce leaned down and motioned for Logan to unlock the door. When he did, Pierce got in and slammed the door shut.

Logan raised a questioning brow.

"I think you're a damned fool, Logan. You're too emotionally involved in this case to be part of the search. I also know I can't stop you, so I'll settle for trying to keep you from getting your head blown off if you do happen upon Bennett somewhere."

"Or Riley," Logan added, his hands tightening on the steering wheel. "Whoever has Amanda, once I find him, he's the one who'll have his fucking brains blown out, not me."

Pierce swore and dramatically covered his ears. "I didn't hear that."

Logan punched the gas and raced out of the parking lot.

Chapter Twenty

Amanda sucked in a sharp breath and eased the handcuffs off the raw, stinging cuts on her wrists. Not that it mattered. As soon as she let the cuffs go, they'd scrape across her cuts again. She'd tried to tear a strip out of her t-shirt to use as a cushion, but without scissors or a knife it was hopeless.

A bead of sweat trickled down between her breasts. She rubbed her shirt and glared at the window on the far wall of the cabin. Inside the air was hot and sticky. Outside the blue sky beckoned through a pane of glass only ten feet away.

It might as well have been a hundred.

Both the window and the door next to it were beyond the reach of the six foot chain that connected Amanda's handcuffs to the metal loop bolted to the floor.

Just like four years ago.

And just like four years ago, her friend had paid a terrible price for being with her. Was Karen still alive? An image of Karen, bloody, beaten, tossed out of the car as if she were garbage, flashed through Amanda's mind. *Please, God, let her be alive.*

A prickling of unease skittered up her spine and she glanced toward the window again. How much longer did she have before he returned? If she was still chained to the floor when he got back, she didn't have a chance. She fisted her hands around the chain, hissing at the sting of metal on her open cuts. Her palms were a mess, slippery with blood from trying to yank the chain free. So far, no amount of tugging had budged that stubborn loop of metal. All she'd managed to do was stir up dust when the chain rapped against the floor. But she couldn't give up. If she did, Logan would blame himself for her death.

She couldn't imagine the anguish he must be suffering right now. For ten years he'd worried that the killer he'd accidentally let go might have hurt someone else. Now he knew the answer was yes, and that she was one of the ones hurt.

If she didn't survive, he would always blame himself. She couldn't give up. She had to make it, for Logan.

She lowered herself to the floor, wrapped the chain around her hands and braced her sneakers against the wall.

One.

Two.

Three. She pushed and strained, gritting her teeth against the sharp, fiery burn in her hands. Her legs quivered and her thighs began to cramp, but she fought through the pain, arching her back, panting with exertion. The wood floor creaked. Did the metal hook move, just a tiny bit? A spark of hope had her pulling harder, but the muscles in her arms gave out. She lost her grip on the chain and pitched backward, crying out when her head smacked the hard floor.

"Damn it." She pounded a fist against the floor and rubbed the back of her head. Unshed tears burned her eyes and clogged her throat. It would be so easy to give in, to lie on the floor and wait for the inevitable. Before she'd met Logan, that's what she would have done. She would have felt she deserved her fate because she owed it to Dana.

Logan had made her whole again. He'd made her realize she had worth, that Dana's death wasn't her fault. She deserved another chance at life, another chance at happiness. The only one responsible for Dana's death was the man who'd killed her. Logan had done that for Amanda, he'd given her back her life. Now she had to return the favor. She had to make it out of here and teach Logan the same lesson he'd taught her. He had to learn to forgive himself. He deserved to be happy again, too.

She took a deep breath, coughing when the humid air hit her tortured lungs. Bracing her feet against the wall again, she gritted her teeth against the sharp stab of pain in her palms and took up the slack in the chain.

One.

Two.

Three.

Pull.

The sun was sinking, along with Logan's hopes of finding Amanda alive. He and Pierce had driven to the park where Carolyn O'Donnell was killed, but the park was flooded with volunteers who were already searching every inch.

They drove to Amanda's house but saw no signs of

anyone having been there since the police finished their last investigation only a few days ago.

They'd driven down I–10 to the condo that was supposed to be a safe house. Even though the fire department had used their hoses to clean the blood from the parking lot, a dark stain still remained. Logan steeled himself against the pain that shot through him, and he steered his Mustang to the edge of the woods that bordered the condominium complex.

He and Pierce searched the woods but didn't find any fresh tracks to indicate the killer had waited there for Amanda, or that he'd taken her back into the woods after abducting her.

FBI agents had searched both Bennett's apartment in town and Riley's home outside of town, but found no signs of Amanda. Riley was still missing. Logan had issued a statewide BOLO alert, telling everyone in law enforcement to be on the lookout for Riley as well as Tom Bennett.

If Riley was innocent, as Pierce still believed, he'd better come back with a damn good excuse for not answering his phone. If he had a good lead on Amanda's location, he should have phoned it in, called for backup. Riley was young, inexperienced. If he tried to be a hero, Amanda might be the one who paid the price.

In desperation, Logan drove back to his house and retraced the route Karen had taken to the safe house, looking for tire tracks along the side of the road, hoping he could spot where the killer might have pulled out behind her. If he could do that, he could backtrack and see where the car came from. Of course that theory only worked if the car had driven through grass or dirt to get to the paved road, definitely a long shot.

Any reasonable man would have given up hours ago.

Pierce had stopped making suggestions and quietly sat in the passenger seat watching the scenery roll by, as if he'd given up hope and was waiting for Logan to come to the same conclusion.

"She's still alive," Logan said, for perhaps the dozenth time in the past half hour, as if by saying it he could somehow make it true.

Pierce looked over at him but didn't say anything. He turned back toward the window.

A few miles down the road from Logan's house, he passed Mill Cove Road, the same road the killer had driven with Amanda four years ago when he took her to the cabin at Black Lake.

"Pierce, they've already searched Mill Cove Road right?"

"I'm sure they have. It was at the top of the list when we organized the search parties. Give me a sec. I'll make sure." Pierce pulled out his cell phone and pushed the speed dial. "Nelson, it's Pierce. No, we haven't found anything. Look, Logan wanted to make sure you'd already checked Black Lake." A minute later his eyes widened. "Why the hell not?"

Logan cursed viciously and braked hard, wheeling the Mustang around in the middle of the road. He gunned the engine and headed back toward Mill Cove Road.

"Hold out your hands so I can take off the chain. Hurry. We have to go." The man who'd hurt Karen and tasered

Amanda glanced behind him at the cabin door. He'd told Amanda his name was Tom, that he'd chained her up to keep her safe. He was trying to help her. Having seen how he'd "helped" Karen, she knew better.

Amanda backed against the wall, holding the chain by her side, ready to wrap it around his neck if she got the chance. Her hands stung from the sweat running into her cuts and her heart felt like it was going to jump out of her chest, but she had to make a stand. The chain was her only weapon. She wasn't giving it up. "If you want to help me, toss me the key and leave. I won't tell anyone about you."

He clutched the handcuff key in his hand, cocking his head to the side. "You're trying to trick me."

Amanda weaved in front of him, waiting for a chance to kick his feet out from under him.

His eyes narrowed and he frowned, crinkling the scar on his face, pulling his lip into a sneer. The effect was startling, disturbing, and even though Amanda's scar wasn't nearly as dramatic as his, she finally understood how difficult it might be for someone to see her for the first time without displaying an outward reaction. If she survived, she'd never again get irritated at someone if they flinched when they saw her scar.

He suddenly charged forward, shoving her against the wall, knocking her down. She fell hard, cracking her head against the floor again. Pain radiated through her skull, pounding through her temples. The metallic taste of blood filled her mouth from her split lip. Her vision blurred—whether from the pain or a concussion, she wasn't sure. She shook her head, desperate to bring "Tom" back into focus, but she only succeeded in making her head pound harder.

"It's your fault you got hurt. Stop fighting me. I'm trying to help you." A quick tug of her wrists, a clicking sound, and the chain pooled onto the floor in a series of loud thuds.

He'd unlocked the cuffs. She was free. He reached out for her and she twisted out of his reach, tripping over the length of chain on the floor. She scrambled to her feet, diving out of the way just as he grabbed for her.

"Pull over here," Pierce said in a low voice. "I see another cabin through those trees." He pointed toward the small square building and Logan nodded.

"I see it."

They left the Mustang parked on the side of the road. Circling around to the back of the cabin, they drew their guns and crept through the edge of the trees, splitting up to go around on either side. They met up at the front of the cabin, facing each other from opposite sides of the door. Logan quietly twisted the doorknob. Locked.

He held up his hand, signaling Pierce. Then he brought his hand down in a short chopping motion.

"Police!" they both yelled.

Logan slammed against the door, busting it open, banging it against the far wall. He ran inside with Pierce close on his heels, both of them crouching down, guns drawn.

The cabin was empty.

Amanda wasn't here. No one had been in this cabin since Logan and his men had checked it out over a week ago.

"We'll check the other cabins. Let's split up so we can

cover the cabins more quickly. If she's here, we'll find her," Pierce assured him.

Logan nodded and led the way out the door.

Amanda had to be here—in one of these cabins on Black Lake—because, God help him, he didn't know where else to look.

Amanda scrambled to her knees and lunged toward the chain.

"You're ruining everything," Tom screeched. "Why do you always ruin everything? Why won't you ever let me help you?"

What was he saying? It made no sense. She grabbed the chain and whirled around.

He stood in front of her, hands on his hips, his face a bright red. "Carrying you is going to slow me down. If you die, you have only yourself to blame."

He started toward her.

Amanda swung the chain, throwing the weight of her body behind the swing. His eyes widened in surprise. He jerked to the side. Not fast enough. The chain struck his temple. He dropped like a rock.

"Police!" a voice yelled outside.

The door burst open and a man ran inside, half-crouched, both hands wrapped around the butt of a pistol. The sun was behind him so Amanda couldn't tell at first who he was. When he got closer, he straightened, and relief swept through Amanda as she finally saw his face.

"Amanda?" He looked down at the man on the floor,

then back at her, his brow raised in surprise. "Thank God I
found you. Are you okay?"

The chain dropped from her fingers, plinking across the
floor. Her body started shaking so hard her teeth chattered.
"I'm f . . . fine. I've never been so g . . . glad to see anyone.
How did you find me?"

Riley smiled and holstered his gun.

Chapter Twenty-One

Tractor-trailers roared past the rest stop, stirring the hot, humid air, but bringing little relief from the smothering heat. Pierce flipped his phone shut and swore.

Logan raised a brow, waiting.

"Riley's alibi for Carolyn O'Donnell's murder is bullshit. He paid another man to go to the conference, a man who looked like him. With Riley missing, I had one of the agents in Alabama go back and pull surveillance tapes from the hotel. They used facial recognition software with Riley's police badge picture and proved the man at the conference wasn't him. I'm sorry, Logan. You were right all along. I should have pushed harder when you first suspected him."

Logan spread a map out onto the hood of his car and smoothed it down. "We don't have time for recriminations. Show me where your men have searched."

Pierce leaned forward and pointed to a spot on the map. "We've searched the entire area near the boxcar where O'Donnell was killed. Some of my guys are on their way to Black Lake in case you and I missed any cabins."

"We didn't." Logan wished to God they had, but he knew there weren't any more cabins at the lake.

Pierce pointed to another circle on the map. "The complex Bennett lived in—did your team search every apartment? Every storage closet? The club house?"

"Every inch." Logan swallowed hard. "Even the storm drains."

Pierce tossed his pen on the hood of the car. "Still no sign of Riley. His house is empty. His car isn't in his garage."

Logan slammed his fist on the hood of the car, leaving a dent. "Think, damn it. Let's go back to basics. Start with the timeline." He grabbed the pen and circled the exit off I-10 where Amanda and Karen were attacked. "The FBI agent heard the commotion outside the condo. He ran outside too late to help, but he immediately called for roadblocks. They were placed here," he drew a line across the interstate, "and here." He drew another line on the highway in the other direction. "Roadblocks also went up around Shadow Falls— here, here, and here."

"Don't forget the county highway, north of town."

Logan marked that too. "Assuming he wouldn't speed so he wouldn't draw attention, we can calculate a relative area he could have covered before the smaller roadblocks were set up. From the condo, he had to take this road." He pointed to the map again. "There's no other option."

"We searched that area."

"He must have driven straight through. Based on when we got our smaller roadblocks set up, I figure he had two options when he got near town. He either drove right down Main Street or he took this route."

Pierce shook his head. "No way would he go down Main Street in front of the police station." He watched Logan draw a line down the alternate route.

Logan paused, considering the various options. There weren't many. He drew the line down several side roads, but none of them felt right. Taking the straightest route, he traced the line further south to the nearest town. His pulse started pounding in his ears when he saw the name of the town.

Pierce's face paled. "Are you kidding me?"

Logan grabbed the map and ran to the driver's side of the car while Pierce ran to the other side. Pierce barely had his door shut before Logan stomped the gas, fishtailing out of the rest stop onto the highway amidst a hail of honking horns, as cars swerved to avoid him.

Pierce grabbed his phone and called the station. "Nelson, it's Pierce," he yelled. "Send backup. We know where Amanda Stockton's being held. Summerville."

A hot breeze blew through the pines, swishing the needles against each other as if the trees were whispering secrets. In spite of the heat, Amanda felt chilled as she rubbed her arms where her t-shirt left them bare. She stood in the clearing outside the cabin, not exactly sure where she was. All she saw were trees, Riley's car, and the cabin. Riley had sent her outside while he checked on Tom Bennett, who was lying on the floor after she'd hit him with the chain.

What was taking Riley so long? Her breath left her in a relieved rush when he finally stepped out of the cabin and strode toward her. That relief was short-lived when she saw the expression on his face.

"What's wrong?" she asked. A sinking feeling went through her stomach. "Did he get away?"

He raked his hand through his hair. "Don't worry, Amanda. He won't hurt you again. He won't hurt anyone else ever again." He pressed his hand on the small of her back and urged her toward his car. "Let's get out of here."

"What do you mean . . . he won't hurt anyone else?"

He grimaced. "How hard did you hit him with that chain?"

She stumbled to a stop. "Are you saying he's . . . that I . . . killed him?"

"It was self-defense. Don't beat yourself up over it." He leaned down and opened the car door for her. "Come on."

She slipped inside the car, her brow wrinkling in confusion. She'd knocked him down, yes, but his eyes were still open. He'd looked stunned, but he was breathing, conscious—wasn't he?

Riley stood in the open passenger doorway.

"I don't understand any of this," Amanda said. "Who was he? How did you find me?"

"His name is Tom Bennett. He works at the police garage. I had a hunch, tracked him down to this place and was lucky enough to find you. How badly are you hurt? Do you need an ambulance?"

"What? No, I'm okay. My hands are cut up, from the chain." She shuddered at the memory. Tom Bennett, charging toward her, shoving her. She tried to envision him with a hood, holding a rose above her, but the picture wouldn't gel in her mind. She tried to imagine him holding the knife in his left hand like she remembered, but he'd held the handcuff key in his right hand, hadn't he? And he didn't seem tall enough to be the hooded stranger.

She stared at her bloody hands, working through the questions in her mind. "I just can't picture him as the man who attacked Dana and me."

Riley gave her an odd look before closing the car door. As he walked around the front of the car, Amanda stilled, watching him. She tried again to picture Bennett with a hood covering his head, but suddenly that image turned into Riley. She looked at his hands, pictured him holding a rose, a knife. A horrible thought, an impossible thought, went through her mind. Hadn't she circled his name on the suspect list she'd created? Yes, but only because he matched the basic description. She'd never seriously considered him as a suspect, had she? She inched her right hand behind her to find the door handle even as she told herself she was crazy.

Riley slid inside next to her and started the engine, flipped the air on.

Music moaned out of the speakers from a CD, low, mournful notes, the same notes that Logan had played on his stereo early this morning.

The same music her attacker had hummed.

Riley's eyes widened. He punched the power button, turning off the CD. His gaze shot to hers, and she knew she was staring into the eyes of the man who'd attacked her all those years ago.

For a moment they both froze, staring at each other.

The knowledge of who he was, what he had done, and—oh, God—what he *would* do, hung between them.

He lunged as she flung open the door. His fingernails scraped across her skin, gouging her arm. She fell to the ground, rolled away from the car. Scrambling to her feet, she took off running toward the trees.

Even before Logan pressed his fingers against the side of Bennett's neck to check for a pulse, he knew Bennett was dead. His skin was still warm, but not as warm as it should be. The side of his head was bloody, but that wasn't what had killed him. "His neck is broken."

"What the hell happened here?" Pierce picked up the chain lying on the floor, attached to a metal hook.

Logan took the chain and held it up so the light from the cabin's window shined on the links. "There's a long, brown hair."

"Amanda's?"

"Count on it." Logan dropped the chain and rushed outside, studying the ground, looking for a trail to tell him where Riley had taken her. His car sat abandoned a hundred yards away, the passenger door flung open. The engine was running when he and Pierce had arrived. Pierce had turned it off and grabbed the keys to ensure Riley couldn't get away if he managed to get back to his car before they found him.

They'd wasted precious minutes going into the cabin, but they had to be sure Amanda wasn't inside. Logan crossed to the car and tried to interpret what he saw in the dirt. He crouched down, mentally sorting through the footprints, piecing together what had happened.

"I'm not sure where Bennett fits into this, but I think Riley must have made Amanda think he was here to help her. She got into the car with him. Then something tipped her off and she jumped out of the car, fell." He walked around the door, picked up the trail again. "She got away from him and ran toward those trees. Riley ran after her."

They jogged the fifty feet to the line of pine trees. Logan tried to find the trail again. "There are too many pine needles, not enough dirt. I can't tell which way they went from here. There are two paths here."

"The brush is thick," Pierce said. "If either of them went off the path we should see some broken branches, maybe some torn clothing."

"Let's go." Logan motioned for Pierce to take the path on the right, while he took the one on the left.

"What have you done?" Amanda cried out.

Pierce had burst into the clearing with his gun raised, apparently surprised the path ended so abruptly. That split second of indecision may have cost him his life. Riley had brought down his own gun on the side of Pierce's skull, dropping him to the ground.

Now he lay unmoving, and Amanda wasn't sure if he was even breathing. She ran toward him, but Riley's arm snaked around her waist and he yanked her against him. She twisted and tried to pull away, but he slapped her across the face, slamming her head back.

She held a hand to her throbbing cheek, blinking back the tears that had sprung to her eyes. Her heart ached for the man she'd known as Riley—and his boyish charm—because the man with her now wasn't the Riley she'd known. "Why are you doing this, Riley? I don't understand."

He reached a hand up toward her face and she shrank back from his touch. His eyes filled with regret. "If I hadn't left that damn CD in my car . . . ah, well. It was just a matter of time. This wasn't how I'd planned to punish you, but as it turns out, this will take any suspicion off me. After I punish you, and eliminate Pierce and Logan, everyone will think my brother is responsible. I'll be a hero."

"Your brother? But, who . . . Tom Bennett is your brother? I don't understand. He attacked Karen. He abducted me."

"Tom knew you'd found me again. But Tom is . . . was . . . weak. He never understood. He thought he could protect you by taking you away. He didn't want me to know where you were, but, of course, as soon as I heard you'd been taken, I knew it was Tom, and I knew he'd come back here. We grew up here." He shook his head. "We argued about you several times. I tried to explain, tried to tell him you had to be punished or we'd never find peace." He tapped the side of his head. "Tom was always a little off. He never understood. He didn't believe me when I told you you'd come back so soon."

The horror of what she'd done filled Amanda. She'd killed a man who was trying to help her. "He was trying to save me," she whispered. "From you."

Riley's hand tightened around her waist, and he leaned down and kissed her forehead. He pulled back, and this time Amanda saw the mad light in his eyes, the same one she'd seen four years ago.

"No, Riley, please. Don't."

"I never really wanted to hurt you, Kate. I just wanted to be left alone."

She shook her head vigorously. "No, Riley. I'm not Kate. I'm Amanda. Remember? Amanda."

He shook her violently. "Don't look at me like I'm crazy. I'm saner than you or anyone else. I see things you don't. I know things. You can call yourself Amanda all you want. I know the real you, the evil that's inside you. You got away once before, but that's not going to happen this time."

Sunlight glinted off the knife that was suddenly in his hand. Amanda sucked in a sharp breath and jerked back. Too late. Fiery, burning pain shot through her side as the knife slipped in between her ribs, once, twice. He let her go and she crumpled to the ground next to Pierce.

The burn faded quickly, replaced by a numbing coldness that crept through her body. She lay there, feeling her lifeblood draining away. She could see Riley beyond Pierce, standing with his gun behind his back, in a deceptively casual stance beside the path where Pierce had emerged only moments earlier.

She realized he was waiting for Logan. Pierce wouldn't have come looking for her without Logan. Did Logan know Riley was the killer? Or would he see Riley and let his guard down, until it was too late?

She had to warn him. If she could draw a deep breath, she could scream, but that might make Logan rush into the clearing, into Riley's trap.

She blinked her eyes to clear her vision and looked at Pierce. Was he breathing? She couldn't tell. She blinked again, trying to refocus. Was that Pierce's gun, lying next to him? Could she reach it? If she did, would she have the strength to fire it? She stretched out her fingers, inching her hand toward the gun.

Muffled footfalls echoed through the trees.

Oh, Logan. Stop, please don't come. Stay away. Stay safe.

A smile of satisfaction lit Riley's face. He slowly raised his gun. "He kills me," he said, his voice a macabre echo of the voice she'd heard so long ago.

"He kills me not, you bastard," Amanda cried out.

Riley whirled around just as Amanda fired Pierce's gun. Her aim was true. The bullet slammed into Riley's forehead, right between the eyes. He jerked backwards and fell to the ground, his eyes rolling up in his head.

The gun dropped from Amanda's numb fingers.

Cold, she was so cold.

A shadow fell across her face. Someone grasped her shoulders. Was Riley back? Had she only imagined shooting him? "No," she whispered.

"Hush, sweetie, it's Logan. It's okay. You're safe."

She went limp against him and he scooped her up, lifting her onto his lap.

She looked up and her vision cleared. Joy filled her at the sight of his beautiful face, his alive, beautiful face. "I won," she whispered. "I finished the game, and I won."

"Yes, you did. You won."

His cheeks were wet. Puzzled, she reached up her hand and wiped away the wetness. He gently pulled her hand to his lips and kissed her palm, then held it against his bristly cheek.

"You always need to shave," she whispered.

"Hang on, baby. The ambulance is on its way. Hang on."

"L . . . Logan," she said. "I can't see you anymore."

"Oh, God." His voice broke. "Stay with me, Mandy, hang on."

"So c . . . cold."

Something hot and wet splashed onto her cheek and Logan awkwardly wiped it away. "Fight, dammit. Don't you dare leave me. I love you."

He'd finally said those three words. Joy spread through her, but the blackness called to her again. "What took you . . . so long . . . to—"

She wanted to ask what took him so long to realize he loved her, but it took more energy than she had to finish the sentence. Her last memory would be of his beautiful voice telling her he loved her. She smiled. It was a good memory to hold and treasure as she died.

CHAPTER TWENTY-TWO

The funeral was three days later.

Nearly everyone on the police force was there, except for the skeleton staff required back at the station. A good number of the town's citizens were in attendance as well, although they were forced to stand behind the rows of Shadow Falls' finest, well back from the tent that covered the grave site.

Even the mayor was there. After all, it wasn't every day a police officer was killed in the line of duty, at least not in Shadow Falls.

The color guard lifted the flag that was draped over Karen Bingham's coffin, and slowly folded it, end over end, into the traditional triangle. The leader of the guard took the flag and neatly tucked the edges in, smoothed the wrinkles. He turned to Karen's husband, handed him the flag. Then he lifted his white-gloved hand and saluted.

Mike cradled the flag against his chest and nodded his thanks to the young man. He jerked in surprise from the sound of gunfire. Logan put his arm around his shoulders and gently turned him to watch the next two volleys from the seven guns that made up the twenty-one-gun salute.

When it was over, the crowd began to disperse. "Karen was a good officer and a good friend," Logan said. "We'll all miss her."

Mike smiled that sad, haunted smile Logan had seen far too often in the past few days as Mike shuffled back and forth from one hospital room to the next. Even though Karen had died during surgery, Mike was a constant shadow in the hospital as he waited to see whether Pierce and Amanda would be okay. He told Logan it's what Karen would have wanted him to do.

Pierce would definitely be okay, but Amanda was still fighting for her life in ICU. The doctors didn't know if she would ever wake up. She'd lost so much blood.

"I hear Special Agent Buchanan might be discharged tomorrow. That's good news," Mike said, as he walked toward his car with Logan by his side.

"Yes, sir. He wanted to be at the funeral, but the doctors wouldn't let him leave. He also wants to stay and wrap up the investigation, but his boss sent another agent to replace him, and ordered him to go home. One of my men will drive him back to Jacksonville once he's released."

"He's going to be okay, though, isn't he?"

"He's too stubborn to let a cracked skull slow him down."

Mike sighed as he stopped beside the police car where an officer waited to drive him home. "You kept your promise, chief. You caught Karen's killer. Thank you."

He extended his hand and Logan shook it, although he felt uncomfortable accepting praise he didn't deserve. He'd worked with Riley, trusted him, and even though Logan had some suspicions toward the end, he'd never fully accepted that Riley could be that twisted, that evil inside.

Turns out, Bennett had been far more aware of Riley's evil than anyone else, and he'd spent his life keeping an eye on his brother. He'd never quite succeeded in helping any of Riley's victims, but he'd tried, and if he hadn't been half-crazy himself, he might have been able to prevent some of those deaths.

Riley had cleverly hid his tracks, falsifying HR records so his vacation days didn't always match the dates of the murders. Pierce's team of agents had found the evidence of his tampering only after knowing Riley was the killer. Too bad they hadn't dug deeper before Karen and Amanda paid such a horrible price.

The police officer opened the passenger door and Mike slid into the seat, cradling the flag in his lap. The officer closed the door and Mike looked out the window, his eyes riveted on the tent that covered Karen's grave, as the car drove away.

Logan's cell phone vibrated again. It had vibrated several times toward the end of the funeral but he'd ignored it. He reached into the pocket of his suit jacket and pulled out the phone. The number on the screen sent a foreboding chill curling through his gut. "Richards here."

After a brief introduction, the nurse on the phone said, "I was told to call you if Ms. Stockton's condition changed."

Logan swallowed the bile rising in his throat as fear clutched at his chest. "Yes? What's wrong?"

"Oh, no, nothing's wrong, sir. She just woke up."

Logan paused in the doorway of Amanda's hospital room. It was still a shock to see so many tubes and machines hooked up to her, even though he'd seen them for the past three days.

She was pale, her skin nearly translucent, and her eyes were closed. Her doctor had assured him she had indeed awakened from her coma, but that she was sleeping now. A natural sleep, not the terrifying deep sleep of a coma.

She was still connected to a ventilator, its obscene hiss the only sound in the darkened room.

He crossed to her bed and sat in the familiar chair next to it. Careful not to bend her arm and interfere with her IV, he entwined his fingers with hers and leaned down and kissed the soft skin of her hand. He listened to the rhythm of her breathing, watched the rise and fall of her chest.

She was a survivor, one of the toughest women he'd ever known. It was because of her remarkable will that she was still alive after suffering not one, but two horrible traumas in her life.

No thanks to him.

Oh, he knew people were calling him a hero, saying that even though Amanda had fired the fatal shot, if Logan hadn't tracked her down she wouldn't have had the gun in the first place. Riley would have killed her and he'd still be out there killing other women.

But those people didn't know the whole story. They didn't realize if it weren't for him, Riley would have been caught ten years ago. Dana Branson, Carolyn O'Donnell, Karen Bingham, and five other women wouldn't have died.

Amanda wouldn't have been attacked, wouldn't have nearly died—twice—if he'd done his job, if he'd followed procedure.

Or if he'd listened to Amanda when she'd tried to show him her list of suspects.

So many women dead. One woman scarred for life, inside, where it mattered. Countless families torn apart.

If things were different, if Amanda could have forgiven him, he might have been able to forgive himself eventually, move on. But he'd looked deep into her eyes when he played that damn CD. He saw the devastation and the horror wash through her, watched her turn away from him, knew they would never be able to navigate the ocean of hurt that lay between them.

And then she'd said those words in the woods, words that stabbed his heart like a knife.

What took you so long?

He didn't blame her for feeling that way, for resenting that he took so long to find the killer, to find her. She'd suffered far too much because of his failings.

In spite of everything, even though he deserved nothing, he wanted the pleasure of seeing her beautiful eyes one last time. But he knew that could never be. He couldn't bear to see them filled with hate or condemnation, and he knew she wouldn't want to see him anyway. Instead, he would remember the way they were filled with awe the first time they made love. He would carry that picture in his heart and it would be enough, would have to be enough.

He pressed a warm kiss against her fingertips and carefully laid her hand on top of the white sheet. He pulled an envelope out of his suit jacket pocket and set it on the side table next to her bed. Then he walked out of her life, and didn't look back.

Amanda's throat was raw, dry. When she tried to swallow it was as if someone had sandpapered her tongue.

When she'd awoken earlier, the doctor explained she had a tube down her throat, a respirator, helping her breathe. That was why her throat was so sore. It would remain in for at least another day until he felt she could breathe adequately on her own.

The doctor told her she'd been unconscious for three days, but he didn't tell her anything else. She tried to ask him questions but couldn't speak with the tube down her throat. When he brought her a pad of paper and a pen, she couldn't grasp the pen to write down her questions. She was still too weak.

After giving her a sympathetic smile and assuring her she was on her way to recovery, he'd left the room, leaving her frustrated and anxious.

She wanted to know if Karen and Pierce were okay.

She wanted reassurance that Riley was really dead, because, even though she was the one who'd pulled the trigger, she still couldn't quite believe the man who'd hurt her and killed Dana was really, finally, gone.

And she wanted Logan. She needed to see him, hold him. She needed to tell him she didn't blame him for anything. She needed to tell him she loved him.

"Ms. Stockton?" A smiling woman in a white smock

entered the room. "My name is Shelly. I'm your nurse this afternoon. It's good to see you doing so much better. I was here when they first brought you in."

She hung a clear plastic bag on the IV pole, replacing the empty one. "Do you need anything for pain?"

Amanda shook her head no.

The nurse patted her hand and leaned over to straighten Amanda's pillow. "Oh, look, someone left you a card." She held up an envelope. "It says *To Amanda, From Logan*. Oh, how sweet. It must be from Chief Richards. He's been pacing the hallway and sleeping in that chair beside your bed night and day since you got here. He only left today to attend that policewoman's funeral. Do you want me to read the card for you?"

Policewoman's funeral? Oh, God. Karen hadn't made it. Amanda shook her head in answer to the nurse's question and choked back her tears.

"I understand. You want to read it in private. I'll put it right here so you can open it when you're ready." She tucked the envelope on the bed next to Amanda's hand and arranged the call button so Amanda could easily reach it. "I'll be back in to check on you soon but if you need anything before then, you press this button, okay?"

Amanda nodded and closed her eyes, hoping Logan would come back from the funeral soon.

She needed him.

CHAPTER TWENTY-THREE

A knock sounded on Amanda's front door, but it didn't send a shiver of dread through her like it had before Riley was killed. She wasn't afraid anymore. Since leaving the hospital three weeks ago, she'd certainly had her share of visitors as well as letters. The major networks had spread the story about what had happened to her all over the country. Mail had poured in from people offering her their support. One sweet, elderly lady named Sadie had even sent her a homemade apple pie.

Nearly every detective, every police officer in Shadow Falls, had dropped by to see her. They all seemed to feel responsible, at least in part, for the heinous crimes Riley had committed. He was one of their own, a brother in uniform they'd trusted and served with for years, a friend. None of them had suspected the evil that lurked inside his twisted mind.

None of them, except Logan.

Amanda couldn't help the surge of jealousy that swept through her. Logan hadn't spoken to her once since Riley had attacked her. But he had all the time in the world for his men. His officers had told her story after story about how Logan had drawn the police force back together in the wake of Riley's death. The officers were a stronger team now, a family, in spite of Riley's betrayal. It might have been Logan who'd figured out who the killer was, but he made sure the entire police department received the credit. SFPD now had a national reputation for having stopped a serial killer. Logan had ensured every man in the department felt valued and took pride in that accomplishment. He'd made each one of them feel special.

He'd made her feel special, too, once—a lifetime ago.

The knock sounded again, louder this time, followed by the doorbell. She shoved thoughts of Logan aside and gently eased herself out of her chair. A couple of Tylenol was usually enough to take away most of the pain from her injuries these days, but there was still a lingering soreness that plagued her when she put any stress on her side.

She moved as quickly as she could to the door and looked through the peephole, smiling when she saw Pierce on her front porch. Ever the vigilant FBI agent, his profile was turned toward her as he scanned the front yard. She wondered if he ever truly relaxed or if the evil he'd witnessed during his career would always haunt him. For her, the dark shadows were finally gone.

She pulled the door open and gifted him with her sunniest smile. "Pierce, it's so good to see you. I didn't know you were back in town."

He stepped into the foyer and kissed her cheek. "You're looking beautiful, as always."

She hugged him, pleased with his compliment. He'd always accepted her and looked past the surface just as Logan had. Not that she worried about her scar anymore. But even if she did, pulling her hair forward to cover her face wasn't an option. One of the first things she'd done after getting out of the hospital was to stop at a salon to have her hair cut off. Now her hair hung in a shoulder-length bob, just below her chin.

"Would you like some iced tea? Soda?" She started to head into the kitchen, but Pierce stopped her with a gentle hand on her shoulder.

"You don't need to wait on me. I should be waiting on you. Can I get *you* anything?" The laugh lines around his eyes crinkled with concern.

"Don't worry about me. I'm fine, just a little sore these days."

She led him into the living room, guiding him through the maze of boxes. The only furniture left in the house was the computer desk, her office chair, and a recliner. Pierce waited for her to sit before he lowered himself into the recliner, a bittersweet reminder of when Logan had once squeezed himself into that same chair. Pierce reminded her so much of Logan that it hurt to look at him.

"I thought you'd gone home to Jacksonville weeks ago," she said.

"I had some unfinished business so I drove back in for the day." He eyed the stacks of boxes. "I guess that "for sale" sign in your yard should be a "sold" sign. Looks like you're all packed up and ready to leave."

"I've had a few nibbles, no firm offers yet. But I didn't

want to wait. The movers are coming tomorrow. Everything will go into storage until I find a permanent place."

"You're leaving tomorrow?" His brows raised in surprise.

"Actually, I'm leaving today, as soon as the taxi arrives. The plane leaves in two hours. I'm moving to Tennessee, renting a furnished apartment down the street from my sister for a couple of months. After that," she shrugged. "Who knows?"

"Heather, right?" At her nod he continued. "I met her at the hospital. She and Madison hit it off, if I remember correctly."

They had indeed. After finding out Amanda had an estranged sister out of town, Madison had made it her personal crusade to shame Heather into coming for a visit. When Heather stepped into the hospital room, Madison had promptly berated her for allowing her husband to come in between her and her family. Once Heather got over her initial shock over the lecture, she and Madison had spent hours debating everything from politics to shoes. They'd enjoyed every minute of it. "They're already planning a shopping trip to New York together. How is Madison?"

"I wouldn't know." His face was impassive, giving nothing away, but his voice sounded guarded, as if he didn't want to reveal too much.

"I thought you two had a thing going?" Madison had been close-mouthed about her relationship with Pierce, but when she went out of town last week Amanda had assumed she was going to Jacksonville to see him.

He shrugged. "We went out a few times. We still talk on occasion."

"I'm sorry it didn't work out." And she was. She'd hoped Madison had finally found that special someone who would see past the bubbly image she projected to the world, and heal the pain Amanda sometimes glimpsed in Madison's eyes when she didn't think anyone was looking.

"Don't be. We only dated a handful of times. Neither of us had much invested in the relationship."

She wasn't sure she believed him, but he obviously didn't want to pursue that topic any further, so she didn't press. "You said you were in Shadow Falls to take care of some business?"

He adjusted his tie, suddenly looking uncomfortable. "I came back to talk to Logan."

Amanda stiffened, no longer feeling enthusiastic about Pierce's visit.

He sat forward, his forearms resting on his knees. "Did you know he'd resigned as chief of police?"

Surprise had her leaning forward as well, wincing when the movement tugged at her side. "Logan resigned? Why? Did he take a job somewhere else?"

"I think you know better than anyone why he quit. He feels guilty, like he failed everyone, especially you, by not stopping Riley after the first murder ten years ago."

She shook her head. "It wasn't his fault."

"Maybe he needs to hear that from you."

If that were true he'd have called her or come to see her when she was in the hospital instead of leaving that cowardly note. "I suppose he's going back to New York."

"As far as I know, he's staying in Shadow Falls. When I spoke to him this morning he didn't mention anything about leaving."

She stared at him, genuinely shocked. "Are you saying he's giving up being a police officer entirely? It's in his blood. It's who he is. How can he throw that away?"

"Maybe you could ask him that question. I tried to change his mind but he wasn't in a talkative mood. He's lost weight, looks like he hasn't been sleeping well." He stared at her pointedly.

Amanda squelched the little nugget of hope that tried to flare to life inside her. Logan wasn't suffering because he missed her. If that were the case, all he had to do was pick up the phone and call her. No, Logan was suffering because of his misguided sense of honor and guilt. "Pierce, I understand what you're trying to do, but it's too late for Logan and me. He doesn't love me. He made his feelings, or lack of them, perfectly clear in the note he left me at the hospital."

"He left you a note? He told you he didn't love you?" He sounded incredulous.

She straightened her spine, her face flaming with embarrassment. It certainly wasn't flattering for the man you loved to dump you with pen and paper. "Not in those exact words, but that's the way I took it."

"Hmm."

"You don't sound like you believe me."

He shrugged. "I'm surprised he left you a note without telling you face-to-face. Maybe he was afraid you wouldn't believe him if you saw his expression when he told a lie that big."

She frowned at him.

Pierce shook his head, as if truly bewildered. "You may

be right. All I can tell you is what I've seen, and from where I sit, you're both crazy in love with each other and too stubborn to do anything about it."

She bit back the angry words she was tempted to say. Pierce didn't know the pain of sitting in a hospital room for weeks, waiting for the person you loved to show, hoping he would finally realize how important you were to him. Pierce didn't know, like she did, that the breach between her and Logan could never be healed. It took an enormous amount of love to go through everything they'd gone through without being torn apart. There was plenty of love from her side but apparently not from Logan's.

"Forgive me for pushing." Pierce stood and reached out a hand to help her to her feet. "I had to try."

She punched him lightly in the arm. "You're forgiven. I'm glad you came by. It was good to see you again." She walked with him into the foyer.

At the front door he paused, a curious expression on his face. "When I went to Logan's house, he was on his deck with his back to me. He was talking on the phone and didn't notice me at first. I couldn't help but overhear his conversation. What he was talking about isn't what I'd expect to hear from a man who supposedly doesn't care about you."

She rolled her eyes at his unsubtle hint. "Go ahead, tell me what you really came here to say."

He gave her a sheepish grin. "Logan was arguing with his investment manager about making sure the money he'd transferred to your account couldn't be traced back to him. He said he wanted to make sure you didn't have to worry about finances while you were recovering." He shrugged. "I figured that meant Logan cared about you. But you're probably right. There must be another reason."

He winked and stepped out the door.

Amanda shut the door behind him with a loud click. She could feel her face flushing with heat. She wasn't sure who she was more annoyed with: Pierce, for goading her to see Logan, or Logan, for giving her money.

Was he trying to assuage his misplaced sense of guilt by paying her off? They'd made love, shared themselves the most intimate way two people could, and then he'd paid her? What did he think that made her?

Tears of hurt and anger burned the backs of her eyes. She paused in the archway between the foyer and the kitchen, and glanced at the clock on the stove. The taxi would be here soon. She wanted, needed, to see Logan one last time. No way was he going to ignore her, then send her money. He was going to hear how she felt about that, whether he wanted to or not.

If she cancelled the taxi and drove herself to the airport from Logan's house, she could still make her flight. It was a hassle. She'd have to put her car in short-term parking, something she'd hoped to avoid since a dealer was due to pick it up at her house tomorrow to sell it for her. She'd call the dealer from the airport and tell him to pick it up there. If she hurried, she could take care of everything and still be on her way to Tennessee to start her new life in just a few hours.

CHAPTER TWENTY-FOUR

Amanda slowed her aging Honda and turned into Logan's achingly familiar driveway. When his house came into view, she braked, unable to resist what might be her last look. Now that she knew that Logan had grown up here, it was so easy to picture an adorable, dark-haired little boy running around the expansive front porch, hurtling down the steps to the front yard, laughing and smiling as he chased his whirlwind of a sister in a game of tag.

The sound of a hammer shattered the silence and destroyed the happy illusion. The sound was coming from the backyard. Amanda continued up the drive and parked on the side, in front of the detached garage. The hammering was louder now. Curious, she crossed to the small flight of stairs and slowly climbed the deck steps, careful not to pull her side.

Pausing at the top, she wasn't at all prepared to see Logan shirtless and glistening with sweat in a pair of khaki shorts. The hunger that jolted through her as she watched his muscles bunch with each swing of the hammer nearly undid her. She ached with the need to be held in his arms again, but the breach between them was too wide to ignore.

He was on his knees, pounding a nail into a bright new piece of decking, and he hadn't noticed her yet. There wasn't a hint of rot in the discarded wood, and yet it looked like he was replacing most of the boards. Why would he tear up a perfectly good deck?

The sudden silence had her looking back at Logan. He was still on his knees, but now he was leaning back, his hands braced on the tops of his thighs, watching her. No smile, no word of welcome. So much for her foolish fantasy that he'd beg her forgiveness for abandoning her when she needed him most.

Her hands tightened into fists. The sound of crumpling paper reminded her why she'd come. She forced her hands to relax and she walked up to him. He still hadn't blinked or moved, but his intense gaze locked on hers and he watched her like a hawk.

When she was directly in front of him, she held up the piece of paper, the printout of her account balance. He grimaced and turned slightly pale.

"It seems that a distant relative left me a small fortune," she said. "Kind of puzzling since Mom and Dad never once mentioned any wealthy relatives on our sparse family tree." She cocked her head sideways. "I don't suppose you know anything about this, do you?"

He sighed and climbed to his feet, towering over her and forcing her to take a step back so she could look him in the eyes.

"You know damn well I know about it, or you wouldn't have come here." His voice was flat, hollow.

"Why did you do it?" she asked, searching his eyes for anger, irritation, *something.*

He bent down and picked up some scraps of wood, tossing them onto a larger pile. Neat, organized, apparently unfazed by his former lover's unexpected visit. *Damn him.*

"Was it guilt money?" she asked, determined to make him react. "It was, wasn't it? Well you know what? I don't want it. Not one damn penny. I already told my bank to reverse the deposit."

His jaw tightened but he continued to pick up the pieces of wood. Amanda was tempted to kick the pile of boards just to scatter them across the deck and see what he would do. How could he be so unfeeling after all that they'd shared?

She wadded the paper into a ball and threw it at him, hitting him in the back. "I didn't sleep with you for your money."

He stiffened and dropped the pieces of wood he was holding. "That's not why I gave it to you."

"Oh? Then why did you?" *Say it's because you love me. Say it.* She searched his eyes, waited, hoped. The words he'd written in that note couldn't be true, could they? Did he really think what they'd shared was just because of the stress of the investigation or was there some other reason he was pushing her away? *Tell me you love me.*

Instead of reaching for her, pulling her close, saying the words she longed to hear, he clenched his fists at his sides. "I knew you wouldn't be able to work for awhile, so I gave you the money to make sure you were taken care of. It was the least I could do after everything you went through."

A fresh wave of pain washed through her. Just as she'd feared, he'd given her the money because he felt responsible. He was still living his life based on guilt, not love. She straightened her shoulders and blinked back the tears she refused to shed. She was stronger now, stronger even than Logan. She'd survived Riley. She could survive *this*. Somehow.

She took a step back, not that it mattered. She couldn't put any more distance between them than there already was. "I put my house up for sale," she said, proud that her voice wasn't shaking the way she was shaking inside. "I'm driving to the airport to catch a flight to Tennessee. I'm moving there to be near my sister."

A shadow of something passed behind his eyes. Pain? Regret?

"I wish you the best, Amanda. Be happy." His voice was tight, strained.

He wished her the best? That was it? He was going to let her go, without even trying? Part of her wanted to hit him, to yell at him. She wanted to shake him, but what else was there to say? She wasn't going to beg him to love her.

She turned around and strode across the deck, ignoring the pain in her side. She kept hoping he'd run after her, call her name, but as she got into her car and drove away, the only sound she heard was her heart shattering into a million pieces.

CHAPTER TWENTY-FIVE

Logan stood frozen in place long after Amanda left. Any doubts he'd had about the way things had ended between them had evaporated when she'd marched across his deck toward him, her face red with anger.

When he'd left her that note, he'd hated not being able to say goodbye to her in person. But after seeing her lying in a hospital bed, so pale and fragile, fighting for her life, he knew he couldn't put her through the ordeal of having to face him again. She'd already made it clear, twice, that she no longer wanted anything to do with him. First, when she'd run from his study after realizing he'd let the killer go, and later, when she'd asked him, "Why did you take so long?"

He wished to God he hadn't taken so long, that he'd been able to put Riley behind bars before Karen and Amanda paid the price for his incompetence. He shuddered at the memory of Amanda lying in his arms, blood soaking through her tank top. He should have kept digging into Riley's background even after Pierce's men verified his alibi. He should have followed his instincts. Hell, he should have listened to Amanda when she'd written up her conclusions about the killer. But he hadn't. He'd put her off, too stubborn to listen to her when he thought he knew what was best for her. All he could think about that day was getting her to a safe house. If he'd listened to her, she'd have never been hurt again.

He'd failed her in every way that mattered. And then, apparently, he'd made it even worse by insulting her with the money he'd put in her account. He shook his head and kicked the pile of lumber, sending boards banging across the deck.

Footsteps sounded from the stairs. Had Amanda come back? Had she changed her mind, decided to give them both one more chance in spite of everything he'd done? The flare of hope inside him died when Pierce appeared at the top of the stairs. He'd already stopped by earlier this morning, arguing with Logan about why he quit as chief of police. Had he come back for round two?

"Save your breath, Pierce. I'm not taking my job back and I'm not in the mood for polite conversation."

"Good. I'm not in the mood to be polite. What the hell is wrong with you? You left Amanda a Dear John note?"

Logan cursed and started re-stacking the lumber he'd just scattered across the floor. "I am not going to discuss this with you. If that's why you drove out here again, you might as well turn around."

"Did you know she's moving to Tennessee?"

"I heard something like that."

Pierce grabbed his arm. "Did you know she's leaving *today*?"

Logan dropped the two-by-four he was holding and shoved Pierce backward. "What do you want me to say? That I screwed up? Okay, I screwed up. I failed her. She nearly died because of me, twice. She doesn't want me anymore. And I . . . respect her decision." He stalked to the French door and threw it open, slamming it against the wall.

Pierce followed him into the kitchen. Logan grabbed a bottle of water out of the refrigerator and took a long drink.

"So that's it? You're just giving up?" Pierce said.

Logan whirled around. "There's nothing to give up. It's over."

"If you really think that, you're a bigger idiot than I thought. Wasn't that her car I saw leaving? What did she say?"

"None of your damned business."

Pierce shook his head. "I'll lay odds she tried to give you one more chance and you threw it away. Damn it, man. What's this really about?"

Logan pushed past him to leave the kitchen but Pierce shoved him up against the wall. "She doesn't blame you, Logan. What are you really afraid of?"

Pain twisted in Logan's gut. Pierce didn't know what he was talking about. She blamed him, but no more than he blamed himself. He leaned his head back against the wall, all the fight inside him draining out. "Did I ever tell you about the research Amanda did? She went through the case files and created a list of suspects. Riley was at the top of that list. She even wrote that we should look into his records to see if he'd falsified his vacation dates. She tried to tell me about the list but I didn't listen."

Pierce let him go and stepped back. "That's it? Good God, man, didn't you hear what I said? She doesn't blame you for what happened. *She told me that.* Besides, you suspected Riley long before she wrote that list. If you're going to blame someone, blame me. I'm the one who told you Riley had an alibi. If I'd made my men dig deeper earlier on, he'd never have gotten his hands on Amanda again. Hell, Karen would probably still be alive."

Pierce pounded his fist on the granite countertop. "Don't think you have the corner on the guilt market. There's plenty of that to share. If you want to feel guilty, feel guilty about making the rest of Amanda's life miserable. You can't change the past, but you can damn well change the future."

Logan stared back at him, afraid to move, afraid to breathe. "She told you she doesn't blame me?"

"Direct quote, man. Haven't you figured it out yet? She's in love with you. She doesn't blame you. I don't know what you think her reason was for coming here, but I'd bet she was giving you one last chance to come to your senses."

Logan shook his head in disbelief. Was it possible she had forgiven him? Was it possible she really did love him, in spite of everything?

He pictured her the way she'd looked, standing in front of him on the deck, her eyes practically shooting sparks at him as she ripped into him for giving her money.

He loved that sassy mouth of hers. She was opinionated, stubborn, as passionate in her beliefs as she was in bed.

In other words, perfect.

He'd thought she'd come to his house just because of the

money. What if there was more to it? What if she'd been waiting for him to tell her he loved her?

Could it really be that simple?

He scrubbed his hands over his face and groaned. "I'm such an idiot."

"No kidding," Pierce said.

"What time is her plane leaving?"

Pierce grinned. "Now you're talking." He looked at his watch and frowned. "You'll never be able to catch her."

"Chief?"

Logan turned around at the sound of Officer Redding's voice, the rookie cop who'd followed Logan around like a lost puppy after being released from the hospital. Apparently Redding's near-death experience when Riley slammed into his patrol car to snatch Branson had changed Redding's outlook on life. He was studying to become a detective now, and was always asking questions about police procedures.

"Redding, I need to get somewhere in a hurry and I don't have time to talk right now. You'll just have to wait."

Logan opened the laundry room door off the kitchen. He grabbed a fresh t-shirt and tugged it on over his head.

"Call her cell," Pierce said. Convince her to wait."

"She doesn't have a cell phone—never saw the point, since she didn't have any family and rarely left her house." He shook his head. "She's probably halfway to the airport by now. I'll have to fly out to Tennessee and track her down. That could take days. By then she'll hate me so much for letting her go in the first place she'll never forgive me." He clenched his fist. "But I still have to try."

Logan grabbed his wallet and keys from the coffee table in the living room. He shoved the wallet into his back pocket, then frowned as he noticed the sawdust covering his shorts and the patches of sweat soaking through his t-shirt. He needed a shower, and a change of clothes. But he didn't have time for that.

Redding was standing in the way when Logan and Pierce headed toward the French doors at the back of the house. "Not now, Redding," Logan said.

The rookie backed out of the way but followed them as they stepped onto the deck. "Maybe I can drive you guys wherever you're going and we can talk on the way. The mayor is after all of us like a pit bull over your resignation, chief. He's determined to get you to come back. He said he'll do whatever it takes. The entire department is at your disposal."

Logan's gaze shot to Pierce. They both stopped and slowly turned around.

Redding glanced back and forth between them, his eyes suddenly wary. "What?"

For what felt like the hundredth time since driving away from Logan's house, Amanda glanced in her rearview mirror, hoping to see his black Mustang. But even though she'd driven well below the speed limit in case he came to his senses and decided to go after her, the mirror remained empty, along with her heart.

She replayed their conversation in her mind, or rather, what she'd said to him. He'd barely listened and had said even less. Maybe she should have been more understanding about the money. But she didn't want his money. She wanted his love. How could he let her drive away? As a police officer he'd fought for countless strangers. Why couldn't he fight for her?

The sound of a siren had her glancing in her mirror again. A police car was coming up fast behind her, red and blue lights flashing. Her pulse sped up as hope wrapped its tentacles around her heart. Had Logan come for her after all?

Closer, right behind her. Not Logan, a state trooper, motioning for her to pull over. Anguish washed through her, leaving her empty inside. She jerked the wheel, pulling to the shoulder of the two-lane highway. Summer heat blasted inside the car when she rolled down the window. Tears threatened, but she fought them back, determined not to cry any more for a man who didn't want her.

Five minutes later, she was back in control of her emotions, but the trooper still hadn't approached her car. She looked back to see what was taking him so long. He was sitting behind the wheel with his head bent as if he were writing something.

Maybe procedures had changed since the last time she'd gotten a ticket, which was a very long time ago, back in college. Or maybe he didn't want to stand in the heat while he wrote the ticket. She couldn't have been speeding. Was he going to give her a ticket for driving below the limit? It wasn't like she'd passed any other cars out on this deserted rural highway. She wasn't exactly a traffic hazard. She blew out a frustrated breath. Leaning against the headrest, she closed her eyes against the bright sun and waited, and waited.

"Afternoon, ma'am."

She looked up to see the trooper standing next to her car with a pad of tickets and a pen. His hat was pulled down low over his face and his eyes were concealed behind a pair of dark sunglasses.

"Officer," she said. "I didn't think I was speeding. Is there something else—"

"License, insurance card, and registration, ma'am," he drawled.

Irritation simmered inside her. She handed the required documents out the window. "Officer," she tried again. "Could you please hurry? I have to catch a—"

"I'll just be a minute, ma'am." He tipped his hat and ambled back toward his car. Was he purposely walking slowly because she'd asked him to hurry up? *Unbelievable.* A quick glance at the dashboard clock confirmed her fears. She'd spent far too long meandering down the road waiting for Logan. If she didn't get going in the next few minutes she would miss her flight.

A shrill noise sounded in the distance. More sirens? She turned in her seat and saw the flashing lights of a police car coming up fast behind her. As it approached, she realized there was another one behind it. And another one behind that. There must be a terrible accident up ahead.

Her eyes widened as she realized there were even more police cars than what she'd originally thought, a whole line of them in the traditional green and white colors of Shadow Falls. As they got closer she counted them—six, seven, eight—good Lord, what in the world was going on?

The first car zoomed past, then another and another,

but instead of continuing down the road, they slowed down and blocked off the highway about fifty yards in front of her, forming a semicircle across the road. They turned off their sirens but left their lights flashing.

She glanced back at the trooper. He sat in his car with a big grin on his face. When he saw her looking at him, he tipped his hat and his grin widened. Amanda shook her head in confusion.

The remaining police cars that hadn't passed her had stopped on the road behind the trooper and formed another semicircle, sirens off, lights flashing. She was completely surrounded. Did they think she was a bank robber or something? Feeling increasingly uneasy, she wasn't sure what to do. Should she get out of her car and put her hands in the air? What if they thought she was dangerous? Would they shoot her before she could surrender?

The silence was broken by the sound of a powerful engine roaring in the distance. What now? Amanda's eyes widened and her heart did a little flip when she saw a familiar black Mustang speeding toward the police cars.

Logan's black Mustang.

He sped through an opening between two of the police cars and skidded to a halt in the middle of the road, twenty feet from her car, fishtailing around until he faced the same direction he'd come from.

Stunned, she watched him get out of his car. He was still wearing the khaki shorts he'd worn earlier, but he'd donned a white t-shirt. His hair was damp and disheveled, so unlike his normal every-hair-in-place look that she couldn't help but smile.

He hadn't let her go after all.

She threw her door open, frowning when the pain in her side forced her to get up slower than she'd like. She rushed toward him, meeting him halfway, stopping just short of touching him.

He took off his sunglasses and hung them on the front of his t-shirt. Damn if he didn't look as sexy as he did in one of those blasted suits of his. She wanted to touch him so badly she had to ball her fists to keep from reaching out. If he wanted her, he would have to make the first move.

His expression hardened as he stared down at her. "You're not getting on that plane."

She raised a brow, disappointed. That wasn't what she'd hoped he would say. "Really? Who's going to stop me?"

He glanced at the ring of police cars surrounding them, then back at her as if he thought she'd lost her mind.

"Okay," she said. "I concede you might have the necessary manpower." Unable to stop herself, she reached up and sifted her fingers through his hair, sweeping some of the dark strands back from his face. One touch, it wasn't enough, but it would do. For now. She drew a shaky breath and dropped her hand.

He closed his eyes briefly and looked like he was struggling for control. She waited, hoping. Was it really that hard for him to tell her he loved her?

"The letter was a lie, every word."

Relief surged through her. She knew he'd lied, but hearing him say it helped ease her fears. She waited for him to say more but he only stared at her. "And?" she prodded.

"I'm sorry," he said, his voice cracking. "Mandy, I'm so sorry I failed you."

"Oh, Logan. You didn't fail me. You've never failed me."

His brows narrowed in confusion. "But the CD, when you heard it, and then later in the clearing, you asked what took me so long. I thought—"

"You thought wrong." Unable to resist the impulse anymore, she reached up and caressed the side of his face. "You've been living with such guilt for so long you automatically assumed I blamed you, too. I didn't. I don't. I ran from the music, not from you. And the only thing that took you too long was telling me you loved me." She dropped her hand and crossed her arms. "I demand you say it again."

His brows rose and the pain on his face slowly eased as he searched her eyes.

"I'm waiting," she said, tapping her foot on the pavement.

Logan's mouth twitched, then he cleared his throat. "I took a new job."

Not what she'd wanted to hear. "You took a new job?" Why was he telling her this?

"Chief of police. Shadow Falls. There's a catch, though."

"A catch?" she whispered. What was he talking about? Why wasn't he telling her he loved her? Why wasn't he kissing her?

He stepped forward, so close that the tips of his shoes brushed against hers. "I have to get married. Apparently the last chief quit after less than a year on the job. The mayor wants the next chief to be married. It shows stability, gives the mayor more confidence the chief won't quit so soon next time."

Amanda's mouth went dry. She couldn't speak. She could barely breathe. What was he babbling about? He couldn't possibly mean. . . .

He smiled that heart-stopping, sexy smile of his. "I would have been here sooner, Mandy, but I had to make a quick stop in town." In ninety-degree heat, in shorts that didn't quite reach his knees, he knelt on the blazing hot asphalt and pulled a small black velvet box out of his pocket.

Tears flowed down Amanda's cheeks as he opened the box. He pulled out a pear-shaped diamond solitaire ring. "Mandy, I've been a complete ass. Can you ever forgive me?"

She punched him in the shoulder. "You know I forgive you. Will you get on with it?"

He grinned. She held out her left hand and he paused with the ring poised to put it on her finger. "Amanda Elizabeth Stockton, I love you. Will you do me the honor of becoming my wife?"

Yes. Yes. "On one condition."

His brows drew up in surprise and he suddenly looked very vulnerable as he kneeled in the middle of the highway with half of the Shadow Falls Police force looking on.

"What condition?" he asked, his voice tight, uncertain.

She gave him a smile with all of her love poured into it. "Tell me you love me again. I've waited so long to hear that."

The worry faded from his eyes and his brow smoothed out. "I love you, Mandy. I love you because you're a beautiful, caring person inside and out. I love you because you believe in me, because you make me want to be a better man. I love you because you're intelligent, and funny and loyal and sexy. I love you because—"

"I only have one question for you, Logan."

He paused, looking uncertain again, and it awed her that a man like him, so strong and appealing he stole her breath—it awed her that he could face her with all her scars and troubles and think for one minute that it was possible she might not want him. She was humbled by his little speech, by the love in his eyes, and she realized that everything in her life that had happened had led her to him, and that she wouldn't change a thing if it meant she wouldn't have met him.

The tears flowed freely now and she had to wipe her eyes to be able to see him. "What took you so long to realize you loved me?" she whispered. "I've loved you since that first time in my kitchen when you pulled me back from a nightmare. The answer is yes, Logan. It's always been yes."

His dark eyes blazed into hers and his hands shook as he slid the ring onto her finger. "I've loved you since the moment you squeezed my foot in your door," he said as he rose to stand before her.

She smiled, then sobered as he pulled her against him. He cupped her face with his hands and slowly ran his thumb along her lower lip, exactly the way she'd imagined that first day in her kitchen, when he'd pulled her back from the nightmare. Then his lips touched hers.

The policemen let loose with a cacophony of whistles and cheers. Abruptly breaking the kiss, Amanda looked up into Logan's laughing eyes. She'd totally forgotten about their audience. Tears clogged her throat as she looked at Logan and saw the naked love shining in his eyes. "You saved me," she whispered. "You saved me from a life of fear, a life of hiding, a life that . . . wasn't a life."

He tenderly kissed the tears from her cheeks, his eyes suspiciously moist. "You've got it all wrong, Mandy. I didn't save you. You saved me."